WANDERING QUEEN

LOST FAE BOOK 1

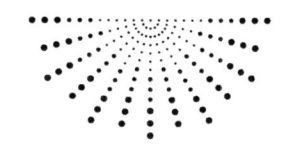

MAY DAWSON

ALSO BY MAY DAWSON

The True and the Crown series:
One Kind of Wicked
Two Kinds of Damned
Three Kinds of Lost
Four Kinds of Cursed
Five Kinds of Love

Their Shifter Princess:
Their Shifter Princess
Their Shifter Princess 2: Pack War
Their Shifter Princess 3: Coven's Revenge

Their Shifter Academy:
Their Shifter Academy: A Prequel Novella
Their Shifter Academy 1: Unwanted
Their Shifter Academy 2: Unclaimed
Their Shifter Academy 3: Undone
Their Shifter Academy 4: Unforgivable
Their Shifter Academy 5: Unwinnable
Their Shifter Academy 6: Unstoppable

The Wild Angels & Hunters Series:
Wild Angels

Fierce Angels

Dirty Angels

Chosen Angels

Academy of the Supernatural

Her Kind of Magic

His Dangerous Ways

Their Dark Imaginings

Ashley Landon, Bad Medium

Dead Girls Club

*For my amazing beta readers, Andrea, Angie, Barb, Becca, Denise, and Lisa,
who helped make Wandering Queen the book it is.
And for everyone on the beta team who helps me with the next book.
I don't know what I would do without you all!*

PROLOGUE

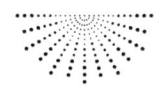

Five Years Ago

I WAS on my knees in the forest. I didn't know how I'd gotten there.

The sun filtered through the green leaves of the trees above. The trees looked wrong somehow, but I didn't know how. In the distance, there was a faint, constant rushing noise, and I tilted my head, trying to understand the sound.

As I rose to my feet, confusion almost tipped into panic. I didn't remember anything. Not my name, not where I'd come from, not how I'd ended up there.

Looking down to make sure I wasn't hurt, I cataloged my narrow wrists and pale skin, and the simple jeans, sneakers, and t-shirt that I wore. There was a note pinned to my chest, and I frowned as I pulled the pin loose.

Your name is Alisa.
You don't have friends. Don't trust anyone who claims to be one.
You're quite good with a sword.

Well then, I supposed that was all I ever needed to know.

My hands shook a little as I folded the note and shoved it in my pocket, as if it might somehow answer more questions later. I touched something else in my pocket, and pulled out a wallet. There was nothing in it except for dozens of crisp hundred dollar bills. Nothing that told me who I was.

I headed toward the source of the strange sound. I had to go somewhere.

The sound led me through the forest to a hard, wide, black path. *A road.* The name followed for the path a few seconds too late. Constant noise rose and ebbed, coming with the cars that raced up and down the road. I knew what they were, but they still felt unfamiliar. Dangerous.

I glanced to both sides along the road. Maybe I should walk down it until I found…what? What was I even looking for?

No one ever found their path by standing still. I didn't remember whoever said that to me, but I had a feeling I'd heard those words plenty of times. I started down the road. Where the hell could I go for help? What could I do?

My Converse sneakers rubbed my heels raw before the forest gave way to houses. Cars whizzed past me, and even though I walked in the grass on the side of the road, they made my heart beat fast when they came so close.

I was limping as I passed a building with several cars parked in front. Two men watched me from the front porch.

"Hey," one of them called. "Where are you going, girl? It looks like your feet hurt."

I didn't know where I was going, but I didn't like the way those men looked at me.

I ignored them, but from the corner of my eye, I saw the two of them exchange glances. Then the second man leaped over the porch railing and crossed toward me.

"Hey," he said. His voice sounded gentler than the first man's had. "Are you okay?"

"I'm fine," I assured him. *Never show weakness.* There was that voice from the past again.

"You need a ride?"

"Thanks, but I'll be fine." I'd been through worse things in my life than a few blisters. I didn't know *what*. But getting into one of those cars with a strange male might lead to something worse than bloodstained sneakers.

"Call you a cab?" he asked.

Cab. Right. That was how people got around with no car of their own, if their destination was too far to walk. I'd forgotten they existed until I heard the word.

I hesitated. "Yes, that would be helpful."

He nodded as he put his cell phone to his ear and took a step back, leading me toward the bar. "Have a drink with me while you wait?"

He wasn't much taller than I was, and his frame looked weak, his shoulders slumped in his white t-shirt. I had a feeling I could kill him if I had to. I just needed to be cautious; any warrior can die if their guard slips or their luck runs out, no matter how weak their opponent.

"Sure," I said.

My shoes crunched across the gritty parking lot. I followed him up the stairs, passing a few peeling rocking chairs and a tin can full of cigarette butts.

He pushed the door open with his back, then stopped, holding it open for me. I made sure I didn't touch him as I walked in.

Faces in the dimly lit bar turned toward me. The scent of stale beer rose to my nostrils, along with a whiff of the man beside me. I'd expected him to smell bad, because his shirt was yellowed at the armpits and his dark hair was greasy, but he smelled like something both pungent and clean. Bleach.

I followed him to a table where his friend was already waiting.

"Cab should be here in about fifteen," the first guy said, slipping his cell phone into his pocket before he held out his hand. "I'm Steve."

I didn't like touching people—how did strangers touching each other ever become the normal person thing to do? But I committed, offering him a grin as I shook his hand. "Alisa."

"And I'm Roger," the other guy said. He was bigger than Steve, wearing a flannel shirt and a trucker hat pulled down low; escaping brown hair curled around his ears.

"Nice to meet you both," I said. One of them signaled for the waitress, who came over glancing at me skeptically. "Water, please."

Neither of them complained I wasn't drinking, so that was a point in their favor. My throat was dry from the long walk.

How the hell had I ended up in the middle of the woods? With no memories?

Did I have a home? A car of my own?

A last name?

The two of them were staring at me, and I knew I'd better let go of my questions about the past for now. Staying alive in the present kept me busy enough.

That note had warned me I didn't have any friends. I didn't think I'd suddenly found some.

I drank my water. The men asked me a lot of questions about my life that I didn't answer. I *couldn't* answer them, but let's be honest, I wouldn't have told them even if I could.

When Tweedle-dum and Tweedle-dee weren't distracting me, I looked around the bar curiously, taking in the bartender that leaned on the bartop to gossip with a cute young blond guy, and a couple of tables of aging good old boys who kept the noise level elevated.

An older woman was drinking by herself at one end of the bar. She slowly sipped a glass of wine. Her posture was perfect and dignified, and even though her hair was gray-streaked in a ponytail, her jeans and halter top clung to her fit frame. One of the good old boys swaggered over and tried to buy her a drink, and from what I overheard, she very politely told him to fuck off.

Okay, okay, she said she was waiting for her boyfriend. But it was obvious what she meant.

It was an interesting cast of characters. I drained the last of my water and set it on the table just as Steven's phone buzzed against the table. "There's your ride," he said, holding up the cell.

"Thanks." Then I lied, "It was nice meeting you both."

Out in the parking lot, a yellow cab was idling. The car looked like it had been through a lot; mud was splattered all across the back of the car, obscuring the license plate.

Steve opened the door for me, which was a little more gallant than I needed, and I slid across the ripped black vinyl of the back seat.

"Where to, little lady?" The driver asked. He might have been looking at me in the rearview mirror, but he was wearing sunglasses and a hat and I couldn't see much of his face.

The passenger door opened just as Steve slid in beside me. I slid over, glimpsing Roger settling into the passenger seat, then I kept moving. Instinct took over. I grabbed the handle and tried to open the door, but the door was locked. I yanked harder on the handle as I heard the doors slamming shut on the passenger side.

"Changed my mind," I said, trying to stay calm. I'd ask them nicely...*once*. "I'd like to get out here."

"Oh, you're going to have to pay the fare, little lady," the driver said with a smile. The car was already rolling, and he turned onto the road.

Steve laughed.

I rolled with my back against the window and kicked Steve hard in the chest. He slammed into the window.

Steve wasn't laughing anymore. I kicked him in the face, my heel catching his nose, which spurted blood. I was already moving, getting my arm around the driver's neck. I yanked him hard against the headrest as he made a choked, shocked noise.

"You're going to want to open that door before I lose my sense of humor," I warned him.

The passenger window exploded open. Steve looked at me with wide, blank eyes. Then he slumped toward me, red suddenly blossoming across his t-shirt like a flower unfurling. Roger let out a strangled scream just before the second sound of a gunshot went off. His blood splattered across the car.

The older woman from the bar gripped her gun in one hand, and she made a hurry-up gesture at the driver. "I think the girl told you she'd like to get out," she said, her voice courteous.

The driver fumbled frantically with the locks. They popped open. I couldn't get out of that bloodied car, full of glass shards and bodies, fast enough.

"Five girls," she said, her voice calm but loud in the quiet air. "She would have been the sixth you stole the life from, wouldn't she? I usually hunt *real* monsters, but you certainly did your best to give the monsters a run for their money."

I knew she was going to pull the trigger. The roar of the gunshot was no surprise.

She wiped the gun down and tossed it into the car with them. "You've got some moves, honey. But it's time to get out of here."

I stared at her. "I think I'd rather go with you, actually."

She scoffed.

"You said you hunt monsters, right?" I said. "I'm great with a sword."

"Why bother being great with a sword when we have guns?" she asked.

A long, sleek black car pulled up just then. I tensed, but she just raised her hand in a wave. "If I were you, I'd get out of here. People don't call the cops for gunfire out in the country, but sooner or later, someone's going to notice the car full of corpses."

The driver's side door opened, and a tall, good looking guy unfolded from the driver's seat. "Hey," he said, in a rough, sexy voice. "You all right?"

She shot him a look. "First of all, you are so late. Second of all, please don't hit on the victim."

"I'm not a victim," I promised her.

She swung into the passenger seat. He shrugged at me—he didn't look sorry—then ducked back into the driver's seat.

I dove for the back door to their car. I managed to get the door open and slid into the leather interior.

She twisted in her seat and gave me an exasperated look. "You just watched me shoot three people and I can guarantee you, I didn't have any heartache about it. Why the hell would you invite yourself into my car?"

I flashed her a smile. "I just want to be friends. We should get out of here before the cops show up."

Fuck whoever left me that note. I could make friends.

For some reason, I wanted to know this icy-eyed old woman with steady hands.

She gave me a look, then said, "Drive, Carter."

He grinned as he pressed down on the accelerator pedal. "Come on, Elly. You're always recruiting."

"Not like this," she told him sharply. Then she said to me, "We'll drop you off somewhere safe. Where were you trying to go?"

I took a deep breath.

This time, I'd have to tell the truth.

"I don't know."

CHAPTER ONE

A *lisa*

I WAS HAVING A PERFECTLY lovely morning, chasing down a vampire, until the damned strange male ruined everything.

"Excuse me, coming through!" I called as I pushed through the morning commuter crowd heading into the D.C. metro, trying to keep my gaze on the vamp racing ahead.

Some people parted to let him through, but no one answered me with anything but a glare. *Sexism.* That's what that was. I hoped they got bitten.

I chased him down the street and into an alleyway, where he finally turned to face me. He'd greased his jet-black hair back, as if he'd watched too many movies before he'd been turned, and now he was trying to live up to the stereotype of a vampire.

His lip peeled back in contempt when he looked me over, and I grinned back at him. *That's right, you sentient stiff tube sock; only one of us is walking out of this alley.*

It was a hot summer day already, even though the sun hadn't been up long. The alley stunk of wet cardboard, piss and the coppery tang of blood coming from the vamp.

He licked his lips as he took a step toward me, those dark eyes gleaming. "Aren't you the hero? I hope you already had your coffee, so I can get my caffeine buzz and my iron all in one."

"No coffee yet. I'm pretty sure I'm still drunk from last night." I flashed him a smile.

He grinned. "You've got a death wish, little girl."

"Not exactly." I disagreed.

I only had a fraction of a death wish.

I had a lot more of a *killing* wish.

I reached back and gripped my sword's hilt, drawing it over my shoulder in one smooth motion.

"This is usually the part where your kind run," I said.

"This is usually the part where my kind *dine*," he corrected.

There was the crunch of a footfall close behind me.

"Trap?" I cocked an eyebrow at him.

His grin widened. "Trap."

"I'm glad you finally realized it," I said.

I whirled, my blade a flash of silver arching through the air. There were two vampires behind me, and my sword sliced deep through the neck of the first one. *Almost* all the way. Fuck. A smooth vamp beheading was a matter of pride to me, but everyone has an off day sometimes.

My head reeled as I spun. *Should've taken it easy at the bar last night, Alisa.*

And by *last night*, I meant three hours ago. Elly was going to kill me if she heard about this. But once I saw the vamp, what was I supposed to do? Walk away? We'd been trying to track this ugly monster for weeks.

I ducked as the second vampire sprang at me, throwing up one arm defensively as I tried to jerk my sword free. He slammed into me, but my sword pulled loose just before he managed to propel us both into the opposing brick wall. My head and shoulder drove into the brick, leaving a jolt of pain in their wake.

We were too close now for a good sword blow, and I grabbed for the knife on my belt.

The vamp got an arm across my chest to pin me and reared back. His eyes dilated as his fangs ripped through his gums. The effect was always gruesome, and I winced as flecks of spit and blood splattered across my face.

"Should've brought a better weapon than some big ol' yellow teeth," I said, just before I slammed my dagger into his guts.

He fell to his knees in front of me, his eyes wide with shock.

I kicked him in the chest, knocking him backward on his ass before he sprawled out across the ground. There was no one else in the alley. My biggest prey had run.

I cursed as I flipped my sword around in my hand, preparing my grip. I ran my knife across the thigh of my jeans, cleaning his blood off the blade, before I slipped it back into the sheath.

Wrapping both hands around the hilt of my sword, I cleaved it down at his throat, striking his head from his body. This time, the sword sliced cleanly through and the blade struck the cement beneath. Blood splattered across my sneakers.

That was why I always wore black. That, and Elly always told me black is classy and sophisticated.

Lord knew I could use any help I could get with being *classy and sophisticated.*

My skin prickled down my neck. Someone was watching me. I kept my grip tight on my sword.

When I looked up, my prey was dangling from the top of the brick building. His wind-milling legs slammed frantically into the brick wall over and over.

A dark-haired man gripped the collar of the vampire who'd escaped me. He crouched easily at the edge of the roof, his face relaxed as he dangled my vampire from five stories up. The vamp bucked hard to escape his grip, despite the distance between him and the concrete.

"Did you lose something?" he called. Even at a distance, he sounded mocking.

"I was about to hunt him down again." What the hell was he? No human would be that comfortable on the edge of a roof like that, gripping a kicking burden. For some reason, the vampire wasn't screaming. "But thanks for the help?"

"No problem. Want me to toss him down?"

"Sure."

The vampire didn't scream as he plummeted to the ground. The fall wouldn't kill something like him, but both his legs shattered when he landed.

I studied the fallen vampire. He couldn't seem to open his mouth to scream, even though his eyes were wide with desperation.

"You look as scared as your victims must have felt," I told him.

I don't love vampires on a good day, but ones like this? Who preyed exclusively on kids? When I was tracking him, I'd found one of the bodies, twisted and broken and so goddamn small it would haunt me at night.

I'd make this vamp's death slow, if I were inclined to be inefficient.

But it was his lucky day; I never wasted my time. There were always more monsters to kill.

I whirled with the sword and cleaved his head from his shoulders. The head bounced across the pavement.

The man on the rooftop started to clap slowly.

I looked back up at him. He stood comfortably at the edge of the rooftop, his toes hanging over the side as if he didn't have a care in the world.

He stopped clapping and put his hands in his pockets. Just the way he stood suggested he was an arrogant bastard, with his broad shoulders and tall, powerfully muscled frame.

"Who are you?" I shouted. We could start there, even though I was also very curious about my follow-on question, which was a toss-up between *what the hell do you want* and *why the hell are you talking to me?*

"Duncan." There was an edge in his voice, as if I were a bit stupid.

Had I met this clown before? I was losing sight of him in the glare of the morning sun, so I cupped my hand over my eyes. I groaned at the light. Maybe I was crossing from *drunk* to *hungover* rather rapidly.

Police sirens blared in the distance.

He lifted his hand, beckoning me onto the rooftop, and I stared at him like he was a lunatic. No one *beckoned* me anywhere. He said, "Let's take this conversation somewhere that your arrest isn't imminent."

"I don't know that I want to talk to you." But curiosity had driven me for the past five years; first I'd been desperate to understand where I'd come from, and then I'd thrown myself into making sense of a world I didn't remember. I sheathed my sword.

"You do," he said. "I know you, Alisa."

Did he know me or *know* me? Did Duncan know the old Alisa, the one I didn't?

I'd tried to let go of my need to make sense of my past. The depth of my need to understand who I was, where I'd come from, felt dangerous. In so many ways, I was reckless with my life, but I needed to be careful with this random man who was trying to entice me into…something.

I backed across the alley, gauging the distance to the bottom of the fire ladder mounted on the building where he stood. I took a deep breath and exhaled.

Then I raced as fast I could, jumping against the brick wall, before propelling myself toward the bottom of the ladder. I caught it with both hands and swung myself up, then climbed quickly until I reached the rooftop.

When I clambered up next to him, he watched me appraisingly. There was nothing friendly in the way he narrowed his eyes, studying me with intensity that sent a prickle down my spine. But now I was close enough to get a good look at his face.

He was *unreasonably* handsome. His cheekbones were high, his cheeks hollow beneath them. His eyes were an eerie light blue, lushly lashed, in contrast with the black hair that fell to his shoulders. His skin was almost unnaturally perfect, as if he was airbrushed, and intricate tattoos that must spread across that powerful chest peeked from the torn collar of his shirt. Either that shirt was a fashion statement, or the vamp had tried to put up a fight.

"I don't know you." And I would remember him, if I'd met him in the last five years.

He cocked his head to one side, studying me. "You don't remember anything, do you? Not your childhood, not your home, not your misspent youth."

"Was my youth misspent?" I rubbed my hand across my head, which was beginning to pound. "I've been trying to misspend my twenties. Good to know I've got some practice."

He looked me over just as curiously as I was looking at him. "At first, this Hunting business made me assume you were trying to help the humans as penance for your sins. But I suppose you would find your way into any career field that involved death and destruction."

"You've been following me?" I demanded.

I should probably just kill him now. But he didn't give me that creepy vibe up the back of my neck; I felt safe enough with him. Just... irritated.

And I also felt a flutter of nerves, an odd reeling in my stomach and a flush of desire that heated my skin. I bit my lip. I spent a lot of time around good-looking, well-built Hunters and I never felt these stirrings. This man was too damned pretty.

His brows rose as if that were ridiculous. "No. I've been trying to track you. You've been missing for a long time."

I couldn't stop staring at him, and I wanted to know what the hell he was talking about, both of which made me feel hot and self-conscious. I forced myself to meet that mocking gaze. "Last chance before I get bored and wander off. Who the hell are you?"

"You're not going to just wander off." He crossed his arms over that broad chest, still holding my gaze. I tried not to notice the way the movement pulled what was left of his shirt lower, revealing the dark lines of hounds and runes tattooed across his chiseled pecs. A perfectly shaped brown nipple winked at me before it was covered by his thick bicep, not that I was looking. "You've never had any control over your curiosity."

God, what a twit. He wanted me to think he knew something I didn't. My desire to uncover my past was a vulnerability, and I wasn't about to let some random jerk—no matter how beautiful —control me.

I cocked my head, staring at him. "Are you a vampire?"

"No…" He frowned impatiently.

I could tell he was about to say something else, so I beat him to the punch. "Shifter?"

He was so big, I could peg him as a shifter easily.

"No," he scoffed.

"Witch?" I asked brightly.

"No."

"Evil?" That was the part that mattered most. I never hurt anyone who didn't hurt someone else first.

His brows arched over those icy eyes. "No."

Must be a Hunter then, to have caught my stray vamp as soon as he broke away. He was an unusually reckless, confident, sexy man, even by Hunter standards. But he was just another human.

"Then I don't give a damn about you," I told him, heading toward the far edge of the roof. "You're cute, Mr. Tall-Dark-and-Mysterious, but you seem like trouble, and I find enough of that on my own."

His lips parted, and he seemed to stumble over what to say to that. Since it was always nice to leave a man speechless, it was the perfect time for me to walk away.

"You need answers, Alisa," he called after me. "I can give you answers."

I started to run, picking up speed. I jumped nimbly onto the ledge of the building and my momentum powered my leap to the next rooftop. I landed cleanly, on my feet, my knees buckling for just a second before I caught myself.

I whirled, taking a step back. He stood there watching me, his light eyes eerie at this distance. I almost faltered, sure he wasn't human, that he was my business after all.

But he wanted something from me, and there was nothing I wanted to give to anyone but my Hunter friends.

I spread my arms out in an exaggerated shrug. "Meh."

Then I turned and sashayed off toward the next rooftop, leaving Duncan-the-gorgeous-weirdo behind.

CHAPTER TWO

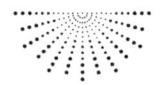

Azrael

"She was *drunk*?" I asked skeptically, staring at my best friend in the dim light of the bar where we'd taken shelter.

The Alisa I knew didn't get drunk, not even during solstice.

"Tell me the part again where she said you're cute." Tiron took a long sip from his Scotch, but even with his face partially concealed by the crystal glass, his eyes danced with mischief.

There were some benefits to being in the human world. Not many, but whiskey in all its various and glorious forms was one.

Duncan snorted at him. "Focusing on the important details, as usual."

"Where did she go?"

"She ran away, like she always does." Duncan sounded dismissive, and I frowned at him.

"You didn't lose her?"

"Of course I didn't lose her," Duncan said. "The hounds and I tracked her back to her pathetic house. It's not even a house. A segment of a house."

He shifted, his hand concealed under the table, and I knew he was reaching to pat one of his hounds. The two hulking creatures hid under the table, not that it mattered; they were invisible to humans, and the barkeep was our servant now anyway.

"The word you're looking for is *apartment*," Tiron supplied helpfully. "You spend enough time in the human world. Are you really too obstinate to learn their culture?"

"Can you call it *culture*, though?" Duncan asked. "Does pigs wallowing in filth a *culture* make?"

He was in a fine mood today, even by Duncan's standards.

"Do you think she truly lost her memories?" I asked.

Duncan nodded. "She didn't recognize me. She was genuinely curious who I am. *What* I am."

"She wouldn't have said you were cute if she recognized you," Tiron observed.

"I am cute, though," Duncan muttered. Then he admitted, "If she'd recognized me, she would have run."

That was wishful thinking on his part. If Alisa had recognized him, she might have put a blade through his gut.

"How'd she survive all these years without any clue who she is or what she can do?" I wondered out loud.

"Princess Alisa is quite good at surviving," Duncan said dryly. "Even though her presence reduces everyone else's odds."

He might hate her more than I did. She simply betrayed me and my court. For Duncan, she betrayed his *brother*. That was a far more serious crime.

"Do you think she might come with us willingly?" I asked. "Once she understands who she is?"

"No." Duncan's lips twisted into a cruel smile. If I didn't know the man beneath the angry mask, that face would terrify even me a little. "I think we'll have to *take* her back."

Tiron tilted his head to one side, studying Duncan. "Why don't you let me go and talk to her? It would be nice if we didn't have to thump the princess over the head and drag her back home unwillingly."

"Would it?" Duncan questioned. "I think the thumping and the dragging sounds nicer. For us."

"Thank you, Tiron," I told the younger man. "But I'll go. She and I have history. Faer wants to know if she has any memories or if the reports are true. She won't be able to fake it with me."

"I need to see for myself," I added to Duncan. I didn't want him to think I didn't trust his judgment.

Tiron nodded. Far from seeming offended, Duncan's dangerous grin widened. Whether he thought an encounter between Alisa and me would punish *me* or punish *her,* I had no idea, but Duncan had a sadistic streak.

"Let's go to this apartment," I suggested.

"That's not a good idea," Tiron said. "You'll scare her."

Duncan snorted. "Proof you do not know Alisa."

"She might try to kill you," Tiron amended.

"Oh yes," I said. "But she has tried that many times before. I don't mind."

My heart quickened at the thought of being face-to-face with my queen, my former fiancé, my betrayer.

But I knew my outward appearance gave no indication of my reaction. I took another long, slow sip, finishing off my whiskey. Duncan still side-eyed me; he was a male of few words who still managed to get his judgments across.

Duncan knew me well enough to know my heart always raced when it came to Alisa—with love, or hate, or a dangerous combination of both.

"This is a bad idea," Tiron said lightly.

"You always say that," Duncan reminded him, rising from his seat. "And you're always outvoted."

"And we always end up in trouble," Tiron shot back. "Maybe you should listen."

"In the end, she's just one spoiled little girl with a sword," Duncan said. "If she gets too feisty, Azrael can throw her over his shoulder and carry her to the portal."

The image was so ridiculous that I smiled. "It almost seems like *you've* been cursed with forgetfulness."

Alisa had indeed always been spoiled and willful.

But she was also dangerous.

Delightfully so.

Or at least, that was how I'd seen her once.

CHAPTER THREE

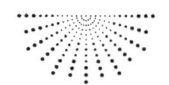

Alisa

"I'm not sure even the baddest vamp would steal a girl away from right under her grandma's nose," Carter said, right before he raised his beer to his lips. The muted light in the bar did nothing to hide how handsome his chiseled features were.

Elly harrumphed at that. "I'm old enough to be her mother, not her grandmother, you ass."

Carter leaned back, yawning and stretching before slinging his arm across my seatback. Julian watched us as he always did with an amused smile across his face.

I turned to regard Carter skeptically. That move would have worked on the girls by the bar who kept eyeing the two sexy Hunters, but I wasn't interested. "If those fingers touch skin, I'll castrate you, you know."

He grinned at me. He had a nice grin that crinkled the corners of his deep brown eyes. "I love it when you're scary."

I rolled my eyes. "Buy me another drink. Get a girl properly drunk, would you?"

That was the plan for the night, after all.

He clapped me on the shoulder—his scarred hand finding just the cloth of my tank, none of his warmth touching my bare skin—and headed for the bar.

"I'll be back too," Julian said, and I groaned and threw a crumpled-up napkin at him as he stood. "Traitor."

He knew Elly would want to talk to me about the messy Hunt that morning. None of us were supposed to work without backup.

Instead, she shook her head in amusement at us. Her hair was freshly permed and dyed into a deep shade of purple-ish red that I was pretty sure didn't occur in nature. It looked good though with her tanned, wrinkled skin and her bright hazel eyes. I'd like to age as gracefully as Elly.

"I wish you two would stop flirting and bow to the inevitable," Elly said.

I smiled non-committedly and swirled my half-drunk beer in the bottle. I knew that Carter and Julian were good-looking, with their handsome faces and their muscular bodies; I admired their competence as Hunters, and I loved the easy friendship between the three of us.

Elly had asked me once why I didn't just *try* to like them the way they liked me, when they were such good guys.

"Or you three," she added. "I wouldn't judge. You go for what you want, Alisa."

"I don't know what I want," I said automatically, then added, "I love them too much as friends to risk ruining it all."

But the truth was, I couldn't see them as anything *but* friends. Carter was over at the bar now, and a slender redhead had sidled over next to him. He braced one big forearm on the bartop, keeping a respectful distance from her, but she kept pressing closer with a thirsty smile on her face.

I laughed and shook my head as I turned back. "They're like my brothers. There's nothing else there—but *brothers* is a lot, you know."

She pursed her lips. "Are you going to feel okay when they move on?"

"Yes," I promised.

"If you're sure," she said, raising her beer for the two of us to toast. I clinked the top of my bottle with hers.

"I'd tell Carter to move on *tonight* if I could," I said. "Yet again."

But I couldn't because we had a mission. It was probably confusing for him because Carter and I flirted like it was our jobs. We had a little road show; he poured 'liquor' down my throat like a sketchball, I flirted with him, showing off a little leg and a lot of neck, I looked drunk, then I ended up lost and alone and inviting... to a vamp.

From the way that redhead was trying to defy physics and press herself against him until their bodies occupied the same space, Carter definitely had the option to move on tonight if he chose.

"I'm not going to change my mind, Elly. You can stop worrying I'll have regrets."

For some reason, I thought about Duncan. The memory of that jawline, the fierceness in those icy blue eyes, all made me feel a strange restless tension. When I thought about him, I wondered about the tattoos I'd glimpsed and what the rest of them looked like. There was something about him that felt... magnetic.

I'd been right to send him away. There was something strange about him, and I knew I should tell Elly about it, but I didn't want to.

Because it would be hard to explain what felt so strange about him.

In five years, I'd learned how to fake normal.

But I hadn't learned how to fall in love.

The way Duncan kept coming back to my mind felt...peculiar.

"What's on your mind?" Elly asked.

I raked my fingers through my hair, pushing it back absently. I shrugged. I didn't want to talk about it.

Julian joined Carter at the bar, helped him carry over a round of beers and shots.

As they walked toward us, Julian passed his hand subtly over the drinks, taking away the alcoholic buzz.

Then Carter set the shot glass in front of me with a self-satisfied thump.

"Drink up," he said, "I'll just keep on getting cuter."

"I don't think you could get any cuter," I half-slurred playfully, leaning forward to slide my hand up the hard muscle of his bicep. A strained look crossed his face, as if my touch really affected him, before he grinned.

"You are definitely drunk," Julian said loudly, before taking a sip. More softly, he added, "We've got company."

"Then I guess Alisa can tell me what's on her mind later," Elly said pointedly. "I know there's something."

"There's always something going on in this wild brain." Carter palmed my head with his big hand, before wobbling my head back and forth. He was lucky I had to pretend to be drunk and infatuated, because I was definitely going to make him pay for that later.

"Let's go play some pool," I said.

We toasted quickly, clinking our shot glasses together. "Swords," Julian murmured for us all, and I knew he had an eye on our vamps to make sure they didn't hear us.

To our swords. Never drawn without cause, never sheathed without honor was the rest of the refrain. But we all had to be genuinely drunk before we started to wax on.

Elly had been lying that day when she said they always preferred guns over swords. Swords were quieter and plenty of monsters were almost bullet-proof.

But rule one of Hunting is that everything dies when you lop off its head.

The harsh whiskey burned down my throat, and I choked. "Lord, Carter, you could spring for the good stuff every now and then." I picked up my beer to wash the taste away.

"That is the good stuff," Carter managed to look hurt. He slung his arm over my shoulders as the two of us swaggered toward the pool tables in the back. The two pool tables were on a raised dais, separated from the rest of the bar by a decorative rail. It was the perfect vantage point to keep an eye on my new friends.

He turned me toward him, his hands on my hips, our bodies intimately close. "Do you need me to distract Elly?" he asked. "Is she nagging you again?"

"Always," I said. He was looking at me with those warm, open eyes —he was my best friend—and I added, "I met someone today who said he knows me. *Knew* me."

Carter's eyes widened. He knew how hard I'd tried to track down my past, and he knew when I'd given up.

"You believe him?" he asked.

"I don't know what to believe," I said. "You know how much I want that."

"Christ, take your sweet time racking," Julian said. His ass bumped my hip familiarly as he set the pool table, and he took the opportunity to mutter, "Company at your eleven."

I ran my hands over Carter's chest intimately, looking over his shoulder as I pretended to nibble his ear. His breath gave against my chest as I found the vamps; they were crowded by the bar, flirting with the redhead and her friends.

"Fuck, you should take those girls home to keep them safe," I whispered to him. Then with a wink I added, "and to give them the best night of their lives."

Not that I would know.

Elly kissed us goodbye, planning to leave us to our game; she'd try to run down the vamps' hive while they were busy here.

"Later," she chided me. "You're coming over for dinner tomorrow."

"I think that's a little much quality time," I teased before I turned to set up my shot.

As I leaned over the pool table, Carter landed a playful smack on my ass.

"Be nice to your grandma," he teased.

She gave him a look. "I'm going to let some beastie eat all three of you."

"What did I do?" Julian demanded.

"No, she's not," Carter said. "She's going to feed us fried chicken and try to fix us, like she always does."

Elly scoffed. "Even I can admit when something is a lost cause."

Carter walked her out to her car just to make sure she was safe—Hunters are never truly alone—and Julian and I kept an eye on the vamps in the meantime. My pool playing was a lot better when I knew there was no risk of Carter smacking the back of my jeans. He embraced playing the obnoxious boyfriend a bit too much.

When he did come back, he brought another round of shots, and I kept getting louder and bouncier as we went through our game.

"Let's do some research into this mysterious new friend of yours," Julian suggested. "Figure out what he wants. What he actually knows."

These two were always on my side.

"I don't know how I'd even find him again," I said, leaning over to take my last shot. "Corner pocket!"

"Was that tank top designed with any intention of keeping your breasts contained?" Carter demanded as I bent over.

"Shoot!" I straightened from the shot I'd sloppily missed, as the cue ball jumped the end of the pool table and rolled across the floor. I had to chase it to catch it, which brought me almost to the vampire's table. I kneeled a few feet away from them, close enough to smell the dark, obnoxious cologne they wore to cover the odor of blood.

"You look good on your knees," one of the vamps muttered, so quietly that if I didn't hunt assholes for a living, I might have doubted I heard him correctly.

I grabbed the cue ball and straightened, rubbing my lipstick with the back of my hand so it smeared across my cheek. I was good at faking messy drunk and looking good at it, too. I gave them a slow, horny once-over—these greasy vamps knew they looked good to humans—and then sashayed back to my friends.

My ass looked luscious in these tight jeans. I knew they were watching.

I was a natural with a sword. I'd learned a lot over the past five years though that hadn't come so easily. Elly and the other female Hunters had to teach me how to walk naturally even when someone was checking me out. They'd taught me how to be deliberately sexy, how to trick a man with his eyes on my boobs, so they never noticed what I was doing with my hands...or a blade.

I held my hands to either side and shimmied to answer Carter, once I was positioned to give the vamps a good look too. "These babies cannot be contained! *I* cannot be contained."

"You're wild," he laughed, wrapping me in his arms and hugging me tight. It was the same warm, affectionate hug that Carter always offered me, wherever we were and whatever we were planning. He added, "And drunk."

"Me?" I asked innocently, then blanched. "I'll be right back."

The bar had a hall that led past the restrooms to a rear exit. When I'd knelt to pick up the cue ball, I'd noted that one of the vamps was positioned to watch down that hallway. If I were going to kidnap someone, I'd force them right out that door into the parking lot.

But I was going to make it extra easy for them. I didn't appreciate the competition from the redhead.

I made a show of being about to hurl and stumbled right past the women's room door, slamming myself into the back door as I stumbled out into the cool night air. I was still bent over pretending to yak across the concrete when arms circled my waist and yanked me to the left. The second vamp threw the car door open just before I reached it, and the first one bundled me into the back.

I screamed, belatedly, and lashed out at the one who had just taken me. I wouldn't want to scream in public and draw some well-intentioned civilian into the fray. I was sure their car was soundproofed.

Now they would discover they had their hands more full than they realized. I twisted to reach my blade as the vamps piled into the backseat with me. The two of them flashed toothy grimaces, their fangs ripping out of their gums. They looked like frat boys—I'd been kidnapped by a couple of bros. The thought of anyone's life ending by bro seemed like an extra tragedy.

The first one lunged at me, but my blade was in my hand, and I caught his throat in my hand. Carter and Julian would be just a step behind. I had to hurry and gut these two before I had to share the win with my friends.

"We heard about you guys, *Alisa*," said the second one just as he pulled a potion bottle out of his pocket.

Fuck. The vamps had probably made Carter and Julian too, then. My friends might need a rescue.

I didn't know what that was in the bottle, but I doubted it was anything good.

I kicked out at him, slamming my booted foot into his face, and he let out a grunt. He dropped the bottle and thrashed around, trying to avoid my next kick. He didn't make it—my heel clipped him across the temple.

The guy I was struggling with managed to croak out a word in Latin just as the other guy smashed the bottle open with his heel.

I inhaled a sharp, sweet tang of magic, and stared at the two bleeding vamps, their long, gleaming fangs biting into their lips and their eyes gleaming with anticipation.

"What exactly is that supposed to do besides piss me off?" I demanded.

The car door was wrenched open. I looked up with a thrill of relief, expecting to find Julian and Carter safe and unharmed.

Duncan filled the doorway. His breath came fast, as if he were enraged, and his eyes on the two men were icy. All three of us paused; the sense of threat that radiated from him was powerful.

Intoxicating, even.

I didn't know where the hell *that* thought had come from, but the wayward horniness was driven away as two shadows shot into the car. I leapt back from the vampire I'd almost strangled as the shadow—no, it was a black dog, an enormous, snarling black dog—slammed into him.

The car rocked as the dogs each leapt onto a vampire. The dogs sounded vicious, growling and snarling, and the vamps screamed, and then there was a wet ripping sound and it was all over.

Blood splattered across my face, cool droplets that I wiped away with the hem of my tank top. My heart was pounding—there was a part of me that was afraid of the dogs—but I knew better than to move fast.

"Thanks for the rescue, boys," I told them, my voice calm.

"What's wrong with you—" Duncan began. That icy glare turned on me, although I didn't feel any fear that the hounds would attack me. In fact, they bounded out of the car and each went to his side, turning around and sitting.

"I wasn't talking to you," I cut him off.

Despite his cold words and even colder gaze, his hands automatically found the dogs' heads. He stroked them and played with their ears, and the dogs butted against his legs as if they'd all but forgotten me.

Duncan's intense gaze, though, never left mine.

"I've got to check on my friends," I said, sliding past him out of the car.

"How peculiar," he said. "Alisa with *friends?*"

"Stay right there," I told him. "Don't move. I want you to meet someone."

He scoffed at that.

I ran into the bar, but I couldn't find Carter and Julian. I glanced around the smoky room where music was blasting and people were playing pool or carrying on colorful conversations, then plunged out through the front doors. Where the hell were they?

I found them mopping up a fight outside the front of the bar. Carter arched his sword through the air, cutting down a vampire. Julian saw a woman at the end of the street who witnessed the whole thing, who saw the bodies scattered across the sidewalk and turned digging into her purse for her phone. He took off running after her to take away her memory.

That was one reason why I could never be with Julian, even though I appreciated our need for a clean-up crew. My own lost memories felt too much like jagged wounds to be with someone who left those holes in other's minds.

Carter saw me and threw his arm around me, hugging me tight, mindless of the blood that covered us both. "Thank God, you're okay. They had us made from the beginning."

"I'm fine," I said. "They had some kind of potion to take me out, but it didn't work."

Carter's jaw tightened with anger that they'd tried to hurt me, but all he said was, "Of course it didn't. You're no mere mortal."

"I wish." I spent an awful lot of time bruised up—I was definitely mortal.

Julian headed back toward us, his hands in his pockets. Even though he wore a leather jacket, his dark hair smoothed back from the hard angles of his face in a normal style, he seemed to carry an air of magic.

"Guys," I said. "My mystery man is back."

"Let's go meet him." Carter sheathed his sword on his back, and Julian touched his back, magicking it out of sight once again. I knelt and tucked my knives smoothly into the tops of my boots.

But when we got around the back of the bar, Duncan was gone, and so were the dogs.

CHAPTER FOUR

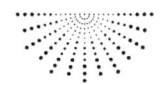

Azrael

IN THE MIDDLE of the night, I joined Duncan outside a six-story tan-brick building. "How is she?"

"She got into a fight with some vampires," he said bluntly. "She's fine."

Cold fury prickled over my skin. She'd been fighting while I slept? "You didn't think to mention that?"

"I was the one on watch," Duncan answered. "There was no reason to disturb you."

There was no good reason I should be angry with Duncan. I leaned against the brick wall beside him, shoving my hands into my pockets. "What happened to the vampires?"

He didn't grace that with an answer.

As we waited there, a homeless man took a piss in the alley to one side. There couldn't be a place more removed from Alisa's former life of opulence.

"She must be losing her mind, living here." A distinct pang of satisfaction strummed in my chest, then I realized how ridiculous it was. She'd toyed with my affections and used my weakness for her to destroy my court. I shouldn't be amused by how far she'd fallen when her only punishment was a cheap apartment and the mortal world.

I should want to destroy her.

Should.

A wayward memory of her rose in my mind. Alisa, glancing at me over her shoulder, a mischievous smile written across her red lips.

Also contained within that memory: Duncan shoulder-checking me, telling me I was an idiot. He'd hissed that Alisa was poison.

Of course she was.

But alcohol was poison too. So was sugar. Everything sweet and addictive was toxic eventually, wasn't it?

"I don't think she is." Duncan watched me, and I knew he was waiting to see how the words landed. "She seems happy enough."

I scoffed.

"Brace yourself," Duncan said, "because here's the strangest part of all. People seem to *like* her."

"We liked her."

"Speak for yourself." Duncan peeled himself off the wall; he wouldn't want to explore that perspective any longer. Duncan wrapped hatred around himself like it was his favorite blanket.

Apparently, that was his version of goodbye. He headed down the street, back to the hotel where the three of us had sheltered for now.

I waited until dawn, making sure that Alisa was safe. When the horizon was a mottled bruise of pinks and blues, I decided the princess had slept long enough.

A woman came toward the door of the building, cradling a paper sack of groceries in her arms. I moved quickly toward the door to intercept her, and she turned wide eyes toward me, her fingers tightening on the keys she'd already fished out of her purse.

"I'm friendly," I told her, letting the truth of it warm my voice. I smiled at her, and her eyes brightened. "I'm going in to surprise an old friend."

"Okay," she said agreeably, and held the once-locked door open for me.

Humans are so easy.

I followed her in, then walked up the three flights of stairs to Alisa's place. The air carried a faint, stale odor. Careful not to brush against the wall or stair railing—I didn't mind getting dirty in battle, but I wasn't trying to catch some human disease—I reached the top and headed down the dim hall of faceless doors.

I stopped in front of her apartment and debated whether to let myself in or knock. Letting myself in did promise a certain entertainment value.

But perhaps she really was a poor little lost lamb with no memories now.

The thought brought a wolfish grin to my face. *Wouldn't want to scare her.*

I banged on her door. When no one answered, I banged on it some more, until I heard someone curse in the distance, the sound muffled by the door. The voice was soft and feminine, no matter how ugly the string of words that carried to me.

I felt her on the other side, as she hovered in front of the peephole. I stared at it, knowing she was looking through.

After all these years, she got to see me before I saw her.

Then the door was wrenched open.

Alisa stood there with a pink flush staining her cheeks. Her hair should have been lavender, but it was brown instead now and hung loose to her waist, slightly wild from bed, which gave her a wanton look. My gaze roamed down her ribbed tank top and sleep shorts. Her eyes narrowed in response, and her fingers twitched, tightening on the hilt of the sword she carried.

"I take it you know me too?" she demanded. "How the hell did you get in my building?"

I tilted my head to one side. Alisa truly didn't remember that we all had the ability to glamor humans.

"May I come in?" I managed politely, even though I didn't appreciate being spoken to in that rude tone. I'd found ways to manage

Alisa's bratty side when we were together, although she'd hardly appreciate that now, from a stranger.

"I already told your brother, I don't need anything from you." Her chin rose imperiously.

"How did you know he's my brother?"

She studied me just as unapologetically as I'd eyed her, her gaze sweeping down my body, then lingering on my face. "I don't see a lot of six-foot-four black-haired, blue-eyed gods wandering the streets of D.C. Safe to say you two are related."

I couldn't help the faint smile that touched my lips. Duncan and I looked different in some ways—for one thing, our scars were different. He wore his hair long enough to cover the points of his ears, and since my ears were blunt, my hair was short, styled to look like a human male who took very good care of himself—but we did look alike.

Alisa thought we looked like *gods*. That was sweet. Her cheeks flushed and her pulse fluttered in her throat. She wouldn't be so unguarded with her attraction if she remembered me.

"He's actually six-foot three," I said.

She rolled her eyes. "I bet he'd say the same about you."

I nodded at the sword she carried. "Do you usually answer the door like that?"

"When someone knocks on my door, they usually either want rent money or revenge. So, yes."

There was a sound down the hall, and she glanced that way, pressing her sword behind her back to conceal it.

"What do you want?" she demanded.

"I want to bring you home."

Her eyes widened as they returned to me. *Got you.* Satisfaction rippled through my body, and I rested my shoulder against the doorframe, studying her face.

"Where's home?" she asked.

"The Fae world."

Her face immediately turned guarded. "Okay. Sure. And who the hell are you to me?"

Let me put this in human terms for her. "I'm your ex-boyfriend."

"Really?" She tilted her head to one side. "How come it took you so long to find me? Weren't looking hard, were you?"

"Not really, no." I'd searched the Fae world for her, thinking Herrick had her killed. Despite what she'd done to me, I'd wanted to make him pay for hurting her.

When I learned she was alive in the mortal world, I'd written her off. *Run away, Alisa. You always do.*

"How do you get to this—" Her lips arched mockingly. "Fae world?"

She didn't believe me.

I demanded, "You slaughter supernatural beasties, and you don't believe in the Fae world?"

"I don't believe in anything I can't see or touch," she said.

"I'm right here. I'm a Fae," I pointed out.

A strange impulse took me over. We were so close right now, and it had been so long since I felt her hands on my body. Just seeing her made my cock throb.

"You can see me." I caught her free hand in mine.

She drew back automatically, then I felt her give, as if she were curious.

That's right, Alisa. You always give in to me. A whisper from the past slipped through my memory, of my own voice, my lips against her throat. *Autumn always conquers summer.*

She'd been summer to me, no matter how cold she acted with the rest of the world.

I guided her slender hand to the hard planes of my chest. "You can feel me."

No matter how cool she acted, her pulse raced even faster now. Not fear. Alisa felt little fear. *Desire.*

"Who was I?" she asked, giving into her curiosity. "In that world?"

"You are Fae royalty," I told her.

She stared at me a second, her eyes widening, then she laughed out loud.

"Does this ever work with anyone?" she asked. "Whatever scam you're running?"

"I assure you, there is no scam." *Besides the truth of what awaited her in the Fae world after she walked through that portal.*

"There's no Fae world," she told me, shaking her head. Laughter bubbled on those beautiful lips of hers as she yanked away. "And I'm no princess."

I jumped to block the door, but her reflexes were as supernaturally fast as mine. She slammed it in my face just a second before my toe caught the door, and instead, I banged my boot harmlessly into the wood.

No, you're right. You're no princess.

You're a damned queen.

CHAPTER FIVE

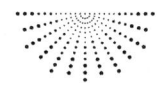

A *zrael*

Seven years *earlier*

It was close to midnight when the first carriages full of new students for the academy began to roll in. Mist cloaked the mountains that surrounded the academy, and a piercing chill hung in the air. It was always cold here, but the thick wool of my coat—and a bit of magic—kept me warm, even though my breath hung in the air.

This miserable place was the winter court's fault. It was only early fall in the rest of the world. This place, though, had been cursed.

And our instructors had seized upon that curse to engineer the most miserable school possible.

As the carriage doors opened, chattering first-year students clambered down. Their desire for warmth and rest was written baldly across their faces; they'd have to learn to hide *those* desires. This place was meant to break spoiled nobles of the need for comfort and safety.

Or perhaps it was just meant to break us, period.

"Glad to see you, little brother," I called to Duncan, catching him in the mass. He turned to me, a look of resignation written across his face. He'd known I'd be his senior here. He'd complained pretty miserably about our training every break, but I wouldn't let him fail here. Better for him to bleed and suffer at home.

"Brother," he said stiffly as he crossed to me. His posture was perfectly erect, even though his lips were dark with cold.

I could tell there was something insolent on the tip of his tongue, but he managed to hold it back for once. We weren't home any longer.

He reached into his thin jacket and drew out a letter, stamped with our father's seal. "Something for you."

"Thank you." I pocketed it to read later. "Bad news; I wasn't able to get you as my junior."

Duncan couldn't hold back his cynical huff. "I'll take my chances."

I hadn't actually tried. I wasn't always kind—he *was* my younger brother—but it didn't seem fair to take him as my junior like I'd threatened.

Every upperclassman at the school had a new student for a roommate, someone to mentor—and to haze. Our students came from wealthy families where they'd been spoiled; the chance to wash someone else's laundry and run their errands was good for them.

And it was fantastic for us as upperclassmen.

There was shouting ahead, and Duncan's head snapped in that direction. The hazing was beginning in earnest.

"You've got this," I promised him, clapping his shoulder. "No matter what I said this summer, you're the toughest male I know. They're going to try to break you, but you're just going to keep your head down and keep fighting until it's all over."

His lips tugged ruefully at the corners, but he didn't answer. He was always reserved, unexpectedly so for a middle child.

He took off running in the direction of the yelling. I remembered that early hazing well.

"Have fun!" I called after him, knowing that here was the only place my brother couldn't hurl a few carefully-selected curse words at me. I grinned.

I went back to my room, expecting that my roommate wouldn't show up until after dawn, bedraggled and shivering and ready to begin a day of fetching-and-carrying.

I hadn't particularly enjoyed being broken of my own spoiled attitude when I arrived at the academy, but it was hard for me to argue that it wasn't effective.

I walked into my room, which was lit only by the moonlight that shone off the snowy mountains and reflected into the room. I slung my coat over the back of the chair, kicked my boots off, and began to yank my shirt over my head.

"Well, hello."

The voice—amused, soft—stopped me dead. I dropped my shirt to the ground and trampled on it as I whirled and drew my sword from where it hung above my desk.

"Easy there, tough guy." The boy on the bed was a slight figure. His lavender hair was short, but wild and ruffled around a heart-shaped face. He grinned at me as if there was something amusing about how I'd come close to decapitating him.

I dropped my hand to my side, but hung onto the sword. He'd only spoken four words, but something about his tone was so irksome that I wasn't taking decapitation off the table quite yet.

"What are you doing?"

"I thought I was sleeping." He yawned. "Until you started your striptease."

I took a step forward, my jaw clenching. "You're lost. You're supposed to be outside with the other first year students."

"Am I?" He glanced out the window, just in time to see the dark snake of freshman cadets twisting up the mountain path. He frowned. "Are they *wet*? They're going to catch a chill."

"You should be with them," I warned. "Get up. Get going."

"I'm where I'm supposed to be," he promised. He extended his hand for me to shake, although he hadn't bothered to stand; he sat cross-legged on the bed now. "Faer of the summer court."

I stared at him, refusing to shake his hand. "Being a prince doesn't get you out of anything around here."

"As well it should not," he said. "I'm glad to hear it. Instructor Tomas told me to report to the barracks. And you are?"

"Why would he do that?" I demanded, irritation in my voice.

He shrugged. "Your name?"

I'd never met anyone who annoyed me so much in so little time.

I grabbed his collar and yanked him off the bed. He was barefoot, his toes dangling off the polished wooden floorboards, and so light and bird-boned that he must be a winged fairy. I was half-tempted to fling him out of the window to see how quick he was with those wings; it would be the fastest way for him to join the other freshmen.

Instead, I set him on the cold wooden floor. He gaped at me slightly, his lips parted as if no one had ever adjusted this brat's attitude in all his life.

"Get your socks and boots on. You're joining the others, and I don't want you too frostbitten to do my laundry in the morning."

He laughed at that. Then he must have seen something in my face. Suddenly, he sat on the end of the bed, hastily dragging on thick wool socks—two pairs, I noticed—then his boots. His uniform didn't quite seem to fit, and I frowned as I hastily dressed myself. Perhaps the princeling had annoyed his own servants so badly that they had wanted to embarrass him once he was out of reach.

"This is a misunderstanding," he said, and since his boots were more-or-less on and he was just trying to tie them, I seized the back of his neck and dragged him down the hall with me like an unruly kitten.

I shoved him through the door to the courtyard, hard enough that he landed on his knees in the snow.

"I've heard about you, Faer," I told him as I followed him out. "You care little about anything but your own pleasure. You're no warrior, and you're not fit to rule."

Anger tightened my chest. I was keenly aware of my own flaws, but I would die to protect my people if I had to. My mother, before she passed, had taken me everywhere with her across the autumn court, teaching me to be a worthy king someday.

"I can't do anything about that," I said. "That's up to you. But you will follow the goddamn rules here, and we'll see what good that will do you."

He got to his feet, clapping his hands off on his trousers. "You don't know me, Autumn."

It was disrespectful to call Fae by the name of their court, and I shoved him again. He landed on his ass in the snow, glaring up at me. It was that look of pure defiance on his face that caused me to drop on top of him, my thighs on either side of his, my hand catching his throat. I pressed down. Maybe the snow could cool that willful temper of his. The stories of how lazy he was in his training were infamous through the courts, and he was paying for his incompetence now. And would pay, for many months to come.

"Why are you too proud to join your peers?" I demanded. I caught a handful of snow and slapped it across his cheek, the motion dismissive and stinging, and he flushed with anger. "Shouldn't a prince be willing to lead by example?"

"This is stupid," he snarled back. "I'm happy to train and fight, but they're just being tortured."

"Some of them are your own nobles of the autumn court." I slapped him across the other cheek with another handful of snow. His cheeks were bright red now in that pale face. "What do you think they'll make of how you've abandoned them?"

"I haven't abandoned them," he said, trying to throw me, and my lips parted to laugh at him. He was such a child.

Then he somehow bucked and knocked me sideways. His leg trapped mine, and the two of us jostled for control across the snow.

"Enough." Professor Vail's voice was darker than the night itself. "Before someone sees the princes of our courts wrestling like children."

The two of us separated and scrambled apart. He was breathing hard, and the look he gave me suggested that if I slept in our room again, I might find myself knifed in my sleep.

Vail and I stared at each other.

"Teach him," he said, then turned and walked back into the house.

I looked at the boy across from me, slight and red-cheeked and still furious.

"Let's go meet your peers," I said, my voice deadly calm.

He was still breathing hard and his fury showed on his face. But he nodded once, curtly.

"I'll run with you," I said, leading the way. He followed, his feet crunching across the snow.

Someone would have to make sure the prince made it to his intended destination. I wasn't afraid to be a part of the group winding up and down the mountain, breaking through the icy river and stumbling up the wind-torn peak, then down again. I'd survived it before. I didn't mind paying the price for my position.

Noblesse oblige, after all.

I'd make sure this boy learned the meaning of the words—or that he quit.

CHAPTER SIX

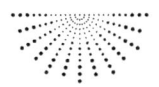

Alisa

WHAT A FUCKING DAY, already. I'd gotten just a few hours of sleep between last night's escapades and this morning's rude awakening. Fae? Really? I'd have to ask around. Maybe the two men were Fae; I didn't know everything about the supernatural world yet, by a long shot.

And they were beautiful to an extent that felt *unreal.* Just thinking about their easy confidence, those tall, powerful bodies, those magnetic eyes and dark hair... my thighs tightened, my core throbbing with sudden longing. Yeah, there was something weird about those guys.

But I was definitely no princess.

The 'Fae' hammered on my front door.

"Go away!" I shouted. I had to figure out what they wanted, but on my own timeline. They were obviously trying to manipulate me, and I didn't want to play their game, whatever it was.

I expected more hammering.

Instead, the hall went quiet. I rolled my eyes, hardly comforted. It was probably a trap.

I'd spent that first year trying everything I could to get my memories back. I'd been to tarot readers and witches and a hypnotherapist. Nothing brought the past back to me.

But I could be sure of one thing: I wasn't a princess.

Besides, someone would've come looking for a missing princess. It wouldn't have taken them five years.

I padded through my threadbare little apartment to the bathroom, rested my sword against the bathroom cabinet, and turned the water on in the shower. The hot water pipes groaned and screamed until the water began to ping against the tile floor, but other than that, the apartment was silent. My neighbors weren't stirring yet.

I kept expecting Prince Charming to somehow magic his way inside my apartment, but I was mercifully alone as I quickly washed my hair. I leaned out of the shower to grab my toothbrush, then brushed my teeth as I stood under the hot spray. My apartment might have been a little the worse for wear, but I loved how compact and efficient it was.

I'd have to use a hot shower and hotter coffee to substitute for sense and sleep last night. I needed to be in good shape for work. I hustled out of the bathroom still toweling off, finger-tousled my waves to make sure they air-dried halfway decently, and then quickly dressed in scrub pants, a long-sleeved t-shirt, and the scrub top over it.

The Hunters had not only helped me find a mission, but they'd helped me find a day job, because slaying vamps didn't pay anyone's rent. Killing was just a hobby of mine.

I had an unusual knack with animals, so despite my lack of any education—or a birth certificate, for that matter—Elly had pulled some strings and found me under-the-table work as a vet tech.

When I saw her tonight anyway, I'd ask her about the Fae. At least I had something to research now. Then I'd figure out what to do with these mysterious strangers.

I grabbed my oversized leather purse, checking to make sure I had my phone, wallet and then, most importantly of all, my knives. I sighed. What I *didn't* have was breakfast or time to make it. Whatever. I could run by the coffee shop. I almost smiled to myself at the thought that no one could yell at me at work today, right? Because I was a *princess*.

I rushed out into the hallway, locking my door behind me.

The hall was empty. Mr. Tall-Dark-and-Gorgeous-Two was gone. I felt disappointed instead of relieved, as I should have.

"No common sense," I muttered, taking the stairs in a hurry. I preferred an interesting life over an easy one, and I had the scars and bruises to prove it. My curiosity about those two handsome assholes was proof too.

I ran to the metro stop, caught the metro, and made it to my destination with minutes to spare. *Coffee time.*

I was waiting in the line when I became keenly aware of a big body behind me. I caught the faint scent of some pleasant aftershave or cologne, something clean and bright that reminded me of pine and crisp snow on an icy winter day.

I whirled, expecting I'd been found once again by the damned 'Fae'.

But the man behind me was unfamiliar. He looked younger, his blond hair ruffled. He was built too, though, all lean, chiseled muscle.

When I made eye contact with him, his green eyes widened, as if he hadn't expected the stranger at the coffee shop to eyeball him. Human then. I twisted back around, my damp hair swishing across my shoulders.

"Excuse me," he said.

I squeezed my eyes shut, wishing I believed in a god to pray to for patience.

Well, too bad. I'd just have to make do without any, and the rest of the world would have to make do with *me*.

"Are you talking to me?" I asked in a voice that suggested that was a mistake.

"Yes," he said. "But I'd like a bit of privacy for what I have to say next."

I almost laughed, raking my fingers through my hair to push it back from my face. "How many more of you are there?"

I wasn't sure I could make it through any more.

"Just the three of us," he said, then pressed his palm to his chest, bowing forward slightly. "My name is Tiron."

"Your friend didn't manage to introduce himself this morning."

"My friends are idiots." His green eyes sparkled with mischief.

I studied him for a second. "I like you a little bit better, but I'm still not going with you to some second location for *privacy*. Sorry."

"Oh, I don't need you to do that." His lips parted in an easy smile. "I'll give us privacy right here."

I arched an eyebrow at him as some wayward combination of concern, curiosity and excitement rushed through my blood. *Death wish.* Maybe the asshole in the alley hadn't been wrong about that.

"Leave, please," he said, glancing around the room at the people who filled it. His voice was warm, soothing. There was something magnetic about it. But just because he sounded nice didn't mean—

People pushed back their chairs, scraping the legs across the linoleum. The people ahead of me abruptly turned and ambled out of line, heading out the door. One of the baristas pulled her apron over her head and dropped it on a table next to someone's steaming, abandoned coffee.

For a second, horror washed over me. He'd spoken. They'd obeyed. The implications of that, of how humans could be abused and forced, rolled over me and left me sick, but I swallowed the surge of fear.

"Oh come on!" I turned to face him, popping my hands onto my hips. "I needed them to get my coffee!"

"Do you?" he asked. He headed behind the counter, turned to face me. "What does Your Majesty desire?"

I rolled my eyes. "I'll get it myself."

"Not used to being *served* anymore, Majesty?"

"You didn't wash your hands," I shot back. I served myself a scone and poured myself a cup of coffee. I'd leave the money behind to pay for both. "So could I do that too? What *was* that?"

"A glamour. And yes, you can make humans do almost anything."

"That seems deeply immoral," I pointed out. Then admitted, "Also useful. Does it work on vamps and shifters and whatnot?"

"I do not know." He carried a glass jar full of chocolate chip cookies in the crook of his arm, already nibbling on one, as he headed past me into the café area. He pushed a chair back from a table with his foot. "Talk with me?"

"Fine," I said. No point in denying my curiosity any longer. I sat across from him, studying him. He was as ridiculously handsome as the other two, but in a different way. His lips were soft and pink, with a pronounced bow and a rounded lower lip, as sensual as the rest of his face was sharp.

He studied me right back, his green eyes seeming to take in far too much. Finally, he waved his hand, encompassing the empty coffee shop. "You can't deny the Fae world is real now."

It wasn't a question.

There was the possibility these males were running some kind of game, but the simplest answer was that they were indeed what they said they were.

"You're Fae," I agreed—at least for now. "Why are you here?"

"You're Fae as well." He lifted a cup to his lips, taking a sip, before I realized he didn't have his own mug. He set my cup back in front of me, flashing me an innocent look as I frowned at him.

"Maybe," I said guardedly. I didn't remember anything from my life before, so it was hard to argue I wasn't. I wrapped my hands around my coffee cup, guarding it from him. "Why did you come looking for me now?"

"You're our queen," he said simply. "The heir to the throne. Your father is dead."

Something dark twisted through my gut at his words. Not a sense of loss, exactly. As if my body felt something, even if my brain couldn't understand.

"Did I like him?" I asked, to buy myself time.

"Not particularly, from what I've heard."

"And would I like being queen?"

"I suppose you would." Tiron tilted his head, studying me. "You were rich and powerful and loved in our world. Who'd turn that down?"

Loved. I'd been ready to snort at the idea of being rich and powerful—as if there wouldn't be strings attached to all that—and then my heart caught on the word *loved.*

As if there wouldn't be strings attached to *that,* too.

"I'm curious," I admitted, and Tiron's eyes sharpened. "But I don't remember anything about my life before."

"I think someone stole your memories," he said.

"Who?"

He shook his head. "We don't know."

"Can I get them back?" I asked. Eagerness broke into my voice, despite my best intentions.

"Maybe. In the Fae world."

I frowned at him, not caring for that answer. They wanted me to go with them a whole lot, and that aroused my suspicion. "Why not in *this* world? So I can make an informed decision on whether I want to stick with my life here or return to the old one?"

He almost laughed. "Do you call this a life?"

What a beautiful, condescending bastard.

"Yes," I said. "I do."

I stood from the table, and his lips pressed shut.

Then he tried again, his voice more kind. "There isn't enough magic in this world to break that kind of enchantment. Whoever cursed you to lose your memories, your identity—that was powerful magic."

I laughed out loud, rubbing my arms absently. "Great. So I have powerful enemies with big magic and I'm supposed to walk back into *that* clueless? I don't think so."

"Alisa. Please. Your brother Faer needs you to come home. He can't rule without you."

"Why?" I demanded.

"You're twins," he said simply. "The throne is yours as much as his."

I had no memory of a brother, no sense of a *twin,* and even though

I'd never thought to miss one before, suddenly that felt like an ache. I'd shared a womb with someone that I didn't even know existed?

My chest tightened. Did my twin miss me?

"I keep hearing an awful lot about what everyone wants from me," I said. "But I want my memories back. I'm not walking into the Fae world with no idea how anything works, or who I am, or who you all are. No, thanks."

"Alisa—"

"You can say my name like that all you want. Figure out how to bring my memories back, and I'll consider going with you."

He stared at me, his eyes wide. I still kind of liked him, despite myself. He was sexy as hell, charming in an odd, quirky way. Something about the way he looked at me drew my touch.

I ruffled his hair with my hand as I went past. Then the bells rang at the café door as I went out.

For a second, the street felt too quiet, as if he'd ordered everyone else to go home, and the sense of something eerie settled over me.

Then a car zoomed by, and a dog barked down the street.

Everything was normal here on Earth.

Well, as normal as Earth ever was.

CHAPTER SEVEN

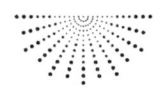

Tiron

"Stunning successes, all around," Azrael said, shaking his head.

As the sun melted into dusk, the three of us lingered outside the veterinary clinic where Alisa worked.

Duncan shrugged, not particularly alarmed by the failure of diplomacy. He never was. "So we execute our fallback plan."

I shook my head at Duncan, and he frowned at me. "What?"

"You just try so hard to be scary," I said, clapping his shoulder with my hand.

"I *am* scary," he pointed out. *"You* used to be scared of me."

"I wouldn't say scared." The badass warrior had knocked me on my ass when I first came to the autumn court, because I'd mistaken him for his brother. He'd knocked me on my ass quite a few times since then, for that matter. But he had a good heart underneath all that grouch.

"I would," he disagreed.

Azrael ignored our banter, seemingly lost in thought.

"She seems…different," he mused.

"Good. Almost anything would be an improvement over the old Alisa," Duncan said.

I hadn't known Alisa. But from what I'd been told of her, her Majesty's current occupation had been a surprise. Most surprisingly of all was what we'd seen, watching her. We'd used magic to cloak ourselves and follow her through the clinic.

She seemed to charm everyone who came into the clinic, whether on two feet or four. She had an easy way with animals that took away their fear. She leaned into doggie kisses, gently coaxed cats out from carriers. When she helped an old woman with an even older cat, who was dying of cancer, there'd been tears in her eyes after she saw them out to spend a few last days together.

"She hardly seems like the villain I've heard so much about," I said.

"She has a way of getting men to let their guard down." Duncan glanced at Azrael pointedly.

"My guard is up," Azrael promised. "I haven't forgotten what she did."

"You've forgiven her a lot in the past," Duncan grumbled. "More than you should have. If you didn't have a tender heart toward her—"

I grinned. No one thought Azrael had a *tender heart,* except for Duncan, apparently.

Azrael pushed him against the brick wall in a sudden flurry of motion. "Shut up."

Duncan's lips quirked at the corners. Normally he'd have come off the wall swinging, but right now, he seemed pleased to have made Azrael lose some of his cool, proving his point. "How has it been, seeing her again? Are you still just as ready to drag her to kneel at Faer's feet?"

"Of course." Azrael patted his brother's shoulder before he stepped back, as if he were dusting him off. "What matters is restoring the autumn court. Protecting the Fae world. Let her face her sins…or at least, some of them."

"The sins she doesn't remember?" I asked, my voice barbed.

I had my own plans for the queen, but I had to admit, her punishment hardly seemed fair.

"She still committed them," Azrael said, his voice as relaxed as ever. "Let's go bring our wayward royal home."

He broke off as Alisa stepped out of the clinic. Her hair was pulled up into a messy bun on top of her head, revealing the long line of her neck. She still wore scrub pants, but her long-sleeved t-shirt cuffs had been pushed halfway up her slender forearms.

A truck turned the corner, moving slowly. As it came close to Alisa, something rang a subconscious alarm bell for me, and I started forward.

The truck slowed. Alisa started down the sidewalk, heading for the metro stop. She turned suddenly, as if she felt the threat coming.

One of the men leaned down and snatched her, picking her up with ease that no human should have.

I broke into a run, chasing the truck. It picked up speed as soon as her feet had left the pavement, even though they were still wrestling with her. She kicked one man in the face, and he almost dropped her back over the side.

Her purse fell on the pavement and exploded open, scattering makeup and a paperback and knives across the ground, and I jumped over the debris.

One of the guys hit her across the head, and she fell to her knees in the back of the truck. Her wide eyes met mine, just for a second, full of fear.

Then she fell forward, into the bed of the pickup.

I launched myself into the air to catch the back of the truck, knowing it was an almost impossible feat.

I almost made it. Landed hard on the pavement. Stumbled, caught myself, kept running, despite the sudden ache in my ankle.

Then another car slammed its brakes to a stop just ahead me. Duncan glowered at me from the driver's side. "You could be smarter."

"I could," I admitted. I threw open the back door and jumped in, and Duncan sped off before I even managed to get the door shut.

But he kept a distance from the truck, staying back so they

wouldn't realize we were following them. Azrael rubbed the back of his neck absently, and Duncan glanced over at him, one eyebrow cocked, as if he knew that Azrael was worried about her.

"Faer doesn't care if we bring her back in pieces," Duncan said.

"Would you shut up?" Azrael said. "I know you want to pretend you never loved her either, but your attempt at keeping your distance is *exasperating*. And it doesn't actually fool anyone."

Duncan's eyes narrowed, his hands tightening on the steering wheel, but he didn't answer.

I desperately wanted to know more about *that*, but from the way Duncan reacted, now wasn't the time to press.

"Let's go rescue a princess." Azrael's tone brightened. "She'll be thrilled to see us again. This couldn't be more perfect. She should be much more compliant when she realizes how much she needs us."

I'd say they were probably both psychopaths, but well, they were Fae and they were royalty. That made them both psychopaths twice over.

CHAPTER EIGHT

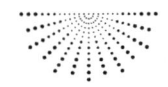

Alisa

I woke up slowly. My head ached, and so did my neck. When I shifted, trying to get comfortable, I couldn't move far. My arms were behind me, my shoulders tense, and I couldn't change position.

Fuck.

My head jerked up as I realized I was tied to a chair. My vision was blurry at first as I looked around. There were two men standing in the room with me, both with big shit-eating, evil grins. I was in what looked like a haunted house.

Or what might soon *become* a haunted house.

"Oh, there she is!" The man in front of me clapped his hands together in an expression of sociopathic joy.

My neck still ached, and I moved my head back and forth, trying to work out the kinks enough to raise my eyes to his face. Right now I was stuck looking at the paunch that strained over the waistband of his jeans.

I blinked at him. "Your ugly face is oddly familiar."

"You're going to have an ugly face by the time we're done with you," he promised.

"Where do I know you from?" It was so hard to remember who I'd pissed off most recently.

"This might refresh your memory." His friend said as he stepped too close to me, then pulled up his shirt to reveal a jagged scar across his blindingly white skin.

I winced. "No, it really doesn't."

I rarely left a bad guy alive behind me, and this was why. If you were going to fight, better finish it.

The first guy stepped close to me, grabbing the back of my chair in one hand as he leaned down. His other hand landed on my thigh, and I gritted my teeth against the burning sensation of an unwanted touch.

I didn't remember anything from my life before, but I hated being crowded at the best of times. I always wondered if something had happened that made me that way.

"A year ago, we were looking for breeders," he said, his voice intimately close to my ear, and I would've leaned away if he wouldn't have interpreted the movement as fear. "You interfered."

"You're shifters," I said. Not all shifters were bad—I'd worked with some before—but there were pockets of evil. Just like humans, only these assholes were furrier. Then understanding dawned. "Oh! You're the pack that was stealing girls off the street and turning them against their will. The assholes with the roofies!"

Yeah, I'd ruined their fun. I'd gone into the bar where they hunted, looking cute and harmless. They'd tried to roofie me, and I'd played their game. Until they got me out into the alleyway, where they discovered I was actually very, very awake.

I hadn't realized I left Mr. Zig-Zag Scar alive. Sloppy work. I shook my head at myself. I still had to talk to Elly about my solo Hunting escapade and now I'd have to tell her I'd Hunted sloppy a year ago. Carter was going to laugh his ass off at me. I'd never hear the end of it.

I'd been headed to dinner at Elly's after work. Would she and the other Hunters be suspicious enough to come looking for me? Would they even have a chance at tracking down these dirtballs before they killed me?

Zig-Zag finally dropped his shirt. Thank Zeus. It was bad enough I was probably going to die here, I didn't need to be blinded by his ugly stomach too.

"Now you're going to be one of our breeders," the first one promised me. "Once you give me a baby, I'm going to cut off little pieces of you until you beg me to let you die."

"That's no way to treat the mother of your child." Thank god, that was a very long-term plan. They didn't plan to kill me today.

Then Mr. Zig-Zag sat on a chair in the corner of the room, preparing a syringe. "Oh, you'll love the way we're going to treat you."

Fuck. They planned to keep me drugged. The first flutters of fear rose in my stomach. I didn't want to lose control. The thought that I wouldn't be able to defend myself made something hollow open in my stomach.

The other guy, the one who still hovered over me, rubbed his hand over my thigh. His touch made my skin crawl, even through the scrubs.

He was close to me, but cautious, not bringing his face into striking range. I couldn't slam my forehead into his nose or sink my teeth into his throat. I was no vamp or shifter, but I didn't need to be something supernatural to be mean.

How the hell was I going to get out of this? I looked around frantically. There was a stained mattress in the corner of the room. I sucked in a breath. Did they have other girls in here?

I thought I'd killed these guys. Fury at myself washed over me. How many other women might they have hurt because of my failure?

"It's going to be such fucking joy to turn you into a breeder," Mr. Handsy promised me as his buddy Zig-Zag strolled over with the syringe.

I struggled harder, the legs of the chair rocking and scraping across the linoleum. But no matter how much my fingers tensed, I couldn't move my duct-taped wrists. Zig-Zag kneeled behind me, out of sight, and then there was a brutal pinch as the syringe went into my arm. Whatever he injected burned through my vein.

"Lucky us." Zig-Zag stood up. "We caught ourselves a Hunter bitch."

"Unluckily for you," a voice said from the doorway, "you also caught yourself a Fae bitch."

The world went blurry around me as the three big Fae men moved into the room. Duncan was flanked by those two enormous black dogs, then they slunk into the shadows and seemed to disappear. I frowned at them. Was I hallucinating them? Were they real? The world seemed to be growing fuzzy.

The gratitude and relief that spiked through my chest at the sight of them could *not* be real.

Tiron strode across the room, his eyes widening as he took in the syringe. "They drugged her."

Zig-Zag scrambled to his feet. "Who the hell are you?"

Tiron slammed him against the wall. His eyes were full of protective fury. Aw, that was sweet.

Tiron pulled him away, then slammed him into the wall again, so hard the drywall cracked. His voice was a growl: "What did you give her?"

"My own special blend," Zig-Zag said, and then Tiron punched him across the face, once, twice. The man fell back against the wall, his eyes fluttering closed.

"Restraint, Tiron!" Duncan scolded him.

Handsy pulled a gun out of the waistband of his jeans, cocking it as he pressed the cold metal to my temple.

I should have been terrified, but I laughed at the cold tickling against my temple. It all seemed so surreal right now. The world tilted.

The third Fae moved so fast he was a blur—was that my imagination or was it real? Because he didn't move like anything human. A gunshot split the room and splintered through the wall. The dogs snarled. Handsy screamed before he was whipped behind me, out of my line of sight.

The third Fae knelt in front of me. He rested his hands lightly on my knees. His face was careful, worried, and that made me want to laugh too. He looked so serious, and I tried to press my lips together, looking just as serious as he did.

"Look at me, Alisa. How are you feeling?"

"Are you even real?" I asked him. "My Faerie? Do I have a guardian faerie instead of a guardian angel?"

His eyes widened. Tiron tried to cover a laugh, turning it into a spectacularly unconvincing cough.

"If you're real, I'm thrilled to see you," I said. There was something that had worried me, something I was forgetting, and I frowned, trying to remember it. "Oh! Could you go see if there are any girls in the house? I tried to stop these guys before, but I failed. I hope they didn't hurt anyone."

The thought made my throat close up, the humor fleeing.

He studied me with curious eyes. "Fight their drugs, Alisa. I'll go check the house."

He squeezed my knees as he rose. For some reason, I didn't mind him touching me.

"She's high as can be," Tiron said.

"This is another part of human culture you made yourself familiar with, didn't you?" Duncan grunted.

"Cut her loose," the lead Fae said as he went to the door. "I'm going to check the house."

"Still following her orders, huh?"

"Shut up, Duncan."

Duncan grunted. "I like her better tied up."

"Why are you such a jackass?" Tiron asked as he knelt behind me. "She must have been scared. Have a heart."

Cold touched my skin—metal, blade—and then my hands came apart. I shook out my shoulders as the tension released.

"You don't realize yet that she doesn't have one," Duncan said. "You're wasting your sympathies."

Tiron knelt in front of me, cutting the duct tape that secured my ankles to the chair. Restless tension swept through my legs in relief at being free, and I stood, only to feel my knees crumble beneath me.

He caught me easily, sweeping me up into his arms. I breathed in his pine scent as he held me against his powerful chest. He carried me as if I weighed nothing.

"You're all right," he murmured in my ear, and his voice was low and sexy, a purr that I could feel through my body, into my bones. It made me want to relax into him and sleep.

But it wasn't for myself that I was afraid, and I struggled to stay awake. "The girls…"

He looked down at me, a frown indenting the skin between his deep green eyes. "You're nothing like I expected, Alisa."

"The house is empty." The leader came back, frowning. "But there are recent signs someone was contained here against their will."

"Human problems," Duncan said shortly. "We have our own problems back home, remember?

Wait. They wanted to take me back home. What was wrong there? I tried to ask, but the words came out slurred. Tiron gazed down at me with worried eyes.

"Let's get her somewhere safe to sleep this off," the other one said, still standing in the doorway. "One of us will keep a watch on the house. See if anyone comes and discovers the bodies, follow them if they do."

Relief flooded my chest. I didn't want to just abandon anyone who might need us. I tried to say something, but by the time I managed to form the first word, I couldn't have imagined the end of the sentence. I frowned at them all, my head aching as I tried to think.

"Don't try to talk," Tiron murmured in my ear. The world was blurring, getting darker at the edges, as he carried me through what felt like endless rooms, as if time were slowing. "We've got you now, Alisa."

Meaningless promises from people I didn't know. And yet as the walls seemed to fall away around me, as the world seemed to fall away, I felt safe in his arms.

Then darkness washed over me, and there was nothing else.

CHAPTER NINE

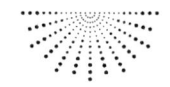

R *aile*

"Where's my bride?" I asked Faer as soon as his blank-eyed human servant showed me into his study.

"Patience." Faer stood at the bar, mixing his own drink, and he turned to me, holding out a pair of crystal goblets. "Nothing good comes without patience."

My lips twisted into a grim smile. Nothing about Alisa was particularly *good*.

"Did you find your hobgoblin?" Faer asked me as I took the goblet from him.

I grunted in response. He didn't need to worry about my antidotes to his sister's old tricks.

He reminded me of Alisa with their shared sharp, mischievous features, though he wore his long lavender hair tied back, revealing the long, narrow points of his ears. He could never pass for human, but Alisa was softer-featured.

I'd thought for a while that perhaps Herrick had killed her. How strange to imagine her in the odd human world instead: the princess buying her food in the cold, bright aisles of a supermarket. Was she *working?* The thought made me want to laugh.

"You remain as sparkling a conversationalist as ever." Faer raised his glass in a toast that I didn't meet.

I took a long sip, studying him.

He went on, "I was going to ask if this was really how you wanted to punish her—it seems like punishing yourself too. But if you are going to be this boring with her, it does seem a fitting punishment. There's nothing Alisa despises so much as boredom."

"Then I don't think she will care for the undersea." But I already knew that. It was one of the many reasons she'd rejected me before.

I moved to the window, where the curtains shimmered, moving faintly in the breeze. The moon shone bright above the ocean tonight, sending silver ripples across the dark. "Will you be sad to send your sister away so soon after the two of you are reunited?"

"I think I'll be able to soothe myself," Faer said. "I've missed her this long, after all."

I could practically feel Faer's gaze as a prickle across my spine. "Perhaps our alliance will comfort your spirit."

Faer used to be quite fond of his sister. I wasn't sure what had changed between them, but his altered feelings left me suspicious.

Still, Faer was much changed from the boy I'd once known anyway. He didn't seem to feel fondly of anyone these days.

"You know, I think it will," Faer said. There was a creak as he took his chair in front of the fire again. "I heard from my scouts that she seems to have lost her memories. It will be interesting to see if she remembers you."

I turned, my brows tilting. What a fascinating development.

"If she doesn't, I would appreciate it if you didn't alert her to our history." Perhaps I could charm her. Perhaps she'd come along readily to her prison under the sea. A smile slipped across my lips.

Faer laughed, a cruel, hard sound. "That look on your face... it even scares me a little."

"I would never harm your sister," I promised him. Just because I wanted my revenge for the trick she'd played on me—and the embarrassment she caused my court and family—didn't mean I intended to be cruel.

Though she might find it so.

He shrugged. "Harm her, don't. I don't care."

I studied him. Once, he'd been a boy who waded into a nest of stinging water-beetles to rescue his sister when she fell into the lagoon outside the castle. Her elaborate gown threatened to drag her under. He'd drawn her out, the two of them both soaked to the skin, their long, pretty hair stuck to their angular faces. Then they'd collapsed in laughter on the bank at the sight of each other.

I'd fallen a bit in love with them both that day, although the next day, my father took me back to the sea. I'd thought about Alisa constantly since then, and when Alisa's father reached out to me with a marriage offer five years ago, I'd jumped at the chance.

Faer was very different now. Was it possible the stories were true, and Faer was enchanted?

Or had he simply grown cold and psychopathic, as happened to almost any man with his kind of power?

"What is it, Raile?" Faer asked without looking up from his goblet. He'd grown tired of my gaze, apparently, even though he seemed to stare at me freely when my back was turned.

My voice came out flat when I said, "I'm simply having trouble containing my excitement at the promise of reunion with my bride."

"I hope you can find a bit more enthusiasm when you greet her," Faer said. "Or she might see through your ruse, even if she truly doesn't remember you."

Rude. The merfolk find me amusing.

I shrugged. I've never been as good on land as I am in the water, in any way.

But once I have my princess, I need never emerge from the sea again.

CHAPTER TEN

A*lisa*

FOR A FEW LONG minutes after I woke, I stared at the ceiling. My mouth was dry, my tongue thick. I swallowed with effort, listening to the low rumble of masculine voices in the next room.

I was in my own apartment.

I was not alone.

I never let anyone come into my apartment. Even Carter and Julian had barely been further than the front door; I didn't want to give either of them the wrong impression.

The unnamed Fae stood in the doorway. His figure was tall and imposing—he looked every bit like a strange Fae god who had wandered into our world, even in a t-shirt and jeans—and I closed my eyes.

He was just too much. Too much arrogance, too much power, too much raw sexual desire when he was near me. Most of all, he was too much *history*. I didn't remember any of that history, but it bothered me to know I had an ex-boyfriend who knew me intimately, while I didn't know a damn thing about him.

Even when I feigned sleep, though, I was keenly aware of his body a few yards away from mine. It felt almost as if there was some kind of connection between us, something that made me hyper aware of his every movement.

"You're awake." His voice was low and sexy, and I felt that honeyed voice seep through my muscles, filling them with warmth. The effect he had on me was undeniable.

I sighed and gave up the ruse. As I raised my head, it felt as if my brain shifted in my skull. I still had a pounding headache.

"Would you like some water?" he asked, stepping into the room. He picked up a glass on the bedside table, then perched on the edge of the bed.

I shifted onto my elbows, then sat back against the padded headboard. "How'd you get in here?" My voice came out a rasp.

He held out the glass, raising his eyebrows, and our fingertips briefly overlapped before I pulled the glass away from him. I took a long sip of cold ice-water, then kept drinking eagerly.

"Duncan picked up your purse for you. Your keys and the like."

"Duncan. That's the grouchy one."

"Indeed." He smiled, a nice smile that crinkled the corners of his eyes.

"Who are you?"

"Azrael."

"What kind of name is Azrael?"

"All right, *Alisa*. It's a Fae name." He tilted his head to one side, studying me. "How do you feel?"

I handed him back the empty glass, and he quirked an eyebrow at me but took it. I glanced down at the covers, at my scrub top. No one had taken off my clothes when they put me in bed. Good. "I seem to be in one piece."

"You aren't upset about what those men tried to do?"

I stared at him, my brows knitting together. Was he trying to *make* me upset? Was he trying to manipulate me into feeling I owed him something?

These guys wanted me to come back to the Fae world for some reason. I wasn't going to trip over myself with gratitude.

"You had nightmares all night," he added. "Do you remember them?"

"No."

"I wonder what you dream about."

I frowned at him. I didn't like his curiosity, the way he studied me. I wondered what he knew about my past that I didn't. The thought that he held answers—that he held *power* over me—made me squeamish.

"Did you find a way to bring my memories back?" I demanded.

"You need to come home," he said. "Whatever enchantment took your memories, it can only be lifted in the world of magic."

I shook my head, even though it felt as if it might wobble right off my aching neck. Lord, last night had left me sore all over, and I ran my hand over the back of my neck, teasing my fingers over the tense muscles in my shoulder blades, trying to press out some of the kinks.

"Why are you so stubborn?" he demanded. "You're royalty, and yet you don't want to go home?"

"I want to go," I said, surprised to hear the truth in the words as I said them. I couldn't say *home*, though. "But *someone* took my memories, right? Someone hurt me there. And you want me to go over there with no idea what I'm walking into? I'm just supposed to trust you?"

Something flashed through his eyes, a look of horror that was there and gone before I could make sense of it.

"Yes, Alisa," he said, reaching toward me, though he didn't quite touch my hand. "You're supposed to trust me."

I cocked my head to one side. "You said you're my ex-boyfriend. Why did we break up?"

He met my gaze levelly. For the first time, I noticed his eyes were purple, but not exactly. A deep blue around his pupil darkened as it radiated outward, specked with red flecks that bled into purple.

Monster eyes. Magnetic eyes. Either way, I could lose myself in his gaze. I blinked, forcing myself to look away, my chin rising.

"You're the only one who knows that," he said, and his voice was bitter. He rose, moving away from the bed. "You didn't let me know in the kindest of ways."

I chewed my lower lip at his tone. I couldn't argue with him, but I doubted what he said. I didn't think I was an unkind person.

"Were you my first boyfriend?" I asked.

He turned at the door. "Stop saying *boyfriend*. That's not a word the Fae use."

Males are so irrational, no matter the species. "It's the word you used with me."

"I was trying to make you feel comfortable." His gaze drifted over me.

No matter how icy, something about the way he looked at me sent a strange thrill of lust throbbing through my body. He hadn't touched me except for that staid touch when he knelt to check on me in the shifters' den, but it was easy for me to imagine what it would be like if he did run his hands up my body. I wondered if his hands would feel cool against my skin or if he ran hot. The thought made me bite my lip.

Nothing about Azrael made me feel *comfortable.*

"In the Fae world, firsts don't matter like they do here. We don't believe in virginity or prize..." He broke off suddenly.

I stared at him, wondering what he was going to say, what he was clearly debating. He seemed so cold and controlled, that I thought he wouldn't speak at all.

Then he said flatly, "But you were my first. You were my first *everything.*"

I frowned at him, but he was already striding out of the room. There was the creak of my front door, distantly, and I swung my feet out of bed. What now?

My head ached and the world reeled for a second, but I found my balance as my toes pressed against the cold hardwood floor.

Finding my balance after being drugged into blissful oblivion? Check.

Finding my balance anywhere around Azrael?

No fucking check marks for me there.

CHAPTER ELEVEN

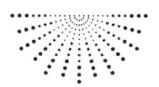

Duncan

"What are you doing back here?" Azrael demanded, entering the living room from the narrow hallway just as I walked in the front door.

"Hello to you too," I grumbled. I ducked under the nonsensical string of flamingo lights hanging across the doorway, slamming the door behind me. "Someone found the bodies. There was much weeping and lamenting."

"Did you follow them back to where they came from?" Azrael threw himself onto the couch, one arm over the leg of the chair, and reached for the cold, sweating beer on the coffee table. It figured he'd made himself comfortable while I was out trailing smelly shifters.

"I did," I said. "To some shifter compound. They seem to be keeping some other girls as breeding stock."

"We have to help them." Alisa clung to the doorway. She swayed on her feet, her pale face even paler than usual.

She was going to lose her balance. Azrael twisted to look at her, but by the time he rose from the couch, he'd be too late.

"Foolish girl," I grumbled, even as I dove across the room to catch her.

She grabbed for the doorway, her eyes widening, as if she realized she was going down. But I caught her first, scooping her up against my chest.

She was so light—bird-boned, built for flight—and she twined her arms around my neck automatically. My muscles tensed, going rigid at the feel of her lithe body pressed against mine so intimately.

I hated her.

But she smelled delicious, like a perfect summer day, like fresh-squeezed lemons and spun sugar and clean cut grass.

Azrael sat back on the couch, a grin spreading across his face.

"I'm just a little dizzy," she protested. "Put me down."

I scoffed at that. She was always independent to a fault. "I'm not sure you can be trusted to *stand*. I never trusted you, but that's a whole new level—"

I broke off as Azrael shook his head at me.

Instead, I sat on the couch opposite him, still holding Alisa in my arms. "Where's Tiron?"

"I sent him to fetch dinner," Azrael said. "We should gather some strength before we head back into the Fae world."

"We need to help those girls first." Alisa sounded sure of herself, earnest. "I have some friends—"

I snorted at that, even though I'd glimpsed her friends at a distance after her run-in with the vamps. Humans were foolish; it was no surprise Alisa had woven her magic around them, even though she didn't know how to cast a glamor consciously.

She gave me a confused look, even as she went on, "They'll help. Then once I know the girls are safe, I'll go into the Fae world with you."

"You trust us?" Azrael sounded pleased.

"No." She struggled against my chest, pushing away, but she still seemed dizzy and weak.

I raised my hands to my shoulders, palms out, making a show of not holding her.

Her ineffective struggle to escape me amused me, as her warm, slender body pressed against mine. Then as she struggled to leave my lap, her ass brushed my cock over and over. My cock hardened, and I didn't know whether I wanted her off me or wanted her to stay.

When she looked at Azrael, I could see just how pale her lips were. High, feverish color still lingered in her cheeks from those damned drugs.

"We don't need your friends." I ran my hand up her arm to her shoulder and pulled her against my chest again. "You are going to hurt yourself. Just relax."

Azrael stared at me with jealousy flaring in his deep purple eyes. I glared back over her shoulder. He'd put me in the position of pretending to care for her. He shouldn't resent how I played the game now.

"We can take care of the shifters on our own," I added.

She rolled her eyes. "Sure. You don't know anything about the shifters but—"

"There are eight of them." I tucked my chin over her head, wrapping her in my arms. "Easy enough."

I didn't know why I pulled her against my body—although it would annoy Azrael, which was always a hobby of mine—but for some reason, she stopped fighting me. She must be exhausted.

I clarified, "Eight male shifters. I think there are two females there, against their will."

"Eight to four, I like our odds," she muttered.

"Eight to three, Majesty," I mocked her. "You don't need to do anything."

She laughed, rubbing her hand across her face as if she were still exhausted. "You want me in a management role? I'll just boss you around?"

"That would be what you usually preferred," I said. "You've generally taken the easy way out."

Azrael shot me another warning look. I gave him my most innocent expression in return.

"You were just injured," Azrael said, sitting on the edge of the couch and leaning toward Alisa.

But *I* was the one holding her. Azrael must relish that.

He seemed to be trying to ignore me, focused on Alisa as he went on. "We can take care of the shifters, and then we'll go home."

"Why don't you want my friends to come?" she asked.

"Fae try not to reveal themselves in the mortal world," Azrael explained.

"The mortal world," she repeated, her lips quirking. "This all seems quite unbelievable, you know."

"From our perspective," Azrael said, "the idea our beloved princess of summer was hidden in this world all this time is unbelievable."

Beloved princess. Azrael was really overselling this.

She glanced up at me skeptically. "I thought he was my ex. Doesn't he hate me?"

"Yes," I said.

The look Azrael shot me was murderous.

Well, he *should* despise her.

I shrugged. It didn't matter what I said. She'd spent so long immersed in the human world, and she knew nothing of ours. She'd laugh off the truth.

The door swung open then, and Tiron came in.

"Did you guys lock the door?" She struggled to sit up. "I have enemies, you know. You shouldn't be leaving the door unlocked."

I could've laughed. *She had enemies.* As if she had to tell us. I was one of her enemies, and here she was, snuggled on my lap. The lamb wrapped up under the lion's paws.

Although it was hard to feel entirely confident that *I* was the lion, while I had a hard-on and kind of wanted to lean forward and breathe in the scent of her hair again. She was so fucking dangerous, even when she seemed sweetest. I knew that.

Tiron glanced at her, then at me, skeptically. "What did I miss?"

"We're going on a mission together," Alisa said cheerfully. She finally struggled off my lap to sit beside me. "Duncan found the shifter compound, and it looks like they're holding some women they abducted against their will."

Tiron set a paper bag on the coffee table between us all, his face troubled. "A mission. In the mortal world."

Azrael shrugged. "Whatever Alisa wants."

Tiron nodded slowly. I didn't know why it mattered so much to Azrael to bring her home willingly. Unless he wanted to increase her distress when she woke in a world where she was surrounded by enemies.

I didn't think my brother was that vengeful, though, even if he should be.

"Why?" Tiron asked Alisa, frowning. "Why do you care?"

Azrael raked his hand through his hair, obviously irritated by us both.

"Because they're in danger?" Alisa frowned up at him. "Because I should have protected them in the first place? I was sloppy, or the shifters wouldn't have been left alive to hurt anyone."

"The Princess Alisa was careless with someone else?" I deadpanned. How unexpected.

She turned to me, frowning. "Did I do something to you in a past life?"

A past life to *her*. Over her head, Azrael fixed me with a dark look, his mouth moving with threats that I didn't bother to lip-read.

I met her gaze. She had luminous eyes, as brilliant and blue as the ocean that Faer was going to bury her under.

"Yes," I said. "You were spoiled and willful, and you hurt everyone who ever got close to you, Princess Alisa."

Her eyes widened, then shuttered, a look of calm coming over her face as her chin rose. But I'd seen the flash of hurt and, more than that, *fear* first.

She was afraid I was right.

"If that's who I was," she said carefully, "and I'm not saying it's true, then I'm not that person anymore. For the last five years, I've tried to protect people. I've hunted down the dangerous things in the night—"

"And you enjoyed it," I finished. She had always enjoyed fighting and killing.

It was the one thing we had in common.

The crease between her eyes deepened. "Yes."

"There's nothing wrong with enjoying your work," Azrael interrupted, as Alisa and I stared at each other. "Tiron, what did you bring back?"

"Chinese takeout," Tiron said cheerfully, although I could feel his gaze fixed on Alisa and me. "I love Chinese."

Azrael groaned. "I do not, but fine."

"Alisa does," Tiron said. He nodded through the doorway to the tiny kitchen, where a scribbled-on Chinese menu was stuck to the door with a magnet.

Alisa pulled her gaze away from mine. I could tell she was shaken by the way her posture was perfect, rigid, her chin held high, and she rested her open hands on her lap as if she were back at court. She didn't even know she sat on this threadbare couch as if she were on a throne.

But anyone who knew her could see it. Already, I could see her shifting, covering her upset with relaxed confidence.

"So Tiron is the charmer," she said, fixing him with a smile that he returned, "and Duncan is the grouch."

"Who am I, then?" Azrael asked, without looking up from the paper bag he rustled through.

"That's a mystery," Alisa said, her voice light.

But I used to be good at reading Alisa. We were alike in some ways, as much as I hated to admit it. The perfect straightness of her spine, the way she folded her hands into her lap and tucked one ankle over the other, was the power pose of a princess.

She'd been taught how to stand, and how to sit, and how to *be* in every moment. When we were young, she'd shattered the glass cage the summer court tried to put around their doll. She'd insisted on being her own person—a person who was messy and flawed and dangerous, but at least her *own*.

When she was nervous, though, she always went back to that pose.

She didn't know how right she was to be afraid.

I knew my brother well, but I didn't know who Azrael was when he was lost to her clutches—whether he was lost in his love for her, or his desire for revenge.

He might still love her, but that love wouldn't save her when we returned to the summer court.

CHAPTER TWELVE

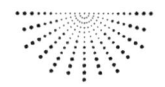

Alisa

WHEN I WAS STEADIER on my feet, I closed the guys out of my bedroom. They refused to leave me until the drugs wore off completely, and I didn't have the energy to pick up my sword and force them out. Honestly, I didn't entirely mind having them here while I recovered. I felt safer with them around.

I felt safe, but I didn't feel comfortable. Even with the door closed between us, I could have sworn I *felt* their presence outside, watchful and waiting.

It was hard to breathe with them around me, even though I never would have admitted that.

I went into my closet, stepping on shoes strewn across the floor, and closed the door behind me. Hidden in the dark, amidst my hanging sweaters and dresses like the fearless badass I was, I called Elly. At least with two doors between us, it felt like I had some space from them, even though my wool coat made my arm itch every time I brushed against it.

Azrael and Duncan and Tiron all made me feel jittery in a strange way. I didn't feel like I was in danger, exactly. They didn't feel like a threat.

It was a feeling I wasn't used to; something sharp and anxious, something aching. The mere presence of their bodies did something to mine. My nipples suddenly hardened painfully against my bra. A strange sensation of emptiness pooled low in my belly. I felt like a horny teenager, noticing everything about the way their muscles rippled when they moved, about their easy, deadly grace. It was easier to think straight when I didn't have to look at them, breathe them, sense them.

"Alisa!" Elly sounded sharp as soon as she picked up. "When you didn't come to dinner and you didn't pick up your phone, I thought the worst. We've been looking for you!"

"Well, the worst was right," I said. "Remember the shifters who were kidnapping humans to turn against their will for breeding stock? They took me off the street."

"I assume they're all dead now?"

The brusque question was touching. She had so much faith in me.

"Yep," I answered. "Well, the ones who took me are. The rest are headed that way."

There were children's voices in the background. Her grandchildren were fighting about something. She cupped her hand over the phone for a second, and her voice was muffled when she said, "Take it to the boxing ring in the basement, I'm not hearing it."

I smiled. Hunters raised their children in what seemed to be strange ways by most human standards.

"Sorry about that," she said. "Are you all right?"

"More or less," I said.

"What's going on, Alisa?"

"I didn't get away on my own." I hated to admit that. "I was rescued. By some men who claim they're Fae... Do you know anything about the Fae?"

"Not much," she said, her voice troubled. "I've heard rumors before. I've never seen one of the rips between worlds, but there are Hunters who swear by them... Hunters I trust."

"But you're still skeptical."

"Whether the Fae are real or not, doesn't mean these men have innocent reasons for claiming you should go with them to another world." When she spoke the words so tartly, my desire to go with Azrael seemed like insanity.

But part of me was curious if there were answers to be discovered, and maybe even a crown...

"They claim I'm a princess."

She snorted. "That sounds too good to be true."

"Doesn't it?" There was something off, but I wasn't sure what it was. The males themselves didn't feel like threats to me. Duncan's little asides suggesting I was someone else in the Fae world were chilling, but I didn't get the feeling my life was in danger.

"Do you need help?"

"No," I said it automatically. Then I added, "I was thinking about going with them. If I really lost my memories in that world, and nothing else can bring them back, maybe I'll find my answers there."

There was hesitation on the line. "Alisa, I don't know how to help you if they're dangerous to you. Once you leave our world..."

"I know," I said.

"You've always wanted to find answers," she said gently. "I understand why you might need to do this. But I'm worried about you."

"Me too," I admitted. "I feel like I know them."

"Like the shifters' mating bond? Fated mates?"

"No!" My voice sounded outraged, and she huffed a laugh in response. I went on, "It just feels like I know them. Like they say."

"They're old friends? What do your instincts say?"

I remembered that note I'd carried from my old life. I wasn't supposed to have any friends.

My voice dropped low, afraid they'd overhear, as I admitted, "I feel like I can trust them."

"I'm coming over," she said. "I want to meet them too. So will Carter and Julian and Amy—"

"We are not having a party."

"Those men hurt you, we'll be having a castrating party," she grumbled, and I smiled.

"Just you," I said.

"And Carter and Julian," she argued. "You can't go off into another world without saying goodbye. They're your best friends."

I sighed. "Okay. Okay, I can do that."

"Damn right you can do that for us. We're your family."

Warmth swelled in my chest, but I went silent. I didn't know what to say to that.

"And if you do go," she went on, ignoring my lack of reaction, as she always did, which made me feel a spike of gratitude too, "you don't stay long. You hear me? Don't run off to the Fae world and never come home. You have friends here."

I closed my eyes. "I'm glad I met you."

"Don't start that," she said sharply. "You're not saying goodbye to me forever."

"No, of course not," I said.

Hunters usually could never admit to any feelings. I fit right in with the bastards, though.

"I'm glad I met you too," she said. "You're a good girl, Alisa. A good Hunter. Good friend."

I nodded, biting my lower lip. Duncan had made it sound like I was a nightmare of a princess back home. But Elly reminded me of all the good I'd done with the Hunters in this world.

"I'm glad I didn't shoot you for your bad manners the day we met. It was fifty-fifty," she added, and I let out a bark of laughter.

"You're awful to me," I said.

"That's because you're one of mine," she said. "Text me so we can plan. I'll let Julian and Carter know they're needed."

Then she hung up before I could figure out what to say to that.

I squeezed my eyes shut, taking a deep, shuddering breath. I didn't know any life but this one, but it was a good life. I didn't want to leave it behind.

When I stepped out of the closet, I was still smiling.

Watchful, purple Fae eyes greeted me. Azrael stood there with his arms crossed over that broad chest, filling the doorway with his imposing frame.

I took an automatic step forward, my fists rising for a fight, before I stopped myself. But maybe I shouldn't have. "What the hell are you doing in my room?"

"Why are you hiding in a closet?" Azrael asked, tilting his head to one side as he studied me. "Were you trying to get away from me?"

"I wasn't hiding in the closet," I said, as if that was outrageous.

"Then what were you doing?"

I wasn't going to answer that. "Stay out of my room."

He glanced around. "You don't need to bring much with you. The clothes you wear here will hardly be suitable."

"What's wrong with my clothes?" I demanded.

His gaze drifted down my baggy scrubs before he lied, "Nothing."

"I wasn't going to wear these." I felt gross in them, in fact, after everything I'd been through, but I was glad no one had undressed me when they put me in bed. I'd have wanted to twist Duncan's pointy Fae ears if he'd touched me. "I've got Hunting clothes for our visit to the shifters. Then we can go to Faerieland."

"Please don't call it that."

Something about annoying Azrael delighted me. He must really be my ex-boyfriend.

He was so tall and broad shouldered that he filled my doorway. I tried to brush past him, but he didn't move. My shoulder hit his hard, chiseled arm, and he tilted an eyebrow as he stared down at me.

"They don't say *excuse me* in the mortal world?" he drawled.

"Let me guess. In your world, males don't just move out of the way after going where they aren't wanted in the first place?"

His lips quirked. "Even when the two of us weren't exactly friends before, Alisa, you never minded having me in your bedroom."

Oh my god. He spoke so knowingly. He was so damned cocky, and at the same time as I wanted to tell him off, traitorous desire throbbed between my thighs when his eyes roamed my body, as if I still belonged to him.

Not that I ever did. I wasn't the kind of girl to *belong* to anyone.

Yet when the two of us were so close that I could feel his body heat radiating against my own skin, I was somehow sure this man and I had history, that we'd known each other deeper than flesh and bone.

"I'm going to take a shower, if you'll get out of my way, and then we can go kick some shifter ass." I said, meeting his eyes as I grabbed the edge of my shirt and pulled it off over my head.

It was supposed to be a sexy power move to bother *him* as much as he bothered me, but I'd tried to take the scrubs top and long-sleeved tee off in one go, and I got tangled up with the arms, my shirt pulled over my face.

"Do you need help?" Azrael asked as I shifted my weight from foot to foot, desperately trying to drag the shirt off my head. His voice was lazy and amused and I really wanted to kick his ass even more than I wanted to screw him when he talked like that.

I finally yanked the shirt off and threw it over my shoulder. Despite his smug attitude, he studied me with open interest, as if he wanted me as much as I might want him.

"What?" I demanded.

"You're still so beautiful," he murmured. "I missed you."

The admission surprised me.

"I wish I remembered you," I said, my voice coming out heated. I felt at a loss. The lack of memories always bothered me, but it was even worse now to be face-to-face with someone who remembered me.

I ducked under his arm and headed down the hall. I felt him watch me go. I'd meant to strip in front of him, to tease him and make him feel the same uncertainty I did, but I already felt too naked under his gaze.

As soon as I closed the bathroom door between us, I took a long, shuddering breath, as if I'd almost forgotten to breathe when he was near me.

CHAPTER THIRTEEN

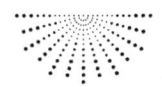

A*zrael*

S*EVEN YEARS earlier*

I WOKE in the shadows of my room. My laundry was hanging across the line over the sink, although it had taken me the last two months to teach Faer how to wash socks competently.

I was generally a level-headed person, but Faer's deliberate incompetence may have driven me to slapping him with wet socks more times than I ever should have. He'd been rendered helpless—rolling with laughter across the wood floor—so it hadn't been much of an educational moment.

Still, I had to admit he'd grown on me over the past two months. I might even call him a friend, strangely enough, even though our courts were enemies. I threw my arm over my face to block out the moonlight seeping in through the window, remembering the training yard that morning.

Faer was exasperatingly lazy when it came to his chores and errands. Playfully lazy when it came to getting out of his studies, although he was so bright it all came easily to him anyway. Cunningly lazy when it came to escaping the various facets of hazing the freshmen suffered, and surprisingly adept at getting his peers out of trouble with him. He'd quickly made himself a favorite among the first year students, although the teachers felt a bit differently.

But with all the different shades of Faer's *lazy* I'd tried to break since we started school, there was one place he threw himself into his work with full effort.

The training pitch.

Despite everything I'd heard about Faer's indifference in regard to fighting, he was fierce on the pitch. Earlier that day, we'd had a competition between houses. Each house in the school had picked their favorite senior and junior combination to represent them in a hand-to-hand fight.

Our house had picked Faer and me. He'd grinned at me, sheer delight in his eyes, the crazy kid, and I'd flicked him lightly in the back of the head. "Don't get smug until we win."

"Why wait?" he'd asked. "You're the one who always tells me not to put things off for tomorrow."

When the four teams fought each other, Faer and I had won easily. We were a flawless team when we worked together.

I rolled over onto my side, curious if he was awake. We hadn't talked about the fight much afterward. He'd been pulled away into the first-years, and I'd been surrounded by the other upperclassman.

The bed was empty, the blankets dripping off the mattress on the floor because he never made the damned bed unless I threatened him.

The bastard was gone.

I glanced at the bathroom door, but it stood open. He wasn't in there.

Swearing, wondering what kind of trouble he could have found to get himself into today, I hurriedly dressed.

His sword brace above his desk was empty. I stood there, my jaw ticking, for just one second as my mind melted down imagining what he was up to. Then I grabbed my sword and stormed into the quiet hallway.

In a moment of wishful thinking, I checked the indoor training field and the library first. Both were open all night for the ambitious and thoughtful students. Of course he wasn't there.

As I headed back down the library steps, I caught a glimpse of movement on the stone wall that surrounded the academy.

There he was, boosting himself up and pausing on the top. Maybe for a brief second, some kind of common sense had disrupted his usual thought processes. Then he dropped out of sight onto the other side of the woods.

The Fae world was always full of danger, but never so badly as at night.

I cursed and started after him. I made sure there were no guards around—their focus was on protecting us from anything that came *in*, because only one student in the entire population was so foolish as to go *out*—and then dropped into the quiet of the woods.

The forest looked like a wonderland right now, with smooth, shiny snow gleaming under the moonlight and the trees all edged with snowy lace.

The snow made it easy to follow the idiot's tracks.

Somewhere along the way the past few months, he'd connived his way into a pair of boots that actually fit. He always talked his way into whatever he wanted. I was normally glad he had *that,* at least. It was noticeable, because his footprints in the snow were as tiny as his brain. The footprints I left beside him as I stormed after him were much larger.

I glimpsed him in front of me, moving through the woods. I almost shouted at him, but just in case he had a good reason for sneaking through the forest, I moved stealthily after him.

I crept up behind him, and I was almost to him before he whirled. His eyes went wide, so bright and luminous that silvery-blue looked like the moonlight itself in that second.

Then he put a finger to his lips and shushed me.

I could not be held responsible if I murdered him on the spot. Anyone who met him would forgive me.

He extended his arm, pointing to the *thing* that moved clumsily through the woods. Some kind of monster, far taller than I was, with wicked, dangerous jaws and arms with long claws.

"They can't live long in the cold," he muttered. "So where did it come from?"

The monster lurched, and I whispered back, "It doesn't look like it'll live long anyway. It's hurt."

"Oh, is it?" he asked me innocently, looking every bit the smartass he so often was.

"You," I said.

"It got away from me last time," he said. "I came to finish it off."

"You came to finish it off," I repeated. "I'm actually going to kill you, Faer, if that monster doesn't."

He grinned at me. "Let's see if you get the chance."

He moved to attack the monster, stalking it through the forest. His feet were silent, but it smelled him and whirled to attack.

His sword was a flash under the moonlight as he fought a brief bloody fight with the monster that left it sprawled on the snow at his feet. The monster's blood spread across the snow as Faer flashed me a cocky grin.

"That's what killed the villager," he said. "Now the town's safe."

"I'm not sure that one killed the villager," I said.

Faer's face changed as he understood what I meant, his face going from smug to terrified in an instant as I threw my knife at the monster behind him.

Blood splattered across his face. My knife had stuck in the monster's eye, and it let out a scream. Then he was moving, finally, diving under the monster's jaws as the monster lunged at him. He cut one of its legs out and then was back up on his feet, and the thing fell heavily, the force of its huge body making the ground heave.

The trees around us shook with the footfalls of the monsters around us. Another monster broke through the trees, then a third.

Faer and I closed up tight enough to watch each other's backs.

"You better win this fight," I warned him. I'd been so proud of him this morning—but that seemed like child's play now.

"I thought you were implying earlier that I was about to be in so much trouble, I'd be better off dead," he said blithely.

The monsters attacked, and the two of us went to work.

At the end, we were blood splattered, breathing hard, exhausted.

But we were both alive, and the monsters were dark lumps in the snow.

I turned to Faer, who was bleeding from a gouge wound in his shoulder. His lips moved in a healing spell, but he was struggling, swaying on his feet.

"Let me help you," I grumbled. "Maybe you deserve to suffer, but I need you to be able to walk back to the academy."

"Have I ever told you how I appreciate the way you look after me?" he demanded. "Because I don't."

He pushed my hands away as I reached for him. I stopped and stared at him.

"You've lost yours gods-damned mind," I said. "Push me one more time, Faer."

"I can take care of it myself," he said, just as he wobbled and went down, sitting heavily in the snow.

I snorted and sank to my knees in front of him, reaching for his jacket. He tried to fight me off, but I was done with his shit today. I pushed him back in the snow, ripping his jacket and his shirt open. "You're too stubborn to listen to correction or to accept help, and both—"

I broke off abruptly as I realized why Faer had tried so hard to keep me from looking closer at the nasty red wound in his shoulder or the scrapes that ran down across his... breast.

Because Faer wasn't *Faer* at all.

CHAPTER FOURTEEN

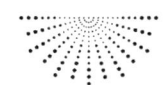

Alisa

My shower turned cold far sooner than it should have. I knew exactly how long it took my hot water heater to give up the ghost: eleven and a half minutes.

My hair was streaming wet down my back, drenching my t-shirt to my spine, as I headed down the hall to the kitchen.

Duncan was doing my dishes. Steam billowed around his broad shoulders, his muscles rippling as he scrubbed out a pan. I'd burned rice in that pot and I'd been seriously considering trashing it rather than trying to deal with the pattern of rice grains singed permanently into the bottom.

"What are you doing?" I asked, just as Tiron, humming cheerfully, mopped his way into the kitchen. I stared between the two of them, "Are you two like…house elves?"

Duncan turned and threw the sponge at me, and I ducked it so it went sailing over my head. He crossed powerful arms over his chest. "House elves?" His tone was affronted.

"Well, what's with the cleaning?" I asked.

"You might want to come back here one day and in that case, it might be best if the place hadn't been condemned." Azrael spoke right over my shoulder, and I jumped. I could almost feel the low timber of his voice rolling through my bones. He'd caught the sponge against his chest—there was a wet spot about his left pec—and he threw it back at Duncan.

Azrael looked at me in exasperation. "You're still a slob."

"I'm not a slob," I began.

He pressed his hand over my mouth, a mischievous look in his eyes. That casual, easy touch made my eyes widen, but instead of wanting to kill him, his touch sent a strange tension rippling down my spine.

His voice was warm as he teased, "Let's not start lying to each other now. Can I show you something?"

"I guess," I said.

Azrael led me into my bedroom, which caused me to give him a distinctly skeptical look. Then I realized all my clothes had been taken off the bed. "What happened to my clothes?"

"They're being laundered. They'll be returned to your apartment tomorrow." He shrugged. "Maybe you could get a laundry hamper."

"I have a laundry hamper," I said, "it's just full of books because I—you know what, I'm not discussing this with you."

My cell phone chimed, and I checked it, then held it up. "Some of my friends are inbound in an hour."

"Fantastic," he said. "I know you still doubt if I'm telling you the truth. I just wanted to show you Princess Alisa."

"Do you have photos or something?"

"No," he said. He hesitated, touching his collar absently, then shook his head. "No, no photos needed. Someone enchanted you to make you look fully human. I can't undo that, not here, but I can show you what you really look like for a few moments."

I raised my eyebrows. "Okay. Except there's no way for me to know it's not just a spell that changes my appearance and has nothing to do with how I *really* look."

"Clever girl," he murmured, the words falling from his lips in a way that made me think he'd said them many times before. "Just humor me. See if your appearance wakes your memories."

My heart began beating fast. It didn't help that Azrael shifted close to me, his gaze focused so intently on my eyes, then my lips, that I thought he might kiss me. It was too easy to imagine caressing those soft pink lips above the hard angle of that jaw.

His big hands rose and cupped my face, and my heart stopped. His thumbs caressed my cheekbones.

"Sometimes it's hard to believe that the first time I saw you, I didn't really *see* you," he murmured.

My hands rose automatically to grip those corded forearms, but I didn't push him away, not yet. "What the hell does that mean? Have you seen me before since I came here?"

"No." He frowned as he said the word.

He released me, but his hand dropped to my lower back to propel me gently forward toward the mirror. I was only used to being touched that way when Julian or Carter were posing as my boyfriend, but this was the first time I'd felt a male's touch so acutely. Each one of his fingers felt distinct and warm, his palm firm.

I stepped quickly away toward the mirror, leaving his hand behind. "Do you have enchantments to make people horny in the Fae world?"

"We do," he said slowly. "Why? Are you afraid someone enchanted you to be…horny?"

I could see his damned face in the mirror over my shoulder. Those beautifully shaped lips twitched in a smile he was trying—and failing—to restrain. From this distance, the devilish specks in his eyes faded; instead, it was hard to tear my eyes away from the magnetic purple.

I decided to ignore him and faced myself in the mirror instead.

Long lavender hair, thick and bountiful, fell around my shoulders and cascaded down my back. My face was still *like* mine, but a gorgeous glow lit my perfect skin, my cheekbones were sharper, and my lips were plusher than ever before. I caught my lip with my lower teeth and worried it, watching the mirror reflect the action.

My reflection was beautiful, but even though I knew it was *me*, it felt like a stranger.

I ran my hands over my small breasts, my narrow waist, realizing my body was more slender than it had been before.

"You're stronger than a mortal," Azrael said, as if he realized I was studying my body in confusion. "You don't need as much muscle."

"Forget muscle," I said, although that mattered to me too; I'd worked hard in the gym and the ring so I could stay alive fighting beasties. I grabbed my boobs through the excess material of my t-shirt and jiggled them—or rather, tried to. There wasn't enough to go anywhere. "What happened to my tits?"

Azrael scrubbed his face with his hand, as if he were seeking strength internally. "Whoever altered your appearance added some extra… curves."

I glanced at him over my shoulder, glaring at him. "I suppose you'd be an expert."

He met my gaze. "I don't want to answer that."

"Good choice." I stormed over to him just as the knock came on my door, two hard raps and then a quick one. Carter was early. Of course he was. "Change me back."

"Are you sure that you don't want your friends to see your real—" Azrael began, then shrugged his shoulders in surrender. He gripped my face lightly, and this time, I noticed a prickling across my skin.

Maybe I'd been too distracted by Azrael before to even notice the damned magic.

He stepped back, dropping his hands to his sides, but I glared at him anyway as I headed for the door.

Duncan was already on his way there, and I shoulder-checked him.

Then I promptly bounced off. The big Fae didn't move.

"I'm making sure that's the company you expected." Duncan looked down at me with amusement as I stumbled across the carpet and caught myself.

"I've survived on my own for the past five years."

"Somehow."

I checked the peephole. Carter, Julian and Elly all waited for me in the hallway. My heart lurched seeing them. I hated the thought of leaving my friends behind.

I swung open the door and stepped back. Carter came in fast, his movements predatorial as if he were looking for a threat. Julian sauntered in behind him, magic sparking at his fingertips even though he looked relaxed.

Duncan snorted a laugh. It was a mean sound, and I turned to fix him with a glare.

He shrugged. "They're cute. If I wanted to hurt you, Alisa, nothing would stop me."

The tension in the room buzzed in the air. *Oh, Duncan.* My friends would take that as a threat. They were already moving...

Julian slammed a blast of magic into Duncan that knocked him into the wall. My framed pictures hit the floor and shattered, and the drywall cracked under the force of Duncan's body. He was plastered to the wall for a fraction of a second, then propelled himself off, already swinging. Carter caught him around the waist and slammed him right back into the wall.

"Stop!" I shouted. Duncan had his hand around Carter's throat and both of them were going for their blades, but Azrael growled too—this inhuman sound, tinged with danger—and both Duncan and Carter froze.

"We're all friends here," I said, knowing that was a damned overstatement, but whatever. "Let's all take it easy."

Elly surveyed the wreckage with her own amusement, shaking her head.

"Put him down," I snapped at Carter and Duncan. "Hands to yourselves. Carter, he's not going to hurt me."

"He's not going to get the chance if he tries," Carter warned him, backing up.

Duncan grinned at that, a psychopathic joyful grin, and Azrael shot him a dark look.

"These are my friends Elly, Carter and Julian," I told the Fae males.

"This is Tiron—" I pointed to the tall rugged blond who filled the doorway, not looking remotely surprised at the mess Duncan had made, "and the giant twins are Azrael and Duncan. Duncan is the surly one."

Duncan raised his eyebrows, crossing his arms over his powerful chest.

"I need you to look at these guys and tell me what's wrong with them," I told Elly.

Her gaze ping-ponged between Duncan, Azrael and Tiron. "Sweetheart, *looking* at them I don't see anything wrong with them at all."

I heaved a sigh, raking my fingers through my hair. I didn't need to discuss how attractive they were; my body was already, always, keenly aware of how attractive they were.

"We'll have to go deeper," Elly said. She glanced at Julian. "You claim you met a Fae once, didn't you?"

He nodded. "They move fast. Manipulate brilliantly. Hard to kill."

"You'd think you'd recognize your crush in that description," Duncan muttered. "It's as if you never really got to know her."

Azrael clipped him in the back of the head without even looking. That male was growing on me a bit.

Elly beckoned Duncan over with a finger. "You don't look quite human."

Duncan gave Azrael a *must I* look, and Azrael gave him a look right back. Maybe the Fae had their own languages, but looking at the two of them, I could believe the Fae could communicate solely in *eyebrow*.

Duncan rolled his eyes—apparently that gesture transferred across worlds—and crossed the room to Elly.

She studied him curiously, then reached up to brush his hair back, revealing the top of a pointed ear. Duncan grabbed her wrist. Julian, Carter and I all started for him automatically.

"Let the old woman touch your ears, Duncan," Azrael snapped.

He sighed. "It's rude."

"Sorry." She didn't sound sorry. She retreated a step to look at Julian.

"They're Fae," Julian said, crossing his arms over his chest. "That's undeniable. That doesn't mean they're nice guys."

"It doesn't seem like such a great idea to go with the strange men into an even stranger world." Carter agreed.

"You're calling our world strange?" Tiron raised one hand to tick things off on his fingers. "You live in America. Land of reality television. Two party political systems. Your entire health care—"

"All right," Azrael interrupted. He sat on the couch, crossed one leg over the other, and rested his arms on the seatback, looking as if he owned the place. "I'm sure you have questions for me. I'll do my best to answer them."

Carter and Elly reluctantly took their seats. Tiron and Duncan continued to lurk against the walls Maybe I should put them back to mopping.

Azrael winked at me, as if we were in on something together.

Julian jerked his jaw toward my refrigerator-box sized kitchen. I walked in front of him, then turned back, almost into his hard chest.

"What is it?" I asked.

"Can you try a spell?" he asked me.

"I've never been any good at magic. You know that."

"Just try," he said "Maybe it was blocked by the other enchantments, but if you're really a Fae princess—you'll be powerful when you get back into your own world. Fae nobility's magic is tied to the courts. You'll be able to do magic almost no one else can do."

His words struck me deeply for some reason.

"I'm already powerful," I reminded him. "I don't need magic."

If I admitted I had more power in the Fae world, it almost seemed as if I could be…better there. As if I belonged there instead of here.

But I didn't believe that. I was just visiting the Fae world.

He smiled down at me fondly. "Yes, you already are."

Then he added, "But I can't wait to see what *Princess Alisa* can do."

The air between us felt charged. I cleared my throat. "Do you really think I should go?"

"No," he said bluntly. "But I know you. I know how much you've wanted answers. And I don't think there's any way we could stop you from walking through that rip in the universe and hunting those answers down."

"Are you joining us?" Elly called. "We're only discussing your true identity in here."

Julian pulled a face at Elly's perpetual teasing, but held his arm out and bowed slightly to usher me ahead of him.

"That's right, my loyal subject," I teased him.

"Watch yourself, Princess," he shot back.

I joined my friends and my new Fae-whatever-they-were in the living room. The guys and I all had a lot of questions, but the truth was, I already knew I was going.

If there was trouble waiting for me in the Fae world, well, I was used to finding trouble. And I was used to getting myself out of it.

CHAPTER FIFTEEN

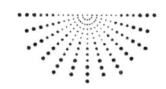

Duncan

THE NEXT DAY, I drove the car we'd borrowed from some helpful mortal to the shifter's compound. Alisa leaned over my shoulder from the backseat, staring at the speedometer.

"Do you always drive like an oversized slug managed to grow limbs just enough to reach the steering wheel, but not the accelerator pedal?" she asked. She was so close to me that the tips of her hair brushed my arm and made me feel on-edge.

"Do you always dress like a pirate?" I asked.

"Pirates don't wear leather pants," she said.

Azrael twisted in his seat to glance over her outfit yet again. "Princesses also don't wear leather pants in our world."

He said that as if I hadn't caught him staring at her ass earlier.

Her eyebrows arched. "If I'm the princess, I guess princesses do."

"You're not the only one," Tiron said. "Every court has their royalty in the Fae world."

She frowned. "What court am I?"

I should remember she'd forgotten everything, but the reminder made my hands tense on the steering wheel. These were the most basic facts she should understand. She really was going to be a lamb to the slaughter in our world.

"Summer," Azrael said, his gaze troubled.

"What does that mean?" she asked. "Is there a winter court?"

"Not anymore," Tiron said shortly.

Azrael glanced at him, and I could almost feel Alisa zero in on that quick exchange.

"What aren't you telling me?" she demanded.

I snorted, rescuing Azrael for once as her gaze flickered to me. "You don't remember anything. There's a whole lot of gaps to fill in."

"Who do you think would've done this to me?" There was vulnerability threaded through her voice as she tucked her hair behind her ears. Finally, it stopped tickling my arm, and the intoxicating, honeysuckle scent she carried faded just a little.

"We'll figure it out together," Azrael promised, as if we weren't going to drop her at Faer's feet and get back to our lives as Fae knights, fighting whatever monsters came through the rips.

"For now, let's go murder some werewolves." Everything about this situation with Alisa made me uncomfortable, from her maddening presence to the way Azrael seemed to come unwound when he was near her. At least we had a mission to lose ourselves in before we completed Mission Spoiled Princess.

I dreaded what Azrael would be like when we left Alisa behind. Stoic, of course, he always was—but I could feel what he felt when he was miserable. Just remembering the last time he lost Alisa made me tense.

I parked our car on the side of the country road where the shifters lived. "Here we are," I said with relief.

The four of us got out of the car. Alisa shrugged her sword harness on, her sword hanging across her narrow back, and drew her hair out from under the straps before gathering it up into a quick knot on top of her head.

She glanced around at all of us. "Weapons?"

I reached down and grabbed the hilt of my sword, which materialized at my hip the second I wished for it. I drew the long, bright blade. "Satisfied, Princess?"

"You could have shown off your magic when you were trying to convince me." She waggled her fingers through the air.

"I always forget how ignorant you are now," I said, just to watch her eyes narrow, her lips pressing together.

Alisa always hated to have any weakness exposed.

Azrael grabbed my shoulder as the two of us headed through the woods toward the shifters' house, making sure we were out of Alisa's ear shot before he demanded, "Why are you baiting her? Teasing her with…"

"The truth?" I raised my eyebrows at him. "Do you think she'll be hurt even worse when she arrives back home to discover just how unwanted she is?"

"That's not true." Azrael shook his head. "Some people think she could take her rightful place as queen, replace Faer—"

I jerked my shoulder out of his grasp, whirling to face him. "Tell me you didn't bring both me *and* the girl here under false pretenses. You are not going to give that brat the throne—"

"If I could *give* anyone the throne, I would take it myself," Azrael muttered back, glancing toward where Tiron and Alisa wound through the woods together. "Keep your voice down."

"You aren't sold on following Faer's orders, are you?" I demanded. "Might I remind you that the girl ruined you, ruined the autumn court—"

"You keep calling her *the girl* as if you didn't love her too."

I went on, ignoring him. "Now she's our chance to get into Faer's good graces and surprise him with our coup. *Keep your friends close and your enemies…*"

"He's keeping us close, in case you hadn't noticed," Azrael said in that arrogant way of his.

"All the more reason you shouldn't make it so painfully obvious you still love her."

"Don't be dramatic," he scoffed.

Gods. He really did. He always insulted me when I struck too close to home. Anger clutched my heart. She'd hurt him before. What would she do to him now?

We had one chance to save the last of the autumn court. We couldn't fail.

I outpaced him, sword in hand, eager for something to hurt and to kill.

Together, the four of us reached the house. Alisa bounced up the steps ahead of us and rang the doorbell.

She glanced over her shoulder at us with a smile arching her lips and touching her face with mischief. Her luminous eyes were heavily lashed, with a tendency to crinkle at the corners when she was genuinely delighted, whether she smiled or not.

"Ding-dong. Girl Scout cookies," she said, as she turned back around. The three of us move to flank her, pressing against either side of the doorway so we would be unseen.

"What is she talking about?" I muttered to Tiron.

"Next time we're Earthside, I'll buy you some Thin Mints, and then you'll know," he said.

Someone yanked the door open.

Azrael grabbed whoever it was by the back of the neck, then threw him over the porch railing so that he tumbled to the ground. Azrael leapt onto the railing, his sword flashing in his hand.

Alisa was already rushing into the house. I cursed and followed her, Tiron on my heels.

Two shifters jumped off the couch and moved to attack us. They didn't have time to shift, but their shouts would warn the others. I drove my blade into the first one, flung him off it onto the wall.

The second one lunged at Alisa. Tiron headed to intersect him, and I lashed out a hand and grabbed the pack of his neck, shoving him away. He turned to me with a wounded look written across his face, but I shook my head.

Alisa made short work of the shifter with a few bloody thrusts of her sword.

The girl was a nightmare, but she didn't need saving. Watching Alisa fight was when I liked her best.

Together the three of us swept through the house. We moved from room to room, killing every shifter that attacked us. Alisa was sharp with a sword, just as she'd been once.

Azrael caught up to us, with blood splatters across his handsome face. A giant, vicious wolf leapt at the two of them, slamming them against the wall. Tiron and I rushed to help, but two more wolves bounded into the room and we turned to face them.

The wolf circled me, and I feinted to my right. The wolf dove toward my exposed left side, just as I'd planned. I drove my sword at its belly, but the wolf was too fast. His flashing jaws managed to wrap around my arm, and I let out a bark of pain. Then Tiron was there, slicing through the shifter's throat, and the wolf fell.

Tiron and I spun to face Azrael and Alisa, just as the wolf dropped at their feet.

"You and I have always been quite the team when we work together." Azrael smiled at her.

She stared back at him without smiling, but I sensed her pulse racing, and I doubted that rapid heartbeat was because of a little thing like a murderous wolf shifter.

"Gods," I muttered. "You should've just let me die, Tiron. It would be better than listening to Azrael's babble."

I swept on, and the others followed me.

Then we found a pair of girls, drugged and tied up in an upstairs bedroom. The air stunk with the kind of sour scent of piss and vomit that sticks in the back of one's mouth.

I lingered in the doorway, rage tightening my stomach. I shouldn't care. They were just mortals. Their lives were short anyway.

The girls were unresponsive as Alisa knelt beside them, her slender fingers pressing against their throats as she checked their vital signs.

There were unshed tears in her luminous eyes as she looked up at me, blinking a bit too quickly. "We have to get them to a hospital."

"Do what you must," I said, cleaning the blood from my sword with a rag. She'd thrown her own sword to one side, careless like a human, when she fell to her knees to check on them.

She cursed at me. "Goddamn it, Duncan, *help me...*"

I stared at her in surprise. Princess Alisa was upset. She didn't even know these mortals.

Perhaps she was a different person, in a different world. The thought stunned me, and I leaned in the doorway, trying to process. If she were a different person now, then delivering her to Faer was wrong.

But her current good nature didn't mean she'd still be someone else once we went home.

"Hey." She snapped her fingers at me. She'd sounded desperate a second ago, but suddenly her face was cool and haughty again.

"This is the job," she told me. "It wasn't about just punishing the bad. It's about helping *the innocent.* You said you'd help me finish my mission, and I said *then* I'd go home."

Azrael said that we'd help her finish her mission. I'd never made any promises to her. But fine. Whatever.

I cut through the duct tape that had bound one girl to the headboard, then lifted her into my arms.

Her head lolled back, and I adjusted the way I held her, so my bicep supported her head. She was filthy, her eyes dark-shadowed, and fury boiled through my blood. I wished there were still shifters left alive to punish for what they did.

When I looked back up, Alisa was watching me, as if she'd noticed the care I took.

"Tell Azrael to make himself useful," I snapped.

Then I carried the mortal girl down to the car.

"We're a good team," she called after me as I went. "Thank you."

I snorted.

We were never a team, and she should not feel gratitude toward me.

Azrael and Tiron and I would be her undoing.

CHAPTER SIXTEEN

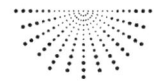

Alisa

AFTER WE HAD DROPPED the girls out at the hospital and I'd called Elly for a clean-up on aisle nine, since we'd left quite a few werewolf bodies behind us at their compound, there was no discussion.

Duncan drove the city streets as rain broke overhead, washing the streets clean and filling the air with the scent of ozone.

We were going home.

The thought struck fear into my heart, but I'd promised I'd go.

Tiron reached out and rested his hand on my leg. I glanced at him, my lips already parting to tell him off. But there was something comforting, not sexual, about his hand on my leg, and when my gaze met his, he gave me a reassuring smile.

I smiled back, barely. It was a struggle.

Duncan parked the car on a busy city street, then tossed the keys under the driver's seat.

"Look at how thoughtful you are," I said, unable to resist teasing him. "Helping the mortal reconnect with his steel carriage."

"Look how condescending you are to mortals and Fae alike," he shot back. "You're returning to your old self as we return to the Fae world."

Lord, I hated him a little.

"You'd think *you* were my ex-boyfriend," I said, "given your inability to ever say anything nice."

He stared at me for a long second, his eyebrows rising above those icy eyes. Something about the ex-boyfriend line had made his jaw tense, but then Azrael didn't like it when I said *boyfriend* either.

"Your ass looks nice in those leather pants, pirate queen," he said. "It's always been the one thing I like about you."

"Shut up," Azrael warned, smacking him in the chest. "I'm still tempted to punch you for that *fae bitch* line."

Why did Azrael care if Duncan called me a bitch?

"You are always welcome to try," Duncan said, offering him a dangerous smile.

"Stop fighting over me and bring a Fae princess home," I said, just because it would piss off both of them.

When the two of them glared at me, Tiron smiled.

"Let's go," Duncan said abruptly, turning on his heel. He led the way to a walk-up Tarot Card reader's office. A purple sign hung above the door, the lights off.

"This doesn't look open for business," I said, already quite confident no one would care. "Did you want me to get my palm read?"

"I can tell you everything that anyone needs to know about you, Princess," Duncan said.

"I doubt that very much," Tiron answered as he reached inside his jacket and pulled out a leather bound kit, unfurling it to remove a pair of slender silver lock picks.

"This place looks familiar," I mused, leaning on the brick wall beside him as Tiron picked the lock. "Yeah, I think I came here before, looking for answers."

"Now you'll find them," Azrael promised, resting his hand on my shoulder.

"And we'll see how much she likes them," Duncan muttered.

I turned to him, my brows rising. "Why don't you just explain to me what I did to you? Not your assessment of my personality—"

"Obnoxious, at best," Duncan inserted.

"—but the actual facts, as best you're capable of," I finished, adding my qualifier because I didn't necessarily trust anything Duncan said to me.

"Later." Azrael interrupted us both. "You two can chit-chat when we're on the other side."

"Does everyone on the other side think I'm some kind of spoiled princess?" I demanded. Anxiety prickled on the back of my neck. "You told me that I'm the missing heir, that my twin needs me, but the details... I don't know what I'm walking into when I go with you..."

Tiron straightened, the door yawing open to the stairs that led up to the tarot reader's studio.

"One second," Azrael growled at the other two men. His hand wrapped around my hip, sparking heat—*don't like being touched, should definitely mind that, why don't I mind that?*—and he pulled me with him through the doorway before he pushed the door shut.

What little light filtered into the room from the streetlight outside passed through purple-and-gold stained glass above the door, casting eerie light over Azrael's beautiful, chiseled face.

"Alisa," he murmured, the name sweet on his lips. God, I wished I understood what had happened between us *before*. He rested his arm on the wall above my shoulder, his body almost brushing mine. I breathed in his scent, a warm, spicy scent, cinnamon and cloves and a hint of wood smoke. He smelled like home on a cold autumn night.

"I'll be there with you," he promised, his gaze meeting mine.

"That doesn't answer any of my questions," I reminded him.

"I know." He brushed the back of his finger up over my jaw, and my knees went weak, damn me.

"I swear it feels sometimes like my body remembers you," I said softly.

I expected him to say something cocky, but instead, he cupped my cheek lightly, his thumb stroking across my cheekbone. "You and I were never supposed to be together, even before."

"Given how it ended, it sounds like maybe that would've been wise advice to follow."

"It would've been boring." His breath was in my hair as he whispered, "And that's one of our faults. Neither you nor I have ever been able to bear being bored."

"Maybe I've changed in my old age."

He laughed. It felt as if he were about to kiss me, but he still held his body away from mine. Somehow I longed to feel his hard, muscular body pressed against mine.

"I don't think so. Not much about the Fae world is boring, Alisa, I can promise you that."

"And you promise you'll be with me." Not that I should care. It would just be nice to have familiar faces, someone around me who seemed to care, even if he was my ex-boyfriend.

"And I'll be with you," he promised. He raised my hand to his face, his thumb caressing my scarred knuckles. "As long as you'll be with me. You've always been a formidable enemy."

"And a good friend?" I was just repeating what Elly had said earlier. It meant nothing to be a dangerous enemy unless one was also a faithful ally.

His lips twisted.

It was just a flicker before his face was as composed as before, his gaze still soft, but it told me everything I needed to know. Tension threaded through my blood, my heartrate accelerating.

I pulled away so fast that my shoulder blades slammed into the wall behind me. Suddenly, I was keenly aware of the fact that the Fae in front of me was tall and broad-shouldered, much bigger than I was. Quite dangerous.

"Alisa," he said, his eyes troubled, as if he hadn't meant to give so much away with a glance.

I reached for my sword, but he got there first, pinning me against the wall. "Alisa. Easy." He took the same tone I did with wild, scared animals in the clinic, but he fixed me with a beautiful smile. "Just trust me."

He waited for my answer, his arm a hard bar across my chest, his gaze on my face. He was feigning patience, but he had me pinned.

I didn't owe him that answer.

I slammed my foot down on his instep, throwing my weight low, breaking out of his hold. I exploded out of his grip.

The door swung open and before I could do a damn thing, Duncan drove his shoulder into my abs so hard that it knocked the breath out of my lungs.

He stood with me, pinning my legs to his powerful chest, slinging me over his shoulder as easily as I carried a bag of dog food at the clinic. Azrael reached out with one hand and unbuckled my sword harness before he ripped it off my back.

"Put me down!" I shouted.

I lifted myself up to get enough leverage to drive my elbow into Duncan's kidneys. He grunted, but continued his implacable journey up the stairs.

"God damn it, I'm supposed to be a princess! Put me down! You're supposed to do what I say!"

"You're not that kind of princess," Duncan told me.

Azrael charged up the stairs ahead of us, then went into the office. Tiron's face was troubled as he followed us up the stairs.

As Duncan shifted, I caught glimpses of Tiron and Azrael from my upside-down vantage point. I drove another elbow into Duncan's kidneys, and this time, I wasn't even rewarded with a grunt.

Azrael ripped down a length of purple silk that hung from the wall, revealing a spot that seemed to shimmer.

I struggled to get free, but instead I was carried ass-first through the portal. Cold and darkness washed over me.

The next second, we were in another world. Lush greenery surrounded us; we were deep in a forest, vibrant green, humid, carrying a sweet, heavy floral scent. It felt like summer here.

"Welcome to your realm, Majesty," Duncan said, his voice cold and dead.

CHAPTER SEVENTEEN

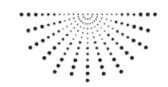

Duncan dropped me unceremoniously on the ground.

"Are you all right?" Azrael asked, his eyes wide as he leaned over me.

I kicked him in the shoulder, and his big body rocked back under the force, although he kept his footing.

I scrambled to my feet and faced him, my chest heaving. Azrael looked at me with hurt written across his face.

"You're no friend of mine," I told him, since he'd made it clear I'd been no friend of *his*. "I don't know what the hell I did to you, but I'm going home."

"This is home," Duncan said calmly, his arms crossed over his chest. "Now, unless you want me to carry you all the way into the palace past your subjects and servants, I suggest you *walk*."

I looked back at the shimmer in the air, past the three males who'd brought me here. Azrael still gripped my sword harness in one hand, regret written across his face. That asshole. I'd show him regret. Tiron offered me a rueful smile.

Duncan glared at me as if he were daring me to get past him.

My jaw was tight as I glanced at the forest around us. "Which way?"

"This way." Tiron gave me a comforting look as he gestured. "Everything is going to be fine, Alisa. You'll see."

Duncan snorted.

I didn't trust Duncan one bit—he hated me, more than anyone else did—but I did think he probably had the most realistic assessment of the situation.

The three of them stared at me as if they were waiting for me to do something, and I made an impatient gesture. "Lead on."

Tiron walked with me, Azrael and Duncan bringing up the rear as if they were afraid I'd make a sudden break back for the portal. I glanced over my shoulder, past them, trying to find the shimmer in the air. Was that it? No magic words? Just walk through the shimmer and I'd be home again, back with Carter and Julian and Elly?

I squared my shoulders. I'd come here for a reason. I'd get my answers, and if I didn't like it here, I'd leave Faerieland behind and go back to the human world.

"I suppose you're happy," Azrael accused Duncan behind us. "You got to carry her kicking and screaming back home."

"I didn't want her here to begin with. But I suppose you're right. I'm happy you're not happy," Duncan replied.

"Trouble in paradise?" I asked, glancing over my shoulder at the feuding brothers. A low-hanging branch hung in my way, and I raised my hand to push it up.

Tiron jumped to push my hand down, and I skidded to a halt, staring at him.

"Bad idea," he chided me. "You really don't know anything about the Fae world, do you?"

"I've only said that eighty-two times now." They seemed to be surprised all over again, over and over, about the fact that I didn't remember anything about my past.

Even if my traitor body seemed to remember that it liked the way Azrael smelled, the way Azrael touched me... no matter what an ass he was.

I studied the branch in front of me. Little barbs ran all along the branch, curling out like so many jagged little splinters. "So the tree's got bite."

"Literal bite," Tiron said. He tugged me to one side, then reached out to catch a crawling beetle from another plant. He carried the bug over in cupped hands, then dropped it onto the tree branch.

The spines snapped closed around the beetle, then the branch jerked up toward the trunk of the tree. I hissed in a breath of surprise at the force with which the branch slammed into the trunk.

When the branch unfurled again, the beetle was gone, although there was a faint slick of bug guts and blood left behind where it had been. Horror wiggled through my gut. Surely I was too big for that tree to *eat*, right?

"Everything in the Fae world is trying to kill you," Tiron warned me.

Including the Fae themselves, a dark voice warned somewhere in the back of my mind.

"Splendid," Duncan said, "Now she's advanced to the level of knowledge of an average two-year-old. The temperament of one, too. If the object lesson is done, can we move on to the palace?"

"You're the one who hauled me over your shoulder like a big bully," I pointed out.

"I was trying to save my brother before you disemboweled him," Duncan said. "Sometimes I think he deserves it, but our mother would have been so unhappy with me, rest her soul."

I couldn't picture Duncan and Azrael ever having a mother who fussed over the two of them.

I stayed close to the males—damn them—since I didn't know anything about the other dangers of the forest. They didn't seem inclined to let me die on their watch, anyway. But it might be trickier than I had thought at first to sneak out here and escape through the portal, until I either regained my memories or learned what I needed to survive in the Fae world.

No, I'd get my memories back. That was the whole point of coming 'home'.

Trees soared impossibly high overhead. Vibrant green and purple leaves shook as birds hopped through the branches, singing. One small white squirrel chased another, chittering back and forth as they leapt through the thick canopy.

Flowers bloomed from vines that wrapped trunks and hung down from the trees, in richer and more beautiful displays than at any wedding. The flowers were not only in a kaleidoscope of colors, but they released tantalizing floral scents. My nostrils flared, trying to tease out the different fragrances as we passed beneath the trees.

As we journeyed through the woods, I had to admit the land was beautiful. Wild and untouched, lush and gorgeous.

We reached a narrow river, where cool blue water coursed over shallow, gray rocks. Creatures dove into the water, filling the air with the sound of splashes, although they'd been a blur I couldn't really see.

"It's gorgeous here," I admitted in surprise. I headed for the river bank, then paused, glancing at Tiron because there might be dangers I couldn't see.

"Let me help you over," he said. "There are dangers in the water, but they're more afraid of us—when we're together—than we need to be of them."

"You don't have to do that," I said, but Tiron was already sweeping me off the ground, holding me against his chest. He waded into the water resolutely, ignoring the way it soaked his clothes to his body. He shifted me higher as the water deepened.

"She doesn't mind when Tiron carries her, did you notice that?" Duncan asked Azrael, his voice barbed.

"Tiron hasn't been an ass to her, as you have," Azrael shot back.

Tiron smiled faintly at the exchange.

"I'm not sure I'd go that far," I whispered. "You know things you aren't telling me."

"But I'm on your side, Princess," Tiron whispered. "I don't think you're evil."

"That's the nicest thing anyone has said to me all day."

"Lies," Tiron responded. "Duncan said you'd make a lovely pirate, or something like that."

At Tiron's teasing, some of my tension ebbed away. The three of them weren't my friends, but I'd figure things out. I'd be fine. I always was. I had a feeling Tiron could easily be turned into an ally—he'd been distressed at the way Duncan dragged me into this world.

On the far side of the river, Tiron set me down on the lush, green grass, then steadied me with his hands on my waist until he was sure I'd regained my balance.

Azrael strode ahead of us now, his face taut with tension. There was a trail on this side of the river that the four of us followed until we stepped out onto a lush, rolling green field that turned into an elaborate garden.

A shining white castle towered above us, and I sucked in a breath of surprise.

"There's your birthright," Duncan muttered in my ear before he passed, adding over his shoulder, "Try not to look so impressed. Look like you belong here, maybe."

"You certainly look like you belong here, with all the other poisonous things," I shot back.

Tiron sighed faintly under his breath.

"What?" I looked up at him as Azrael and Duncan strode ahead of us toward the castle, winding through the enormous, elaborate gardens. "Is he always such a grouch?"

"Yes," he said without hesitating. "He's the worst, until you get to know him."

"He seems to know me, and he doesn't care for me much."

"You hurt Azrael." Tiron stopped, turning to face me, and I looked up at him. "Azrael can forgive you that, perhaps. Duncan will be a bit harder to win over."

"What about you?"

A faint smile played over Tiron's lips. "Maybe I was already won over from the first time I watched you kick ass in the mortal world to save a mortal life."

He reached toward my face, and I took a step back automatically, my hands rising.

"I was just going to fix your hair before you see Faer," he told me. "You look a bit of a mess, thanks to Duncan's persuasion techniques."

I hesitated, then nodded. It wasn't as if I had a mirror and comb before I strode back into my kingdom. Tiron's fingers were gentle and adept as they stroked over my hair, tucking it back behind my ears. Then he gave me a slow once-over before he reached out and pinched my cheeks.

I pulled away, staring up at him.

"Trying to get some color in your face from something other than boiling rage," he said, humor in his voice. "All right, shall we?"

"Whenever you're ready." Duncan's voice was distant, irritated.

Tiron winked at me, unimpressed by his friend's ire. It was impossible not to smile back at his playful air. The two of us made our way to the guys.

There were guards on the grounds, pointy-eared or horned Fae, dressed in black tunics. My eyes flickered between their unusual features and the pointy weapons they carried.

Suddenly, one of the guard's eyes widened, and he dropped to his knees, his head bowing.

"Here we go," Duncan muttered. "This should be good for her."

A few guards gaped at him, then looked back at me, and suddenly they were all falling to their knees.

I stared at them. I wanted to tell them it was all right, they didn't need to do that, but it didn't sound very princess-y. I wasn't sure what I was supposed to say.

Then Azrael's voice, in my ear: "Tell them to rise and be at ease, if you want them to go back about their business."

I nodded my acknowledgement—and maybe my thanks—before I said loudly, "Rise. At ease."

Then I headed toward the castle doors, my feet crunching over the colorful marble gravel underfoot, passing through an arch into a big courtyard. There were people training in here with swords and bows and in hand-to-hand combat, Fae knights of every size and shape, with strange ears and stranger faces. I caught a flicker of a tail and stopped, trying not to gawk but letting my gaze roam. A cacophony of noise rose in the air, but this felt, for the first time, like coming home. Like someplace I knew, someplace where I belonged.

"Princess Alisa." A woman in an elaborate gown, her hair trussed up to expose her long, jeweled ears, fell to her knees in front of me. Her voice sounded choked with emotion, and I took a step back before I could stop myself. She looked up at me with her pink eyes, shining with tears that leaked onto her unnaturally pale skin.

"Oh, here we go again," Duncan muttered.

The bustle and noise of training ceased as attention rippled through the crowd, and one by one, people dropped their weapons and fell to their knees.

"Rise! At ease!" I called.

"She can be taught," Duncan said in a tone of wonder, to no one in particular, then I heard a *whap* as Azrael's fist found his brother's chest.

People rose to their feet again, and so did the woman in front of me. She wiped away her tears as she rose, although more immediately sprang to her eyes.

"It's really you," she murmured. "We thought you were dead all this time."

"No such luck," Duncan said. Another *whap*. Duncan didn't seem particularly moved.

Then she drew me into her arms, hugging me, beginning to cry into my hair. I froze.

I was never good at tears, never knew what to do when a friend needed encouragement. If someone hurt you and you wanted me to kick ass, I was your girl. I would always have a friend's back.

But if someone hurt you and you wanted tissues, cuddles, and encouraging words, there had to be a more competent friend that you could find. After *whoever hurt you sounds like an asshole, do you want me to bury him alive?* I was pretty much spent.

Over her shoulder, Azrael raised his eyebrows at me, as if to say *go on*.

I raised my eyebrows right back. *What? How?* Then I closed my arms around her back.

"There, there," Azrael mouthed at me, frowning as if he wondered how anyone could be so bad at this.

"There, there," I patted her back, remembering to say something, anything. "I'm home again."

For now. Against my will. But still, home again.

She pulled back, studying my face, cupping my face in her hands. Her nose was starting to turn as pink as her eyes as she wept. "I've missed you *so*. Do you remember me? Is it true you lost your memories?"

"It's true," I admitted. She looked a bit younger than me, but not by much.

"We were best friends." There was a hitch in her voice.

Duncan snorted. "An overstatement."

Azrael stepped in front of him, blocking Duncan from me and the tearful girl, although I could still hear him demand, "Why are you like this?"

"Someone should tell Alisa the truth." Duncan returned.

"But you only tell her 'the truth' because you hate her," Azrael pointed out.

"It's still helpful." Duncan said, then added, to me, "She was a glorified servant that your parents paid to be your friend."

She bit her plush pink lip and didn't deny it. "But I genuinely came to love you, Alisa. My name is Nikia."

"Nice to meet you," I said automatically, before thinking it through, which set her off crying again.

"All right, okay, let's continue the reunion later." Duncan shoved me forward with his hand on my shoulder blade.

I glared at him. "How come you don't drop to your knees like the rest?"

Duncan winked at me. "I only do that for women I like, Princess."

Azrael rubbed his hand over his face as if we both exhausted him.

"King Faer would like to see his sister alone," Nikia said. "I will take her from here. You three can wait in his antechamber."

Tiron closed his eyes, as if he were praying for strength. Azrael and Duncan exchanged a glance, and I could almost swear I saw the word pass between them. *King?*

As if something had changed while they'd been away. I had a funny feeling, though, that they knew they might come home to a king on the throne.

They'd said I was queen, that Faer needed me to rule. Would we rule together? Or did the king not feel like he needed me at all?

Tension boiled in my stomach at the thought of seeing the twin brother I'd grown up with, who I didn't remember at all. I swallowed, suddenly more anxious than I'd ever been facing down shifters or vamps.

"I have so many questions," I told them, my voice tight with anger. "Questions you should have answered."

The look Azrael gave me was full of regret, but it didn't help me now.

"Come along, Princess," Nikia said gently. She gave them all a dirty look, as if she didn't know why I was angry but she was on my side, and that made me like her a little.

Nikia swept away through the stone halls, expecting me to follow.

The three males were terrible, and I hated them, but I still hated to leave them behind.

It's only because they're the only familiar faces in this world.

It isn't because I feel anything for them at all.

CHAPTER EIGHTEEN

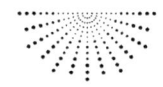

A*zrael*

S*EVEN YEARS earlier*

"W*HO THE HELL ARE YOU?*" I demanded as I faced the lavender-haired girl in the snow.

She had to be in pain from the wound in her shoulder, but she still managed to pull quite the insolent face.

"My name's Alisa," she said. "Faer is my twin brother."

I stumbled over my words—and my thoughts—for a second. There had been a girl in my room all along? We shared a private bathroom, and I'd never seen Faer—Alisa—naked. She'd never seen me. But we'd still be so close. The memory of whipping her with those wet socks, the two of us tussling across the ground while she laughed helplessly, rose again in my mind. But this time felt different.

"I've got to deal with your wound," I reminded myself as much as her. She gritted her teeth, trying to press her hand over the wound and spark her magic to life. Blood rapidly pumped from the wound, soaking the remnants of her tunic and flowing into the snow. Magic flashed around her fingertips, then died. She was weaker than she wanted to admit, and her head fell back against the trunk of the tree.

"Don't give up," I warned her. "You're not going to enjoy the combat medicine class that comes up in a few months. That's going to be far worse than this little bite."

"I don't think anything here is made for my *enjoyment*," she managed.

I pushed her hands out of my way and raised my own magic. She grimaced as my healing magic poured into her. Healing isn't an autumn strength, though winter is the worst at it, and I knew I was hurting her. The grimace turned into a panting of pain, and finally she couldn't hold back a whimper, though she tried to swallow the sound.

Normally, I'd have felt just fine about my idiot roommate feeling the pain from his poor decisions. On the other hand, I was protective of females. I had conflicted feelings seeing Alisa in pain.

"You are terrible at this," she managed through her gritted teeth.

Actually, my feelings were becoming less conflicted by the moment.

The wound knit together between my touch, then her skin healed over. When the wound was red with tender new skin, I pulled away and stood to my feet. I towered over her.

"Does King Herrick know where you are?" I demanded.

She scooped a handful of snow and held it against the red skin where the wound had been; apparently my healing magic felt like a burn. She hadn't exactly expressed any gratitude either for the fact that she was no longer bleeding out. Her face looked drawn and tired, but Alisa's eyes were still bright. She always looked as if she were plotting some bit of mischief.

I nudged her calf with the toe of my boot. "I'm waiting."

She sighed. "Yes, Herrick knows where I am."

"The king gave his blessing for you to sneak into an all-male academy?" I asked skeptically.

She smiled mirthlessly. "Not his blessing, no."

"Then what the hell are you doing here?"

She turned that insolent gaze up to me, the same one she'd given me posing as *Faer* that always tested my patience. As if she were speaking to a child, she said slowly, "I don't need anyone's *blessing* besides my own, Azrael."

I dropped to a crouch beside her. "You know that by law, entering the academy under a false name is a ticket to the hanging tree?"

"I'm sure they're going to string up the high king's daughter. Even the masochistic assholes teaching here aren't that stupid," she scoffed.

"Why are you here?" I demanded. "You don't even like it here."

She met my gaze, her eyes blazing with challenge. "Faer didn't want to come. *I* did."

"Why?"

"You ask so many questions, Azrael." She yawned as if those questions tired her.

Now that I knew who she really was, I wondered how I ever mistook her delicate features, her slender body, for Faer's. I knew from his reputation that he was slight, that he didn't care much for the training yard, but Alisa... with her beautiful lush lips, her bright eyes and those rounded cheekbones, she was gorgeous. No matter how short her lavender hair was cropped.

"Let's focus on the important ones then," I said. "Why the hell shouldn't I tell people who you really are?"

She tried to pull together the bloodstained rags of her tunic, and I sighed in exasperation and yanked mine over my head.

She shook her head, rejecting the gift. "I don't need anything from you."

My voice came out icy. "Oh, really?"

She looked up at me, something flashing through her eyes at my threat. Then she smiled, confidently, as if she already knew just how I'd react. "Azrael. You can't tell on me. We're having so much fun together."

I laughed at that. "You're breaking the laws that govern the four kingdoms. Your father might be high king, but maybe you could pretend to care about those laws."

"I do," she said, her voice brittle, as if she didn't appreciate the accusation.

My mind raced. I held out my hand, offering her help up. I still gripped my shirt in my other hand. "Let me tell you how this is going to go, Princess."

She ducked her head to hide a laugh at my high-handedness. Irritation flickered inside me, but I pushed it away.

Vail had assigned me to mentor and help my younger charge. I intended to do just that.

"You're going to get up," I said patiently. "And put this shirt on, and you're going to say *thank you*, you ungovernable brat. And then we're going to go back to our room before we're caught, and keep up this little charade. But you're going to explain it all to me, Alisa. Why the hell are you here, really?"

She glowered up at me for a few long seconds. I held out my hand, waiting. She suddenly slapped her hand into mine, and I pulled her easily to her feet.

It was hard to let go of her hand, and she didn't move to pull away. Tension seemed to shimmer in the air between us. I'd grown fond of 'Faer' the past few months, despite his many faults.

When I looked at Alisa, I knew I could feel fonder of her, in a very different way. At a bare minimum, she'd be sent off from the academy in disgrace if she were found out.

But most of all, perhaps, I didn't want to say goodbye to Alisa. The academy seemed like it would be boring without her.

"You're going to keep my secret?" she asked, her body close to mine.

"For some reason," I grumbled. "You must have infected me with your foolishness. If I'd known that your kind of stupidity would be contagious, I would've asked for another roommate back when you first strolled into our room—"

Her smile was like the sun coming out after a heavy rain. "You would have done no such thing. I keep your life interesting, Azrael. You need me."

I scoffed at that. "Not at all. And for the record, just because I know your true identity, don't think I won't hesitate to—"

"Be absolutely miserable to me?" Her eyes widened innocently. "Oh, I wouldn't dream of it. I enjoy our little game. You don't even realize the half of what I manage to get away with under your nose. And our instructors, oh..." She trailed off meaningfully, a mischievous smile teasing at the corners of that beautiful mouth.

"I don't understand," I said frankly. "What are you doing here if you don't take any of this seriously?"

She looked genuinely surprised at that. "I do take it seriously. Our training—what we do matters. Every Fae royal should be able to fight for our kingdom."

"What about Faer?"

An unpleasant expression crossed her face, and she murmured, "I don't know what's become of my brother. He's always had a lazy side but now... the way he sides with Father... I almost wonder if he's enchanted."

She shook herself, as if she'd realized she was revealing too much, and her expression changed in an instant. "Nevermind about that. I always wanted to come here, since I was a kid listening to bedtime stories about the Fae knights, and when Faer turned down his place, I saw my chance."

I scoffed. "Some fairy tale."

She inclined her head, admitting I was right. The realities of what faced us in the ever-growing rift was worse than any story.

"I just wanted to prove myself," she said.

"To who? No one even knows who you are. And you'll never be allowed to fight, since you're a summer court princess." My words came out brusque, but they were the truth. "Sooner or later, if you succeed in getting through the academy and sneaking off, you'll have to return to reality. And no one will ever know what you did."

She smiled up at me. "I'll know, Azrael. And now, you will too."

She pulled my shirt from my hand and despite the blood loss that should've left her staggering, she managed to sashay back toward the walls guarding the academy.

CHAPTER NINETEEN

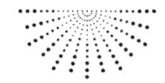

Alisa

Nikia led me into a spacious room with gold-streaked marble floors and walls. Even the flowers blooming in pots everywhere couldn't quite warm this space. She gestured toward a wooden door at the end of the room.

"No one enters King Faer's private apartments," she said, "except for family."

"And servants?" I asked.

"Human servants," she said, as if that was supposed to mean something to me. I frowned.

"What did I come back to, Nikia?" I asked.

She glanced toward the closed door. "I'll come to your chamber tonight to help you get ready for the ball." Her voice was hushed as if she were afraid someone would hear. "We can talk then."

"The ball?" I demanded.

Her wide smile lit her eyes with amusement. "Yes! Faer has been planning for your homecoming for a long time! Tonight there will be a big celebration. Bigger than solstice."

"I've got jet-lag," I said, except my current sense of *lag* came from moving between worlds and possibly from dealing with *exhausting* Fae men, "but all right."

"I have some other errands to attend to while you meet with the king, to make sure you're ready for tonight," she said, then glanced at the door again, as if there was a ticking clock for me to go through it. But she smiled at me widely.

I wondered what went into being *ready for tonight.* Pirate pants probably weren't going to cut it for the party.

"Thank you, Nikia." I wasn't sure if there was something else I was supposed to say, without Azrael here to whisper into my ear. Damn him. He was useful, at least.

I headed toward the door, then stopped and looked back at Nikia. "Do I knock? Just let myself in?"

"He's expecting you," she said, which didn't answer my damn question in the least.

Whatever. I only cared so much right now because I was nervous about coming face-to-face with a twin I didn't remember. *The only way out is through.*

I pushed the door open and stepped in.

Inside was a big, comfortable living room. Balcony doors stood open to the sea, which was blindingly bright and blue.

A man with a face that looked eerily like mine came from the balcony into the room, his face brightening with a smile.

I stared at him, my stomach bottoming out with a sudden, bitter ache. I hadn't entirely believed I had a twin until we were face-to-face. He had my cheekbones and generous lips, although his jawline was sharp and masculine, his face broader. His lavender hair was brushed back from his face.

"Alisa." His tone was warm with wonder.

"Faer?" I didn't sound nearly as confident as he did.

"You're home." He met me in a few quick strides and wrapped me up in a hug. I was enveloped in the scent of fresh-cut grass and honey.

He smelled like summer. "Oh, Alisa. I thought I'd never see you again."

Maybe coming home wasn't going to be all bad after all.

The way he seemed to have genuinely missed me warmed my heart, and I wrapped my arms around him without hesitating as much as I had with Nikia.

"I'm sorry I don't remember you," I blurted out. "It must be strange."

"It must be so terrible for you," he said, pulling away but resting his hands on my shoulders so he could study my face, as if he couldn't get enough of looking at me. His silvery-gray eyes were definitely not human, and they might have been alarming, but they sparkled and danced with warmth.

"We'll figure out what happened to your memories. We'll get them back," he promised me.

"Thank you. I tried in the human world—I didn't know who I was or how I got there."

"Come and sit and have a drink and tell me all about it," Faer said. He led me onto the expansive balcony, to one of the couches that looked out over the sea. He smiled as he handed me a glass, inclining his head to the ocean. "I'm waiting for an old friend of both of ours to arrive for the dance tonight. I wanted to keep an eye out for his arrival."

"Oh? An old friend?"

"His name is Raile," he said, "Not that you would remember him. Not yet."

He settled himself into the couch, and I sat beside him. He sprawled back, but I sat on the edge, not quite comfortable yet. It was warmer here in the Fae world, and my leather pants and the thick shirt I'd worn for Hunting seemed to cling to my body, as if I weren't uncomfortable enough already.

I glanced into the crystal goblet he had just handed me. "What is this?"

"Storm wine. A favorite of yours, if I remember correctly."

I shrugged. It wasn't as if I disagreed, or could. I took a sip, and something sweet and satisfying and slightly numbing bloomed across my tongue.

I wouldn't get drunk in the Fae world, not until I understood what lay around me, but one sip had me thinking that I could misspend my twenties here just as well as I had in the mortal world.

I studied Faer's face. The resemblance was easy to see; his face reminded me of looking in a mirror, except at a masculine version of myself. His jaw was a little bigger. He was slender, but fit.

It felt wrong not to remember my own brother. I'd come to terms with my lack of memories in the mortal world, but here I stumbled with grief over everything I didn't know.

"How were Azrael and Duncan and Tiron, bringing you home?" he asked.

I didn't want to get them into trouble, not that they deserved that loyalty, so I evaded the question. "Why did it take you so long to find me?"

Or had Fae scouts found me long before, and this was just the first time I was wanted?

"Truth be told, we thought you were dead," he said. "It never occurred to me that someone would have hidden you in the mortal world."

"Do you have any idea who?"

He shook his head. "You and I both have enemies, Alisa. But now we can look out for each other."

Maybe. "I have another question."

"Of course." He sounded warm and generous, the expression on his face open.

There was affection in that gaze, and it made me soften my words. I didn't want to ruin things with my twin. When he was a stranger to me, everything between us felt strange and tenuous. But he probably didn't feel awkward and uncertain like I did.

"Why did you send someone I used to have a relationship with?" I asked. "To bring me back? It made things...strange."

But now I didn't have to see the brothers or Tiron again. I wasn't sure if I felt relief or dread at the thought that they'd be gone, and I wouldn't have to see them again.

"Because Azrael and Duncan and Tiron are the best," he said simply. "And this was the most important mission I've ever sent anyone on."

"Why?"

"Because you're my sister," he said. "My twin. The other heir to the throne."

"Do we rule together?" I asked.

He glanced away at the sea, the wind ruffling his long hair, which fell, thick and lush, to his waist. "From the time we were children, our father trained me to rule. But you always had the answers to his questions, Alisa—at least, you always had half of them." His lips quirked up. "I always thought we *should* rule together."

Something curdled in my stomach at his words.

"We're twins, right?" I said.

He said slowly, "Inheritance passes to the son in a set of twins."

"Why?" I asked sharply.

He grinned at that. "Same old Alisa. I love the way you challenge the world."

Either we weren't meant to rule together, or he wasn't sure he wanted to share the throne.

"Azrael implied I was the heir to the throne. The *equal* heir to the throne," I said flatly.

He frowned. "You just came home. You didn't remember our world existed a week ago. Do you even want to rule?"

Did I? I didn't know how to be their queen. I didn't even know how to be Alisa of the summer court. But I wanted things to be fair. To be *right*. And for the inheritance to go to the son, regardless that we were born from the same womb, didn't seem fair or right.

"Then why did Azrael tell me that you needed me?" I demanded.

"I don't know why Azrael does many of the things he does," he admitted. "But he wasn't wrong, Alisa. I do need you. My sister—my family. I've been lost without you."

The breeze teased his long hair around that serious, concerned face. His eyes were intent on mine.

He was lying to me about something. There were no signs in that beautiful face that I could identify, no tell in his tall, still frame. But maybe some part of me knew him and remembered him.

Because I was sure my twin was lying to my face.

"Surely we make the rules now?" I said. "If you want us to rule together, we will."

He smiled. "You're right. Now, we make the rules."

When he raised his glass in a toast, I clinked the edge of my goblet with his.

CHAPTER TWENTY

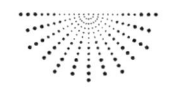

"Take time to rest before tonight's festivities," Faer said to me as we reached the door to his apartment.

"About that," I said. "I'm exhausted. I haven't even gotten used to this world. Could we do it another night?"

"Everyone wants to celebrate your return, Alisa," he said gently. "This is part of the duty of the throne."

Well, that was hard to argue with.

"That sounds all well and good, until I fall asleep with my head in the punch bowl."

He pulled the door open. "If you start to nod off, I'm sure one of them will poke you."

One of them? Anticipation ran down my spine as he stepped into the antechamber ahead of me.

Azrael. Duncan. Tiron. The three of them faced us. Their jeans were gone. Instead they wore black tunics and trousers, fitted to reveal their muscular, powerful bodies. They carried their swords openly, strapped to their hips, a curved, bejeweled dagger on the other side of their belts. So, they were some kind of soldiers. Something else they'd neglected to mention, although I could've guessed it from the dangerous way they carried themselves.

They sank to their knees, the movement graceful and practiced. I glanced from them to Faer in surprise. I hadn't expected them to kneel—not to anyone—from what I'd known of them so far.

"Rise," Faer said, his expression magnanimous. "Thank you for your service and for bringing my sister home."

His voice was warm, and yet when the three of them rose, they looked at Faer with hard eyes and cautious faces.

"Do you want us back at the front, your Majesty?" Duncan asked, an eagerness in his voice as if he were desperate to get away from me. Which he probably was. He'd made it very clear he despised me, so while *the front* didn't sound like a pleasure cruise, maybe it was for him compared to seeing my face.

Meanwhile, Azrael looked stoic and immutable, as if no mission could give him pause.

I caught Tiron's eye, and he winked at me, a quick flicker of his lashes. Something lightened in my chest.

"No," Faer said. "I know how much you three love to fight, but I need my best men here. To protect my sister."

Duncan's lips tightened. "Is there some particular threat you're concerned about?"

"All of them." Faer went on cheerfully, "But also, she needs someone to teach her how to live in this world again. You three can serve as bodyguards and as teachers while we work to restore her memories."

Oh, lord help me.

I couldn't get away from the beautiful men on either side of the rip, and they couldn't get away from me either, apparently.

"Surely there's someone else," I said, and Duncan's eyes widened faintly, as if he were relieved by the idea. Meanwhile, Tiron's lips pressed together, as if Duncan's irritation had shifted to him.

"They are the best," Faer repeated. He touched my back, flashing me a warm smile. "Rest well, sister. They will show you to your quarters."

He closed himself back in his apartment. The door clicked shut definitively, leaving the four of us staring at each other in the airy room.

"Well, *fuck*," Duncan said.

"Duncan," Azrael said, his voice warning.

Duncan strode toward the door that led back into the rest of the castle. "Come on, Princess. Time for the tour, so maybe you won't get lost in your own home."

"Do you want me to kick his ass?" Tiron asked, resting his hand on my shoulder. "Because he's technically my senior, and he's saved my life four or five times, but I *would* be willing to kick his ass if it would make you feel better."

"Seven," Duncan corrected, without looking back.

They led me on a whirlwind tour of the castle, then brought me back to an apartment that was warmer but far more modest than Faer's lodging above. From the living room, I could see my balcony that overhung the sea; the room was filled with flowering vines and an enormous sunken tub in the corner, so large that might actually be a pool.

Books filled the shelves on one side of the room, and all kinds of weapons and armor hung from the walls. I turned to take in the room, then said, "I see my interests haven't changed much."

An enormous tree grew *inside* the room, its flower-laden branches twisting to hang over the shimmering blue water of the pool. Two doors, to either side of the room, were open to bedrooms.

"It's lovely," I said, then added, "Why is it so much smaller than Faer's rooms?"

"He moved into the king's quarters when your father died." Azrael said. "When the two of you were children, you shared this set of rooms."

"Seems very practical. In my world, they put up fences to keep children out of pools. We slept in a room with one. Makes perfect sense."

"This *is* your world," Azrael reminded me.

"Not until I remember it," I said, "and I'm rather put out with you, as I'm just now remembering. You lied to me—"

The door opened, and Nikia bustled in, followed by several women.

"Time for us to leave," Azrael said.

"Run away, Azrael," I told him, and his jaw tensed.

I expected him to swipe back at me, but instead he bowed at the waist. There was mockery in his graceful motion, though his face was blank.

Then the three of them swept out of the room and left me to my doom.

"I thought I was going to take a nap," I protested as Nikia and the others bustled around, beginning to prepare me for the party hours from now. Apparently, I needed a bath, I needed to be dressed and made up and my hair done, and I couldn't do any of that on my own.

"I do not need to be bathed," I said, scandalized. "Go away!"

Duncan had said I was spoiled and willful, and when I chased my reluctant servants out of my apartment, I could see where perhaps I'd earned that reputation before.

But the day had been a whirlwind, and I needed to be alone.

I went out onto the balcony and rested my forearms on the railing. There was no one else in sight; Faer's balcony overhung mine, but I couldn't see him and he couldn't see me, so it felt as if I was alone here at the edge of the sea.

The wind ruffled my hair, and I breathed in the fresh, bright scent of salt. As I watched the waves roll in and out, listening to the crashing of the waves, peace settled over me. I'd always loved the ocean.

So this was home.

When I had been alone for a while, I turned to the pool, shedding my clothes before I stepped into the water. The water was warm and pleasant, and I swam a few laps before I let myself float. Some of my tension floated away too.

When I heard a faint knocking at the door, I expected it was Nikia. I tried to fix a smile on my face as I lifted myself easily out of the water. I picked up a towel from the rose quartz bench by the pool's edge and flinging it around my body, anchoring it with one hand as I left wet footprints across the marble.

I hadn't meant to be ungrateful; I was just exhausted by people.

But it was Azrael who stood in the doorway, his hands folded behind his back. My breath stuttered at the sight of him. His eyes dropped to my towel, and then widened.

"I heard you wanted to be alone," he said.

"And so you thought you should come to torment me?" I left the door open as I strode back into the room. He could take that as an invitation, or not.

"I thought you should have some help preparing for tonight's festivities," he said, "unless you want me to find you an eye patch and you can go as a pirate."

"Will it be a costume party?"

"No," he said. "But Duncan would be delighted if you wore one."

"Well, I do live to please Duncan." I tucked my hair behind my ears, studying him. "You came to make sure I don't embarrass myself at the party."

"Let's not set goals that are too lofty," he said.

"You're a jackass," I said. "I'm still mad at you. You don't even like me, you forced me through the portal—"

"If I truly hated you, Alisa, I could have told Faer we couldn't find you," he interrupted me. "I think the Fae courts need you."

I stared at him uncertainly.

"For tonight," he said, his voice low, controlled again, "you should just become reacquainted with your people, your world. But you do need to do that in a gown. Is playing dress-up really so terrible to you now? You used to love a good costume. A good prank."

My lips pursed to one side. He caught my hand in his and towed me with him into the bedroom on the left. An enormous, engraved, wooden wardrobe ran across one wall, the one opposite the windows, and he pulled it open to reveal dozens of gowns.

"Where did these come from?" I asked.

"They're yours from before," he said. "Not the latest style."

I ran my fingertips over the rows of colorful silk gowns, many of them elaborately embroidered or heavy with pearls and jewels, and I frowned. "This all seems…ridiculous."

"Royalty are ridiculous," he said drily. "It never bothered you before."

"Please stop talking about who I was before." I felt like I was going to lose my mind every time he alluded to a shared past that only he remembered.

He paused, then said, "You're right. It must be difficult."

I shook my head, glancing away from the gowns to his face, then dropping my gaze to his chest, which was easier to talk to. His face was too beautiful. "I don't know how to do this, Azrael. Whoever I was before, I'm no princess now."

"You'll get through it," he said. He hesitated, then admitted, "You've always been amazing, Alisa. Whatever else I've ever thought about you —you've always been strong. Clever."

"It's hard to feel clever when you don't know the rules of the game. When you don't even know the game, for that matter."

"You have me."

"Do I?" I asked. "You're keeping secrets from me. And I kicked you, and I have to wonder how genuinely forgiving—"

"You and I used to be rougher than that with each other in bed," he said, his voice rich with amusement. He touched the spot on his shoulder where I'd kicked him. "I'll heal."

Whenever Azrael mentioned our past sex life, my imagination ran away with me.

"Usually, you'd be attended as you dressed," he said, his voice taking on a warm, teasing edge. "But you sent all the servants away."

"Did I?" There was a teasing note in my voice too, as I raised my eyebrows at him. The flirtatious tone of my voice surprised me so much that I cleared my throat. I wasn't used to speaking to males like that, but I felt different around Azrael.

"I'm no servant, Majesty," he said. His thumb brushed over my cheekbone. "You were right earlier when you said I'm no friend. But what's between us has always been more complicated…more *interesting*…than that."

"Well, I do hate to be bored, or so I've been told." My voice was arch.

He tucked a strand of hair behind my ear, hesitating. He was so close that it felt as if he might kiss me, and my heart was suddenly racing. It really felt as if my body remembered him, because longing throbbed at my core, and I bit my lower lip.

When Azrael leaned close, my breath stuttered in my chest.

I'd lost my mind, I knew that. This was no fairy tale, and yet part of me wondered if his kiss would restore my memories. I let my eyes drift shut as his long fingers slid across my jaw.

I swayed in toward him, my lips parting as my eyes closed, shutting out the world outside.

Even the sound of the ocean rushing against the shore outside fell away. There was only me and Azrael.

CHAPTER TWENTY-ONE

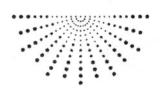

"I'll help you dress," he said, pulling away suddenly, as though with effort. "Pick a gown."

My heart was racing so fast that I almost felt as if I'd stumble. Was I *blushing?* I never blushed, but my cheeks felt hot. God, I'd tried to kiss him. "Are any of them better suited for the occasion than others?"

"They're all out of season," he said. "You'll look out of place tonight."

"Then I'll look how I feel, at least." The memory of my flat t-shirt in the mirror back in my own apartment rose to mind. I was thicker in my mortal guise. "They won't even fit…"

"We'll make do," he said, as if there was a *we*. As if we were a team.

I chose a dress with a tight rose-gold bodice that shimmered with jewels under the lights. It plunged low to reveal the shape of my cleavage, and a long, tulle skirt would drift around my legs.

I was pleased to find rose gold leather slippers to match, which apparently was what most Fae wore, among all the rest. "Flats!"

"How else would anyone make shoes than flat, for walking in?" Azrael asked, frowning.

"You have no idea what kind of wild stuff humans think up."

He turned his back before I dropped the towel and slipped the bodice up over my hips. I hauled the bodice over my breasts, breathing in. Why didn't the Fae world have Spanx? "You can look now. Not like it's anything you haven't seen before…"

He turned, his gaze widening with appreciation as if he liked me in any form.

"It's different when you aren't comfortable in front of me." He moved behind me, pulling at the laces of the corset. When his fingers swept against my spine, my back arched faintly. I bit my lip, unable to completely hide the way my body responded to his touch. He added, "And it's been five years."

"Did you do this for me often before?" I asked.

He seemed comfortable with his hands on my body, helping me into this elaborate gown. Meanwhile, I fluttered with nerves. I had to get a grip.

"Often enough," he said. "There's always some debauched party in the summer court. And you've always been…difficult…with the servants."

His voice sounded amused as he added, "And everyone else."

Debauchery sounded promising right now. Something about the tease of having him dress me was causing me to imagine him *undressing* me. I'd asked Azrael if there was an enchantment to make people horny, but I needed the opposite. I needed a cold-shower spell, pronto.

"Do you have some new girlfriend?" I asked, teasing him, using those human words he despised.

He drew the corset tight enough that it squeezed my chest, and I exhaled a huff.

"No." The playful note had left his voice.

"Why do you say that as if it's so ridiculous? Was I so amazing…or so terrible…that you can't move on?" I was teasing, but he fell suddenly silent behind me.

When he didn't answer, I twisted, trying to see his face.

He yanked on the corset again. "Hold still. I'm barely qualified to lace you up as it is, but since you terrify the servants…"

"I don't *terrify* anyone."

"Nonsense," he said. "Look at how you scare Duncan."

I laughed out loud. "It doesn't seem like anything or anyone scares Duncan."

"He'd like you to believe that." His fingers brushed my bare shoulder blades as he tied the ribbons at the back of the bodice. "There. *Now* you can turn around."

I spun, the skirt twirling out from my legs. It made me feel silly and alive, just for a second. As if I were a storybook princess, and not the somewhat terrible princess I was now.

"How do I look?"

"Beautiful." But his eyes were guarded as he watched me. "So beautiful it hurts."

"That's funny," I said. "That's how I'd describe your face."

His brows arched. Why had I just said that? But it was true; everything about the sharp plane of his cheekbones, his beautifully shaped lips, his jaw, drew my gaze and left me aching all at the same time. I bit my lower lip, glancing away.

"You're less guarded than you were before you…left," he said.

I shook my head, hating how I felt at a loss when he reminded me of a shared past I didn't remember. "I told you to stop telling me about who I was before. I want to remember for myself."

"Right," he said. "I'll stop. It's just sometimes I think perhaps you're a different person than you were."

He sounded as if the thought troubled him.

"From what Duncan said, that would be a good thing. He made it seem as if I were pretty terrible before."

He shrugged. He'd liked me anyway, before; maybe he was disappointed by the changes. I tilted my head, staring at him for as long as I could bear to; it felt like staring into the sun. It was impossible to look away, and yet I knew that gazing too long would hurt.

"You're going to look out of place," he said, touching my hair and brushing it back with his fingertips. "Perhaps you might as well embrace it. Leave your hair down."

"Everyone else will have theirs up?"

He nodded. "You'll look a bit wild."

"I *am* a bit wild." I didn't know anything about how to be a civilized Fae princess.

He smiled, a real, genuine smile that crinkled the edges of his eyes, and held out his arm. "Time for the princess to survey her chaotic kingdom."

I hesitated at leaving the room.

"I will be right by your side when you have a question," Azrael promised me. "I won't let you look foolish."

I couldn't hide my smile. "Well, you can try. And I appreciate it."

Azrael offered me his arm gallantly and escorted me to the ballroom. Just before the servants swung open the doors, I murmured, "They're going to go to their knees, aren't they?"

"Yes, they are," Azrael said. "Even Duncan if he's in the crowd, much as he despises it. I try to keep him away from these things, though."

"Does he despise it as much when he kneels in front of Faer?"

"Oh yes." There was a fervency to his words.

I wanted to know more about how Duncan—and Azrael—felt about Faer, but the servants were opening the doors and music spilled out and I had more pressing questions. "Do I say the same thing?"

"Just stand there and smile and look like a princess. After a few seconds, the music will start back up and people will rise and come to greet you until you go to your throne on the dais." He smiled down at me. "If you need to retreat, go sit up there and look queenly. You'll have to invite me up, though, so if you want me to come with you, say so."

"Wait." I grabbed his arm, and his lips parted in surprise. "Azrael. This sounds like a nightmare."

"Being a princess isn't easy." His words were light and mocking, but I had a feeling he meant them.

I groaned. "Why did I come back here?"

"Just make it through tonight, and tomorrow, we'll go to work restoring your memories," he promised.

That was well and good in theory, but I still had to make it through tonight, and apparently, that included talking to half the kingdom. I faced an endless sea of Fae, of tails sticking out of dresses and elaborate hairstyles wrapped between horns, of faces that might be human and mouths with forked tongues.

Princess lesson one: No introvert should ever take the crown.

The noise and lights washed over us, and then the music stopped. Everyone sank to their knees. I stood there with a frozen smile on my face until the music began again.

Being a royal seemed merciless.

For a second, the lively fiddle music that started up again relaxed me.

Then I felt someone bearing down on me like a missile, and I glanced up expecting a threat, only to see a beautiful redheaded Fae bearing down on me.

Azrael pressed his body against mine from behind, and I was acutely aware of all that hard muscle against me. I started to twist to give him a look—not that I wanted him to pull away—but he whispered, "Elena Beure. Autumn court. You need to greet her first, or she can't approach you without violating proper etiquette—she hates that. She'll probably pretend to be your long-lost best friend, but you couldn't abide her. Watch for her little insults. The old Alisa would never tolerate them."

My mind reeled. He squeezed my shoulder, the gesture strangely comforting, and pulled away.

So this was a mean girl, according to him? What were mean girls like in the Fae world?

"Elena," I said, imitating Faer's magnanimous tone earlier, as if she were lucky I was speaking to her.

Annoyance flickered across her lovely features before she cooed, "Alisa, I'm so glad you made it home safely. Were you rescued by this handsome man?" She caught Azrael's forearm with one hand, smiling up at him winsomely.

Azrael didn't bother to smile back. "Princess Alisa has always been able to rescue herself, Elena."

"Oh, so it's true," she said sympathetically. "You lost your memories. Listen, you must come to tea tomorrow, and I'll catch you up on everything that's happened."

"Thank you, but I have a plan to *catch up.*" I wasn't sure why I'd hated her before, but something about the way she looked at Azrael was like fingernails scraping metal for me. "Perhaps we could socialize some other time."

"Of course," she said.

"Why did I hate her so much?" I whispered to Azrael as she left, picking up a dance partner along the way. The two of them began to swirl across the dance floor with a flicker of skirts—oh, and I glimpsed a tail—to the music.

When Azrael hesitated, I was tempted to slap him.

I told him in a fierce whisper, "You lied to me that Faer wanted me to rule alongside him. You'd better get a lot more forthcoming in a hurry, or I'll tell Faer I need another bodyguard."

I realized I'd misstepped as soon as I said the words. Duncan would have called my bluff, eager to escape to a warzone rather than spend any more time with me.

Azrael studied my face with his purple eyes, which looked dark under the pulsing lights strung across the ceiling, then sighed under his breath.

"When we were all younger, Elena was determined to sleep with me," he said. "I believe she hoped to find her way to serving at my side as queen. You didn't particularly want to marry me yourself, but you certainly didn't want her to."

I frowned. "I meddled in your relationships?"

That was hardly fair. If I hadn't wanted to marry him myself, I shouldn't have prevented him from marrying anyone else. I'd encouraged Carter and Julian to move on, instead of hoping our friendship would tip over into something... hotter.

"I didn't want her." His voice was clipped, as if he were offended by the implication. Then he softened, his eyes sparking. "You always meddled, Alisa."

I didn't know what to say to that, but someone else was already approaching us.

And so the night spun on.

I met person after person who remembered me, but I didn't know them.

Azrael whispered in my ear, telling me the right royal protocol to follow. He was subtle and smiling and seamless, and I had to admire how smooth he was.

Of course, he'd almost *smoothed* me right through that portal without an inkling of how wrong things were.

But despite his best efforts, I felt as if my uncertainty was on display. Some Fae stared at me with disappointment, some could barely contain their glee—but either way, I was left feeling insufficient.

"What a lovely party," I muttered to Azrael. "Can I go yet?"

"Protocol—" Azrael began, then hesitated.

"Let me guess," I said. "the old princess Alisa didn't care much for etiquette?"

Azrael said slowly, "The old princess Alisa used it to her advantage. Give me a moment, and I'll get you out of here without causing any chittering."

I wasn't sure what Azrael did, but before I knew it, the two of us were slipping out of the room and back down the halls to my room.

"Thank you," I said softly when we reached my door.

He looked at me as if he were going to kiss me. But maybe those lush-lashed, deep purple eyes were just bedroom eyes. Maybe he didn't mean to smolder in my direction.

He stepped close to me, looking down at my face as he came so intimately close that my breath caught, right before he pushed open the door to my room over my shoulder.

"It's my duty. Goodnight, Princess."

His duty. Anger tightened my chest. Gods, the beautiful man could go fuck himself.

And I wouldn't even think about what that would look like, his hand wrapped around a cock that I was willing to be was long and thick, his eyes heavy-lidded as he jerked his hand up and down...

"Goodnight," I managed, before fleeing into my room.

"Wait," he said, reaching for me. My heart galloped, but all he did was step behind me and unfasten the damned corset.

Did I really have to tolerate these ridiculous clothes? The tight corset around my chest suddenly released, and I drew a deep, full breath. "This whole place is a trap. Even the goddamn *gowns*."

He hesitated, then said, "I'm sorry, Alisa."

I would have pressed him on what he was sorry for, but he was already moving on silent feet through the door. It closed softly behind him.

I shed the gown and crawled into the thick, luxurious bed. The crisp sheets and soft, thick blankets all carried a faint, sweet floral scent, even better than Tide.

I was exhausted, and I should have fallen asleep immediately. Instead I lay there wishing for sleep, listening to the endless rush of the ocean through the open doors to the balcony.

It sounded as if the old Princess Alisa played a fierce game with no prisoners and no regrets.

I wondered if she was still buried deep inside me.

CHAPTER TWENTY-TWO

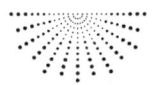

Azrael

Seven years earlier

Our next few months at the academy passed without trouble. Well, without any more trouble than seemed inevitable with Alisa at my side.

She continued to pretend she was a boy. I continued to pretend to be exasperated by *him* on a regular basis.

Actually, the exasperation didn't take much pretending.

"You know your junior and mine missed a class together," Galic stopped me in the hall. "I intend to find out just what they were up to, in case they need to be punished for more than skipping."

I stared back at Galic. He had his books clutched in his arm and a smug look written across his face. He'd annoyed me since we began at the academy. His confident smile flickered when I didn't answer him with anything but an icy glare.

"I'll speak to Faer," I said finally, making it clear that I didn't take anything Galic said at face value

I was halfway down the hall when Galic called after me, "Are you afraid of what the High Princeling will do to you when he comes to power?"

The hall went silent. It was crowded with students, all waiting to see how I responded. I glimpsed Duncan in the crowd, his brow furrowed as if my own brother didn't know what to think.

When I turned to face him, Galic had found his smirk once again. The accusation of cowardice sparked cold rage for me, and I wanted to tear Galic's insolent head from his shoulders.

"Galic," I said, letting my voice roll through the hall, no longer speaking quietly, "We're supposed to cheer on our juniors. Your jealousy that both Faer and Keral can kick your ass? Well, you might not have the sense to be embarrassed, but believe me, everyone else feels ashamed on your behalf."

Galic's cheeks went dusky. "I'm not jealous of either of them."

"Right," I said. "That's why you live to beat the hell out of Keral not on the pitch, but in your room, when he can't fight back. What a joke."

There. I'd staked it out clearly; I didn't beat 'Faer' because I was proud of him, not weak and jealous like Galic. Even before I knew who he really was, I'd had no interest in carrying out the academy's traditions of punishment. Although 'Faer' had told me—twice—that it would be better to take a beating than listen to me talk.

'Faer' was really testing the strength of my convictions.

I turned my back on Galic, a deliberate provocation I hoped he'd take.

Duncan whistled to warn me at the same time as I heard Galic's soft footfalls racing down the hall. I'd expected that, though.

I juked to one side just as he lunged at me. His body rushed by instead of tackling me. As soon as he slammed into the ground, I was on top of him. He'd managed to roll, and he got in one solid punch across my jaw before I was able to pin him to the ground. Then I made up for my sore jaw, punching him more than once.

He glared up at me balefully and his split lips parted to speak. Galic never knew when to quit.

He spat out, "You know, when you become Faer's servant, you became Herrick's too. I thought you were supposed to be the autumn prince—not a maidservant."

I leaned close to him, eye-to-eye. The hall was still silent, students having stopped to watch the fight.

"Faer's nothing like Herrick," I warned him. Everyone knew how much I despised the High King; there was no denying how I felt. "He's honorable, and a good fighter, and he cares about his people. As much as I think it's time for summer's reign to end, he'd be a far better king than his father."

I knew everyone could hear what I'd said. And suddenly, I realized how much I might regret what I'd said. Sooner or later, my words would certainly carry beyond the walls of the academy.

Alisa and Faer might be very different people, but to the world, it looked as if I was throwing my lot in with Faer. I was supposed to be the rebel prince of the autumn court—the one my people hoped would one day overthrow the high king.

I rose slowly from Galic and dusted my hands off dismissively. He didn't move to rise until I'd walked away, staying submissive, even though he glared after me through narrowed eyes.

I knew I'd have to watch that one. Galic would try to get revenge on me, or on Faer.

When I came into our room from battle training at the end of the day, exhausted with the taste of salt clinging to my lips despite the cold outside, Alisa was lolling on the bed, somehow already bathed and dressed.

She looked up at me from her book—*look at that, Alisa with a book, maybe she truly was turning over a new leaf*—and asked, "So it's time for summer's reign to end, hm?"

Of course she'd focus on that comment. Regardless, she was

reminding me I'd praised her publicly, which I regretted already. She was cocky enough.

I scoffed. "I'm in no mood to deal with you yet."

I stepped into the bathroom connected to our room. The wooden floor was cold under my bare feet as I began to strip off my sweaty, dirty tunic and trousers, but a snap of my fingers had the bathwater steaming in the huge sunken tub. I plunged myself into the water, letting out a sigh as the hot water helped unkink some of my sore and bruised muscles.

I was floating in the water when I heard her soft voice from the doorway. "I won't look. I've got a test to study for tonight so I'd like to get the laundry out of the way."

I nodded without looking her way, pretending as if I weren't suddenly hard just from having her in the same room when I was naked.

I shouldn't have said what I said about Faer in that hallway.

But I'd meant every word I'd said about her.

I'd fallen in love with her steadily over the past few months.

"Since when do you study for tests?" I asked her as she began to wash both our clothes in the sink.

"Since I realized my graduation would be even sweeter if it came at the top of the class, before I show them all who I really am," she said. Before I could point out yet again that this was a terrible idea, not that she listened, she went on, "Since when do you say nice things about the *prince of the summer court?*"

"Nice things?" I snorted. "I'd never say nice things about you, Alisa."

I never dared use her real name, even in the privacy of our room, in case I slipped. But something about this room, further from the hall, felt safer.

She closed the door softly behind us, enclosing us in the steam. "No, never," she agreed with a smile as she draped both our socks over the line that hung across the bathroom. "Autumn and summer are always enemies, after all."

"And autumn always conquers summer," I reminded her.

"Does it? Summer comes first, every time," she returned just as quickly.

I splashed her. "Your tongue is always so quick. You'd better be able to fight—if you weren't a princess, you'd have people queuing up to kick your ass."

"I can," she returned, crouching at the edge of the tub, "and I don't need you to fight my battles for me."

I had been floating, but I quickly sat up in the tub, raking my wet hair back from my face with one hand so I could give her an incredulous look. "I wasn't fighting your battles. Galic spoke out of turn and he needed to be reminded of that."

She rolled her eyes. "You're unbelievable. Most nobles are pretentious, but you're the only one I know who *pretends* to be extra-insufferable to cover—"

She broke off abruptly.

"To cover what, Alisa?" I leaned toward her.

Her gaze fell to the water, and she absently skimmed her fingertips over the water. It was one of the few times I ever saw her look uncertain, even shy, and it made my heart beat faster in my chest.

Because suddenly, I had the feeling Alisa might feel the same way I did about her.

"To cover the fact that you're actually halfway decent," she said, suddenly raising her gaze toward mine. Her eyes sparkled with mischief, and she abruptly scooped a handful of water up and threw it into my face.

I sputtered water, but I was already moving. I grabbed her under the arms and yanked her into the water with me. She fell on top of me, letting out a squeal, her lithe body pressing against mine as we fell into the water with a splash.

"I'm fully dressed, you ass," she said, although she didn't sound truly mad.

"Don't start games you don't want to play, then," I returned.

She was still pressing against me in the water, and her hand idly stroked down my side. Her fingertips on my skin did something for me that no other woman's touch ever had, and my breath caught in my chest.

"When it comes to you, Azrael," she said, and her voice had gone husky, "I always want to play."

I sat up against the back of the tub, pulling her with me. She straddled my lap in the water, then leaned forward, pressing a tentative kiss against my lips.

Her mouth was soft and sweet and reminded me of lemonade. That was perfect for her—she certainly had her sour side.

And I loved every part of her—even the bits that drove me mad.

I wrapped my hand around the back of her head, my fingers twining in her hair, and she smiled against my lips.

"What?" I whispered.

"Always so domineering," she murmured, then kissed the side of my mouth anyway. "Even when you kiss me."

"Just wait," I promised her, and her smile widened, as if she liked the idea. Then I turned my head and captured her lips with mine.

We shared slow, tender kisses. She caressed my lower lip with hers, sucked it into her mouth, and the sensation made me want to lose it and plunge deep into her. Instead, I pushed her damp hair back behind her ear; steam billowed behind the tub, and she was soaked, and her hair clung to her glowing skin.

But no matter how gentle those kisses, she was still straddling my lap, grinding down on my cock, her thighs pressed against mine tightly as if she wanted more of me. I'd let her take the lead, though.

I wrapped my hands around her hips, feeling her sway toward me, and she let out a moan. "Azrael... should we do this?"

"No," I said, my own voice coming out husky.

"*Are* we going to do this?" she asked, a smile in her voice.

"It's a mistake," I said, kissing the corner of her mouth anyway. "Our courts are enemies. That's probably why the instructors placed us together."

"Mm. True." She nipped at my earlobe, and the sensation throbbed all the way to my cock.

"You shouldn't even be here," I said.

"You'd be lost without me." She ran her fingernails over my bare shoulder, tracing her way down my chest. She stopped at the black shapes that covered my chest, looking at them carefully for the first time; we always wore so many layers in this frozen hell hole. "What are these?"

I hesitated. "In my family, we don't talk about our marks."

"In my family, we don't run away from home to have sex with handsome Fae princes in the tub, but here we are," she said, her eyes shining.

"Are you sure?" I asked, because I didn't want her to rush into anything.

"Azrael," she said, cupping my face with her hand. "Have you ever known me to shy away from any ill-advised adventure?"

"No, no I haven't," I said.

"Be brave with me," she challenged.

"You are such a brat," I murmured, but I kissed her anyway. Every time I pressed my lips to hers, it felt as if something inside me, something wound tight for a long time, unspooled a little more.

Her hand still lingered on my chest, and I covered her hand with mine, our fingertips overlapping on the dark lines there. "In my family, everyone is born with three spirits connected to them. Three animals. It's an ancient form of magic—a legacy passed down from an ancient hero."

"What kind of animals?" she asked irreverently. "Squirrels?"

I smacked her ass in the water, and she laughed at me, then bit my earlobe again a bit more fiercely. I kept my hand on her ass, massaging gently up and down the curve to take away the sting.

"It's different for everyone. Hounds for my brother. Birds for my little sister." Telling her felt as if I were revealing something deep and precious about myself, and it gave me a strange, dangerous feeling to trust the princess of summer with any secret. "And bears for me."

"Bears," she murmured. "Ah, I see it now." She bowed her head and pressed a kiss to my bare skin, just above the line of the tattoo. "Will I ever get to see these bears? Have you ever called them out before?"

"No. They're for the most dangerous of times," I said. "Most people in our line—in times of peace—go their whole lives without ever calling on their animals."

Something sad came into her eyes, as she stared into mine. "You know that's not our world, Azrael. Not this age."

"I know." I wanted to chase away the sadness in her eyes. She had been so light and playful just a moment before.

I kissed her neck, and she tilted her head to one side, welcoming me in. Then I began to suck a bruise, and she groaned even as her hand lifted to my shoulder, as if she might push me away. But she stayed still, her heated thighs pressed against mine, her fingernails sinking into my skin. I pulled away from the bruise and pressed a kiss in its place.

"Are you being gentle with me?" she asked, her brows lifting as she stared down at me. "Or am I supposed to be gentle with you?"

I huffed a laugh of surprise. "Gentle's not really my style or yours, is it?"

She shook her head.

I ran my finger across her cheekbone, down her neck. Her breath seemed to pause in her chest, despite all her teasing. She bit her lower lip as my hand delved lower, until my thumb stroked over her nipple through her wet, clinging clothes, right before I palmed her breast. She ground down on my hips.

I yanked the tunic up, and she raised her arms, helping me. Beneath the tunic, her breasts were covered with a white compression wrap. I ran my fingertips over it, and it dematerialized; ash rained down into the bathwater, then was lost in the swirling bubbles.

"When you're with me," I said, "I want the real you, Alisa."

"Are you sure?" There was something vulnerable in her eyes, even though her lips turned up at the corners with her usual liveliness. "You know I'm trouble."

"My kind of trouble," I promised her.

She rose onto her knees. I skimmed my hands over her hips, pressing her pants down, and that brought her small but perfect breasts into my face. With my fingertips pressing into the curve of her ass, I caught one of those pert pink nipples in my mouth, and she let out a breath as I swirled my tongue around her nipple. I sucked on it, then nipped it gently, and she gasped and pushed me away.

She shed her pants in a hurry, the waves she created rocking against my chest. Then she pressed her breasts against my face again. "Do the other one."

"And you say I'm bossy," I said, but I didn't mind. I teased her other nipple with my tongue, flicking against it, then drew it into my mouth, sucking and swirling and devouring, until she moaned, her eyes falling closed.

My hands ran up her hips to her slender waist. She leaned into me, pressing her lips to mine in eager, frantic kisses. These kisses weren't gentle now, and when she ground down onto my cock, my tip slid inside her. She went very still, and I paused too.

"Okay?" I asked her, running my thumb over her cheekbone.

She smiled then. "Oh, Azrael, if it's just *okay* I'm going to be very disappointed. You know our rooms are pretty well sound proofed. Make me scream."

I laughed and caught her hips in my hands, dragging her further down onto my cock. She was so tight and narrow, and having our first time in the bathtub wasn't ideal. Her lips parted, maybe in pain, and I paused.

But she slammed herself down on me, driving my cock deep inside her. She felt so good, and I exhaled hard.

Then I caught her hair with my hand, dragging her head to mine, kissing her over and over. When she leaned toward me, I could feel how full of my cock she was, how she pressed herself hard down against my abs as if she only wanted more.

"It hurts a little," she admitted, as if she knew I wanted to know, "but in the best way, Azrael."

I nodded, waiting for her, and she began to move slowly up and down my cock. She was so beautiful, with her lavender hair clinging to her forehead, those mischievous eyes dark and luminous. She looked at times as if she were made of moonlight and magic itself, more full of life than anyone else I'd ever met in this world.

Then as if she felt my thoughts, as if I were getting too serious for her, she leaned forward and bit me, her teeth scraping against my shoulder before they pinched my skin painfully.

"Ouch," I said, and slapped her ass again, even though she just laughed against my wounded skin.

She was still moving up and down my cock, and I took her hips in my hands, helping her move steadily up and down my cock, quickening the cadence. She let out a moan and then she tightened around me, her channel pulsing over and over. She shook her head back and forth, her hair flying around that delicate face, her eyes closed now. Her hands rose to her chest, cupping her breasts briefly, before they slid up her face and into her hair, as if the pleasure was overwhelming to her.

"Azrael," she moaned, and I shattered inside her. I yanked her close to me, holding her tight as I emptied into her and she pulsed around me.

I bit my lip at the waves of pleasure washing through me, then buried my face in her hair, feeling warm and content in a way I wasn't sure I'd felt in years. The two of us clung to each other, trading kisses already even as our bodies shuddered from the powerful waves of sensation.

I always had the feeling that the two of us would cause each other pain, but I was innocent enough then to believe that it would all be *in the best way.*

CHAPTER TWENTY-THREE

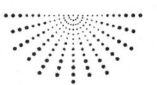

Alisa

THE NEXT MORNING, I woke up and stumbled out of my bedroom to find Nikia sleeping on the couch.

I stared at her, wondering if she was drunk. I'd barely noticed her at the party last night but then, I'd been so focused on saying all the right things with eyes constantly on me, judging me, assessing me…

Just thinking about the night was enough to give me hives. I needed coffee.

I pulled on my own leather pants—maybe I should have worn something more low-key for my return to the Fae world—and headed into the maze of the palace. The long marble corridors seemed strangely empty, sparking a suspicion that made me wish for my sword.

But Azrael still had it, damn him. We'd have to discuss that today.

I wasn't sure I could find my way back to my bedroom. Coffee first, then I'd find Azrael and Duncan and Tiron.

I realized I must be headed in the right direction when I walked through a door and instead of cold marble floors, found honey-colored hardwood. I must be moving toward the servant's quarters.

I headed down a flight of stairs, and inhaled the scent of bacon. Promising sign; my stomach rumbled with hunger.

When I pushed open the door to the kitchen, I heard a sob.

I went in slowly, looking for the source of the sound. I couldn't see anyone in here at first; the kitchen was enormous. A long bank of butcher-block countertops lay in front of me, with pots and pans hanging down and shelves of stacked plates blocking my view of what lay on the other side. Early morning light seeped in through the high windows above the kitchen.

There was clattering further in the kitchen and I could see people stirring and working near the big brick ovens.

Then I heard the sob again, on the other side of the counter, followed by an angry growl of a voice. I edged backward, away from the servants by the ovens—I could do without any more kneeling—and skirted the end of the countertops.

The angry growling voice was scolding someone. Then I heard the sob again, and then a voice, a small, uncertain voice that sounded like a child's—but maybe it was a small, full-grown Fae of some kind—and then there was a *smack*. Whoever it was sobbed harder.

Fuck going around the long counter. I jumped up and caught the edge of the hanging wrought iron pot rack as my feet landed on the top of the butcher block. I rolled under the hanging cast-iron pans and came up on the other side.

A stunned Fae male stared at me, his mouth hanging open, and I longed to close those lips for him.

There was a girl at his feet.

A child. If she'd been human, I would have pegged her for eight or nine, but her huge, tear-filled eyes were golden, and little horns curled out of her blond hair near her forehead.

"What the hell are you doing?" he demanded, and then I saw the strap in his hand. Red hot anger flashed over me.

I punched him in the face, a quick one-two combination that burst his nose open and then sent his chin flying skyward. He landed hard on his ass.

"No one's beating a kid in my castle," I warned him.

He scoffed at me, as much as anyone can scoff with blood pouring from their nose. It came out as a bit of a sob itself. "Your castle? You're going to be strung up on the wall for what you just did."

Right, I looked mortal. The word might not have gotten around about my peculiar appearance.

I offered my hand to the kid, who looked up at me with terrified eyes. There were mottled bruises across her arms—old wounds and new—and someone had split her lip.

"Where did you come from?" I demanded.

She looked at me uncertainly, and didn't take my hand.

That was probably for the best, since the next second, a whirring noise flickered above my head. I glanced up to see the flying Fae above me, just before he let himself fall. He slammed me into the wooden floor.

He was light and I was already rolling to throw him when two other Fae piled on top of me. I struggled to buck them off. I could really use that damned sword right about now.

"Run!" I hissed at the girl, at least wanting her out of danger until I had the situation under control.

She started to slide under the butcher block counter, but one of the Fae snapped at her, "Stay. Stand against the wall."

She rose to her feet on the other side of the counter and I thought she was going to make a run for it, but instead she backed up until she bumped the wall. I willed her to run; then she stopped and stared forward. There was a glazed look in her eyes. Fuck. That damned Fae glamor. I thought it only worked on humans, but maybe it worked on kids too.

I had better learn to do that myself, and fast.

I slammed my elbow into the nearest face. And hey, it turned out those Fae noses are just as crunchy and blood-gushy as human noses, despite the Fae's superiority complex.

But they were so strong—stronger than a shifter, even—and as one of them rolled out from under me, so quick he was a flash, I found myself pinned on my stomach. One of them was half-on top of me, his weight pressing the breath out of my lungs, his elbow bearing down hard into a pinch point in my shoulder that sent pain rippling through my shoulders.

The one I'd hurt earlier kicked me in the side, his boot catching my ribs, and the world went red with pain.

He tried again and this time, I managed to explode up and flip myself. The man on top of me hadn't expected it—his elbow dug in until I wanted to scream and then suddenly, I was free, no one on top of me—so I got loose, right before the kick landed across my breast. I let out a half-feral scream that surprised even me and grabbed his boot, yanking him with me as I rolled. He lost his balance, tripping over my body, and slammed into the countertop.

Then I scrambled up, grabbing a frying pan off the rack and whirling to face my attackers.

Three familiar, big Fae bodies flashed through the kitchen, and the males who had attacked me screamed. Duncan decapitated one of the cringing Fae with a brutal flash of his bright sword. Another Fae tried to fly away, only for Azrael to pounce on his back and drag him down, before slitting his throat with the bejeweled dagger he carried from his belt. Apparently it wasn't just ceremonial.

The Fae who tried to run from Tiron slipped on the ice suddenly underfoot, and Tiron kicked him over onto his back. The Fae tried to say something about mercy, but his words were cut off by Tiron's blade.

"There's no mercy if you hurt our princess," Tiron warned him.

The Fae was a corpse, so there was no real need for that one-liner. Tiron looked up at me and winked.

Blood was splattered across the kitchen, across me and across the still-petrified child who stood pressed against the wall.

Then it felt as if time slowed down to a normal speed. Tiron picked up a kitchen towel and wiped the blood off the blade of his knife. The Fae who Azrael had killed thumped down onto the ground behind him.

Duncan surveyed me and the pan I still carried skeptically. "Are you going to make me a cobbler, Alisa? Cobbler is my favorite."

"You'd think they'd have better sense than to attack the Princess in a room full of knives and...cast iron," Tiron said, giving me a saucy grin.

"Why did you kill them?" I demanded, pressing a hand to my side, then jerking it away as pain blossomed through my chest so intensely that I could barely breathe. Fuck. I'd need to baby those ribs; I was pretty sure I'd broken a few.

"They were dead once they hurt you," Azrael said bleakly.

The countertop pressed into my hip, and I realized I'd backed into it.

"They didn't even know who she was," Duncan said, his voice amused. "They thought some random human came in here and told them to fuck off—"

"Are you all right?" Tiron asked. He threw a look over his shoulder at Duncan and Azrael that I couldn't quite read, then tried to pull me away from them.

"Fine," I said. "I don't need to be babied." *Just my ribs.* "What's the girl's story?"

Tiron followed my gaze to the girl who still stood against the wall. "She must have been one of the tithes from a village that couldn't raise enough funds. The summer court still takes servants as payment."

"Excuse me?"

"For the tithe," Tiron said, as if that added any clarity.

"Remember our precious princess is an idiot now," Duncan called. There was a dragging sound; apparently he was on clean-up duty.

I watched him and Azrael each tow a body by their ankles, leaving a smear of blood across the floor behind them. Tiron followed my gaze, then said, "Faer would have them tortured to death. They assaulted you. They were lucky to go out this way."

"Faer didn't strike me as the protective type."

"It's not about protection. It's about honor and respect."

I huffed a skeptical laugh at that. "Where does the girl come from? How do we help her?"

Tiron gave me a long look. "You're going to make someone very unhappy."

"Ask me if I give a shit," I said.

What's the point of being a queen if you can't set the world right?

CHAPTER TWENTY-FOUR

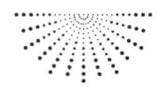

T*iron*

"Stay with Alisa and keep her out of trouble," Azrael told Duncan.

He glanced at the girl, who sat across from Alisa, wide-eyed and kicking her feet. We were in Alisa's lavish little apartment. Nikia bustled around uselessly, obviously distressed but trying to focus on a hearty breakfast.

Duncan raised his eyebrows, dusting his hands absently against his pants even though he'd already washed off the dead Fae's blood.

"I'll tell her to do the same with you," Azrael added.

Duncan's lips tilted into a smirk.

Azrael jerked his head, gesturing for me to come with him.

"Important job, Tiron. He needs you to keep him out of trouble while he talks to daddy," Duncan called.

I'd never seen the princes come to blows, but watching Azrael's jaw tense, I thought it might just be a matter of time.

We went to see Faer. The prince was still in bed, and he sat up, his face languid. There was a female massaging his shoulders and the blankets kept rippling down by his knees until I realized there was someone down there too. I averted my eyes as his eyelashes fluttered in pleasure.

"What?" he demanded, his voice surly.

"Thank you for seeing us," Azrael managed. He was far more diplomatic than I was. "There was an incident this morning when Alisa visited the kitchen."

"Oh? Was her toast burned? Pulp in her juice? Pits in her cherries? Did my sister kill anyone?" He didn't seem too concerned.

"She ran across an indentured girl who was being…mistreated… and she became involved. She would like to return her to her home."

His eyes snapped open, although his lips were still parted, his breath coming in short pants, as if he were close to orgasm. Rage twisted his face.

Azrael said quickly, "I think it would be best if you freed the girl from her obligation, and we took Alisa to see her home. She might get the wrong idea about the Fae world—she might become obsessed with going home herself." Then he corrected himself. "What she *thinks* is home, since it's what she remembers."

She might be obsessed with home. Or with revolution. From the fierce glint in Alisa's eyes, I thought Azrael might be saving the ungrateful prince's life.

Faer scoffed. "She won't be going home."

"By law, she can't be married against her will," Azrael began.

"I'd never want her to be," Faer said, the lie rolling off his tongue smoothly. He raised a hand, shooing us out. "Fine. Take her on a tour. Let her save one little girl. Soften the realities. But make sure she's back for the gala tonight."

Azrael's lips parted, as if he wanted to ask *another?* But instead he bowed and headed out of the room.

He was just as much of royal blood as Faer. I wondered how he felt, bowing to him. I didn't dare ask; I never wanted to tip my own hand.

I was going to gut Faer one day. I'd dreamt of it so often it felt almost like a memory.

But I smiled like a fool, bowed, and walked out with Azrael.

Azrael exhaled in the hallway, running his hand through his hair to push it back from his face.

"Why did you ask me to come?" I hadn't said a word.

Azrael glanced over his shoulder. Then he whispered, "Every time I'm within ten feet about him, I have completely inappropriate daydreams of assassination."

I hadn't realized Azrael and I had so much in common.

I glanced around, making sure we were truly alone, before I said, "He'll give up one servant. But she's not stupid—she's going to know there are more."

"I know," he said.

A muscle ticked in his jaw, and I wondered how he felt about Alisa's reaction. The autumn court had given up both living tithes and glamored human servants long ago. The summer court would fight tooth and nail to keep both.

"She can't save the whole world," he said. "And once she gets her memories back, she won't care anymore."

There was a bitter edge in his voice. I wasn't sure if he really believed that about Alisa, though.

As if he couldn't abide the topic anymore, Azrael swiveled on his heel and strode down the halls. "The princess will be waiting."

I followed him through the labyrinth of the palace, then he led the way into Alisa's room. She looked up from the table, frowning.

The girl at the table was silent, dazed. Nikia was trying, gods bless her, spooning tea into her mouth.

"Faer agreed we could bring her home," Azrael said.

Alisa leapt from the chair and crossed to Azrael. He moved into a defensive posture automatically, but she threw her arms around his neck.

He smiled a true, delighted smile before he buried his face in her hair to hide it, and from the way Duncan scoffed, he saw it too.

"It will give you a chance to see more of the summer court," Azrael added. "It's time you got to know your kingdom again, Princess. And it's time they got to know you."

Her smile back was shy but genuine.

Somehow Azrael's gentle moments had the feeling of a long con to me. Maybe I shouldn't judge, as I was in the midst of the longest con on all three of them, but cold fingers of anger clutched my chest. "I'll get the horses ready."

I was headed down the long marble hall toward the sweeping stairs when I heard the door fly open behind me. That would be Duncan; Azrael didn't slam doors.

"What the hell," Duncan growled when he caught up to me. "You're jealous?"

Jealousy wasn't really the issue. I hated that we were all trying to use her to restore our kingdoms; I hated Duncan and Azrael for it, even as I did the same thing. But it was best if they read my emotion as jealousy.

I stared back at his grim face. "Are we going to keep pretending that you're not?"

When he opened his mouth, I knew what he would say, so I said the words right along with him, *"I know her too well for that."*

His bright blue eyes blazed.

I cut him off before he could say anything else, "You're usually obnoxiously honest, Duncan. But this time around, you're lying to yourself."

"You don't understand what she did—how she betrayed us—"

"Then help me understand." I threw out an arm toward the apartment. "Because that girl in there, she just seems *good*. She seems kind. Better than any of us."

We'd all been hardened by our losses and by what we must do to protect our people. But maybe that was no excuse for who we'd all become.

Duncan's face was suddenly overcome by pretend pity. "That girl just oozes deceit. I suppose she's beguiled you."

"Sure, Duncan. Your hatred is all about what she did to the autumn court—and not at all because she chose your brother."

I was usually pretty good at reading Duncan, but I didn't see his right hook coming until the world went red.

Azrael and Alisa walked out of the room, and their faces were a distant blur. I was already in motion. When I slammed into Duncan, the two of us rolled down the stairs. Horned servants scattered; we slammed into some poor glamored human, who fell down the last few steps.

"Enough," Azrael shouted, his voice full of fire that he rarely called upon. It even made Duncan look up, as careless as he usually seemed of his older brother's authority.

Azrael didn't storm down the stairs. He waited for Alisa, then swept down the stairs, as graceful as ever, taking his time.

I picked myself off the ground, ignoring Duncan. My shoulders throbbed where I'd hit the stairs, and my ankle was stiff along with my jaw. I resisted the impulse to rub any of the pain away, instead straightening my shoulders.

Azrael barely looked at me; his attention was focused on Duncan, who glanced away, his jaw stiff, as if his brother could scold him with a look.

"Tiron, take Alisa and go saddle the horses," he said, his voice quiet. "We'll be along shortly."

I nodded. Azrael and Duncan walked away together, their postures straight and erect, the movement synchronized without discussion.

"He's in trouble," I mouthed at Alisa.

She rolled her eyes. "You should be too," she chided me as we headed for the doors to the courtyard. Servants swung open the doors for us, and sunshine spilled across the marble lobby. She glanced at them, then swallowed whatever she was going to say.

I led her through the courtyard, past the gardens and the training pitch into the stables. When we walked into the quiet of the horse barn, she caught my arm and swung me around to face her. I thought she was going to ask what Duncan and I had fought about, but instead she asked me quietly, "Are you all right?"

For some reason, the question struck me hard. "Yes, of course. I take harder hits every day in the training yard."

Her gaze was searching. She touched the edge of my swollen jaw. Her knuckles were calloused from fighting, and peeling black nail polish still covered part of her thumbnail. They weren't a princess's hands. But they were gentle.

"You two seem so close." she said softly. Then she studied my face, and she must've realized I didn't want to talk about it. She smiled as she stepped back, but I felt a lurch of loss as the space between us grew.

"We are, but we fight," I said, as if it were nothing.

But Alisa's presence felt as if it changed all my feelings, even though I knew it should change nothing. I needed to stick with the plan.

"Duncan can be difficult," I added.

"No? I hadn't noticed."

I began to saddle the horses, and she watched me. There was something bothering her still, but I didn't want to talk about Duncan.

"This is my horse," I said, stroking the white stallion's neck. "Duncan rides the grouchy black one two stalls over, and Azrael's got the chestnut mare."

"What's his name?"

"We aren't supposed to name our animals," I said. "That's a human affectation."

She scoffed at that. "Nonsense. You don't talk to him? There's no way I can believe you don't talk to that horse, unless you're actually the villain of this whole affair..."

I laughed at that, because she was smiling. But I felt a strange prickle at the word *villain*, given that I had my own secrets.

"Are you going to help me get the horses ready, Princess?" I asked. "You could go make friends with Duncan's horse—that will irritate the hell out of him."

She hesitated. "I don't know how to ride, Tiron."

"You know how to ride," I assured her. "I'm sure you've been in the saddle since you could walk, just like every other Fae noble."

"Maybe. But I don't remember."

I tightened the last cinch. My horse side-eyed me skeptically, and I patted his side.

"They never have to know," I promised. "I'll cover for you."

She smiled. "That's good of you, Tiron."

That smile of hers made something twist in my chest. But I'd seen how Carter and Julian fell over themselves for her, and they certainly hadn't won her heart.

I led her horse over and helped her get the toe of her slipper into the stirrup, then showed her where to grip the pommel.

She rose into the saddle with the grace of an ambitious slug. But confidence building first. She glanced down at me, waiting to see how I'd react, and I told her, "You're a natural."

"And you're a liar," she said, but there was no bite in it.

"It'll come back to you," I promised. I chewed my lip, debating how I could keep the others from noticing her lack of grace. "You know, with the child along... it would probably be best if we took the carriage."

Relief—and gratitude—spread across her face. "Thank you, Tiron."

I held out my arms as she unfolded herself awkwardly from the horse. I knew that she didn't need me.

But she still slid off the horse into my arms. And for a second, I held her tight, breathing in her sweet scent of summer.

She lingered close to me, her gaze on mine. Her eyes were wide and dark-lashed, and there was a scar at the edge of one of those eyes. When I touched the scar curiously with my fingertips, she didn't pull away.

"What happened here?" I asked. "It left a mark."

"I don't remember." She raised her fingertips to the same scar. "It seems like you should have a memory of all the things that left a scar. But that's not how humans are. Some of the worst scars are from wounds we don't even remember."

"Maybe it would be easier to forget," I said, then realized how stupid that was to say, and I winced. "I'm sorry."

"You're not going to hurt my feelings." Her gaze on mine was a bit too keen. "Maybe one day, Tiron, you'll want to tell me what it is you wish you could forget."

My lips twisted. "Maybe."

The day I told Alisa the truth would probably be a bad day for us both.

CHAPTER TWENTY-FIVE

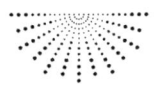

Alisa

AT FIRST, Duncan wanted to still ride his horse, then Tiron volunteered to ride in the carriage to keep me company, and that prompted Azrael to offer to stay with me as well, and then Duncan insisted on riding in the carriage too, to babysit us all.

The carriage moved briskly down the hill into the forest, leaving the glittering ocean and the strip of city along the shore behind us. The sway of the carriage was strange, and a few times my shoulder bumped Azrael's. Every time, heat washed over me, even though he seemed lost in thought and never noticed. Something was bothering him.

I smiled around at them all, but I smiled especially hard at Duncan, who was grim-faced and sporting a black eye. "Well, this is pleasant."

Duncan grunted in response.

Tiron leaned forward, bracing his elbows on his knees as he smiled at the Fae girl who sat beside me. She leaned into me, the little horns that jutted from her soft blond hair poking into my arm. I wrapped my arm around her protectively, but told her, "You don't have to worry about him. That's just Tiron."

Duncan snorted. "Something his enemies have said many times."

"Strange that I don't see any of them still around," Tiron murmured, the smile never leaving his face. "What's your name?"

"Eulia," she finally managed, her voice a whisper.

"That's a beautiful name," Tiron said. "I have a cousin named Eulia."

He leaned back, shifting so he could get his hand into his pocket. He pulled out a coin that he walked over his knuckles, until he pretended to drop it. He tried to catch it in mid-air, but it vanished.

Eulia was watching him curiously.

Duncan never would have admitted it, but he was too. I hid a smirk as I looked past him at the wild orchards we were passing, where tree limbs tangled together and red fruit dripped from between the leaves.

Tiron spread his hands. "I lost the coin."

Eulia gave in and smiled.

"I know," he admitted. "I'm so clumsy. Wait—what's this?"

He frowned down at his hand, which suddenly contained one of the red fruits from outside. He offered it to Eulia. She hesitated, staring at him, then reached out and took it from him. I almost smiled. Tiron's charm was irresistible.

The carriage rocked and swayed through villages and past mountains. Then the road looped around, and we began to wind up the mountain.

The air turned slowly cooler. I craned my head to see out the window. Two Fae knights on horseback rode ahead of us, and another rode beside the man controlling the carriage.

We crested the top, and suddenly the world on the other side was spread out below us, revealing lush greenery in contrast to the snow that surrounded us.

"A pocket of winter." Tiron produced a snowball, holding it out to the girl, and I wondered how he managed that trick. "I wish I could show you both how beautiful the winter court is."

She took the snowball from him, her eyes lighting up with wonder. "I only saw the snow when they brought me over the mountain, and I didn't get to touch it..."

Azrael held out his hands, and Tiron tossed another snowball to him. There was a flicker of darkness in Azrael's eyes, but it was gone when Eulia looked at him, replaced by an easy smile. I never saw Azrael smile at me like that, so uncomplicated and genuinely *sweet*, and it made something ache in my chest. I couldn't remember what I did to him that I'd never see that smile aimed my way.

"You know what these are good for?" Azrael said, just as Duncan began, "Don't you dare."

Azrael whipped the snowball at him. The snowball exploded across Duncan's face, dusting his dark hair with white. For a second, tension squeezed in my chest, wondering how Duncan would react.

Duncan scraped the remnants of snow slowly from his face, his trousers. The look on his face was grim as ever.

He launched himself suddenly at Azrael, a grin springing to his lips as he tried to slap him in the face with the snow. Tiron already had new snowballs in both palms, and he went after them both.

An instant snowball fight erupted, rocking the carriage. When Eulia began to giggle, the sound rose thin and shaky into the air.

"Help me," Azrael begged, pinned on the floor of the carriage by Duncan, while Tiron pelted them both with snowballs mercilessly. I was laughing at them all so hard I could barely peel myself off the wall of the carriage, but Eulia scraped up some of the snow and launched it at Tiron's face.

She froze for a second at her own daring. But when he laughed, as he wiped snow from his eyes, she visibly relaxed.

"Maybe someday, you could come be one of our knights of the winter court, Eulia," he teased.

If only there was still a winter court. The thought rolled over me heavily. Did Tiron think his court would rise again? From what Azrael had told me, the royal family had been murdered. I didn't know how the laws and lineage worked to know who would take the throne. Could it be Tiron?

His green eyes crinkled at the corners as he teased Eulia and tormented Azrael for her amusement. Watching him, I could imagine him as the king of the winter court.

And Azrael—seeing him being playful, when he was usually so imposing, made my heart lurch in my chest. My traitorous body always responded to Azrael's too-gorgeous face, those sharp cheekbones and the sweep of his jaw, his mesmerizing purple eyes. But his kindness made me ache for him in another way.

Duncan had been smiling too, but now he was back on the bench across from me, nestled into the corner. Tiron and Azrael were still throwing snowballs at each other, both of them trying to persuade Eulia to join their side.

Duncan was watching me, his gaze hard. It felt as if he could see right through me.

I stuck my tongue out at him.

The next second, something exploded outside the carriage.

The carriage tilted onto its side. I grabbed for Eulia, trying to protect her. Azrael was already launching himself off the floor of the carriage, wrapping both her and me in his arms as his broad shoulders shielded us.

The carriage hesitated for a second, tilted at that terrifying angle. Over Azrael's shoulder, I saw Tiron raise his arms, and I heard the wind blow up outside as the temperature suddenly sank. Duncan ripped off his shirt, exposing those big biceps and his tanned skin, and the tattoos on his chest seemed to be moving.

Then the carriage slammed into the ground. The force of it was jarring, and Eulia let out a whimper, then fell silent. Her small body was tense and strained as if she was ready to flee.

Duncan was already moving, throwing open the carriage door and skimming himself up and out. Tiron glanced back at us and followed him. Azrael pulled his dagger from his belt and gripped the blade, extending the hilt to me.

MAY DAWSON

"Stay here and protect her," Azrael told me, and then he was gone too.

Eulia and I were left alone in the dark of the carriage. Outside, I heard shouts and the clash of swords. I pulled away from Eulia, intending to go after the males and help them, but she clung to me.

"It's all right," I told her.

Suddenly, the dim light of the carriage grew even darker. At the door of the carriage, a huge horned Fae reached toward us with an enormous hand.

I pushed Eulia behind me so I could swing the blade, but before I could, a snarling filled the air. The male looked back in horror just before one of the shadow hounds slammed into him. The hound's teeth flashed, tearing open the male's throat, and then both of them tumbled off the top of the carriage.

Eulia's eyes were closed tightly, tears leaking down her cheeks.

"Open your eyes," I told her, my voice coming out sterner than I intended. "You've got to be ready to fight."

"I'm scared of the hounds," she whispered.

"The dogs are the least of our problems," I told her. "They're on our side."

I wanted to know who the Fae were who had attacked us, and why. I jumped and caught the edge of the doorway, my fingertips straining against the polished wood as I tried to skim myself up. I got my elbow onto the smooth side of the carriage, and stared around me.

Tiron, Azrael and Duncan fought furiously with two enormous horned Fae, both of whom were the size of giants—easily half again their height, if not more. But the ground was scattered with other giant Fae. Our carriage's driver and the guard with his long lilac-colored cloak both lay in the snow, their uniforms—and their blood—vivid against the crisp white snow.

The shadow hounds were a blur as they moved between the Fae, snarling and tearing with their wicked teeth. They'd make short work of the giants that were left.

I pulled myself the rest of the way out and looked down.

Eulia stared at me with wide, alarmed eyes.

"I'm not leaving you," I promised, leaning back in and offering her a hand up.

She looked at me skeptically. Then her wings burst out of her tunic, long and shimmering and iridescent, and she used them to fly up beside me. I scrambled out of her way, and she landed lightly beside me on top of the carriage.

The last of the giants fell.

Azrael and Duncan and Tiron turned to us, their swords bloodstained.

"Brigands," Azrael said shortly. "They must have seen the royal carriage and assumed something of value was on board."

Duncan snorted. "Too bad they didn't realize it was just Alisa."

He whistled to his hounds, and they came bounding toward him. He dropped to his knees, petting their heads and dare I say, *cooing* to them. He babied them despite the blood on their muzzles.

Eulia stiffened beside me. Her eyes were wide with fear.

"Duncan," I said softly, not knowing how he'd react. Would he be the gruff asshole he always was? Or would he respond to her fear and send the hounds away again?

Duncan looked at me with that smirk across his face, as if he were about to say something cutting, then his gaze found Eulia. His expression changed, her fear mirrored in his face as sudden protectiveness.

"They're friendly," he promised her. "They'd die to protect someone like you, they would never hurt you."

He murmured a word, and the two dogs sat. Their tongues lolled out of their broad muzzles, giving them a goofy look despite the blood matting their dark fur. I was relieved that the blood didn't seem to be their own.

Azrael and Tiron set to work checking on the corpses that scattered the clearing, then pushing the carriage back up onto its damaged wheels. Neither of them complained that Duncan and I didn't help, both of us focused on Eulia.

When she finally reached out and stroked her hand over one of the dog's heads, between its ears, Duncan grinned triumphantly. For a second, the two of us smiled at each other.

Then he seemed to remember who he was, and that smile disappeared, replaced by his usual grim nature.

"We should move." But his cold words were belied by the way his hand rested on the dogs' backs, his fingers absently stroking through their wiry black fur.

We abandoned the carriage and began the trek down the mountain on foot. Duncan fell behind us, and when he caught up, the dogs were nowhere to be seen.

I wanted to ask him about his hounds. But Duncan's moment of light-heartedness had fled. Azrael and Tiron took turns carrying Eulia on their shoulders because she was so small. Duncan stayed behind the rest of us as we wound our way down the mountain trail, gradually leaving behind the snow and ice and walking through the thick green foliage of summer.

Tiron carried Eulia ahead, and Azrael walked beside me, thrusting his hands into his pockets.

"Do you think the brigands knew that I would be there?" I asked.

"I'm not sure I believe in that much coincidence." Azrael watched Tiron, who was pretending to lurch back and forth as he carried Eulia, who was laughing. Then he said carefully, "I wanted to warn you... there's a possibility she's not wanted at home, Alisa. There might be a reason why she was the one bartered for the taxes."

Those words felt like a slap. I started to ask why he hadn't told me that *before* I became set on bringing her home to a situation that might be terrible.

But before I could form the words, he said, "I hope that's not the case. I just wanted to warn you."

Around us, the mountain sloped down into green hills, dotted with farms. The trees were heavy with flowers, big white and pink blooms that released a sweet fragrance like spun sugar that drifted through the air. The Fae world seemed so beautiful and magical.

But we'd left bodies behind us. This world might be even darker than earth.

As we headed down the road, Eulia sprinted ahead. Tiron jogged to catch up with her.

We reached a weathered gray farmhouse, the fields behind it tidily plowed and dotted with outbuildings. A woman ran out of the house and hugged Eulia, beginning to cry, and Eulia clung to her.

The scene made Azrael smile, but he jerked his head toward the road. "Come on. We don't belong here."

I hugged Eulia goodbye, and we left the happy scene behind.

As we headed for the soaring mountaintop, Tiron's fingers brushed mine. The two of us exchanged a quick look, and I was almost tempted to reach out and take his hand. But I didn't.

Instead, all four of us seemed lost in thought as we began the long trek back to that damned gilded prison of mine.

CHAPTER TWENTY-SIX

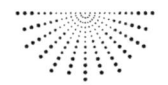

Another night, another party. The night before must have worked so well for Faer's agenda.

Azrael leaned in close to me, his exhalation against the shell of my ear sending a strange tingle down my neck, and I resisted the urge to touch the bare skin caressed by his warm breath.

"General Winspar was loyal to your father, but he barely tolerates your brother. He hates Faer's incompetence in the training ring and takes it as a personal affront that your brother avoids all combat sports. He might be a good ally… if you ever need one. Just know that, like a lot of men who form their identity around being tough, he crumples into a tantrum if anyone disrespects them."

With that thought, Azrael straightened.

"Is there any particular way I'm supposed to greet him or address him?" I asked in a whisper.

"*General* would be ideal. Genuine warmth and respect if you can muster them would do a good deal to win him over."

I nodded and turned to face the General, who was beckoning over a female Fae with long, dark hair.

"Welcome home," he said. "I wanted you to meet my wife, Bitta."

"It's a pleasure," I said, extending my hand to clasp the way I'd noticed other Fae greeted each other.

I managed to make small talk with them both. I might need an ally given how confusing the conversation with my brother had been.

When Bitta mentioned that she had just given birth to a baby—not that I could tell from her sleek gown, the Fae really were impossible—I steered her over to the chairs, taking a seat with her so she wouldn't have to look up.

The startled faces around me suggested I'd just broken some kind of protocol, and I glanced at Azrael, but he was smiling. The General seemed pleased by the concern I'd shown his wife.

A tall Fae wound through the crowd, his gaze fixed on Azrael.

"Forgive me, Princess," the General said. "This is the master of training—he runs the military academy for highborn Fae."

He sighed under his breath, his eyes flickering toward Faer—who was holding court on the stairs to the dais, surrounded by laughing Fae females—and then added, "Such as it is now."

I glanced at Azrael, but he didn't have time to explain anything, except to add, "His name is Lanin."

The Fae who ran the academy was tall even by their standards, with sharp dark eyes and a mass of dark red hair.

The general tried to intercept him, but Lanin had eyes only for Azrael.

"Your autumn court nobles are about to be slaughtered," he said.

Azrael rose to his full height, eyes flashing. It would be alarming to be on the opposite side of that fierce glare, and Lanin raised his hands. "I can't stop them from being pulled early to command battalions at the front, unless you—"

The General broke into this urgent conversation with a smile. "Did you somehow miss that the princess has returned?"

Lanin stiffened, then turned to me as if he hadn't recognized me. Understandable enough.

"Forgive me," Lanin said, and seemed to hesitate. Apparently by sitting down I had caused a significant portion of the crowd's brains

MAY DAWSON

to spontaneously melt out their ears. I needed princess lessons, and fast.

I hated that my brother had thrown me to the wolves. I would prefer actual wolves to awkward social moments, actually.

Faer was still laughing at the other end of the room, surrounded by chittering females.

"Nothing to forgive," I said, then read on their faces that perhaps the old Alisa was not quite that quick to let a slight go. "Tell me more about this situation."

My voice came out sounding imperious. I hadn't quite meant that tone, but whatever.

Lanin scoffed. "I doubt Faer would tolerate that."

Azrael looked at me with unexpected deference softening his features—a show for these two, and somehow it warmed my heart.

"As you wish, Princess," Azrael said. "This might be the wrong time for a discussion, but we will have it. Soon."

The look he flashed Lanin might have been a threat.

I wanted to talk to him about all this desperately.

Once they had gone, I touched Azrael's arm. "Can you get me out of here? This is miserable..."

He gave me a sympathetic look. "Take a break. Dance with me."

"I don't know this dance either, Azrael."

"Try following for once," he said, taking my hand and pulling me out on the dance floor with him. "Perhaps your body knows the dance by heart."

Just like my body seemed to know *Azrael* by heart, and tried to respond to him, no matter how unwise that was?

"What's going on?" I asked him softly.

"The rift keeps getting worse, more and more monsters coming through. So Faer keeps sending officers from the academy. They're not done with their training, they're...young." Azrael's Adam's apple bobbed. He couldn't hide his worry.

"He sends autumn Fae," I clarified.

He jerked his head in a nod, although his head was still high, a smile fixed on his face, as if he were focused on the dancing. "If I beg him not to, he might listen. The game wouldn't be any fun if I lost all hope."

Anger clutched my chest. I hated the thought of Faer manipulating Azrael. *Hurting* him. Azrael might not be my friend, but he clearly loved the autumn court.

Azrael took me around the ball room. He was all lean, muscular grace, moving with ease around the room. The music seemed to sing through my blood, the room beginning to spin around me, the dance carrying me along. *Magic.* It felt as if magic was in the air.

"See?" he murmured into my ear. "You do still know the steps."

"I'd like to cut in." A tall Fae loomed at my shoulder, glaring at Azrael as if Azrael'd personally offended the male somehow.

Suddenly, the spinning room came to a halt; the magic died, even though the music played on.

I'd just begun to relax, and now I stiffened again. "No, thank you."

The man turned the glare on me. He was tall and handsome, his bones slender and sharp, his eyes a deep, magnetic silver.

"You can't deny me," he grumbled.

"Excuse me?" My hands slipped apart from Azrael's.

"Raile," Azrael started. "Good gods. She *just* came home. Give her time."

"Give her time? More time? I waited five years for her," Raile said. "And for that damned hobgoblin to die."

"Hobgoblin?" I frowned. "What are you talking about?"

Faer was making his way through the crowd behind Raile. Everyone melted out of his way. He had an easy smile on his face, and his jeweled tunic shone under the lights.

"You're a princess," Raile said bluntly. "You dance with everyone who asks."

Azrael ran his hand over his face in exasperation. "You didn't learn how to court a woman any better in the past five years, apparently."

"Perhaps I should be queen instead of a princess then," I shot back. "Because I don't intend to dance with anyone who doesn't please me."

I didn't know where that came from, the barbed words that slipped out, but Faer's eyes widened.

Azrael's hand slid across my back, and he leaned in close to me as if he'd whisper in my ear like he had so many other times tonight.

"Oh, no," I said softly, my voice meant to carry only to his ears. "Whoever this is... You knew about him, didn't you? You could have warned me I'd have some determined suitors."

The guilt that flickered through his expression left no doubt.

"I hate you, Azrael," I said, my voice very low. "Just as much as Duncan hates me, I hate you."

He shook his head. "You don't understand anything."

"You're right, I don't," I admitted. "But I know that this is a miserable place full of miserable people."

Azrael leaned in close to me, his lips almost brushing my ear. When I started to pull away, he caught my arm, his grip tight and commanding. "If you run out of here like a child, Faer will use that as one more example that you aren't fit to rule."

One more example. Apparently, there had been many conversations about me. I was beginning to understand the big pieces, at least, of this puzzle. Faer and I were twins, so either of us could rule, perhaps. But Faer wasn't my friend. He'd brought me back for a reason.

He'd sent Azrael to do his bidding, and Azrael always would. After what I'd just heard about the autumn court, I could almost understand why.

But that didn't mean I could ever trust Azrael.

"I'm not going to dance with you," I told Raile, pulling my arm out of Azrael's grip. "Or any other man. Not tonight."

Raile's cold, cruel eyes never left my face. He bowed. "I'm at your service."

If only anyone was.

Azrael had said I'd be left alone on the dais, so I headed for the dais. I could at least pretend to be alone in this crowd full of people, as the music played and the party went on.

I took my seat on the cold throne, high above the party and all the dancing and laughter.

CHAPTER TWENTY-SEVEN

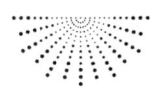

Nikia was in my room when I came back. I stopped in the doorway, horrified, as she melted off the couch and toward me, her eyes bright.

"What is this?" I asked, all out of juice for asking questions nicely.

She stopped, looking at me in confusion, and I asked more gently, "Why are you in my room?"

"To help you with anything you need," she said.

"I don't need anything between the hours of nine pm and nine am, I promise," I said, holding the door open for her. "Thank you for everything, Nikia. I'll see you tomorrow."

"Royalty doesn't sleep alone," she said.

I'll tell Azrael that popped into my mind, completely inappropriately.

"Royalty gets to make the rules." I waved my arm, ushering her out into the hallway.

"Actually, they don't," a deep masculine voice said from the hall.

I jumped, automatically reaching for a sword that wasn't there.

Raile leaned against the wall opposite my door, his hands in his pockets pushing up the hem of his suit jacket. He went on, "It's a surprisingly bad deal, being king, and I hear it's an even worse one being a princess. Or even a queen."

"Why are you here?" I demanded.

"I wanted to see you."

I was on the verge of telling him I never wanted to see him—*ever*—but he added, "I felt we had an awkward start earlier."

"Do you think?"

He frowned. "I do. That's why I thought we could start over."

I stared at him. Nikia was finally out in the hall, but she took a step forward, raising her hand. "Princess, it's not considered appropriate to have male guests in your room without a chaperone—"

"I'll make him stand on the balcony then," I said, my decision made —just because I was stubborn and at the moment, exasperated with all the rules I neither knew nor wanted to follow—and I reached out and grabbed Raile's sleeve. I towed him into my room before I swung the door shut on Nikia's protests.

"You are not a very good princess," he observed.

I shrugged. "Maybe. But I think I'd make a kickass queen."

His lips parted in a sudden smile—a dazzling one. "Perhaps you would."

I headed for the balcony. "Now that I have you in my room, I don't really know what to do with you."

"Go for a swim with me."

"What?" I shook my head, glancing at the pool. "It's too small."

The thought of being in such close quarters with Raile, who radiated confidence and power as if he were larger than life, overwhelmed me.

"Not there." Raile headed past me to the balcony, where he rested his elbows on the railing. I studied his back, his wide shoulders and the narrow taper of his waist. He looked like a swimmer based off his build. "Out there."

I followed his gaze to the ocean, which looked deep and dark and terrifying under the cloudy night sky.

"I don't think so," I said with a laugh.

He turned to me, leaning against the railing. His eyes looked as deep and dark as the ocean beyond.

"Why not?"

"It's dangerous," I said. "The ocean is dangerous in my world. It's got to be even worse here, where everything wants to eat us—"

"It's not dangerous when you're with me," he promised.

"Are you some kind of monster-whisperer?" I asked.

"Something like that." He gave me a smile that was sharp and sly. "Maybe I'm the king of monsters. Sea monsters, at least."

"I hunted monsters when I was in the mortal world." I didn't fear them—at least, I didn't fear them on land, if I could reach a sword.

"That doesn't surprise me," he said, reminding me that he, too, had known me before.

"How do we know each other?" I asked curiously. "What did I do to you?"

He shrugged one big shoulder, his hand in his pocket, a lazy, non-committal answer. "I thought we were starting over."

"All right, let's start over." I held out my hand. "My name is Alisa, and I have no interest in dancing with domineering men."

Although if that's true, I'll definitely have to cross Azrael off my dance card forever and ever.

He cocked an eyebrow at me. "That's a strange way to say hello, but all right. My name is Raile, and I have no interest in parties."

"Doesn't your court have parties? What court are you from?"

"I don't like to have fun," he said. "That's what anyone would tell you."

I joined him at the rail. "I can just imagine what people would tell you about me."

"Do you want to know?" he asked bluntly.

I sighed, putting my thumb nail into my mouth as I tried to chew off the last flecks of my black nail polish.

"Yes," I said. "I guess so."

Maybe I needed to know, even if I dreaded what I would hear.

"Diplomatic affairs have not gone well lately in the Fae courts, not on land or sea. There have been questions about how well Faer manages all the courts, and rumblings that perhaps the time of the summer court to rule the Fae kingdom has passed." He glanced sidelong at me. "Your memory has faded enough that people thought perhaps you would make a wise queen in his stead, though."

Well, there was a dig. He and Duncan must have gone to the same school of taunts. "Wait, the summer court rules the Fae? But it hasn't always been that way?"

"No, not at all," he said. "The Fae courts used to all be independent, although the council of royals came together to deal with attacks outside our borders—like at the front."

"I'd like to discuss the front more later," I said, because I had no idea what was going on within my own kingdom. "But first, let's talk about me."

"I assumed that would be your desire," he deadpanned, and I pulled a face. He went on, "Tonight and last, you blundered, Alisa. You insulted people and didn't respond—perhaps didn't even understand —when others insulted you. Without Azrael whispering in your ear, you would have fallen completely flat, and his presence did not go unnoticed."

"I don't remember anything here." I pressed my lips together, afraid I'd revealed something I shouldn't. Raile was not my friend, even if he spoke as bluntly as one in this particular moment.

Raile nodded. "Nonetheless. Some Fae hope for a ruler to guide the courts through this turbulent time, and you... you butchered that idea tonight. You are not qualified to rule, not right now."

"That's why Faer wanted to have the parties right away and not once I had the chance to catch up," I said, filling in the details.

"Would a day or two have been enough time to catch up anyway?" Raile asked. "Faer may have pressed your disadvantage, but you were already lost."

"Thanks," I said drily. "You really know how to give a girl a pep talk. I don't know that I would want to be queen, anyway."

"You don't have a choice, really." Raile flashed me a slow smile. "Maybe you'll be my queen."

Once I realized he was implying marriage, I laughed out loud. I couldn't help it. Marry this sexy but ridiculous man that I'd just met?

"I was almost starting to like you," I warned him. "But I don't like when you say stuff like that."

"Alisa, you forget I already know you," he said. "I know you don't like anyone."

He headed for the door, his hand still in his pocket.

"That's not true," I called after him. "And you don't know me that well. You don't know who I became when I was on the other side."

"People don't change," he said, glancing over his shoulder.

"That's a lie."

He stopped in the doorway, added, *"Fae* don't change."

Then he was gone before I could argue with him anymore.

CHAPTER TWENTY-EIGHT

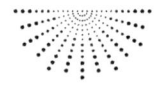

Azrael

Seven years earlier

I woke up in a dark and quiet room, and even before I turned my head, I knew she was missing. The room felt empty without her; even in her sleep, Alisa had a certain presence.

An annoying presence. That damned, incorrigible princess, off doing something she shouldn't yet again. I wasn't even surprised.

I got up, taking a moment to pull on my socks and boots. As I was grumbling to myself and getting dressed, she slipped in through the door, stealthy as a shadow.

"You even yell at me when I'm not here," she said, her lips quirking in amusement. "That's dedication."

"You drive me crazy whether you're here or not," I shot back, beginning to pull off my boots again.

"Don't bother getting comfortable," she said. "The campus is shut down because there were reports of a Ravager attacking a nearby village. You and I have a mission!"

"What part of *the village is shut down* makes you think that you and I should go out? Why do you think students should save the world?" I asked.

Alisa just smiled. I was already lacing my boots back up.

The two of us slipped over the wall. When we dropped onto the other side, I told her, "Well, my academy education lacked in *sneaking* until I got to know you."

"And here you're hardly even grateful." She grinned and bumped her shoulder against mine. Her warmth radiated against mine, soaking through my coat and into my skin. I had to work harder for the magic that kept me comfortable despite the stiff winter breeze; for the summer princess, it came easy.

The two of us skirted the village, looking for signs of the Ravager. We passed an empty farmhouse, the roof beginning to cave in with snow.

"The village seems so empty," she noted, looking past the farmhouse to the village below, where smoke curled from just a few rooftops. "Did they all decide to relocate to warmer courts?"

I glanced at her, not sure if Alisa genuinely didn't know or if she were being glib. Deciding to give her the benefit of the doubt, I said, "The war's decimated the Winter court."

She gave me a wide-eyed look. "There's no nobility there."

"War doesn't just touch the people who started it, Alisa." My voice came out bitter. "In fact, it usually barely touches *them*."

There was something wild in her eyes, and that was when I realized that—despite the reputation she and Faer had—she cared for everyone, not just her own court. Seeking out this Ravager wasn't just for her own glory.

I saw one of the houses ahead also had a caved-in roof, but there was no snow on this one. "Come on."

She'd seen the same thing I had, though. She was already darting ahead.

Alisa pulled her sword as she ran. I matched her pace, the two of us sprinting furiously for the house. A last curl of smoke rose from the chimney, as if the fire were just beginning to die.

The front door was splintered open. The monster that forced its way in had taken out part of the wall.

And the dry, dusty scent of the Ravagers lingered in the air. They were still here.

She and I stopped at the door, looking at each other. I saw the same understanding reflected in her eyes.

Then we moved in sync through the doorway.

Inside the house, the oak table at the center of the room was turned over, and chairs and plates and candles were scattered around the room. Alisa moved to the door on the left as I headed for the stairs.

She pushed open the door and took in the dark room. "Workshop. Untouched."

A scream came from upstairs.

"That's why," I said. I went up the stairs fast. She cursed—probably because I'd gotten ahead of her, I doubted she'd actually be upset about the danger we found ourselves in—and followed me.

As I reached the top of the stairs, the Ravager stepped in front of me. It was so big that it filled the entire passageway. It stared at me with its lizard eyes, but it was the mouthful of sharp, twisted teeth that caught my attention.

"You don't belong here, friend," I told him. "Time to go back to your own world."

Instead, it whirled, its powerful thick tail slamming into the wall, pluming dust over me as the wall disintegrated. I ducked, barely keeping my balance on the stairs, so that the tail passed harmlessly over me.

Then I jumped and caught the damned thing around the neck.

It hadn't been expecting that, and it whirled, shaking its head. Those dangerous teeth flashed close by me, and it tilted its head, trying to fix me with one of those huge, rolling eyes. But I was too close for it to turn its neck and bite me as long as I stayed close.

"You're not supposed to ride the thing, Azrael!" she shouted at me. She was already lunging forward, slamming her sword into its legs. The beast howled. It snapped at her, but she was already gone, dancing to one side.

My grip on its neck was slipping, and when I lost my balance, I'd be at its mercy for a moment. I struck with my knife, plunging it into the monster's eye. It roared as I finally slipped, and when it bucked, I was slammed into the wall.

But Alisa was there, finishing it off. I'd known she would be, and that was why I lay on the floor for a second, catching my breath. The floor shook beneath me as the monster collapsed.

I looked into the untouched eye as it stared into mine, as it gave its last breath.

"Where did you come from?" I asked it, before I tore my knife from the other eye.

"I think that's what we need to figure out," she said, offering me her hand. I let her pull me to my feet, and she winced as she strained. "Wow, you really are letting me carry your weight these days, aren't you?"

"I know how strong you are." I planted a kiss on the top of her head.

Then I looked past her to see a tear-stained woman carrying a small child.

"Thank you," the woman whispered. Her gaze was fixed on the monster at our feet; I didn't think she'd seen evidence of our forbidden tryst.

"Is everyone else in the house all right?" I asked.

"Tis just me and the babe," she said, using the more formal cadences that were so common for winter court fae. We barely saw any of them, despite living in their territory. "My husband died this summer in—"

The moment she registered Alisa's short lavender hair, curling around her ears, she stopped talking.

"Thank you," she repeated, but it sounded mechanical now.

"Will you be able to repair your house?" Alisa asked. "Or do you need help?"

She shook her head. Alisa frowned, as if she were confused by her reaction. How innocent had Herrick managed to keep her of what the summer court was doing to winter? I elbowed her, then pointed at the beast.

"We're not done yet," I reminded her.

"I hate this part," she grumbled.

Together, the two of us maneuvered the Ravager down the stairs and out of the house. We used magic to drag it deep out into the woods, and abandoned the carcass there.

"I've been doing some research," she said. She was still frowning slightly, as if she were troubled by our encounter, but she forged on. "I thought we could use a merge spell, so we can track where they're coming from."

I laughed, but she was looking at me with her brows lifted, so I stopped. "You're serious."

"You and I are both royalty," she said. "I know it's a difficult spell, but if anyone can do it, we can."

"Your confidence level is going to get you killed," I grumbled. "Or me. Probably me."

"You're not saying no," she said lightly.

I sighed. "I'm not saying no."

Together, the two of us worked the spell, which allowed her to *see* through the eyes of the Ravager. She trusted me to lead her while she was running blind, lost in the beast's past.

We found our way to a place in a cave where a portal had been constructed.

She gasped as she studied it. "Someone built this. Why?"

I ran my hand over the frame, which was etched with runes. "To destroy the winter court," I said, my voice somber. "The last of it. Every male, female or child who might rebel."

The blood drained from her face. "Herrick."

"Or those on his orders," I said.

"Help me destroy it," she said.

And we did.

That night, we finally stumbled into bed with only a few hours to sleep before dawn came and the start of our training. But I could feel how she was restless and worried, lying in bed without sleeping.

I lifted myself onto my elbow, then stared at her in the dim light. Her lavender hair seemed to shine, no matter how dark the night around us.

I didn't know what to say, so I got up and slid into bed beside her. She smiled and shifted, settling her head into the curve of my shoulder.

We never cuddled; we had sex, in furtive moments, behind two locked doors. Cuddling was dangerous.

But so was leaving Alisa alone with her own thoughts, as she sorted through the darkness of the summer court.

"You're going to change the world," I whispered, before dropping a kiss into her hair. Maybe she could fix what was broken in the summer court, but I didn't dare say that out loud, not while she was still wrestling with Herrick and Faer's misdeeds. "Maybe they'll let girls into the academy when they see what you've done."

She scoffed. "They're going to be so furious I got one over on them… I've probably made things worse."

She was almost always so irrepressibly optimistic, in her own way, that I knew she was hurting.

"Can you keep a secret?" she asked softly.

"I'm pretty deep in your secrets already, Alisa," I reminded her.

"It's not mine." She turned her face up, studying me in the moonlight.

"I'll never betray your trust," I promised her, smoothing her hair back from that beautiful face.

Her eyes shone silver and bright. "I'm not the only girl at the academy. There's a winter court girl hiding here too. We've gotten to be friends. Maybe together we really can change the world."

I was silent for a few long seconds, processing that news. "Just be careful. If she gets caught, she won't have the High King's protection."

"I'm not so sure even I do anymore," she muttered.

She nestled into me, and she fell asleep, as if she'd just needed to tell me her secret hopes and dreams before she could sleep. But now I couldn't fall asleep. For Alisa, trusting me with a secret like that was a far greater intimacy than biting my shoulder to hold back her scream during sex.

I held her tight, overwhelmed by how much she trusted me.

And by how hard it was going to be to protect her.

CHAPTER TWENTY-NINE

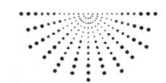

Alisa

THE NEXT MORNING, I woke to a pounding on the door to my apartment. I was still bleary-headed from sleep, but I grabbed my sword, which I'd slept with that night, and headed for the source of the racket.

When I swung the door open, Duncan stood framed in the doorway.

"Oh no," I said. "It's too early for you."

"I'm supposed to teach you," he said impatiently. "So get on your clothes and let's go train."

"Duncan, I don't think there's a damn thing *you* can teach me that I need to learn." I was sick of all the arrogant Fae men in my life.

His lips twisted as if that were amusing. "Fine. Then come with me to train, and show me how little need you have of a bodyguard."

"You saw me fight the other day," I shot back.

"You fought shifters," he said. "Not Fae."

"Same difference." I started to close the door.

So quick he was a flicker of movement, he stepped forward to block the door, which brought us chest-to-chest—well, almost. He was so much taller than me that it was more like nose-to-chest. He looked down at me, his eyebrows tilting.

"I forgot you're lazy," he said. "Or is cowardice a thrilling new addition to your personality?"

I shook my head as I turned on my heel and headed away from him. "Bait me all you want. I'm not impressed."

"Competence in fighting is a hallmark of Fae royalty," he said. "Faer aside. If you cannot do this, you'll never rule."

"I *can* fight, though. I just don't want to play with you. And I don't know if I want to rule, for that matter."

"You tire me," he said, ducking his head and covering his sudden yawn with his bicep. "I didn't ask to discuss your innermost longings. I asked you to come out to the field and allow me to assess your capabilities, because that's my job."

"Sorry to bore you."

"If you aren't dressed and walking out that door in two minutes," he told me, "I'll throw you over my shoulder and carry you out—in whatever you're wearing, or *not*—to the training yard where the squires are practicing. Then you can go through your paces in front of them."

"Through my paces?" My brows arched. "You've got to be kidding me."

"One-and-nineteen," he said, crossing his arms over his big chest. He stared into my eyes as he said, "One-and-eighteen."

"You know, I was a Hunter, I don't exactly mind beating people around the head and shoulders," I said, heading back into my room because I didn't particularly want to be carried anywhere by Duncan ever again. "You don't have to burst in here with threats and insults. You could've brought me coffee and asked me nicely."

"One-and-thirteen. There is no coffee," he called back as I went through the drawers, trying to find something that looked like workout gear.

Did I own a sports bra?

"And I don't *ask nicely*," he added.

"Yeah, I was picking up on that. Quite the character flaw." I glanced back out the room at him. He was still standing in my living room looking as if he owned the place. He wore a fitted black tunic, black trousers, and what looked like black leather slippers. So, the same thing he wore yesterday. That didn't help me with my current wardrobe conundrum. "Are you wearing your dirty laundry?"

"Why do you ask so many stupid questions?"

"Why do you?" I rifled through another drawer.

"One-hundred-and-six," he said ominously. "One-hundred-and-five."

"I didn't hear you counting down the whole time."

"I was counting in my head."

"You're just making stuff up." I gave up, straightening from my search of the bottom dresser drawer. "Duncan. What do I wear to work out? Now that I'm in Faelandia?"

He came into my room with a sigh, searched through my closet, and pulled open a set of drawers hanging beneath the long line of jackets that I never even noticed. He pulled out a soft black tunic and pants like his, and tossed them to me.

"I thought I was a princess. This looks like a soldier's uniform."

"I'm a prince," he said simply.

"What?" I thought of what Raile had said the night before, about how there were many courts of the Fae. But then, why was Duncan here, inflicting all his sunshiney personality on me?

"Thirty-two."

What an unsatisfying answer. But I hurriedly pulled off the shirt I'd worn to bed and yanked on the tunic and pants. They were comfortable, at least.

"Two," he said, and then a beat later, "One."

"Shoes?" I demanded, heading for the closet. I searched through the rows of shoes on the shelves. "I'm trying here, you know. I said I'd come out with you. No need to treat me like a *squire*. I don't know what that is, but I bet you're terrible to them."

"You'd be right," he said. "Shoes."

"That's what I just said—" I started, right before something stung across my ass. I glared up at him as Duncan handed me the shoe he'd just swatted me with. He held the other one up, staring at it, as if he were considering going after me with that one as well.

"Shoes," he said. "As I said."

"Did you really just spank me with a shoe?" I wrenched the shoe out of his hand before he could get any more ideas.

"Did you really just fail to notice I was offering your shoes?" he asked.

"If I didn't know better, *Prince* Duncan, between the fact that you complimented my ass *and* smacked it, I'd think you like me."

"I don't like *you*. I do like your ass, specifically."

"Well, maybe I'll win you over one—" I stopped myself just as I was about to say *maybe I'll win you over one body part at a time.* It sounded as if I were flirting with Duncan, and Duncan was not worthy of flirtation. I slipped my feet into my shoes. "Let's go."

As we headed through the halls, I asked, "What's the plan for today?"

"We're going for a horseback ride to see if you remember how not to fall off," he said, "and then you're going to try to hit me for a while."

"Sounds delightful."

"We'll see." He stepped through the door ahead of me, into the soft diffused early sunshine, and held it open for me to pass.

As we walked through, I glanced at the young Fae warriors already training in the yard. Even though the sun had just risen, they were already covered in sweat and sand. They looked miserable, and I would prefer not to join them.

Instead, I followed Duncan into the stables. "Did you and I ever train like that?" I asked.

He snorted. "No. We're royalty—they are low Fae, apprentices to the knights. Our training was completely different."

His condescending tone exasperated me. He complained about my stupid questions, but also about my ignorance. He should at least pick one consistently.

"Our training was also miserable," he added, "but completely different."

He started to saddle his horse, and I tried to imitate him with the second horse until he turned to me, his eyes widening. "You don't know how to saddle a horse."

"Why do you keep being surprised?" I demanded. "Can't you hold a thought in your head longer than five minutes?"

He saddled a horse for me, grumbling the entire time, and then led both our horses out into the yard. "Am I going to have to put you onto the horse, too?"

I didn't answer him, because maybe? I put my toe into the stirrup uncertainly, trying to figure out where to put my hands for a second, and then swung up easily onto the horse's back. Muscle memory must have taken over.

He grunted. "Small mercies."

The two of us rode out through the gardens, heading for the woods. I glanced behind us. "Don't want an audience in case I kick your ass, huh?"

He grunted in response.

"Are you going to be surly all morning just because you're stuck with me? I can be fun, you know."

"I do know," he said, surprising me. "I also know it's a trick."

"Why don't you tell me what I did to you?"

"Because it's Azrael's story," he said. "Ask Azrael."

"Why are you so mad at me about something I did to Azrael?"

His jaw set. "You don't know anything about what it means to be family."

"Maybe not," I said. "I don't remember having any."

I wondered if Faer had ever really been my family, for that matter. My brother acted warm and caring when I was near him, but he'd kept his distance at the parties, leaving me to embarrass myself. There was nothing loving in that.

He glanced at me, his brows drawing together. We were nearing the woods, and I could've sworn I heard an eerie singing coming from the forest, although it faded into the breeze as we neared the trees.

"Stay close," he said. "I'm supposed to return you alive. Bruised at most."

I rolled my eyes, but the shoulder of my horse grazed the shoulder of his, as if I'd accidentally leaned and encouraged the horse that way. I was keenly aware that I didn't know everything when we were out here in the woods.

"What if I return *you* bruised? Would Azrael scold me?"

"It used to seem like you enjoyed Azrael's scoldings," he deadpanned, "and what came after them."

My jaw tensed. I was so curious about the relationship I'd had with Azrael before, but Duncan was never going to give me meaningful answers. "I thought you were going to stop talking about my relationship with Azrael."

"I'll talk to you about whatever I please." He drew up his horse. We'd come to a clearing, ringed with trees. Mossy stones covered half the ground, wild grass the other. Mushrooms dotted a fallen log nearby, the mushroom caps red and shining, and I glanced at them suspiciously. Surely the mushrooms here were trying to kill me, but they were probably less dangerous than the Fae who paused his black horse just ahead of me.

"What kind of prince goes to the front?" I demanded.

He slid off his horse in one deft move, then offered me a hand.

"Hard pass," I said, swinging down from my horse on my own.

He spoke quietly to our horses, then unstrapped a bundle from the back of his saddle. He pulled out a wooden training sword and threw it to me. "Here. A familiar weapon to better your odds."

I caught the wooden hilt and brought it down to my side with a *swish*, testing its weight and balance. "Is 'shit talking' a thing in the Fae world too, then?"

He cocked an eyebrow at me. Then without any further preamble, he moved forward, his footing sure over the loose rocks, pressing an attack.

I raised my sword at his first blow, which was almost desultory, and the wooden swords crossed with a *crack*.

Then the two of us began to parry for real, fighting back and forth, blocking each other's blows.

When he left me an opening, I managed to slip behind him and slapped the blade of my sword across his ass. He spun, already knocking my sword with his so hard that the force of the blow traveled up my wrist and stung my forearm, but I grinned in triumph anyway.

"Payback," I said.

"You don't want to play a game of playback with me, Princess."

"Maybe I do, *Prince.*"

The two of us fought back and forth. He was a more than competent opponent, and I found myself smiling. I'd felt so unsettled the last few days, but it was a release to lose myself in a game I knew and understood.

"You're not bad," he admitted, the two of us facing each other, chests heaving and swords still crossed.

"You either." I moved into the ready, eager to fight again.

Duncan never smiled around me, but I could've sworn he looked pleased as he moved forward and I met him. The sound of our swords broke the quiet of the woods.

I could fight with this fool of a man forever.

CHAPTER THIRTY

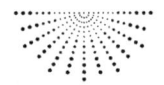

D*uncan*

WHEN WE RETURNED, Alisa followed me into the barn and watched me as I started to stable the horses.

She chewed her lower lip, her eyes wide and beguiling even when she worried. A strange protective urge ran through me whenever she looked anxious.

So I flicked that pouty lower lip.

She stared at me, her fire returning. "Touch me again and I'll murder you in your sleep, Prince."

"You can try," I said. "Even unconscious, I like my chances."

"How do you even walk while carrying all that ego?" she asked, but despite herself, her gaze lingered on my body.

I nodded at the brush, telling her to get to work. "You're not nervous, are you? You worked with animals dirtside."

"Two things are hard for me now," she admitted, tucking her hair behind her ears, plastering it to her head. Then she picked up the brush. "First of all, I work in an urban veterinary clinic. I can handle guinea pigs—I've never been anywhere near a horse until now."

Then she corrected herself, "Well, that I remember. That's what's really hard now. People expect me to know everything, but I don't know how to ride well. Or…how to *princess* well."

I stared at her, shocked by her vulnerability. I'd never known her to lack confidence, let alone admit to it.

Then her lips twisted into a familiar smirk, as if she realized she'd shocked me speechless.

I'd been tempted to tell what a natural she'd always been. That smirk caused the soft words to die in my chest. That smirk might be a defense mechanism now, but once it had signaled danger.

Instead, I closed my hand over hers as it gripped the brush and pressed behind her.

"I'll show you what to do," I said. "Your useless brother and his knights have the stable staff to care for their horses. We do things differently."

"We?" she asked, glancing over her shoulder at me.

I huffed a laugh. *"We.* Until I manage to get rid of you, we're going to do things the right way."

As I showed her how to safely approach the horse and how to brush it down, her hand was in mine. Her bones were so fine that she made me feel like a monster in comparison. Her ass brushed against my cock, which instantly hardened, and I took a step back so she wouldn't feel me against her.

I let my hand fall, watching her delicate muscles ripple as she brushed the horse in long, sure strides. My cock throbbed as it pressed against my pants, as if just watching her was going to make me explode.

"It's a matter of pride for all academy grads to care for their horses themselves. Our warhorses would go to hell and back for us, we could saddle them and muck their stalls ourselves," I said.

"Even princes?"

"Even *princesses.*"

"I went to the academy with you and Azrael?" She frowned at the thought.

I nodded impatiently. I didn't want to discuss that either, so I changed the subject.

"We should get you a real horse instead of one of these ponies, so you can keep up when we ride," I told her, then realized the act of getting a horse like ours would be a commitment she wasn't ready for.

She turned to me, her eyes wide.

God, she was beautiful when she looked at me, giving me the full weight of her attention. Her eyes were large and luminous. Her curvy, heavier mortal frame was unfamiliar, but strangely mouthwatering.

But it was the way she'd fought for the humans we'd seen that made some stupid part of me ache to protect her. Before we knew it, she'd have her memories back. She might murder Faer and take the throne, but unlike what my foolish brother thought, she'd never be a better ruler than he was. He was stupid and mean; she was brilliant and cruel.

Maybe she wasn't that woman right now, the one with an angel's face and a demon's mind. But she'd find that old Alisa again, deep inside.

She'd be far more destructive than Faer, if it suited her. Alisa did as she wished no matter what it cost.

"What's the name of your horse?" she asked, startling me out of my own thoughts.

I shook my head. "We don't name our horses."

She raised an eyebrow. "So I've heard. Doesn't that make it confusing to talk about them?"

"They're not pets," I said.

"You're full of shit," she said. "I don't believe you."

"They're war animals."

"They deserve names." She cocked her head to one side. "What about your dogs?"

"My hounds?" I touched the tattoos on my chest absently, as if they felt me speak of them. "No. Not pets either."

She looked at me curiously as if she'd noticed the motion.

Before she could pry, I told her, "Go find Azrael. He's got the next round of teaching-you-how-not-to-be-useless."

"I'd like to see you adapt to my world as quickly as I'm adapting to yours," she shot back.

"This is your world," I said.

Something sad came over her face. "Maybe someday."

When she looked so uncertain, so *vulnerable,* my own body responded. I almost reached out to her. Then, the second after that impulse, anger flared through my chest.

I turned my back and left her behind me, striding out of the stables and into the bright sun of the courtyard. Swords clashed against swords and shields as a dozen of the knights trained, along with the prince himself.

Faer broke off mid-blow and wandered over to me, leaving his opponent standing alone.

"So, how was she?" Faer asked me. Sweat beaded along his hairline, and as we spoke, a human servant came up with lowered head, offering him a tray with a bowl of cool water and a towel. He splashed water over his face and wiped it off with the towel.

"Sloppy." I crossed my arms, leaning against the wooden rail that surrounded the fighting pit.

I wasn't even sure why I lied. It was a decision made before conscious thought caught up. Whatever—it would give her a better chance of surviving Faer and Raile, and it cost me nothing. I wanted them to suffer too; let them all make each other miserable. "She learned some things in the human world, but not enough to replace all she has forgotten."

He nodded. "She'll need you three to protect her, then." For a second, he sounded as if he actually gave a damn what happened to her.

"Yes," I said. "I suppose so."

"How is it, seeing her again?" Faer asked curiously.

"It's nothing," I said simply. "She doesn't matter to me."

"Then it won't trouble you to watch Raile take her." He watched her with bright, curious eyes as she moved about in the distance, heading into the palace.

I shrugged. Faer didn't care about my feelings any more than I cared to discuss them. He was asking for his own amusement.

She'd almost reached the palace when Azrael and Tiron emerged. Azrael touched her arm as he spoke to her.

She'd seemed to be boiling with rage last night after she met Raile, but for some reason, she seemed to have forgiven him a little today. She didn't punch him in the face, no matter that he deserved it. My chest tightened as I watched them together.

"Does he still care for her?" Faer asked, his tone light, though there was nothing light about the question at all.

"It doesn't matter," I said. "He'll do his job."

"I don't doubt that," Faer said.

I grunted and moved toward them, leaving Faer behind. He whistled to one of the squires and his feet crunched over gravel as he moved to practice with another one. I wondered if they were terror-struck to strike the king or if they were good opponents to better his skills, and I wondered which Faer preferred.

When I reached them, Azrael said, "Good. The four of us are going to the Delphin to see if she can restore Alisa's memories."

"She's not ready for the Delphin," I scoffed. "She'll eat Alisa alive."

"Literally?" Alisa asked, crossing her arms.

Neither of us bothered to answer her. It took me a second to realize that she meant the question, and by then Tiron was whispering to her that the Delphin was just grouchy—not deadly. "Just like Duncan," he assured her.

"Of course she doesn't know anything about the Delphin," I told Azrael. "This is a bad idea."

"I'll teach her along the way," Azrael promised.

I grunted again. "Giving her princess lessons. What a perfect job for you."

At least I'd been assigned to test her skills and make sure she could still defend herself, as the summer royalty was rather prone to assassination attempts—for good reason. And yet, I had to admit that as much as I might joke about wanting her dead, the thought of anyone trying to kill her sparked rage that tightened my fists.

But I didn't mind her being hurt a little, at least in the ring, and especially if I was the one who got to do the hurting.

It was a long ride to the Delphin, and along the way, we encountered a pack of creepers, animals that clung to the branches and dropped down to attack their prey.

"Time to move." Azrael reached out and smacked Alisa's horse across its hindquarters, stirring it into a gallop. "Go with her!" he barked at Tiron.

Tiron and Alisa's horses darted ahead into the forest as the creepers raced through the trees above, chittering with excitement. Leaves drifted down from above.

The four of us raced at top speed, trying to get out from beneath the cover of the spreading canopy. My spine tingled at the possibility of having a creeper leap down at me.

"Get to open ground!" I shouted at Tiron and Alisa. "Out of the cover of the trees! They won't be able to surprise us there."

Tiron urged his horse to the left, and Alisa hesitated. Just for a second. Then she decided to follow Tiron.

Her horse jumped to the left and tried to leap over the same fallen bough as Tiron's horse, but their timing was off. Her horse stumbled, but caught itself.

A creeper dropped down from the woods onto the two of them, a furry body that flashed with teeth and fangs as it slammed into Alisa's shoulders.

She cried out, somehow staying on her horse as the terrified animal raced out of control, mindless through the woods, completely careless of its rider.

"Throw yourself off!" I shouted. She'd be hurt, at this speed, but it would give us a chance to kill the creeper that clung to her shoulders despite her best efforts to throw it off. She reached for her sword, but she was still wearing her damned sword harness, the one she thought she was comfortable with, and she couldn't reach the hilt with the creeper snarling and snapping at her throat.

"Gods be damned, Alisa, listen!" I shouted at her, fear spiking through my chest.

I glimpsed sunlight through the gloom of the trees, then realized she was still heading for the clearing up ahead. She didn't want to stop until she reached open sky, where we'd have a better chance at fighting the creepers. The rest of the pack wouldn't come to the rescue of their companion if we were in sunshine.

The creeper sank its teeth into her shoulder, and she screamed, still trying to guide the horse. Then she and the horse were out in the sunlight. Her feet came out of the stirrups, then she threw herself to one side, launching herself off the horse.

I was off my horse and to her side in seconds. Tiron and Azrael dismounted just as quickly, their feet slapping the earth.

I grabbed the creeper's fur at the back of its neck, slicing my blade through its neck. She screamed again as the teeth sank deeper before the thing relaxed into death.

Her horse was already thundering off, through the woods, heading back for home. I watched it go, sure that the horse, at least, would make it home safely. Fae horses knew the dangers well of the forest and knew how to evade most of them. They were smarter than our princess.

I looked down at the ugly face of the creature I'd just killed, stained with Alisa's blood. My heart was still racing. As if I'd been afraid for her.

The cursed girl didn't listen. I stood with my sword ready, looking out at the trees that ringed us. There were yellow eyes in the trees, glistening from the shadows, but they didn't dare attack us out here.

I picked up the furry body and slung it toward them. "Have your friend back."

The corpse crashed into the underbrush. After a few long seconds, I heard a flutter as some scavenger fell on the creeper and dragged it away.

I turned to Alisa, worried how hurt she'd been, now that the worst of the danger had passed.

She was on the ground, blood staining her throat and her shoulder and her hair. Tiron sat beside her, his hand on her shoulder as if he could loan her strength to deal with the pain. Azrael knelt beside her, his face calm as he checked her wounds.

They no longer needed me.

My jaw stiffened.

"Are we still going to see the Delphin?" I asked. "She's lost her horse. She barely seems competent to stay on one to begin with."

Tiron flashed me a warning look that made me want to throttle him. He was my friend, someone I'd grown as close to these last few years as if he were my younger brother. But he sided with her, and for no reason. She wasn't loyal to him; she was never loyal to anyone.

"Yes, we'll go on," Azrael said decisively. "There's no reason not to. But she'll need to ride with someone."

Tiron's lips parted, and before he could eagerly offer his horse to her, I snapped, "She can ride with me."

Azrael glanced at me skeptically.

"I'm the best horseman of the three of us," I said.

"Debatable," Azrael put in.

"I can help her not fall off her horse again."

She gazed up at me with a frown dimpling the space between her blue eyes. *"You* told me to fall off my horse."

"You didn't listen." My voice came out hot.

"I did. I simply waited for an opportune time." She tried to raise her arm to indicate the open sky above us, but she winced when she did, and it twisted something inside me to see her hurt.

"When I give you an order, you can follow it, Princess. No need to think for yourself when you don't know a damned thing about our world. Your pathetic attempts don't serve you much."

"Duncan," Azrael said warningly. "Tiron, patch her up. Then we'll move out again."

I glanced at him meaningfully.

He added, "Alisa will ride with Duncan."

Good. Tiron couldn't be trusted with that minx any more than Azrael could.

I'd save my friends from themselves, if it were even possible.

Alisa always had a gift for driving men half-mad.

Memories of her body against mine, her lips, stirred me, and I glanced away out to the woods again, ignoring the sound of Tiron ministering to her wounds, coddling her.

If they couldn't remember what she truly was, I wasn't sure how either of them would survive another round with her.

And I couldn't survive losing them again.

CHAPTER THIRTY-ONE

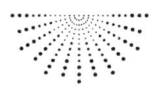

A *lisa*

I SWUNG up onto Duncan's horse first, then he slid behind me. "At least you're small enough that I can see over your head," he grumbled.

"So grouchy. And yet, you wanted me here on your horse with you," I reminded him as he looped his arm around my waist lightly. His hard abs and chest pressed against my back. There was no escaping; we had to be intimately close together now.

He snorted. "I don't even want you in my *world*."

He just didn't want me anywhere near his friends. I saw the looks he threw my way, as if he were jealous when they were near me. It was strange, given how much he hated me.

The four of us set off again, moving quickly through the woods. "Will my horse be all right?" I asked as we galloped through the forest.

He paused. "Yes. She knows her way home, and *she* knows how to stay out of trouble."

His tone implied I didn't share the common sense of the horse.

For a few minutes, we traveled in silence. I sat uncomfortably in front of him, keenly aware of how he despised my body against his. My spine was stiff, which made me bounce uncomfortably in the saddle as I leaned away from him.

His voice was disarmingly sexy, despite his gruff tone, when he asked me, "Why did you work with animals in the mortal world?"

"They're easier than people," I said bluntly, still too shocked from the encounter with the creepers to keep my guard up. "You must be able to understand that. You don't like people."

"Is it that obvious?" he asked dryly.

"But you like some people," I murmured. "Azrael. Tiron."

"*Like* is an overstatement," he corrected.

"You love them." I didn't say it just to rile him, although I enjoyed that. It was true.

He grunted. "It's not too late for me to turn around and feed you to the creepers, you know."

"I can see it in the way you look at them. You want to protect them. Take care of them." It was too hard to stay away from him. I leaned some of my weight against his chest, relaxing into his grip.

He huffed a laugh. "They should be able to take care of themselves. If they're so useless, I don't see why I'd care."

I rolled my eyes, but gave up on that line of conversation. For a few minutes, there was no sound but the horses' soft footfalls on the ground and the rustle of the branches above. His body against mine moved as if it was one with the horse, all grace and strength. I admired the way he rode, even if I hated everything else about him.

"Why is everything so dangerous in this world?" I mused. We were traveling through a grove of trees that reminded me of weeping willows, their long tendrils dangling to the ground shimmering in an array of whites and grays. As the wind moved through the tendrils, soft music rose in the air, as if they were chimes. "And yet, it's all so beautiful."

He grunted.

"You're not a very good conversationalist," I said.

"Maybe I just don't want to talk to you."

And yet, as the two of us rode together, his powerful arms were looped tightly around my waist. His cock stiffened, brushing against the curve of my ass. I hid my smile. Maybe he didn't want to *talk* to me.

But, here we were. I had a captive audience for my questions.

"You told me to talk to Azrael, but you have your own story. I did something to you too," I said.

"Why don't you wait until you get your memories back, and then it can be a pleasant surprise?"

I chewed my lower lip. "I'm sorry if I did something that hurt you."

He froze, just for a second, before he scoffed. "You can't be sorry for something you don't remember."

"Can't you be?" I asked. "I obviously made bad choices. Hurt people. I don't remember any of it, and it's hard to believe I would have, but... I wish you'd tell me what I did. Otherwise, I can't begin to make up for it."

"You can't begin to make up for it anyway," he said, his tone flat and unyielding. His arm tightened around my waist, as if his body gave him away no matter what he said.

It was the same unthinking way that my body responded to Azrael.

"You loved me," I said slowly, understanding dawning. "But we weren't together? Not like Azrael and I were?"

His body went rigid. *Bingo.*

Then he growled into my ear, "Shut up."

"Let me take her for a while," Azrael called. "I need to explain to her about the Delphin."

Duncan had been so eager to keep me away from Azrael before, but now it seemed as if he could not hand me off fast enough.

He hadn't even denied that he loved me once before.

Azrael spent the rest of the ride telling me about royal protocol I needed to know, about what it would be like to meet the Delphin and what she'd expect from me, but I couldn't stop my mind from wandering.

My gaze kept returning to Duncan as he rode ahead of us, his spine as straight as a sword, his shoulders wide and commanding.

When I leaned back into Azrael's grip, resting my head on his shoulder, he smiled faintly as if he were surprised, but he said nothing.

And when he caught me staring after Duncan, he said nothing then too. He just kept telling me what he thought I needed to know.

But I had my own set of questions.

WE RODE past a foreboding stone castle on a hill.

"Who lives there?" I asked.

"The Sisters of Arms," Azrael answered. "That used to be a nunnery back when they sent misbehaving women off to the convent. Before our world ripped into its different fragments: Dirtside and Avalon and the Grayworld and the others."

"What do they do with misbehaving women now?" I asked.

Azrael's lips quirked, but whatever he was thinking, he kept his own counsel. "Now the nunneries house the Sisters of Arms. Orphaned children, destitute women. They train as warriors and serve as a last line of defense when the monsters from the rips come too close to home."

Duncan snorted. "As if the monsters don't come *from* home, often enough."

Azrael sighed faintly. "Enough with your superstitions."

"The monsters of the summer court aren't superstitions, no matter how much you wish it so."

"The summer court has monsters?" I demanded.

"The summer court has *stories*," Azrael corrected. His hard body against mine was distracting. "Anyway, this Delphin is a seer who grew up in that keep since she was very young."

Duncan snorted.

"Now you're bringing up children's stories to try to torment Alisa," Azrael chided him. "Bringing up the nightmare creatures like the Shadow Man."

"There's more than one Delphin?"

"Not enough," Duncan muttered.

"Yes," Azrael said, ignoring his brother, although I couldn't do the same.

I kept finding my gaze drawn to the grumpy knight.

Azrael went on, "The Delphine can see the future, or at least, they see glimpses of it. They protect the Sisters by warning them when the monsters approach."

"The Delphin have incredible gifts of magic," Tiron said. "If anyone can restore your memories, I'm sure the Delphin can."

If anyone can. He meant to be encouraging, but those words struck deep. What if no one could?

Azrael drew up his horse. I glanced up at him, wondering why, and he jerked his jaw toward a gravel path that stretched away into the woods. The rocks almost seemed to shimmer, despite the gloom of the forest.

"You'll need to go alone from here," Azrael said. "The Delphine won't see anyone from outside the Sisterhood unless they come alone."

"That's a creepy rule," I said.

I'd just barely swung off the horse when Duncan raised his hand in a shooing motion. "Off you go. Be brave."

Tiron leaned over to him and said, in a conspiratorial stage whisper, "If she slices off your head—or any other part—I won't feel sorry for you."

I stared down the path. Trees seemed to tangle together above the path, the branches woven together as if they were embracing—or strangling each other.

When I glanced over my shoulder at Azrael, he gave me an encouraging nod.

"Why is she hesitating?" Duncan cupped his hand over his mouth and stage-whispered to Azrael. "Do you think she's lost her nerve?"

Duncan had leaned close enough to Azrael to bring him into punching distance, and once again, Azrael reached out and smacked his fist in Duncan's chest. Duncan let out a cough that turned into a laugh as he watched me, those blue eyes of his bright and wicked.

I tossed my hair over my shoulders and headed down the path, more irritated than I was unnerved now. My feet crunched over loose rock, and the deeper I went, the more it felt as if I were walking into darkness. The air grew gloomier and strangely cold. My skin tingled.

Then I reached the end and stepped out into the sunlight. I was in a clearing, tightly ringed by trees as if they formed a fence, and at its center was a small house. In front of the house, a woman surrounded by dogs took a silver kettle from above a flickering fire.

"Come in, Alisa," she said, looking up at me. Her eyes crinkled at the corners, and all the other wrinkles in her face seemed to ripple at the motion. "Say hi to my pets and have some tea."

"Hi," I said cautiously. I knelt so I wouldn't be much of a threat and held out the back of my hands for the dogs to sniff as they bounded toward me. Then I was surrounded by half-a-dozen enormous tan hounds, all eagerly sniffing me. One of them knocked me over onto my ass, and I laughed. They were panting and friendly, and I began to rub their heads and pet their long bodies. One of them fell over, offering me his stomach, squirming his head into my lap.

"They like you," she said.

"I bet they like everyone," I said. I crooned to one, petting his ears, "Don't you? Aren't you a good doggo?"

"Oh, not everyone," the Delphin said mysteriously. She carried over two cups of tea and sank cross-legged into the grass, offering me a cup. She seemed as spry as a young woman, even though she looked as if she was very, very old.

"Thank you," I said, accepting the cup of tea.

"Why are you here?" she asked.

"Well, given that you know my name, I'm sure it's no surprise I'm seeking answers."

"I want to hear it from you," she said. "Sometimes what you want and what you *believe* you want are two very different things."

"I want my memories back," I said. "It seems like someone used some kind of enchantment to steal my memories."

She nodded thoughtfully before taking a sip of her tea. "What kind of monster would steal a person's memories? They're part of our identity."

"Yes." I huffed a sigh. "Do you know who it was? Or can you look back and see?

She shook her head. "I don't have a spell to return your memories to you. And I have a sense for the *future,* not the past. I can only see what lays ahead for people I've met. I can predict what will happen to the Sisters, because I know them all."

I frowned. "Then how did you know my name?"

"I saw that one of my Sisters would meet a Fae princess and that trouble would follow where royalty went—as it usually does."

"Oh."

"If there is another Delphin you met before you lost your memories, she might have seen something in your future she can tell you," she said. "Or she might not."

Great.

She reached over and gripped my hand in hers comfortingly. "If you truly want answers, you'll have to journey to the Cursed Caves."

"That doesn't sound inviting at all," I responded. "The Cursed Caves really need to work on their marketing."

She smiled faintly. "In the Cursed Caves, whatever enchantments you carry come to life. You'll be able to see whoever your enemy was."

"And then what?" I asked.

"Once you understand what happened, you can reclaim your memories," she said. "If you wish. Some people find their pasts are overrated."

I snorted. "Mine very well might be, but I can't bear not knowing."

Worst of all, I couldn't begin to make up for anything I might have done.

"Then here's hoping you're strong enough to bear the truth," she said. She raised her cup. "Drink up, Alisa."

Drinking tea and petting dogs always comforted me, but I still didn't know how to find myself again.

CHAPTER THIRTY-TWO

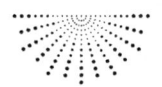

Another night, another damned insufferable party.

Nikia was helping me into my dress when there was a sharp knock on the door. The two of us exchanged a look, then she went to the front door.

Azrael stared her down, something dark and fierce in his eyes. Instead of his usual warm, sexy voice, he growled, "Get out."

"Excuse me," Nikia began, then let out a squeak.

I clutched the bodice of my dress and rushed to the doorway to see Azrael gripping her elbow firmly as he shoved her out the door. He slammed the door shut, then stood there facing it, his spine as straight as a sword. I didn't have to see his face; I could imagine the tension in his jaw when he radiated this kind of fury.

"What are you doing?" I demanded. "I thought you said *I* terrified servants. Are you trying to fight me for my spot as head bitch around here?"

He turned to me, folding his hands behind his back. Azrael was tall and commanding—almost intimidating—when his dark eyes flashed with fury.

But he spoke in calm, controlled tones when he said, "Tiron overheard her giving a report to Eilick—the captain of Faer's guard. We believe she's been reporting to him all along."

A chill raced down my spine. I hated the thought of being spied on.

"Fine," I said off-handedly. "I guess you've earned yourself a position as my maid."

"I don't think so."

I crossed the floor to him slowly, lifting my hands off the bodice of my gown. The tension in his face changed, the anger in his eyes shifting into heat, as the strapless gown slowly slid down my body, exposing my round human breasts, my stomach, the width of my hips.

I'd heard muttering from other Fae in the ballroom about how ugly mortals were, but he watched me with nothing but desire.

Then his gaze swept up to my face. "Are you proud of this little display?"

"I am, in fact," I said. "As you can see, without help, I'll end up naked in court, and that will be awkward for everyone."

"You're a demon with a crown," he grumbled.

I took that to mean I won, and I smiled as I turned. There was some strange pleasure in bending Azrael to my will, no matter how small the victory.

I'd felt restless and stupid since the long, silent ride back from the Delphin, and riling him was comforting.

When he stepped in close behind me, I breathed in the scent that was distinctly Azrael, spicy and warm. He smelled like home and it made my breath stutter in my chest, even before he knelt behind me. He was so close that I could feel his breath against the small of my back, and I bit my lip. Thank god he couldn't see me react.

His hands gripped the material of my dress and he stood slowly, drawing it up my body. I hadn't been sure if he was teasing me deliberately, but now I knew, because his hands traced along with the silk, running up my calves, over my thighs, over my hips.

"Nikia is quite a bit more efficient than you are." My voice came out cool. That was a relief, because when his hands brushed over my skin, heat tingled in their wake.

"It must be because she has more practice." His voice was intimately close to my ear, reminding me of how he murmured into my ear at those damned parties, preserving me from humiliation as best he could.

I raised my arms as he lifted the gown over my chest. His hands lingered there, just underneath my arms, his fingertips resting so near my breasts that I wondered what it would feel like if he caressed me.

I'd had sex dirtside, wondering if it would wake the feelings I didn't seem to have. My attempts to explore sex had all been disastrous. Now Azrael's lightest touch did more to spark desire than any eager man with his face between my thighs.

He reached for my corset strings and began to tighten them. It was strange to think he was as comfortable dressing me as my maid had been; how many times had he done this for me before? He said I didn't want to marry him, but the act of letting a man dress me seemed so intimate and vulnerable.

I couldn't imagine the old Alisa without imagining how she'd loved him.

"Will you need help with your bath later?" His voice was a purr in my ear.

"I'll let you know." I cocked my head to one side. "Where do you all sleep?"

"Why? Do you want to come torment us during the night too?"

Coming from Duncan, I would have been sure those words were barbed. But Azrael seemed as if he might very well feel tormented now, touching me without giving way to his own desires.

I bit my lip, sure that they were *my* desires too. He yanked on the corset, hard enough that I swayed back and forth with every tug.

If it were anyone but Azrael—or Duncan—I would have turned to him and pressed my lips to his. I wouldn't have held myself back from what I wanted.

And I couldn't deny any longer that I wanted Azrael.

But our past changed everything. Until I remembered it, I didn't know what it would mean to him if I kissed him.

His fingertips brushed my back as he tied the corset into a bow at the top.

"I don't know when I might need my servant." I stepped away from him quickly as if his touch stung me, even though the truth was dangerously opposite.

He looked at me with quiet intensity, looking ridiculously handsome in even that plain tunic.

"Why don't you dress like a prince?" I asked. If Duncan was a prince, Azrael must be one too.

His face shuttered. "We don't have time to even begin that discussion."

"Then we can discuss it tonight when you undress me," I said, a teasing—almost husky—note in my voice.

"I don't think so."

His tone was harsh, instantly dousing the fire that I'd started to feel toward him.

"Azrael." I frowned at him. "It's your duty to explain to me how things work around here, isn't it?"

His lips quirked at one corner. "That doesn't mean I owe you *myself*, Princess."

"I'm just asking for your story."

"And I'm just telling you no."

The two of us stared at each other for several long beats.

"You know I'll win eventually," I told him.

He stepped close to me, so intimately close I could breathe in the scent of his body. He looked down at me, his gaze fixed on mine. He was so close that it seemed like he should kiss me.

Purple eyes smoldered down at me. But his voice was soft when he warned, "When you and I play, Princess, no one wins."

I stared at him in exasperation for a heartbeat, then whirled and went to find my slippers. Maybe it was because I'd daydreamed about kissing him right before he slipped in another of those barbs, but I was suddenly furious. I found a pair of dainty silver slippers and turned to face him, shaking the shoe at him from across the room.

"You are ridiculous, you know that? All your little one-liners. Do you ever think about what it's like for me? Being here without my memories? Does it ever occur to you to walk in my—" Something boiled over in me, and I tossed a slipper at him. "In my goddamn shoes!"

The slipper bounced off his chest, and he took a step forward, anger flaring in his eyes.

"I'm so sorry," I said, as if I hadn't meant to hit him. Then I chucked the second shoe. "My aim was terrible!"

His arm flashed, knocking the slipper out of the air, before it could clock him in the face. He stared at me, those dark eyes intense on my face.

I regretted my ridiculous behavior as soon as it was over. I would've regretted it even more if I'd actually hit him in the face.

This goddamn place was making me come unwound, and my feelings for Azrael weren't helping. I crossed my arms over my chest and stared into the distance, somewhere over his head.

Calmly, Azrael picked up my slippers from the floor. I didn't look at him as he walked toward me, his movements slow and predatory.

He stepped right in front of me, so close my eyes were level with his chest.

"Once upon a time, I would've spanked your spoiled royal ass for trying to hurt me, Princess," he murmured.

As if my body remembered him, my core clutched at the threat and at that low, seductive voice.

It'd be nice if I could *remember* the relationship where he and I once played those kinds of games. My body felt tight as a strung bow, waiting for him to touch me. I didn't know how, if he'd be rough or tender, but it didn't matter much. I ached for his hands on my body.

Suddenly he sank to his knees. Those broad shoulders bowed before me, his head intimately close to my inner thighs.

But all he did was lift my foot and gently slip one shoe on. I set my foot down, fury lancing through me as intense as his had been a moment earlier.

"I don't need you to dress me like a child," I said, but he was already grabbing my foot. I struggled to pull away, but though his fingers were gentle on my skin, his hands were steel. I wobbled, about to fall, and almost had to reach out to catch his shoulders to steady myself.

I stopped then, drawing myself to my full height, and let him slip the damned shoe onto my foot.

He rose in front of me again. There was a spark of challenge in his eyes when he said, "But now I intend to be a good servant."

I stared at him, feeling anger like a fist pressing into my chest. I shouldn't give a damn what he thought—I barely knew him, he should be nothing to me—but he could hurt me, somehow.

"I hate you," I warned him.

But I hated myself more, for letting him hurt me.

"If only it were that simple," he assured me. He swept his arm toward the door. "Well, Majesty?"

CHAPTER THIRTY-THREE

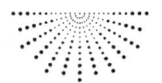

Azrael

Seven years *earlier*

They called a formation in the middle of one day, when we were supposed to be going to lunch. That was always a big deal, and when I saw Alisa in the crowd running to join the group, I grabbed her sleeve.

"What did you do now?" I joked, before I really saw the pale, drawn look on her face.

She *had* done something.

I pulled her close to whisper in her ear, "If there's any chance you might get away with it, you'd better wipe that look off your face. You look guilty as sin itself."

She nodded. I wished I had time to talk to her about what was going on, but the alarm gong was chiming incessantly, making it almost impossible to speak to each other. She was already rearranging her face though, writing her usual blasé expression across it.

"It was for a good cause," she said softly. "Unavoidable. I don't want you to think I'm stupid."

I'd never think that. But she was already running for the first-year assembly, and I fell in with the other seniors.

Galic was smirking, the asshole. I was sure he was connected somehow.

The incessant ringing of the gong had set us all on edge, even before Vail stepped up before us all. The look on his face was somber with disappointment. I'd always known Vail to be heavy-handed but fair.

"Someone stole from my office," he said, his voice heavy. "Riders this morning brought the mail from the city, but all of my mail seems to have disappeared. I hope the guilty party will step forward."

I glanced from the corner of my eye, but no one stirred in the crowd. I couldn't imagine walking to the front of the assembly, past all these students standing at attention, to face Vail publicly. The thought of Alisa strolling forward made my chest tight.

"I know who it was." Galic's voice broke the silence. He cut his eyes my way, his gaze malevolent, as he stepped forward from the crowd. "I saw Faer leave the office and I followed him."

"And then what?" Vail demanded, his voice icy.

I couldn't see Alisa from here. She was shorter than most of the other first years, so she blended into the crowd. Duncan was there at the front, though, standing head-and-shoulders above the rest of the Fae. He glowered at Galic, his eyes narrowed with hatred. I hadn't realized he and 'Faer' had grown to be friends.

"And then he burned them!" Galic delivered this damning news as if it were delicious in his mouth.

"Did it occur to you to stop him?" Vail asked coldly.

Some of Galic's exuberance fled.

"Faer, come here, please." Vail's chilly voice was frightening.

Alisa stepped out of the crowd and made her way up to face him. Galic had that damned smile plastered across his face again, the one that made me want to force him to choke down every tooth he had on display.

Vail and Alisa spoke quietly. I couldn't see what he said to her, or what she said. Knowing Alisa, she had some spin, some story.

But she must have confessed to *something*. Because he looked up and out at the crowd, and said, "Very well. We'll take care of this immediately."

My heart seized in my chest as Vail nodded at two of the academy instructors, who seized Alisa's arms. Floggings were rare at the academy, but when they did happen, some students tried to run. Not Alisa, though. She went with them calmly, her head held high.

But her eyes met mine, just for a second, across the distance. A rueful smile came to her lips.

She was about to be uncovered. Maybe they wouldn't whip her when they found out who she was—that thought sparked relief for me—but she'd certainly be escorted back to Herrick's castle. Or maybe they'd beat her senseless for the prank she'd played on them all, making the all-male academy look like a pack of fools.

Vail murmured a word, and the trees that framed him unfurled their branches, opening up to bind her to the trunk.

"Stop," I called, pushing through my fellow students. Duncan gaped at me from the front of the first-years.

Vail turned, shock written across his face. I was always a model student.

And I'd be one now, too.

"According to rule thirty-seven in our guide book, Faer is my responsibility as my junior," I said. "His mistakes are my fault as well, and correcting him is up to me."

Vail stared at me, amusement entering his cold gray eyes. "Always so studious, Azrael. But rule seventy-nine allows instructors to select their own punishments for students who fail in particularly spectacular ways."

Alisa shrugged at that, as if she at least were *spectacularly* in trouble. It made me want to shake her when I was all keyed up, but I was committed now.

"True, but I think it's in paragraph D of rule thirty-seven that any student can take a fellow student's punishment," I said. "Then I regain my right to beat Faer mercilessly myself."

I fixed Alisa with a cold smile. This play might work just because Faer and I were so obviously often at odds throughout this year. And because I was famously proud and *insufferable,* as Alisa had so kindly put it.

Vail sighed as he glanced between us. "I will never understand royalty. But very well. If you insist."

He stood back, sweeping his arm with a half-bow toward the tree.

To Faer, he said, "You can stand close by and watch."

"No," Alisa began.

I grabbed her shoulder and leaned close, letting my temper flare in front of the audience. I let my words carry to them. "For once in your life, Faer, try to pay attention. Learn something."

With our faces close together, my back to Vail and our fellow students, I could wink at her. This was the only way to keep her secret safe. I would do anything for her, and I hoped she really would learn that she could trust my love.

I knew she understood what I was doing. For a second, her eyes looked luminous, as if she were about to cry. Then her chin rose.

I drew off my gloves without hesitating, unbuttoned my coat, and passed both to her. Despite the fact she was still dressed, her legs trembled, as if she'd forgotten to warm herself and the cold was beginning to seep in. I drew my tunic off over my head and draped it over the pile in her arms.

Then I pressed my bare chest against the trunk of the tree, feeling the rough bark against my cheek. I felt a tic begin in my jaw, as fear of what was to come washed over me, and I hoped no one else saw it.

The branches wrapped around my arms and spread them wide. Another one crept across my lower back, immobilizing me completely.

I promised myself I wouldn't scream.

CHAPTER THIRTY-FOUR

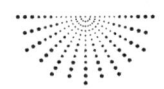

A*lisa*

FAER SEEMED to be enjoying himself at his party, as he usually did.

There'd be no running to the throne to escape the crowds tonight. Faer already sat on the throne. One Fae female perched on his lap, trading kisses with him. A second stood behind him, massaging his shoulders. She seemed content to be all-but-ignored, smiling widely and staring down at the back of his head with affection written across her face.

Faer looked dissolute and pleased with himself as he steadily worked the skirt up of the girl in his lap, his hands gliding over ever-more-apparent pale silvery flesh.

"Who are they?" I asked Azrael abruptly. He stood at my left shoulder, ready to whisper into my ear.

"Laina, a summer court noble who would love to be Queen," he said, his gaze flickering to the one who all but writhed across Faer's lap as he smiled smugly. "And Tresa, of the sea court. Faer seems to find them both pleasing, but they're two of...several."

"Do you think they feel debased?" I asked. "Or are they genuinely... enjoying themselves?"

"I think those are questions best not asked in the court." His voice was matter-of-fact.

He showed no signs of any reaction, despite the fact we'd just had that ugly fight.

He was my blank-faced, handsome servant.

I knew better than to believe that was his true identity.

"You're loyal to your duty, at least," I told him, taking the drink out of his hand as soon as he'd taken it from a passing servant. I raised the glass to him in a brief toast. "Though not to me."

He stared down at me, his face still expressionless, but something dangerous sparked in those dark eyes.

"Once, Alisa, I owed the autumn court my loyalty, and I gave it to you instead. Drink to that." His tone was cool.

His words were a harsh reminder that I hadn't gained my memories today. Without them, I didn't know how to fight my brother for the crown, or if I even wanted to. Perhaps I should go back to the human world.

But the summer court seemed to be falling into pieces. That felt like my fault. My responsibility.

"How many other children work in the summer court because their villages couldn't pay their taxes any other way?" I demanded.

"I don't know the count," Azrael said.

"Don't be insufferable."

He shrugged one shoulder. "I'd guess dozens, if not hundreds."

"That's barbaric." My fingers were wrapped so tightly around my glass they ached, and I forced myself to relax my grip. "Why don't you do anything about it, Azrael?"

He smiled humorlessly. "If there even *was* anything *I* could do about it, I'd still tell you once again to keep your mouth shut in the midst of the court."

"Everyone around here keeps their mouths shut, don't they?" I said.

I'd been mistaken for a mortal this morning. These people would never see me as a potential queen until they saw me as Fae, just like them. They didn't see humans as being worthy of any consideration.

"Change me back," I said. "You said you could break the enchantment once we were on this side. So change me back."

"I can't," he said.

"You can't or you won't?" I demanded. I glanced at Azrael, wondering if this was an order of Faer's.

Azrael's gaze followed mine, then flickered back to my face. His lip curled faintly on one side, as if he read my thoughts. As if he still knew me that well.

"You're a good servant, as you said." I leaned against him, my hands sliding up the hard planes of that chest so I could raise my lips close to his ear. "But you're not *my* servant, are you?"

His gaze caught mine. "Find a way to make me yours, then."

His words were a puzzle to untangle later. He was trying to tell me something important. I stared back into those vivid purple eyes.

"Where are Tiron and Duncan?" I asked.

"Duncan can't be trusted in a crowd," he said, "and you can't be trusted with Tiron."

I scoffed at that. "I want them to attend tomorrow, if we have another one of these damned parties."

Azrael's lips tightened into a line. "Tiron is too outspoken for this setting, Alisa."

After a moment, he added, "You shouldn't be here either. But I can't help that."

"Feeling protective of me, Azrael?" I teased. "Or just afraid I'll embarrass you? Or that I'll accidentally start a war?"

His gaze met mine levelly. "Why choose just one?"

I patted his cheek—his eyes sharpened at the condescending gesture. Despite myself, it was hard not to notice how smooth and warm his skin was against my palm, how his cheekbones and strong jaw seemed to have been carved from marble by an artist, making him obnoxiously beautiful.

"I wish you were on my side," I told him softly. "But I'm not afraid to be alone."

His jaw tensed, but I didn't wait to hear whatever he was going to say next. Trading barbs might be a pleasant pastime, but it wasn't going to set my kingdom to rights.

I crossed the ballroom toward the dais, ignoring the people who tried to speak to me. I'd spent the past few nights being *polite* and apparently, it had only increased the whispering about how I no longer knew how to play the game.

Raile fell into step beside me. His tall, powerful body in a gray uniform carried a presence that was hard to ignore.

"What kind of trouble have you found lately, Princess?"

"Not now, Raile," I told him.

He stopped me with a hand on my shoulder, turning me to face him, and I gave him a look.

"You're lucky that my ire is reserved for someone else tonight," I warned him.

"I'll take your ire over being ignored," he told me, his jaw tense. "I'm not accustomed to being *dismissed* so rudely."

"Then something so new and novel must be exciting for you," I told him, before continuing across the ballroom. I had to wind my way around the clusters of people conversing, then duck the couples spinning across the dance floor.

They'd melted aside for Faer when he passed. I promised myself that one day they would do the same for me.

Faer was still reclining in his throne on the dais. My twin throne was beside it, but Tresa perched on the arm. Faer had his hand on her thigh and was leaning over to kiss her while the other girl straddled his lap.

As I climbed the stairs, Faer noticed me. He watched me with one eye, not bothering to take his lips from Tresa's. I reached the top and faced the three of them, crossing my arms.

"You'll both need to leave," I said softly. "My brother and I need to speak."

Tresa smiled against Faer's lips. "I don't think your brother wants to *speak*..."

I couldn't keep standing here awkwardly in front of Faer while another girl sat on my throne. The entire court was watching, waiting to see what I'd do next.

Raile had warned me that when people disrespected me and I did nothing, the Fae thought I wasn't worthy to rule.

I grabbed her by the back of the neck. She let out a squeal. *God, I hope she's a terrible person, or I'm being one myself.*

"I don't like to repeat myself," I told her as I dragged her toward the edge of the dais. I hoped she'd take the message she couldn't win, and she'd walk away. I didn't want to hurt her.

She tried to pull back out of my hold. Her feet slipped out from under her as she struggled. I tried to pull her back onto the dais as she teetered on the edge of the stairs.

There was no saving her, though. I was about to fall down the steps with her, so I let go, taking a step back. I forced myself to compose my face into a cruel mask as she rolled down the steps with a squeal.

I watched her until she came to a stop at the base of the stairs.

The music had stopped. The room was silent and everyone was staring at me. Azrael's face was shocked, then he composed himself.

Raile smirked, crossing his arms over his chest. He looked almost proud of me.

She rose to her knees, letting out a shaky sob, then looked up at me with hatred written across her face. I smiled back at her. Too late to do anything now but play the game. I raised my hand, waving her off.

"Music, please," I ordered softly.

Bright strains of fiddle music began instantly. She stumbled to her feet and ran toward the entrance to the ballroom.

I didn't wait to watch her go. I turned my back on the crowd and faced Alaina. She stood beside Faer, who had propped his face on his hand and his elbow on the throne. He was watching me with open curiosity.

And she was no longer touching him.

"Leave us, please," I said.

She fled past—giving me a wide berth—before she rushed down the steps. Her skirts fluttered behind her and she yanked her untied corset against her breasts.

I sat down on my own throne. "We need to talk, brother of mine."

"I'm always here at your pleasure, sister of mine." He leaned back in his chair. His eyes were intent and watchful. "You don't even need to manhandle my friends to get my attention."

"Tell your *friends* to stay off my throne, then."

"No disrespect meant, I'm sure," he said.

"I'm sure." I leaned back, matching his expression of careless ease. The court had returned to dancing, talking and—from this vantage point, I could see for the first time—fucking against the walls, for a particularly adventurous couple. They seemed to have tails, which whipped around them with ecstasy. But I had the feeling we were being watched closely, no matter how busy the court looked now.

"I like it up here," I said.

We had quite the view of the dancers in their colorful gowns and suits. I glimpsed tails and ears and horns, Fae with faces like cats and like dragons. The high goblins and the trolls lurked around the edges of the dance floor, and they looked wistful, as if they might like to dance too.

I'd barely noticed before, when I ran up here to pout. *Never again.* It was time to put that uncertain version of Alisa behind.

Even though I felt quite fondly of her; that Alisa was warm and comfortable in her skin, even if she didn't know her way in this world. She was loved in the human world, at least by her friends. I didn't know if I'd ever see her face again, more rounded and flawed than the Fae face that Azrael had shown me in the mirror. Something in me ached and rebelled, but I forced the words out.

"I don't think this mortal enchantment suits me, do you?" I asked.

"I thought you liked it," he said.

It seemed like a betrayal of *myself* to lie and say I didn't like my mortal body, my mortal face. I refused to say those words.

"I'm a Fae queen, not a mortal. It's time I let it go." As soon as I said the words, I knew they were true.

This face had been my escape plan. As long as I looked mortal, I could walk back into the rip and escape back to my old life. If I changed my face, I committed myself to staying in this place, with these people—at least until I learned how to enchant myself.

No more escape plans.

His lips parted, then twisted as he corrected, "A Fae princess."

He'd fashion himself a king and turn me into nothing. I could see it on his face. He wanted me to be Raile's queen—and I needed to figure out what Raile offered him—but never the queen of the summer court.

"Of course," I said with a smile. "You'll forgive me. I don't remember how anything works."

Let him think me as clueless as I felt.

He sat forward, frowning. He was deliberating—he wanted me to keep looking as if I didn't belong here—and I decided to talk over his internal dialogue.

"I've heard people whispering how ugly I am as a mortal," I said, imagining stabby deaths for those people, but Faer didn't need to know my dreams. "How foolish the summer court looks."

His eyes narrowed. He didn't like that.

"Of course I'll help you, sister." He rose from his chair in one smooth movement, already holding his hand out to me.

I took his fingers lightly, and he helped me off the throne.

I smiled at him warmly. One day I'd help *him* out of his throne.

"Summer magic," he murmured, facing me. "Lift this enchantment and reveal my sister's true face."

A glow suffused us both, and I heard a sharp gasp from the crowd.

He looked beautiful in that moment, his lavender hair floating around his face, his silver eyes bright in that cruelly handsome face. He was limned by light, his power glowing around him in a soft golden blur.

No wonder humans followed Fae into the immortal gardens. With that gorgeous face and a slight smile curving his mouth, he was the perfect predator.

His magic felt like sunlight on my face, and the light around us glowed brighter, deeper. I struggled to keep my eyes open as they watered because the brightness was blinding. I finally had to shut them, but before that, I saw him grit his teeth, as if it were a struggle to break my magic.

The heat on my face had felt welcome, comforting, but suddenly it was too intense. It burned my skin, beat against my eyeballs. My lips felt as if they'd gone dry. Every muscle grew heavy, then weak. Pain swept through my body, deep as bone. Every muscle cramped.

As I fell to my knees, my hand slipped out of his. The pain was unbearable, and I let out a scream.

Then the agony faded, as abruptly as it had begun.

I opened my eyes to find Faer on his knees. He gasped for breath, and he stared at me with narrowed eyes as if he hated me.

"I know who enchanted your face," he spat. "I remember the feel of their magic."

"Who?" The word came out cracked, my voice parched.

A cruel smile spread across his face. "You're not their queen, Alisa. And you never will be. You were happier dirtside than you'll ever be here."

I might have tried to murder him just then, but my legs felt as if they were made of gelatin. Exhaustion weighed on me, all the heavier a burden because I had to hold my shoulders steady and chin high. I couldn't show any weakness.

Then suddenly, I saw Azrael standing at the very bottom of the dais. He couldn't come up to the dais unless I invited him.

I raised my fingers, beckoning him.

The room had gone so silent during the flare of Faer's magic that each of Azrael's footfalls rising up the stone steps rang through the cavernous space. There was only the faintest whisper of voices, beginning to murmur.

My mind raced; if Azrael carried me out of here, how weak would I look?

Faer rose and, still half bent over, stumbled the few feet to his throne. Somehow breaking that enchantment had almost destroyed him; he must have thought it would be easy, though. He'd never risk looking foolish in front of the court.

There'd been some kind of special power in that enchantment. I'd need to find a way to drag the secret from his unwilling, lying lips.

Azrael slid his arm around my waist. His body blocked me from the crowd. I expected him to sweep me up to his chest, but he murmured into my ear, "Show them how much stronger you are than Faer, Majesty."

He lifted me easily to my feet. I swayed on my aching legs—I felt drained as if I'd just run for my life—then caught myself, wrapping my hand around his corded forearm.

He pressed his arm tightly against his body, holding me up as much as he could, though I walked on my own.

Together, the two of us swept down the dais and through the crowd. I heard the crowd murmur around us as they melted away, making space for us to pass. I held my chin high, a smile fixed on my face.

The music began to play along, a slower song, almost a dignified one. I glimpsed the fiddle players from the corner of my eye. Their faces were intent on their instruments as their bows swept back and forth.

I looked for Raile, for some reason, but I didn't see him in the crowd. Most of the faces tonight were unfamiliar, despite all the whirlwind introductions I'd been through lately.

Then we were out into the hall, leaving all the noise behind as the guards closed the doors behind us. We were in the long moonlit marble hall, which was filled with statues. At one end, the hall stood open to a flower-filled verandah, to the ocean outside and the depth of the dark night.

I stumbled, and Azrael was there without hesitation, catching me in his arms and bearing me up against his chest.

I shouldn't be so vulnerable with him, but everything ached and I wasn't sure I could walk.

I let my head fall against his chest as he carried me up the stairs. Sleep seemed to crowd my mind even as he was carrying me. The swaying of his arms felt like safety.

"Well played, my queen," he said softly into my ear. He carried me into my bedroom and lay me on the bed.

I woke up hours later, still in my gown and slippers. As I stared up at the dark ceiling, I wondered if I'd really heard those words, or if I'd just dreamt them.

Well played, my queen.

Everything in the summer court was mysterious, but the biggest puzzles of all were the visiting princes of the autumn court.

Or were they the *trapped* princes of the autumn court?

CHAPTER THIRTY-FIVE

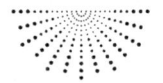

Tiron

I WAS DOZING against Alisa's door when I sensed movement on the other side. I started to scramble to my feet, but when the door was wrenched open, I tumbled backward into the room.

I landed on my back on the marble, and before I could rise, Alisa straddled me. Her ass slammed into my stomach—with more force than was natural, given her delicate bones—and knocked the breath out of me.

That beautiful face rose above mine, similar but different than before, her lavender hair hanging around us both. Her face was resolute, beautiful but dangerous.

Her lips parted and her eyes widened as she registered who I was. Oh good—once she recognized me, she didn't feel like stabbing me. I'd bet Duncan couldn't have said the same.

"Tiron, why are you sleeping against my door?" she demanded.

"Because you never invited me in." I winked at her.

She gave me a skeptical look and rose to her feet. "Well, apparently inviting you would be unacceptable behavior for a princess. And we all know I'd never want to be a bad princess. Would you flag someone down for breakfast, please? I'm starving."

I was willing to bet that she was drained from the magic last night. Azrael had told us all about her transformation the previous night—as best he could, above the sound of Duncan alternating between scoffing and throwing back glasses of whiskey. Somehow Duncan had found time to smuggle a bottle back from dirtside. He was resourceful when it came to his bad habits.

I stepped back into the hall and stopped a passing servant. When I came back, Alisa stood before the mirror built into a vine-covered stone archway. Her fingertips rested lightly on her chiseled cheekbones, and she studied her face. Her eyes were dark and shadowed in that lovely, expressionless face.

"Breakfast is on its way," I promised her, walking up behind her. I cocked my head, looking at our shared reflections. "What do you think?"

Her eyes flickered to my reflection. "You're very handsome, Tiron. But you knew that already."

Her lips turned up, her tone teasing. I could almost see her press any genuine emotions she felt down into a box, deep inside.

"I'm glad I please your Majesty," I returned.

As she turned to face me, she ran her hand over the stiff, jeweled bodice of her gown. "Where is Azrael?"

Somehow it bothered me to hear his name on her lips. She was focused on him even when we were face-to-face.

"He had some…autumn court…business to deal with."

She cocked her head to one side. "Tell me more about that."

I huffed a laugh. "You should ask him yourself."

"Azrael's not exactly forthright with me." She tilted her head to one side, studying me with those bright eyes. "You destroy a man's little kingdom one time, and he just can't get over it."

She was gauging me somehow, testing me. I stared back at her, unanswering.

She patted my cheek. "I hope someday you have that same loyalty for me, Tiron."

My lips parted, but she was already turning. She ran her fingers through her hair, pulling it on top of her head, displaying her long neck and the bare lines of her shoulders. "Azrael has been filling in as my maidservant since Nikia made herself...unreliable. Since he's gone, I need you to undress me."

"Ah," I said, eloquently.

"Come on, brave knight. Don't tell me you're afraid of a little ribbon and lace."

"I'm afraid of *you* specifically," I said dryly, "and a bit afraid of Azrael."

"Why Azrael?" she asked.

Did she really not see the protective, possessive fury he radiated around her? Maybe they were both blind to their own feelings.

And Duncan looked at me as if he wanted to slap me every time I looked at Alisa twice. Duncan would claim it was for my own protection, because he was even more of an emotional dunce than the other two.

I liked them all, but the three of them might well be hopeless.

I sighed and began to undo the corset. She stepped away as soon as I'd unknotted the top.

"Never mind. It's so loose now." She wriggled it down over her body, and I turned my back. She kept on talking anyway, and from my peripheral vision I caught a glimpse of her stepping out of the skirt. "The hems of the dresses used to drag on the ground. They don't now. I'm just a bit taller, I guess—and quite a bit thinner."

She didn't sound happy at the idea. "I worked hard for my muscles. Now they're gone overnight."

If she was going to stand there naked and stare in the mirror, I guessed I could open my eyes. She examined her body, which was tall and narrow, straight as an arrow. She ran her hands over small, high breasts and the delicate flare of her narrow hips. I was instantly hard, my cock straining at the front of my pants. Shouldn't have looked.

Then she turned and took a few quick steps before plunging into the pool, raising a splash that soaked my pants. The sight of her bare shoulders, the taper of her waist, the curve of her ass... I glanced away, but I was too late. That memory would surface in my dreams.

"Sorry," she called. She was treading water, looking up at me with a worried expression. "I needed a bath after sleeping in my clothes. I didn't mean to offend you. I thought the Fae were comfortable with nudity."

"Quite comfortable, yes," I said, wiping my face absently. Men and women bathed together all the time.

Of course that didn't mean the bathing was always innocent, either.

No matter how comfortable I was with swimming naked with other females, I wasn't comfortable with how I felt around Alisa. It might be best for my mission to seduce the princess and win her to my side.

But it felt like the deepest betrayal, when I didn't want to betray her at all.

"I just thought you were thoroughly... mortalized now," I added.

"You make me want to splash you," she said with a laugh. "Come join me."

"As your Majesty wishes." I deadpanned.

"I need you to stop doing that, or I'm going to do more than splash you," she warned. "Call me Alisa, and don't be a jerk about my title."

"I'm sure it's temporary anyway." I grabbed my shirt hem one-handed, then dragged it up over my head.

She was floating in the water, her hair floating around her face, but despite her relaxed pose, I was sure she was watching me. I untied my pants and let them slide down my hips. I knew she was probably used to wearing underwear now, but Fae didn't.

"What do you mean?" she frowned.

"You'll be a queen soon." Instead of diving in as she had, I waded down the steps. "The water's surprisingly cold."

"One way or another, I guess," she said, but I had no doubt that Alisa would find a way out of avoiding Raile unless it pleased her. Even if it meant gutting him instead. "And I like it cold."

"Why? That's an odd preference... except for the deep-sea merfolk, of course." Maybe she had some mermaid in her lineage.

She tilted her head to one side, considering. "I don't know."

I was tempted to ask her if she'd always had that preference, but of course she didn't know. It was hard to make small talk with someone who didn't have memories of their life growing up or anything else.

I might very well know Faer better than she did. Lucky me.

"Duncan wants me to fetch you for the training yard," I told her as I floated on my back. My outstretched hand bumped hers, and I started to pull away, but she turned her face in the water and smiled at me. She looked like an angel floating in the water.

"Come with me," she said. "I feel like he and Azrael are keeping us apart, when you're the only one I like."

I laughed. "Perhaps they are. They both have a mission they've given themselves. Azrael is teaching you etiquette and Duncan gets the pleasure of playing swords with you daily. Meanwhile, I've been left in the cold."

"I think there are other things I need to learn. Like magic," she murmured. Then she turned to me and added, "You'll come? Help me tease Duncan out of his shell?"

Her voice was arch and playful. But she looked at me with drops of water clinging to her lashes, her eyes wide and luminous and aching.

"Yes," I said, already able to picture the look on Duncan's face. "There are other things you need to learn too, Alisa. Like how to use your wings."

A look of wonder—and uncertainty—spread across her face. "Wings?"

"One night soon," I promised her. "You and I will sneak out."

"Do we have to sneak?" she asked, a teasing edge in her voice. "Doesn't a princess get to make some decisions for herself?"

I would've answered her seriously, but she was already going on,

"Sneaking is always more fun, of course. It will add a bit of excitement to our tutoring sessions."

She must already know the answer, and she didn't want to hear it.

Maybe Alisa would rewrite what it meant to be a princess, just as Azrael said she had before.

CHAPTER THIRTY-SIX

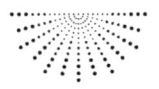

Duncan

"Why are the two of you wet?" I looked between the two idiots in front of me.

Tiron's wet blond hair curled around his ears, just beginning to dry, and Alisa's long, damp lavender hair was pulled into a messy bun on top of her head. Tiron gave me a fake innocent look that was familiar—but never stopped irritating me nonetheless—and Alisa smiled and shrugged, never particularly sorry.

It was far too easy for me to imagine the two of them swimming in that pool together, Tiron's hands tracing the slender lines of her body, palming her breasts in the water. The image pissed me off and made me hard all at once.

I turned my back on them so neither of them would see how I felt. "Get on your goddamn horses. You're late."

Tiron went to her side, helping her saddle her horse. Then he hovered beside her, watching her mount up.

"Don't coddle her," I snapped.

Alisa's gaze rose to mine, her eyes widening, before a smile spread across her face. "You're right, Duncan. Thank you for expressing your faith in my abilities. I know that can be hard for you."

Tiron ducked his head, hiding a grin as he went to his own horse.

During our entire ride, no matter what I said, Alisa found a way to twist every complaint about her failings into some compliment. She responded warmly, as if every grouchy remark I made was some sweet and tender affirmation. I fell silent before we reached the clearing. She was impossible. She just liked to irritate me.

And she was so very good at it.

We reached the clearing where we'd practiced before. I dismounted and enchanted my horse, and left Tiron to help Alisa, since he clearly loved to do so.

As soon as I pulled my training sword, I said, "Ready."

Alisa rushed to draw her own sword. She was too late though, and I tapped her outer thigh with my blade, pulling the blow so it would sting but shouldn't bruise deep.

She brought her sword to the ready, grinning at me over the blade. I already regretted the unfair move just because I was out of sorts, until she exclaimed, "You're right, it's so important to always be ready! Thanks for the reminder."

The only creature worse than Evil Alisa was Perky Alisa.

"Why don't the two of you team up and press an attack," I said, since they liked to form a team so much already, "Maybe I'll be lucky and one of you will get in a blow to the head that knocks me as senseless as the pair of you."

Tiron considered this, his sword at the ready. "Hardly seems fair."

"Try me," I said.

For a few minutes, the only sounds were the thwack of our training swords against each other's, ringing out in the clearing. In the end, the two of them bested me—barely. I swept Alisa's leg, but she rolled out from under my killing blow and Tiron stepped in, catching me with the blade to my throat.

"Decent," I admitted grudgingly.

"Ha," Alisa said, panting. Her hair had come a bit undone, strands hanging into her face, which emphasized the fine cut of her cheekbones. "You're being generous, Duncan, how unexpected. It shouldn't be so hard for the two of us to bring you down."

She wasn't twisting my words now to say I was *generous*. Her voice was her natural one, not the light affect she took on when she was teasing me.

"To be fair to us," Tiron said before I could decide how to respond, "Duncan is the best of the king's knights."

I scoffed--not at the thought that I was the best, but at the thought that I was one of the king's. "Maybe. It depends on the day."

"You only came here a few years ago," Alisa said to Tiron, as if to confirm.

He nodded and pulled off his sweat-soaked shirt, revealing the hard planes and muscles formed by years of daily training for combat. "One day I might be as good as Duncan, though."

I snorted at the compliment. "You two are more annoying than usual. Were you drinking wine at breakfast?"

"Maybe you're hungover from last night," Tiron gave me a meaningful look before he took his flask off his horse and guzzled water.

"Were you two at a different party?" Alisa asked, her brows arching. "I'd rather go to that one. I bet it was much more fun."

"Only because you weren't there," I said, but my heart wasn't quite in it. The knights had their own revelry, and it was far more pleasant then being anywhere near Faer.

"What brought you to the autumn court?" Alisa asked Tiron curiously.

He hesitated, and I knew he didn't want to answer that question. He kept the truth of his past hidden deep under that sunny exterior. I suspected I didn't even know the half of it.

"Are you two going to gab all day like a couple of scullery maids peeling potatoes, or are we going to train?" I demanded.

I tapped Alisa's sword with mine impatiently. She couldn't hide her faint smile as she moved into position—as if she found me harmless, or even amusing.

"I'll make you a deal," she said. "I want a story. I barely know the two of you."

"I'm not in the bedtime story business," I warned her.

"I said a deal. I'll go up against the two of you. If I win, you tell me."

"That's ridiculous," I scoffed.

"If it's ridiculous," she tapped my sword's blade with hers, the way I'd done to her a moment before, "then you'll easily beat me and gloat. What do you have to lose?"

"I wouldn't bother to gloat about beating you," I said.

She rolled her eyes and turned to Tiron in an appeal for help.

"Come on, Duncan," Tiron said. "The queen of summer is going to need to fight, sooner or later. No matter how much we intend to protect her. Might as well practice now."

He gave me a long look. Alisa glanced between the two of us, her eyes narrowing as if she were about to demand to know what we were talking about.

"Okay, fine," I said, simply because I didn't want to get drawn into a long conversation about what it would mean for her to be *the queen of summer*. "I'll play your little games, Alisa."

My condescending tone just made her smile. She said archly, "I know you will."

The three of us all moved to the ready. Alisa faced the two of us, who stood about ten feet apart. As soon as I took a step toward her, she darted toward Tiron, trying to use her speed and agility against the two of us.

She was quick and clever, but in the end, the two of us beat her.

Tiron reached his hand down to her, and she grabbed his forearm. He pulled her up.

"Fine, keep your secrets," she said, leaping to her feet. She pressed her elbow into her ribs as if she'd been hurt, but she must be trying to keep it from showing on her face.

If I didn't know Alisa's true nature, I would've felt like a real dick for making her work so hard for the simplest scrap of information. She was tough and hard-working. I hesitated, hating myself for the way I softened.

Then I tossed my water bottle to her. "The first time I met Tiron, he came into an open competition to become an apprentice. Believe it or not, people *fight* each other for those spots and the torture that comes with them. Azrael or I both would've picked him out as a royal for some other court."

"But I was thinking," Tiron pressed two fingers to the side of his head dramatically, "so I wore a mask."

"You looked like a moron," I scoffed. "Only spring court knights wear those silly little masks. And it didn't do much to hide the way you carry yourself."

"That almost sounded like a compliment," Tiron said.

"He won round after round. Day after day. The last competition round was fighting knights of the court so they could be assessed. But the night before, there was a feast to celebrate." I shook my head at Tiron, before I asked him, "Were you drunk? Maybe you were drunk."

To Alisa, I added, "He called me *Azrael*."

Tiron spread his arms. "It was an honest mistake. You two are practically twins."

I scoffed at that. "I could kick your ass for old time's sake, if you want to go down that road."

Alisa was smiling at the banter between the two of us; seeing that genuine, warm expression that crinkled the corner of her eyes, my chest grew light.

Danger. Her smile had brought my guard down before, and I'd paid for that sin.

"Anyway, I asked him to apologize and he copped that winter court attitude," I finished. "Then I accidentally broke his nose and two ribs."

"There was nothing accidental about it," Tiron said, sounding exasperated.

"I didn't *mean* to break your nose. If you're going to drop your fists, though, it can't be helped." I crossed my arms over my chest.

Tiron rolled his eyes. "Anyway, one of the fun things about this whole affair was that we were enchanted so we couldn't just heal ourselves. It was a week of cumulative damage. I was half-wrecked going into the fights the next day. I knew I was going to lose—I'd be lucky not to puncture a lung."

"What happened?" Alisa prompted.

Tiron glanced at me, his eyebrows arching mischievously. "You want to tell it, Duncan?"

I shook my head. "Go ahead."

"I really think you should," he insisted.

Maybe I should puncture his lungs now after all.

"I'm dying of curiosity," Alisa said.

"If only it were that easy to get rid of you," I told her, but she just smiled at the dig.

Tiron was looking at me as if he'd win if I refused to finish, so I finally uncrossed my arms and gave in.

I admitted, "I let him win. Pretended he knocked me out."

"He's a really good actor when he tries," Tiron confided to her.

Alisa looked at me curiously, as if she were seeing something about me that she hadn't before.

I opened my mouth, about to try to justify it all to her, but then I snapped my jaw shut. I didn't owe her anything.

"Let's fight," she said, before I could say it myself.

CHAPTER THIRTY-SEVEN

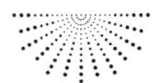

A *lisa*

As we were riding back to the castle, a male on a horse appeared down the road, such a distance away that I couldn't see his face. His posture was erect though, his shoulders broad, and he looked sexy even from here.

"What does Azrael want?" Duncan frowned.

Of course. Of course it was Azrael.

Why was I so attracted to all three of these jerks?

Duncan clucked to his horse, and the warhorse shot off, Duncan kept his seat easily, his fine ass bouncing against the saddle as he raced toward Azrael.

Tiron kept his horse at a sedate pace, matching mine.

"Do you guys really not name your horses?" I demanded. "As if they're just tools?"

He raised his eyebrows. "Between you and me, Alisa… but if you tell anyone, I'll put spiders in your bed…"

"Does this world have spiders? Why? Why would there be spiders here too?"

"Every world has spiders," he said. "Some of them are huge."

Well, that made interdimensional travel a bit less exciting.

I almost asked another question, but I interrupted myself. "I don't want to talk about spiders. What were you going to tell me?"

He patted his horse's neck. "Meet Merlin."

"Merlin?" I raised my eyebrows. "I thought he was a dirtside story."

"Not just dirtside," he corrected, "and not just a story."

His horse's ears flickered as if he'd recognized his name.

"It's a good name," I said.

"Azrael's been trying to get you a warhorse of your own," Tiron said. "That pony's already thrown you once. She's too volatile to ride to the Cursed Caves, since we're likely to go through hell to get there."

"You don't have extra horses in the stables?"

He shook his head. "The horses bind to their rider."

I fell silent, thinking about whether I dared *bind* to any animal. What would happen when I left the horse behind—if I ever did?

The truth was, I had no intention of returning to that shimmering door in the forest anytime soon. I couldn't explain why I felt tied here, or what I truly wanted. Once I had my memories back, could I walk away and leave this world behind?

I didn't think so. But I didn't know what was locked away in my brain, either. My memories might change everything.

"What does it take to get a warhorse?" I asked.

Tiron snorted. "The permission of the stablemaster, for one. Which comes from the head of the guard. Which comes…"

He broke off abruptly, and faint color rose in his cheeks.

No wonder Duncan and Azrael had tried to keep us apart. Tiron told me too much. As long as I didn't have a more reliable mount, I couldn't safely travel to the Cursed Caves. Faer might not want to forbid me from going—god help him if he tried—but he could confound the trip in subtler ways.

I had a feeling Faer was doing his best to keep me from breaking the spell on my memories. I'd bet that either he placed the spell on me himself, or my father Herrick had, with Faer's knowledge.

"Did you know Herrick at all?" I asked.

He shook his head. "No."

"You didn't go to the academy with the rest of us?" I asked curiously. Tiron didn't seem like he knew me from before.

"No. I should have. I was the sixth son of a mere lord. I was never going to inherit anything but an empty title, pocket change and half a drawer of fancy silverware."

"What happened?"

"The winter court was destroyed," he said, his voice sharp. "You must have traveled in your carriage past the ruins of my family's home when you went to that academy."

I stared at him,

"Not that you remember," he finished in a softer tone.

I hoped his family was alive and well somewhere despite all the devastation of the war. "What happened to your five brothers?"

"A tidy row of unmarked graves behind the house," he said. "Along with the graves of my parents and my two little sisters."

His jaw was tight, his head bowed above the horn of his saddle. I wanted to reach out to touch him but I didn't dare console him. My family had been the ones to murder his.

He looked up, and I could almost see him decide to let go of the past—for now—as his shoulders straightened and his chin rose. "Sorry, Majesty. It's not the lightest subject."

I'd threatened him before if he kept calling me that, but right now I didn't mind any nickname. He had every reason to hate my family—to hate me. "I don't mind talking to you about it, Tiron. I wish…"

I wished I could change the past. But I couldn't.

He shook his head, as if he were desperate for a subject change. I should find an easier topic, but I was burning to know if Faer was as bad as our father.

"Is Faer any better than Herrick, do you think?" I asked.

He glanced at me sidelong, then confessed, "I don't think I want to answer that, Alisa. He's your brother."

"I think I need to know," I said. "Please, Tiron. I don't want to go make other friends..."

I trailed off as I realized I had no way to make other friends. I was isolated. There was no one in the court I could trust; I wasn't going to strike up a lovely friendship with one of the horned girls sipping wine between dances at Faer's parties. Faer had spent the last five years building relationships and loyalties and alliances and *fear*. The court belonged to him.

Sometimes it felt, though, as if these three men belonged to *me*.

Maybe that was enough to go to war with Faer... if I could ever truly trust them, if they could ever trust me. Despite the past.

"The truth?" he gritted, his voice low. He looked ahead steadily, and I followed his gaze toward where Duncan and Azrael rode back toward me.

"Please," I said hurriedly, knowing he wouldn't speak openly once they were back.

"I think the summer court needs a queen, not a king," he managed. He glanced at me with something open and vulnerable in his green-eyed gaze that I'd never seen before. "I think your kingdom needs a hero, Alisa. And I think that hero has to be you."

I stared at him, not sure how to answer that. I'd felt like a hero at times as a Hunter, when I rescued people from monsters. But I wasn't *that* kind of hero.

But then, Azrael and Duncan cantered into earshot, so we both let the subject drop.

"Faer wants to have lunch with us all," Duncan announced, his tone so dour that it sounded more like an invitation to a hanging.

"How dreadful," I said, matching my tone to his, which just earned me a baleful glare.

Azrael's face was perfectly blank—the way it always was when he didn't like something and he was making sure no one saw his emotions. He was always guarded that way when he was anywhere near Faer, or even in the court. But he was animated—for Azrael, at least—with Duncan and Tiron.

And with me.

Usually.

"What's bothering you?" I demanded.

"He might be embarrassed from that show on the dais," Azrael said. "I'm curious what he wants this morning."

When Azrael said he was curious, I had a feeling what he truly felt was *dread*.

What had Faer done to Duncan and Azrael before? They seemed wary around him, as if he'd cost them something before.

I knew they wouldn't want to answer the question. But I was furious at the thought, and sooner or later, I'd find out if Faer had hurt them.

So what? What are you going to do then? They're not even your friends.

My inner voice was an asshole, and I decided to ignore it.

"Do you think Raile will be at this lunch too?" I asked as we rode toward the castle. I hated the thought of seeing him. Raile himself seemed like an interesting male, but I hated that he represented my brother's desire to control me. "Then it'll be like a party of princes!"

"Delightful," Duncan muttered.

Tiron glanced at me, a look that I couldn't quite read; I hadn't meant to leave him out. Given life for Azrael, Duncan and myself, it certainly wasn't as if there was anything so great about being nobility.

But maybe Duncan and Azrael were having their own debauched princely parties. I picture those two figures against the wall the other night, lips parted and tails lashing in ecstasy. I imagined these men surrounding me instead of the horned figures, their hands tracing my body, their lips against mine as they spun me between them…

I glanced at Duncan sidelong, trying to imagine his O-face when he always looked so grumpy. Duncan probably managed to scowl his way through an orgasm.

Duncan met my gaze. "What?"

"Nothing," I murmured. "Nothing."

When we reached the castle, I quickly bathed. I debated between wearing one of those damned gowns—it was ridiculous that my everyday clothes were a two-man job—and the Hunter garb I was comfortable in. Was it best if Faer didn't see me as a threat? If I looked lost in this world? I needed to get to the Cursed Caves.

There was a knock on the door. I threw my towel around me and padded across the floor to find Azrael leaning in the doorway.

Something loosened in my chest as soon as I saw him, with his handsome face and his deep purple eyes. That was when I realized how nervous I was about facing Faer again, after last night's escapades. I felt better as soon as I saw Azrael.

"That's a great look," he said. "Definitely wear that to lunch. If Raile is there, I'm pretty sure he'll throw you over his shoulder and dive into the ocean. Swim you all the way to the undersea."

He teased me, but heat flared in his gaze.

"Help me choose my clothes, maidservant of mine," I teased as I padded across the room. "My old battle armor or twirly princess clothes?"

"Those twirly princess clothes can be your armor just as well," he promised me. He followed me into my room and to my surprise, he actually began to flip through my gowns. He let out a scoff. "I think you need a wardrobe makeover, Majesty."

"I'll have to ask my brother for an allowance," I said. My voice was light, but the frustration I felt was real. "Or do I have bank accounts somewhere? Not that I'd remember my pin. How does that even work here, anyway?"

"We'll figure something out," he promised.

I never knew how seriously to take it when he sounded as if he were on my side. He pulled out a dark blue gown, heavily embroidered and beaded at the bottom to look like the night sky over a forest.

"It's pretty," I said. While it was lovely, it seemed like a bit much for lunch.

"It used to be a favorite of yours." He looked at it as if it had memories for him, then put it back in the closet. He pulled out a sleeveless gray dress with a lace overlay. "Maybe this one. What do you think?"

"Sure," I said. "Clothes don't matter much to me."

"You have changed." He smiled, and I could've sworn there was real affection in the way his eyes crinkled at the edges. "I always wondered how it was you managed to wear boys' clothes for almost a year."

This dress at least didn't have a corset. Once I'd stepped into it, I pulled my hair up on top of my head, and he began to button it for me.

"When was that? At that military academy?"

"Yes." The back of his fingers brushed against my bare skin over and over as he fastened the tiny pearl buttons, and I bit my lip at the touch.

I'd felt so little for so long for any man, but Azrael's slightest touch set my heart racing.

"Tell me about what happened."

"Faer was supposed to go, but he didn't want to. Females weren't allowed at the academy at that time. So you took his place."

"I'm curious what *that* conversation looked like between me and Faer."

"I wonder as well. Of course, he adored you when the two of you were young. I'm not sure when that changed. Maybe you two were still on good terms."

Wistfulness twisted through me when I tried to imagine Faer and I being *close*. "Funny that I think he's a total asshole, but imagining how we lost each other still hurts."

"I wish I had an answer for you."

"How did you and I meet?"

"We were roommates." He must be finished buttoning, because his hands dropped to my waist. His big hands seemed to span my waist, hot and individual, and my breath paused in my chest. Into my ear, he said softly, "You were a terrible roommate, by the way."

"Oh? I bet you were insufferable." I could just imagine Azrael arranging his socks by color and complaining if I left a towel on the floor. He'd seemed so uptight in my apartment, although I'd treasure the memories of the three of them doing dishes and mopping.

"I was," he said, to my surprise. "But that was part of my job."

His hands fell away from my body. "Come on. Let's go face…"

He trailed off, and I knew he'd been about to call my brother something uncomplimentary, but he restrained himself.

I wondered if he held himself back because he didn't want to hurt me or because he didn't trust me.

CHAPTER THIRTY-EIGHT

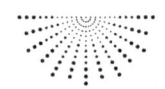

*A*zrael

WHEN WE WALKED into Faer's apartments, he greeted us with sparkling wine and equally bubbly conversation. But I couldn't forget the way he'd stared at Alisa the night before with narrowed eyes and a grim twist to his lips.

He hated her.

"Sister of mine," he said, slinging his arm over her shoulders. "How are the lessons going?"

I never trusted him less than when he seemed happy.

"Lovely," she said. She didn't pull away, but there were faint lines of tension around her eyes, even as she looped her arm around his waist. "What have you been up to today while I've been ducking Duncan's blade?"

"Trying to arrange some trade with the sea court even though we've offended them lately." He squeezed her shoulders. She glanced at him quickly, and he added, "Oh, it's fine. If Raile can't take a bit of rejection, forget him. We'll figure out another way."

Alisa twisted to give him the full weight of her skeptical expression. "You and he seemed pretty intent on sending me off on an underwater journey ASAP."

"It's not as if you've ever been in love," he said airily. "I thought it wouldn't matter so much to you. But maybe this newly reinvented Alisa is more of a romantic."

She stared at him, and he added, "I approve. You be whatever *Alisa* you want to be." He pressed a kiss to her forehead. She froze, but he didn't seem to notice. He released her and added, "Okay, let's eat."

"Is he drunk?" Alisa mouthed at me behind his back as he headed for the table, which was set up inside for once.

I shook my head hastily. I'd never seen Faer drunk; he didn't need to drink to give into his base impulses. Just like the old Alisa, he never let his control slip. He often acted as if he was drunk, to encourage the idiocy of the unobservant around him, but it was always one of his games.

Faer intended some audience for this act; I wondered who it was.

The five of us took seats around a round table. The table was heaped with a fancy seafood lunch. A chocolate tower bubbled in the center, just low enough to let us all look over at each other's faces.

Alisa skipped everything else and immediately speared a strawberry to dip into the chocolate. When she popped it into her mouth, she closed her eyes for a split-second.

"I know how much you love chocolate." Faer sounded pleased. "I'm glad that didn't change."

"I need one of these for my room," Alisa murmured.

"Have you been eating in the knights' quarters when we aren't together?" Faer asked her.

I hated the image of Alisa eating alone every day in her room, with the sun shining on the ocean beyond. Now she didn't even have Nikia hovering around her.

She chewed and swallowed slowly before she answered. "No, I've been dining in my quarters."

"I'm sure you've all been enjoying finer fare then you're accustomed to in the knights' hall then." Faer glanced between the three of us.

Fuck. Faer was reminding her she was alone. He surely already knew the answer to every question before he asked.

Alisa said coolly, "It'd be inappropriate to have them in my quarters, Faer."

Faer's eyes narrowed. Before he could speak again, as if she wanted to cover for his mistake, she added, "What court business do we have next week?"

Faer raised his glass to his lips for a long sip. Then as he set the crystal goblet down, he said, "It's all rather boring. Hopefully I can wrap up business with Raile this week, and there are appeals to hear. Next week is all council meetings and tax collections."

Alisa's eyes sharpened on the word *tax*. If I could beam thoughts directly into her brain, I'd tell her not to pursue the tax payment situation, not now; she'd need to be in a stable position in this court before she challenged something that benefited the lower nobility.

But she said lightly, "I'd hate to leave you bored on your own, Faer, but that sounds like the perfect time for me to take a trip."

"A trip?" He raised his eyebrows. "I worry about your safety, Alisa, but where is it that you want to go?"

Don't say the cursed caves, don't say the cursed caves...

"I'd like to see some of our kingdom," she said. "It's another gap in my knowledge."

"There are so many places I'd like to show you," he said warmly. He launched into a long description of many beautiful places: the fountains of Eleid, the singing forest, the wild gardens in the north.

Alisa ran her finger around the top of her glass. "That sounds lovely. I'll need a few things, of course: a more suitable horse, funds for a travel wardrobe."

"We'll tell the bursar to inform the local shops to give you an open line of credit," he said. "Anything you want, Alisa, I'm happy to buy you."

He took another sip then said, "You really should order new dresses. Your current wardrobe is a bit of a disgrace."

Alisa ignored that and said, "That's kind of you, thank you, but I should be able to pay my own way."

"You don't have a job," he said with a smile. "You're the princess of the summer court, of the high court. You never have to worry about money. Everything that belongs to the court, belongs to you."

She nodded. "All right."

"I'm so sorry," Faer said, raising his gaze to the rest of us. "We've left you out of the conversation. Duncan, how are her lessons going?"

Duncan stared at the prince long enough that I thought he might not answer. Worry sat heavily in my stomach whenever he and Tiron were around the prince. Diplomacy was not Duncan's strength.

"She's an adequate pupil," he said. "She almost put up a fight today."

"I've got such a warm and encouraging teacher." Alisa attempted to clink her glass against his.

Duncan looked at her as if she had spontaneously grown a set of horns and might try to gore him.

"And Azrael? The etiquette lessons?" Faer's pale eyes locked on mine. The pale silver of his irises almost faded at times, leaving his pupils like pin-points.

"I'm still hopelessly unsuited for polite company," Alisa said. "Luckily, I spend most of my time with the three of them."

Tiron smiled at her. "Aren't we all lucky."

Yes, *lucky* was what I felt right now.

"Once I've managed the intricacies of Fae social etiquette," Alisa began, "I was thinking we could expand my curriculum a bit."

No, Alisa. No. Somehow I had a feeling she'd guessed that Faer had given me a very specific set of directions regarding what the princess could and couldn't be taught. But I'd planned to teach her whatever was needed, and play dumb. Most soldiers develop a knack for that.

"What were you thinking of?" Fae asked her over the glass of his wine before he took a sip.

"A magic tutor," Alisa said brightly, but the words seemed to hang in the air.

"I can teach her anything she needs to know," I said. Faer would want to control whatever she learned, and any tutor he assigned would likely be his spy.

"Of course you can," Faer said. "Yes, Alisa, whatever you like. That's a great idea."

For a few minutes we ate in silence.

"Oh, Alisa," Faer said suddenly, as if something had just occurred to him. "I thought you might need a new maid. The head of staff told me today that Nikia's mother had gotten sick and she needed to return home."

"Poor girl," Alisa murmured.

"I thought of the perfect company for you." There was the faintest smile twitching at Faer's lips, a smile that I didn't like at all. He glanced up at me then. "Zora! What a treat for us all it would be to have her here at court!"

My breath froze in my chest.

Zora.

My little sister.

My hands curled into fists under the table, knotting around the napkin. "That would be a treat," I said, my voice calm. "Zora is busy with her studies, though—and she's about as surly as Duncan. I'm sure there are more pleasant ladies."

Alisa's eyes widened. Then she said smoothly, "I don't need a maid. I'm not used to it; it makes me uncomfortable after my time in the mortal world."

"Oh?" Faer asked. "You don't need one? Then who laces your corsets, Alisa?"

He raised his eyebrows. "It must be difficult for you. After all, you told me just a few minutes ago how you'd never invite these men into your rooms."

"I manage," she said.

He flashed her a bright smile that didn't reach his eyes. "I insist. Nothing but the best for my twin."

The rest of the meal went by quietly. Duncan sat stone-faced, but Tiron covered for him, chatting animatedly with Faer. Tiron had a knack for harmless, winning chit-chat. He'd make the perfect spy; he could talk to anyone and convince them that they were friends.

As soon as we reached her apartment, Alisa grabbed my wrist and towed me toward the door. "You two as well."

I glanced down the hall, making sure we weren't being seen, then followed her in.

As soon as the door was closed behind us, Alisa spun to face us. "How do we protect your sister? I know that was a threat. Faer wants to make sure you two stay under his control."

Duncan snorted.

"I understand you want to protect her," Alisa snapped. "Tell me how to help."

"You're very sweet," Duncan deadpanned. He threw the door open so hard that it slammed into the wall.

Alisa jumped at the bit of violence, and my fury re-focused on Duncan. It was tempting to punch him in the face when I was angry.

Well, really, it was *always* tempting to punch Duncan in the face. He was always doing something to deserve it.

"We'll figure something out," Tiron said.

"You say that a lot," she said. "So far the list seems to be growing, and not a lot is getting crossed off."

"You haven't been in this world a week," Tiron said.

"Would you go look after Duncan?" I asked impatiently. I couldn't tolerate Tiron's signature brand of optimism at the moment.

Alisa meant well, but she didn't understand what Faer was capable of. An autumn court village rebelled against Faer a few years ago. Faer had kept the news from me until the damned hunting party came back.

I'd found an excuse to escape and ride past a few weeks later. The men, women and children of that village still dangled against the walls of the keep, strung from different heights. Their bodies twisted in the breeze, slowly decaying as they bumped against the stone walls. One of Faer's assholes had killed a kid's cat and tied it into her arms.

That was when I'd known that one day I'd kill him.

It was too easy for me to imagine Zora blank-eyed too, swaying against that stone wall.

"We'll figure it out together," Tiron said, right before he slipped out the door.

"No we won't," I said. Zora wasn't Alisa's problem, and I didn't want to owe her anything. "I'll take care of it."

Alisa's brows arched, her eyes flashing. "I'm trying to look out for you all."

"You can't even look out for yourself, Princess." I bowed my head to her. "Let's have our lessons in the garden this afternoon. I'll see you in an hour."

I headed for the door.

She got there first, pressing her back against it. She looked up at me with those luminous eyes. "Don't run away, Azrael."

I met her gaze evenly. "My family is in danger at the moment, Princess. I don't have it in me to be nice right now. You'd be wise to give me that hour."

"I'm trying to help."

Since she'd trapped me, I trapped her too, bracing a hand to either side of her head. I leaned in close. She looked up at me, her breath stuttering in her chest.

"You helped me once before, and I lost a kingdom," I growled. "It was my sworn duty to protect the autumn court and every person in it. I failed them."

My voice came out husky when I said I failed them, no matter how little I wanted to display that vulnerability now. I couldn't afford to be vulnerable.

"She's the last thing I have to protect," I managed. "So you'll excuse me, Princess, but I won't gamble on you again. Not with her."

Her cheeks flushed, bright red as a slap. Knowing Alisa, she might have far preferred I hit her than insult her. *Truly* insult her, because this was different than the usual banter between us.

She stepped aside from the door, sweeping her arm to indicate I should go.

I waited in the garden for an hour, but she never came.

CHAPTER THIRTY-NINE

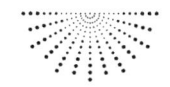

Azrael

SEVEN YEARS *earlier*

I COLLAPSED ON THE BED, groaning. The beating had shredded my flesh, and bitten into the muscle beneath. Alisa moved rapidly to the door and closed it, making sure it was really closed before she rushed to me. She collapsed to her knees beside the bed, her eyes wide.

"It was a letter from the male whose place my friend took," she whispered to me. "I had to protect her."

"And I had to protect you."

"No, you didn't," her voice came out hot. "I was ready to use my magic to conceal myself."

I scoffed. "As if your magic would hold under the lash."

"It would," she said stoutly.

I buried my head in my arm. "I can't take your impudence on top of the pain. I'd prefer to be tortured in just one way, thank you."

"So dramatic." She perched on the bed beside me. I heard a hiss under her breath as she took in just how bad the wounds were.

Fae royalty could heal ourselves with relative ease, so Vail had beaten me far more fiercely than he would've beaten anyone else, I knew that. He'd had to make his impression in the moment. I'd left a trail of blood across the snow and down the hall, though I'd walked proudly back to the dorm, and only collapsed here in privacy.

Her hands moved across my back, the soft glow of her magic sweeping over the deep cuts. "Lord, I think I see bone."

"That's not a helpful thought," I managed, because I didn't want to visualize just how bad it was. The pain was so intense that my stomach roiled. "I think I'm going to be sick."

But I didn't have the energy to move. The worst of the pain began to fade, replaced by a terrible itching sensation as my wounds began to heal under her touch. I could heal myself, but I had a feeling that—no matter how glib she was—she needed to be the one to fix the damage.

"I was prepared to take my own punishment, you know," she said softly. "I wouldn't do something that I wasn't willing to pay for."

I scoffed. "You would've been discovered."

"That wasn't the only reason you did it. You are obnoxiously heroic, you know that? Quite the show-off."

She phrased it all in the most ridiculous way, but she wasn't exactly wrong. I'd had motives beyond the practical for protecting her body. I said finally, "The whip hurt less than standing by while someone else hurt you."

She huffed a breath of exasperation. "And don't you think it's exactly the same for me, you big oaf?"

"Watch it," I said. "No name calling."

Her hand caressed my skin, which was healed now. "You're so damned stubborn."

"Me?" I sat up, twisting to face her. My exhaustion was rapidly fading into irritation. "You're ridiculous. So determined to be a hero instead of a princess—"

"I don't think I have to choose," she shot back.

"You don't think half the time at all," I told her. "You fixed things for your friend this time. So what? You think she won't be discovered sooner or later?"

Her jaw set and she looked away. She knew that already.

"She doesn't have anywhere else to go," she said softly. "Herrick had her family killed. She'll be killed too, if she's found out."

"So you think you owe her."

"I do owe her. I haven't stopped him." When she turned her wide eyes toward me, I knew she was devastated that she couldn't stop Herrick.

She might have been innocent when she came here, but being emerged into the world of all four courts had stripped that away.

I hesitated. I shouldn't trust a summer Fae with anything so precious about my own court. My first loyalty should always be to them.

And yet...

"I'll take care of her," I promised. "I have connections, Alisa. If things go sideways... I'll get her out of Herrick's grip."

She smiled sadly. "Can you do that for me too?"

"What?" I asked, instantly hot with anger at the thought she was trapped by Herrick.

But that sadness was already gone, chased by mischief. She straddled my lap suddenly, her fingernails biting into the fresh skin that covered my shoulders.

"You promised Vail you'd punish me," she purred into my ear, and I was instantly hard when her lips brushed my cheek. "Are you going to keep your promises, Autumn?"

"Always, Summer."

She was laughing as I fell back on the bed, rolling over with her until I could trap her legs with mine. I smacked the pert curve of her ass, the sound ringing out in the room. I yanked her pants down, revealing the pale orbs that rapidly turned red under my palm, and her laughter turned into little moans and wiggles across the bed.

"Can I distract you?" She rolled over onto her side, reaching for my cock.

"Not yet," I said, rolling her back over and smacking her ass again, hard enough to leave the marks of my fingers across her beautiful skin. She let out a little cry and then wiggled her ass, unable to resist begging for more even as she tried to convince me to stop. "Someone should've done this a long time ago. And regularly. But I'm happy to try to catch you up."

She laughed. "I'll never understand how you can be such a—"

I interrupted her with a flurry of spanks that had her trying to writhe away, but I wrestled her across my lap, pinning her leg with mine to keep her across my knee, where she belonged. With her in that position, I could see her pink, glistening clit and see just how wet she was from her *punishment*. Well, maybe there was more than one way to tame her; maybe the power of orgasms would be good for her attitude.

I aimed a few more smacks at the spots where she sat, determined she'd still feel me as she went about her classes tomorrow. "What did I say about name calling?"

"I was going to say you're *such my favorite*."

"Mm, and lying too." I continued spanking her cheeks, loving the sight of her spread in front of me, the way her bottom turned pink, the way she alternately tried to buck away and waved her ass in front of my face if I paused, wanting more.

I paused, rubbing the overlapping red marks my fingers had left, and she let out a soft moan. That sound always drove me crazy. I ran my fingertips across her inner thighs, caressing her, and her hips bucked, trying to get my fingers against her clit. I laughed and smacked her ass again. "You're so demanding, even when you're in no position to put up a fight."

"I know what I want," she corrected, glancing at me over her shoulder, "and I'm *always* in a position to put up a fight. If anyone thinks I'm not, they're underestimating me."

I grinned at that and lobbed a few more hard smacks at her ass. She buried her face in the sheets, but she was smiling too.

"I'd never underestimate you," I promised, finally releasing her, and she rolled over onto her side. "You're a terrible roommate, but besides that, you're pretty perfect."

She grinned, reaching back to rub her bottom. "I'm the furthest thing from perfect and you know it."

"Not to me," I promised. I pushed her shoulder, knocking her onto her side. She was laughing even as I pressed a kiss to her inner thigh, and then the laughter died as my lips traveled steadily upward.

When I kissed her center, she writhed just a little. I looped my arms around her thighs, holding her still as I ran my tongue across her, lapping up her sweet honey as her fingernails slid back and forth across the sheets. Then I teased my tongue inside her, working my mouth steadily against her clit, and her hands fisted the sheets, yanking them loose.

Her hips began to buck, or try to, but I held her still. She tossed her head, her lips parting, then ran her fingers through her hair, pressing her palms against her head as if she were trying to keep from flying apart.

But of course, I wanted her to come to pieces, and she did. She moaned my name as she began to pulse around me, her body shuddering around my tongue as her orgasm rippled through her body. I was painfully hard, and I was afraid I'd come in my pants from the pleasure of seeing her come for me. She was so beautiful when she was like this, her pale skin flushed with pleasure, her body vulnerable and open and *mine.*

Then she went still, smiling at me. She ran her hand through my hair, and I climbed up to collapse on the bed beside her. My fingers stroked idly over the flat planes of her abs as she lay there, still shuddering with the occasional aftermath of the orgasm.

"You are too good to me, you know that," she said softly.

"No such thing." I kissed her naked shoulder. "You deserve the world, Alisa. And all I can give you..."

I trailed off, because our life together was all secrets and sin.

"All you can give me is all I want," she assured me, capturing my lips with hers. The two of us traded long, slow kisses. Then she settled her head onto my shoulder, the two of us lying together.

"The truth is, Summer, I don't want to be at this academy without you," I whispered into her ear. "And I don't think I want to live without you anywhere."

She looked up at me. "The odds that you and I are going to have a happy ending..."

She trailed off, but I finished it for her. "They aren't good."

"Then let's enjoy now," she said, right before she nipped my earlobe with her teeth, and I had to start all over trying to punish her.

As if Princess Alisa could ever be reformed.

CHAPTER FORTY

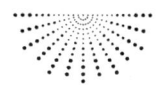

A*zrael*

THE NEXT FEW days passed more-or-less peacefully. Most of the time, I was with Alisa, teaching her royal protocol and history. She was cold, but a conscientious student. She fled as soon as we'd finished our discussion. It made me think of Duncan's accusation that she always ran away.

When I wasn't with her, I was in the library, searching for answers about her magic. The cursed caves were a long, dangerous journey that Faer refused to agree to. He didn't want Alisa to slip that far out of his reach, I was sure.

I wasn't convinced he wanted her to have her memories back at all.

I closed the book I'd been searching through and rubbed my hand over my face. She'd always be a bit helpless as long as she didn't have her memories, and I could see how much that wore on her. I dreaded what would happen when she remembered and she no longer needed us, yet it made me ache to see her suffer at all.

"You look like you need a break."

I startled at Alisa's voice. She stood in the doorway.

"How did you find me?" I asked.

"I only got lost half-a-dozen times," she admitted. "One of the servants finally helped me."

Her brows drew together, her voice changing, when she asked, "Are some of them… humans?"

"Yes," I said. Then, defensively, already knowing it would bother her, I added, "They all came here willingly."

"And can they go back willingly?" she asked, a barb in her voice.

The old Alisa hadn't minded the plight of humans in the Fae world at all. I shook my head. Any evidence she'd changed always left me unsettled. How could I hate her when I caught glimpses of the woman I'd loved, and not the faintest glimmer of the one I'd come to hate?

I leaned back in my chair. "Why are you here?"

She hesitated, then admitted, "I'm tired of fighting with you. How are things with Zora?"

"I sent word for her to go to the Sisters and pretend it was a spontaneous conviction on her part. If she listened… then she's out of danger. Faer respects them and won't take her away." The odds that my sister would actually listen for once worried me, though. If she left the Sisters, then Faer might manage to snatch her away.

She came and perched on the edge of the desk, flipping idly through the pages of one of the books I'd discarded. Her honeysuckle scent teased my nose. The memory of burying my face in her hair, of wrapping her tight in my arms as she laughed and twined her arms around my neck, made me ache.

"You're trying to figure out what happened to me," she said.

"I told you I would."

"I know," she said, but she still said it as if it meant something to her.

She leaned forward, and my lips parted in surprise right before her mouth covered mine.

Her lips were still soft and tender, the perfect counterpoint to the quick blade of her words. Her words could be a lie, but could those lips? I struggled not to believe she meant it when she kissed me, even after everything. My mouth parted against hers, welcoming her in.

She was too far away, leaning in to kiss me when I wanted her body against mine. I reached for her, threading my hand through her soft hair until my hand cupped the back of her head.

That first kiss had been tentative, but now her lips were urgent against mine. My heart quickened, beating so quickly that I could hear it thundering in my ears.

Her skin carried a clear, cool scent, like greenery and mint and honey. The scent reminded me of the clear, cold lake where Alisa and I used to swim. We'd slip away from the academy and swim under the moonlight. It was worth losing sleep to share those stolen moments. Magic warmed our bodies as we swam, the air so cold our breath hung in the air in an icy fog. The shock of a cold bath still jolted sweet memories into my mind.

My arm circled her waist, and I yanked her off the tabletop into my lap. I kissed her back just as fervently, just as wildly, and when the two of us broke apart, we were both short of breath. I kept my arm around her waist, anchoring to me, just for a little longer.

"What brought that on?" I asked, trying to cover how much emotion it stirred for me.

"I had a silly thought," she admitted, tucking her hair back behind her ear. "Sometimes in fairy tales, an enchantment is broken with a kiss, and I thought…"

She trailed off and glanced away across the expansive library, but made no move to escape my lap. After a second, she added, "And also, I wanted to. I've wanted to for a while."

"Oh?"

"It feels like parts of me remember you," she admitted with a small laugh, as if it embarrassed her. Her teeth flashed white, a little sharper than a mortal's now, and I caught her chin with my two fingers and turned her face back to mine.

I kissed her again, greedily. The tip of her tongue teased against my upper lip, and I opened to her. Our tongues swirled together as she kissed me hungrily. My fingers ran through her hair, caught at the back of her head as I held her still.

She moaned against my lips, shifting closer to me, as if desire had swept over her as quickly as it had me. My cock was suddenly, achingly hard. The librarians would disapprove.

It was hard to stop, to pull away, before doing things that the librarians would never recover from. I pressed my lips to her forehead instead, a chaste kiss.

"Do you want me to tell you what I found?" I managed, a hitch in my voice. Facts and myths couldn't do anything to relax the tension that throbbed in my cock right now. But Alisa and I couldn't go any further into our desire.

"Sure," she said, curling against me easily, and despite my best judgment, I held her close.

"I haven't been able to identify the enchantment that stole your memories. I imagine it might be a series of complex spells, because it seems like an almost impossible thing. The magic might have sealed off your brain's pathways to everything you knew before—"

She tensed, but didn't move her head from my shoulder. "That sounds...final."

"I think another spell could unblock those neural pathways," I said. "I just don't know *what* spell."

"That's not your only theory." She looked up at me, hope bright in her eyes.

"No," I admitted. "I think maybe you're under some kind of spell of continuous forgetting. You *do* remember everything, but as soon as it begins to rise in your mind, the enchantment makes you forget. All your memories are in your mind right now—you might be remembering the enchantment itself right now—but the *memory* of remembering is forgotten as soon as it rises."

She was silent for a second. "That gives me a headache just to imagine, Azrael."

"It would take a lot of power," I admitted. It gave me a headache too.

"Faer knows who changed my face." She rested her fingertips lightly on her cheekbone. She pulled away from me, sitting up, although she was still on my lap. I missed her body against mine, but that didn't matter.

"Let me guess. He's holding the knowledge hostage?" I asked. "We can't even trust him to tell you the truth."

"Why does he hate me so much?"

"I don't know. When I visited the summer court as a boy, you two seemed close. You weren't just brother-and-sister, you were best friends."

"I need to know what happened." She sounded determined, and Alisa was always unstoppable once she made up her mind. "Is Faer still refusing to let me travel freely?"

I nodded. There had been no more parties. Faer had insisted his sister was *unwell* and needed to recover. The lie irritated me, but there was nothing I could do about it.

Although thanks to Tiron, who seemed to have a friend everywhere, rumors were spreading about the queen being stronger than ever before. Duncan had shaken his head and grumbled that the two of us were playing a dangerous, senseless game. He insisted we let her go to Raile and be done with it.

As if Faer could be trusted to keep any of his promises.

As if Alisa would *just go* to the gown fittings, the wedding, the undersea, like an obedient princess.

As if the three of us would be able to bear her being forced.

Nothing about my life had been simple since I met Alisa, that day in the forest outside the academy when I discovered who she truly was.

I pushed all that aside for now. "I'm sorry it's not better news. It might be a perilous journey, but I think the answer might still be in the caves, as the Delphin said."

"Then we should go there." Then, after a second, she said, "It's good to have a familiar face here, Azrael. An old friend. Even if I don't remember you. Thank you."

"Don't thank me." Guilt and regret twisted through my gut. But I had to say something else, something true but sweet. "I'd do almost anything for you, Alisa."

Almost anything.

But my top priority was still freeing the autumn court from Faer's clutches.

If I could just restore her memories, she'd be the same person again, the woman who wasn't worth throwing away a kingdom for. Wouldn't she?

The question haunted me, because the girl who lay her head against my heart now?

I knew I truly would do *anything* for her, all over again.

CHAPTER FORTY-ONE

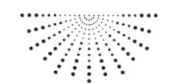

A *lisa*

WHEN I LEFT AZRAEL, I was reluctant. Faer had asked me to have lunch with him privately. I felt more comfortable with Azrael or Tiron by my side. Hell, maybe I was even happier with Duncan by my side, even though he growled insults at me.

At least it was a chance to press Faer on the Cursed Caves. He'd been avoiding me. I wasn't going to bemoan the recent lack of parties, but I knew he had his own motives.

But when I walked out onto Faer's balcony, he wasn't alone. Raile was with him.

"Why are you dressed like that?" Faer frowned. "Well, never mind. Raile's never minded your quirks."

"Or yours," Raile told him, which almost made me smile.

The table was set for three, out on the balcony. It was blindingly bright out here with the sun reflecting off the ocean, and a crisp wind kept ruffling the tablecloth up so that it almost covered the plates.

"Raile is more comfortable out here," Faer said, as if he recognized my unspoken question. "Closer to the sea."

"Right," I said. "You're from the sea court?"

Raile nodded. He pulled my chair out for me, and I sat awkwardly. I'd been on some dates in the human world, and no one had pulled my chair out for me. My dates had been more *pay-for-your-own-burrito*, then *hey-want-to-give-me-a-blowjob*. They had not prepared me for the niceties of the Fae world.

"How long are you staying here?" I raised my cup to my lips and sipped something sweet and unfamiliar, the action covering up my nerves. I found Raile unnerving—sexy, but unnerving.

"I'll need to go home and tend some matters soon," Raile said. "I thought perhaps you'd come with me."

I almost snorted whatever-Fae-fruit-juice-this-was out of my nose. "Why would you think that?"

"Raile," Faer said, "Perhaps this isn't the time."

"I would like you to marry me," Raile said.

Faer pinched the bridge of his nose with two fingers.

"I would like to not marry anyone," I said. My fingers were suddenly so tense on the goblet I thought I might shatter it. I looked to Faer, my voice coming out barbed when I demanded, "Brother?"

"You are a princess," he said. "You'll have to marry someone, for the good of the kingdom."

"Why don't you marry Raile, then?" I demanded. "You'll also have to marry, won't you?"

"An alliance with the sea court is essential to final victory for the summer court," Faer said, as if I hadn't offered a perfectly reasonable solution. "Otherwise, our enemies can attack us by sea."

"An *alliance* sounds lovely. Great idea. There's no reason I need to wear a white gown and carry flowers down the aisle with this dickwad—no offense, Raile—for us to form an alliance."

I'd probably just failed all of Azrael's princess lessons in one paragraph.

"You don't need to wear a white gown," Raile said, his tone reasonable. "You just need to come with me to the undersea."

"The undersea," I repeated. I rose from my seat, pushing away from the table. The wind whipped my hair into my face as I reeled, trying to figure out what to say. "I won't marry anyone."

"You will," Faer said, his voice laced with steel. "Not today or tomorrow, but you are a princess. And Raile is patient."

"I've already waited five years," he said.

"Charming." My hands shook with rage. "Why do you even want to marry me?"

A smile twisted Raile's lips. Faer leaned toward him, shaking his head.

But Raile ignored him.

"Revenge," Raile told me, the word falling heavily between us.

And I thought relationships were fucked-up in the mortal world.

"Stay away from me," I told him, my voice tight with fury. "I won't marry you, it doesn't matter how patient you are."

"You will," Raile called as I headed for the doors to Faer's apartment. "You promised yourself to me, and I to you, long ago. There's nothing stopping us from finding love, Princess Alisa."

"You're a madman!" I shouted before I ducked through the doors.

"You made me that way!" he yelled back, rising from the table. "With your tricks! With your cruelty!"

Then I was gone, running through the long marble antechamber and back through the maze of halls. I should've run to someplace private, to my own quarters, someplace I could think.

Instead, my feet carried me to the library where I'd found Azrael earlier.

I threw open the door and barged in. He looked up from his book, then rose, his face clouding as he took in my expression. I glimpsed Tiron and Duncan, who must have joined him in his search for answers, but neither of them mattered to me now. I was fixed on Azrael.

"You absolute *asshole*," I told him, right before I punched him across the face.

He stumbled back, catching himself against the shelves of books. I was already swinging for him again, but he didn't let the second blow land; he ducked to one side, trying to catch my arm, but he and I were pretty evenly matched, except for his greater size. He kept trying to parry my blows, because he wouldn't strike me, but I wanted him to.

Hit me back, Azrael. Hurt me. You can't hurt me any worse than you already have.

"What is it exactly that you are accusing me of?" he demanded, as if I were the crazy one in this situation.

"You know that Faer brought me back here to marry Raile!" I exploded. "You let me think the Fae needed me. That I was supposed to come back here and rule. Instead, you brought me back for what—to be a slave in the undersea?"

"Don't be dramatic." He ducked a book as I threw it at him.

I ripped another off the shelf. I *was* being dramatic—and childish—but the hurt that tightened my chest felt as if it would crush me.

"No," Duncan egged me on, "Be dramatic. He *is* an asshole."

"Stop helping," Azrael warned him, glancing over my shoulder at him.

"Oh, I'm not helping." Duncan grinned.

"I told you I appreciated your friendship." My eyes widened at my own stupidity as I lashed out at Azrael again, who just barely danced around the table, evading me. "I kissed you! Like an idiot. And you let me kiss you."

Even Duncan wasn't smiling now. He shook his head.

"I'm sorry," Azrael said, and this time, maybe on purpose, he didn't duck when I hit him. My fist slammed into his jaw, knocking him backward against the shelves. The shelf rocked, and Tiron rushed to steady it. Books rained down from the shelves, and Azrael raised his arms to cover his head as they slammed into him and fell to the floor.

I shook my hand out. My knuckles ached. I didn't feel any better.

Azrael faced me, his eyes wary, as he rubbed his jaw with one hand.

"I hate you," I whispered, but the room had gone so quiet I could be heard in any corner. "You could have told me what Raile was plotting that first night, didn't you? But you didn't. You said you'd keep me from looking foolish, but you're the one who played me for a fool."

I stalked for the door, ignoring how miserable Azrael looked. Tiron started to follow me, but Duncan grabbed his arm.

"You don't deserve anything else, Princess," Duncan called after me. "You don't remember that, but we do."

Then he muttered, almost to himself, "At least, we do at times."

"You know what?" I spun in the doorway. *"Bullshit.* I call bullshit on that. I know who I am, and I'm not the villain you want to paint me. That's just a lie you tell yourself because it means you don't owe me a damn thing—that you don't have to be anything but villains yourselves."

Then I ran to my chambers, my leather slippers whispering over the marble floors. The sound raised what might have been the thinnest thread of memory—running like this as a child, Faer pursuing me, both of us laughing.

Or maybe it was just my imagination.

Whatever it was, it had me crying as soon as I slammed the door between the Fae world and myself.

I wasn't going to stay here. Not for long. Not lost in my tears, and not trapped in my gilded cage.

This princess was going to save herself.

CHAPTER FORTY-TWO

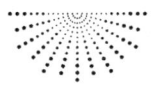

A*lisa*

THERE WAS a rustling sound at my window. I whirled to find Tiron floating outside my window, with a self-satisfied grin spread across his face.

I ran to the stone arch that formed the window. Beautiful iridescent white wings spread to either side of his body.

"You look like an angel," I said.

He laughed at that, then reached out to grab the edge of the arch. "Not quite. Look out."

I stepped to one side as he thrust his legs inside, letting his momentum carry him inside as his wings snapped back into his body. His upper body was bare, and his powerful shoulders and lean abs rippled with the motion.

He took a few quick steps to catch himself, before shoving one hand in his pocket. The movement brought the two of us close together, and the clean pine-and-snow scent of his body washed over me. My nostrils flared before I could resist the impulse, eager to breathe in more of him.

"Show-off," I accused him.

"I'm just showing you what you can do, Princess." He winked at me. "Time to reclaim those wings."

I hesitated. "Do Duncan and Azrael know you're here?"

He shook his head.

"Are you going to get in trouble?"

He grinned, the corners of his green eyes crinkling, and I felt silly for asking.

"Would Duncan try to kick my ass if he knew where I was?" he asked lightly. "Absolutely. Do I care?"

The mischievous look on his face suggested that he did not, in fact, care. Warmth lit my chest. It felt good to have someone on my side.

"That conversation... with Azrael..." I began. I didn't want him to choose between his friends and me.

"Azrael's..." he hesitated. "Azrael is a good man. But he's got some baggage, Alisa. He lost a lot..."

"I know." I managed a smile. "If I were him, I think I'd hate myself for forgetting."

Sometimes I hated Azrael for remembering.

"That's not your fault." Tiron sounded sure about it. He shifted, as if he were about to reach out and touch me, then tucked his hands behind his back.

"No, but..." I stared out the window at the bright reflection of the sinking sun off the ocean. "Whoever I was before... maybe I deserved what happened. What if whoever took my memories and shoved me through that portal is the actual hero of this story? What if I'm the villain here, Tiron? Just as much as Faer..."

"You're nothing like Faer." The words exploded out of him, surprising us both.

He cleared his throat. I was still staring at him, reeling from the power in his voice. His fire lit a spark of warmth in my chest. It was nice someone believed in me in a palace where everyone saw me as either weak or dangerous.

He stepped up easily into the window, and the light framed his tall powerful body. He held his hand out to me.

Apparently Tiron was the master of the subject change.

"Fly with me."

"Promise I won't fall." I put my hand in his.

His hands were warm and firm, calloused across the palms and the knuckles. They didn't feel like the hands of a nobleman, not even a sixth son.

He pulled me easily up onto the windowsill beside him and wrapped his big arm around my waist. I was suddenly pulled against all those lean, hard muscles that rippled against my body with his motion.

He grinned at me. "Falling is just a part of flying. You can't have one without the other."

He let himself fall back.

I closed my eyes, holding back a scream. The two of us tumbled toward the ocean, and a splash of cold water slammed into my feet. I opened my eyes in shock, just in time to see Tiron's wings shimmering around him. His wings beat, and the two of us shot up through the air.

He held me close as we flew back and forth over the white-capped waves, as the sunk sank low beneath the ocean. Once I was sure that we weren't going to die, I couldn't hold back a giddy laugh.

The two of us swooped to shore and he landed lightly, still holding me tightly in his arms. My toes touched the sand, but I didn't unloop my arms from his waist. Instead, the two of us lingered there at the edge of the sea, as night fell around us.

"Ready to fall?" he teased me.

"I don't even remember having wings," I confessed. "I'm not sure how to…"

I glanced over my shoulder at the empty space.

"If you don't want to shred your clothes you might want to…" he trailed off. "Not that clothes matter to you, you can always get new ones…"

Of course fairies flew half-naked most of the time. They were so comfortable in their skins, so different than humans.

"No," I said. "It's all right, I'll..."

"Of course." His words were smooth but his eyes had gone wide, as if he hadn't just seen me naked in the pool earlier that week.

I pulled the simple black tunic over my head and held it gripped loosely in one hand. He kept his gaze fixed determinedly on my face, but a muscle ticked in his jaw, as if the act physically hurt him. I hid a smile.

Was I a terrible person for enjoying the way these males reacted to me?

I didn't think so, especially when I felt the same wayward impulses.

He rested his hands on my shoulders. "Your wings were probably hidden by your enchantment—it would have been pretty awkward if you'd unfurled them on a city bus or in a Burger King or on a date—but they've been there all along. You just need to call on them."

His own wings suddenly unfurled, with a quick *pop* at first, followed by a slower curl as they spread to their full, immense size.

He stared at me, the cool, salty breeze ruffling his blond hair. He looked as if he expected my wings to emerge just as easily. I closed my eyes, imagining my wings unfurling to either side, how it might hurt as they ripped out of my back.

Nothing happened.

I opened my eyes again. "That was incredibly non-specific. Just so you know. You're not going to be recruited to write a book on flying for dummies anytime soon."

"Was it?" He grinned.

Something hung over us both. I looked up to see my wings—luminous, lavender wings dappled with gold and silver. They were so beautiful they took my breath away. I raised a hand to run it over the curve of my wing, and sensation fluttered through my wing, down my shoulder, all through my body—a sudden, intense sense that seemed to strike all the way to my core.

"I should tell you," he said suddenly, "Fae don't touch each other's wings...not without permission. Just as a matter of etiquette."

"Why?" I asked.

"Our wings are so sensitive. It's incredibly erotic... as intimate as a kiss."

He was still standing close to me. His defined jawline and his beautiful lips—a plush lower lip, a pronounced bow in the top—were in my line of vision, and I could barely draw my gaze away from him.

"How do I learn to use these things?" I asked, forcing myself to look away from him before I gave into impulse and kissed him.

He shifted ever-so-subtly closer to me as I started to speak, then paused, and suddenly I had regrets. I shouldn't have distracted Tiron from the subject of kissing.

I looked out over the immense dark of the ocean now. The sea in front of us seemed to be mirrored by the sea of brilliant stars above. Clusters of luminescent flowers floated on the waves, and the tide was a constant soft rush.

"You trust me," he said softly. "Falling is part of the game, but I won't let you get hurt."

"I do," I said, the words quick and glib. I didn't trust easily.

All my life—that I remembered—I'd carried the weight of that note. *You don't have any friends.* I'd let the Hunters into my life, carefully. I loved being with Elly, Carter, Julian and the other Hunters. I laughed at their boisterous drinking and the casual Hunter's code that involved a lot of fighting and flirting and... well. I trusted them to watch my back. I thought of them as friends.

I'd taken time—a long time—to grow that comfortable with them all, though. What I felt when I was close to Tiron was... different. Intense.

But I had to trust him to learn to fly. I told myself that the way I was acting made sense, even though it felt very....un-Alisa.

Tiron gripped my hand in his. "Trust yourself," he murmured. "You knew how to do this. Deep inside, you do."

"Unless the enchantment that blocks my memories could also cause me to plummet to my death," I said lightly. "Well, let's do this."

"Beat your wings," he said. "You should feel the contraction in your shoulders."

Sure enough, I felt a ripple through my shoulder muscles and then beyond. I frowned in concentration, continuing to beat my wings.

He was smirking at me.

"What?" I demanded.

He didn't answer me. He just glanced down.

At the dark ocean, far below our feet.

CHAPTER FORTY-THREE

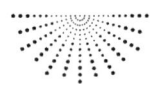

Tiron

ALISA WAS ALWAYS BEAUTIFUL, but when that smile of wonder lit her face as she was limned by the moonlight, she was so gorgeous that my chest ached.

The two of us flew together over the ocean, swooping back and forth.

When we landed and she'd pulled her shirt back on, she said, "It was good to see the city from above. I hate that I don't remember anything about my own kingdom."

"You know, you and Azrael have more in common than you realize." Azrael cared so intently about the autumn court; I knew it was painful for him to stay away from his people and the autumn court lands. But he felt they were safer without him, given Faer's attention.

She groaned. "Do we have to talk about Azrael? It feels like my life revolves around Azrael. *Will Azrael help me? How does Azrael feel today?*

What stupid one-line insults will he deliver if I ask him to fill in my memory?"

Color lingered in her cheeks; the mere mention of Azrael seemed to leave her heated. Perhaps in more ways than one.

"We don't have to talk about Azrael," I said slowly, "but you seem like you need to."

She shook her head, then tucked her hand through my arm. "You know, you give excellent side-eye."

"Just one of the many services I provide." I patted her hand over my forearm, enjoying just being close to her. "Let's go see your city, Alisa."

The city stretched across the hill above us. On the other side lay the forest. We padded barefoot through the thick sand, then stepped onto the cobblestone street. Flowering trees and low stone walls separated the city from the docks and its buildings and the faint fishy scent underlying the clean salt breeze. Between the fragrant flowers and the sea, the aroma in the air seemed to change every time the wind shifted.

As we wandered through the city that lay beyond the castle's gates, Alisa looked around curiously, and regret washed over me. She was all but trapped in that castle. We had to find a way to rescue her.

At night, the city was vibrant and loud; most of the low Fae were nocturnal. They had to adapt to the preferred working hours of the high Fae, but they stayed awake late in the night.

The cobblestone streets shone under the moonlight, and awnings decorated the rows of small, colorfully painted shops with apartments above.

At this time of evening, the low Fae owned the streets. A pair of female goblins loped past us arm-in-arm, their long, quivering ears pierced a dozen times and decorated with hoops.

A troll stomped by, his toothy face irritated. He passed a family of wood sprites, who appeared to be carved out of wood. Despite being almost all leg, with long arms dangling from their knotted bodies, they moved at a slow, languorous pace. Somehow the wood nymph children moved even slower than their parents, falling slowly behind until their parents turned to whisper at them. Then they managed to lope a little faster to catch up.

Alisa smiled at the sight. "I guess not much changes between worlds."

"I don't know if that's a comforting thought or a terrifying one." I glanced up and down the street, then squeezed her hand. "Let's get you a disguise before someone recognizes you."

"How are you going to disguise this?" she said, tugging on the ends of her long lavender hair—hair that symbolized to all just who she and Faer were.

"Trust me, I'm resourceful."

"I know you're *resourceful,* and that's exactly why I wonder sometimes how trustworthy you are," she teased.

I felt a jolt at her words, even though she was just being glib.

I pulled her into a shop. Clothes hung from pegs all over the walls and were stacked up on tables; mannequins with eerie, enormous eyes stared blankly into the distance as they modeled gowns.

"We need to cover up all this hair," I murmured, picking up a red hood embroidered with gold thread and seed pearls.

She looked at me skeptically. "I don't know what to make of that. The shape says *nun,* but the colors say *mardi gras.*"

"Nun, huh?" I picked up the gauzy wisp of red that went with it as a shirt.

"If I can dress myself, I'll take it." She swiped it from me.

The two of us pulled a few things for her to try on, then as the shopkeeper left her counter in the back and headed down the aisle, I pushed Alisa through the curtain into the dressing room. I didn't want anyone to know who she truly was.

She emerged a few minutes later, a bemused smile on her face. Every bit of her hair was hidden by the cowl, but her shoulders and flat stomach were exposed by the wisps of red fabric that clung to her body like flames. Matching pants hung low on her hips, the satiny fabric loose and flowing.

"These feel like fancy pajamas," she said. "So comfy and easy to move in. If I weren't afraid I'd accidentally flash someone, this would be a great Hunting outfit."

"If your prey is male, it might help you get the jump on them," I managed.

We each picked out a pair of shoes since we'd gone barefoot. Once we paid, we headed out into the night. Street vendors were roasting food over fires as we neared the main square, and the scent of smoking meat and toasting nuts filled the air.

Raucous fiddle music played loudly from the square, and Alisa groaned at the sound. "I've had enough of parties for a lifetime."

"No *party* with Faer is much of a celebration," I said. "Just come see."

I held out my hand, and I felt oddly gratified when she gave me a skeptical smile and clasped my fingers with hers.

"What are they celebrating?" she asked.

"Does there need to be something to celebrate?" I asked. "Life is hard around here. Maybe the harder life is, the more desperate we become for whatever joy we can find."

Her mouth opened, but I didn't want to answer the question that might form on those beautiful lips.

"Dance with me," I said, tugging her toward me. She might look at me skeptically, but she still let me pull her close and slip my arm around her waist. I reminded her, "Azrael kept me away from all those parties. Let me dance with you now."

She came with me as I danced her across the cobblestones, moving ever closer to the music, but the expression on her face was pensive.

"Why did Azrael keep you away? *Really?*" she asked, a frown creasing between her brows.

I hated for her to think badly of Azrael. Maybe she shouldn't trust him—or any of us—completely. But Azrael was one of the best Fae I'd ever met.

"Faer barely tolerates me," I admitted. "Because I come from the Winter court, he doesn't trust me. Azrael has always protected me in the past, but now he's just about all out of favors, all out of influence."

"Because of you?"

I winced at her blunt words. "Yes, I suppose so. That's part of why Duncan misses the front so much. In a strange way, it felt safer for us all there."

"It's not just because Duncan lives to tear things apart with his bare hands?"

"Well, you know we don't have television here," I said.

The two of us emerged from the street and the shadows of the towering buildings around us into the square.

"He grows on you, you know," I said quietly. "He's gruff and mean, but he'd do anything for the people he cares about."

"I can see that," she said, "but it's not much of a redeeming feature unless you're one of those people."

She was one of those people, no matter how hard Duncan tried to pretend she wasn't. But that was something they both needed to figure out for themselves.

Still, when the two of us began to dance, she seemed to lose herself for a while in the whirling crowd. Horns and tails and faces both monstrous and beautiful flashed behind her, but once she began to smile, I could barely register anything but her face. Her body was warm and lithe against mine, the music bright, and for a few moments, nothing mattered but the two of us and the way our bodies moved in easy rhythm together.

When the two of us finally stumbled out of the crowd, I felt lighter than I had in years, with my arm around her waist.

"Let's buy something to drink," I began, then felt someone loom ahead of me. I pulled my gaze away from Alisa's laughing face and stared right into a belly-button. An enormous expanse of white belly floated in front of me.

I looked up to find a snow troll.

The snow troll. Gior, the only snow troll who was both smart enough to survive and foolish enough to live openly in summer court territory.

Now wasn't an awesome time, not with Alisa.

He stared down at me with that surly expression on his face that all trolls had, no matter the occasion. I shook my head, trying to warn him off.

Gior looked at Alisa, cocking his head to one side. His body swung as he looked back at me. He looked again at Alisa. The frown-lines of confusion that ran across his enormous forehead puckered deeper than usual.

"This one is pretty," he said to me. "Why?"

"Why what?" she asked sharply.

"Why are you with him?"

Her tension evaporated like the morning mist, and she laughed. "We're not together."

Gior let out a low grumble that could have meant just about anything. I didn't particularly want to find out what.

"I'd love to catch up," I told Gior, "but Al…ah, *Alandra*… and I have plans tonight. We should talk soon!"

I caught Alisa's narrow wrist and began to pull her past him. Gior lagged for a second; he was always slow to move that big body around. I wondered how he had possibly survived the butchering of the winter court.

But before I could go far, his big hand settled on my shoulder, and my knees buckled as if I'd just been slammed with a shovel.

Alisa swung around, stepping into a fighting stance, ready to fight for me. It was oddly touching, but I knew Gior didn't mean any harm. He gripped my shoulder so I wouldn't fall.

"Sorry, sorry," he said. "I always forget how flimsy you bird-fairies are."

"Not bird-fairies," I disagreed.

"Bug fairies," he tried again.

"What do you want, Gior?" I demanded, then realized I shouldn't have asked that.

I was in trouble if Gior spoke openly in front of Alisa. He meant well, but it wasn't his nature to be guarded.

Trolls didn't bother with deception; they usually worked out their problems with more of a *smashing* technique.

"Two winter troll cubs," he began.

I shook my head frantically; I'd have slapped my hand over his big meaty jaw if I could've reached it. "Not here."

"It has to be now," he grumbled. "They're out of time."

Alisa looked at me curiously.

"Okay, okay," I said. "I'll take care of it. Where are they?"

I wished I could meet with him secretly instead of asking in front of Alisa, but the odds weren't good I could sneak out of the castle again tonight.

He checked our surroundings, his knuckles dragging the cobblestone as his body swung. I pinched the bridge of my nose; trolls make terrible spies. But he was brave enough to go against Faer and his cronies to protect our court. I couldn't fault him for that.

Although, as I watched him slowly try to maneuver his body in a circle, there were plenty of other things I faulted him for.

I said, "Out with it, Gior. By the time you finish looking around, there'll be a squad of kings' guard behind you."

It was the wrong thing to say. He stopped to turn around completely, revolving slowly in front of us.

Meanwhile, Alisa eyed me curiously. I didn't want her to have any inklings of my true identity, but Gior's request was a pretty inconvenient clue.

Gior finally finished his runway turn and leaned in to whisper, "The old north den."

The scent of rotted fish washed over me along with the hot whisper, and I winced. "All right, Gior. I'll take care of them. Don't go back there. I worry you're being watched."

He winked at me, but whenever Gior winked, it took both eyes.

"Goodbye, friend," I briefly clasped his arm—and staggered as his big hand wrapped around mine with too much force—then finally, finally managed to break away.

Alisa let me take her hand as we walked through streets that seemed even busier now, even though the moon was at its peak, full and bright like a coin above us.

"Tiron," she said sweetly as soon as we started down a quiet side street, "I have some questions."

"I don't have any answers for you, Princess," I told her, but I already knew that answer wouldn't fly.

CHAPTER FORTY-FOUR

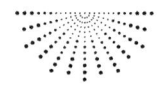

A*lisa*

I STOPPED AND FACED TIRON, chewing my lower lip. His mind was obviously racing, even though he offered me that usual easy handsome smile when he told me that he didn't have any answers.

Because he didn't trust me.

Clearly, he was trying to protect those trolls from his own court, which had almost been destroyed. We didn't know each other well. It made sense that he didn't trust me…not with the shreds of his kingdom.

"Okay," I said. "Is there some trick to getting back into the castle? Or can I fly back on my own?"

His eyes widened in surprise. "That's not happening. I'll… I'll fly you home."

"Okay."

He glanced at me as we headed down the streets toward the docks, the scent of the sea growing ever sharper and more pungent. The air between us felt thick with tension.

"What are you up to, Alisa?" he asked finally.

"Nothing. Looking forward to going home and curling up, drinking some—" I cut myself off as I realized I was down a maid, and every time I left my room I found myself in trouble, and I lived in a world without Diet Coke now. "Tea, I guess. If I'm lucky."

I missed my crappy little apartment and Wi-Fi and grocery shopping and doing whatever the hell I wanted, without having the entire summer court judging my every movement.

But I wasn't going to try to go back, even though I missed the human world. Something was very wrong; Tiron was trying to help those trolls because my kingdom had turned rotten.

I understood if he didn't trust me. But one day, I was going to earn his trust.

He glanced at me sharply. "It's that easy? I have that very weird conversation with the troll—although to be honest, there's no *other* kind of conversation to have with a troll—and you just smile and move on? What are you really up to, Alisa?"

"Oh my god." Males, no matter the species, were impossible. "You don't want me to pry, correct? So here I am. *Not prying*. Or did you want a different response?"

He was still frowning, so I decided to try the different response out for size and see how he liked them. I caught his arm and told him, "Tiron, don't you dare leave me out. I insist on going with you and helping you."

His frown deepened. He was beginning to look as confused as the troll.

"What do you want from me?" I demanded, letting go of him so I could spread my arms in exasperation.

"I don't know," he admitted. Then he shook his head slowly, a smile crossing those lush, kissable lips. "You're not what I expected."

"Isn't that a good thing?" Even though Duncan made it clear he didn't expect the new Alisa to last.

"Maybe, maybe not." One corner of his lips lifted. "Maybe my life would be easier if you were the villain, Alisa."

"Don't you mean, *Ah-Alandra?*"

His smile widened into something real. "Never going to let me live that down, are you?"

"Never," I promised him. "You're usually so smooth. It was kind of nice to see your human side."

He huffed a laugh at that, and I said, "You know what I mean."

"Come on, we've got a journey ahead of us," he said. "And we have to make it back to the castle before Duncan comes looking for us to train in the morning."

I could have groaned at the thought of facing Duncan's quips—and the stinging flat blade of Duncan's practice sword—without any rest. But a warm glow spread through my chest, and I held my tongue. Tiron wanted me with him.

"Lead on," I said.

The city gates rose ahead of us, closed; the shadowy figures of two guards stood in front of them. I followed Tiron's gaze to spot enormous winged Fae squatting on top of the walls, so still that at first I mistook them for statues. Maybe we could fly over the sea undetected, but I supposed it would take us a while. I glanced at Tiron curiously, but he pulled me to one side down an alleyway.

"There's an aqueduct," he told me, opening a door covered with ornate scrollwork in the side of a building.

"Are you sure it's not a sewer?"

His grin spread. "Travel with me and you'll only ever travel in style, Princess."

His infectious smile was impossible not to resist, no matter where he took me. I followed his broad shoulders as he led the way down unending circular steps. We descended into darkness, and I heard a low, constant rush of water. At least it smelled no worse than the sea.

It grew dark enough that I had to feel with my toes for each step. Tiron muttered a word, and a ball of light formed in his palm. He said another word, and the ball of light shot upward and followed us, illuminating our path.

If I couldn't trust Tiron, if he had some grudge against me, I could die down here.

The thought came to my mind once—I was a Hunter, after all—and then I dismissed it. I was taking a risk, but my gut said Tiron was a friend.

Why would I trust a note from the same person who stole my memories and shoved me out of my world, anyway? The note nagged at me. Why would my enemy want to make sure I knew my name and that I could defend myself? Had it been someone close to me—someone who still cared about me?

There were just a few names on that list.

Tiron raised his hand, white sparks forming at his fingertips. The water ahead of us froze, forming a long trail that led down the tunnel ahead of us. He held his other hand out to me, and I wrapped my fingers around his.

"Winter court powers?" I asked.

"Being the sixth son might mean I don't inherit material things, but it didn't change what kind of *magic* I inherited."

"I need to learn about my summer magic." The ice was slick under my slippers, but Tiron seemed surefooted, so I matched his pace. I knew he'd catch me if I started to slip. "I know Azrael can't teach me much without getting on the wrong side of Faer. Maybe I can find a tutor from the summer court."

Somehow. Even though I didn't know who to trust here.

"I don't know summer magic," he said, "But I'll teach you what I can, Alisa."

He taught me the words to his light spell as we walked along the icy path. The sound of water rushing underfoot and the constant crackle of the ice breaking apart faded as I focused.

Warmth swept over my skin as I formed the words. The light that blossomed in my hand was so bright I closed my eyes, and the sound of cracking ice was suddenly loud in my ears.

"Things I learned today," Tiron said hastily. "Summer magic is hot."

I tossed my ball of light into the air the same way he had, and the two of us ran as the ice began to crack apart under our feet. He muttered his spell again, magic sparking at his fingertips, as he began to try to heal our icy path underneath our feet.

The ice broke apart between us, and he leapt onto my ice floe, which rocked under his weight. He grabbed me close, pulling me against all that ropy muscle. The tunnel was too narrow for his wings, but suddenly the water was all ice around us again.

"Wrong place to practice," I said with a laugh.

He was still holding me tight, and he made no move to pull away.

"I'm a terrible teacher," he murmured. "Don't tell Azrael."

"Your secrets are safe with me," I promised.

I meant that promise in every way, and I hoped he knew that.

I couldn't imagine anything I'd find in my memories that would change how I felt.

"I know," he said.

The ice rocked underfoot, our bodies swaying with the movement of the water that still rushed underneath. There were little flecks of silver and gold in his emerald green eyes.

His hand on my one hip was icy cold, tingling through the fabric of my pants, and the other hand felt warm. Tiron was more complicated than the handsome, cheerful knight he'd seemed at first glance. But I didn't mind that. I was complicated too.

His lips were so near mine, and I thought he was going to lean in and kiss me. My breath froze in my chest. I wanted him so badly.

He shifted subtly closer to me, his hands pressing my hips against his.

Then he let out a groan, dropping his forehead against mine. "You know we shouldn't be doing any of this."

I pulled away so I could look up at him, studying his face. "Why not?"

No matter what he said, his hands were still on my body. "We snuck out of the castle for flying lessons and now... what I'm doing is treason in Faer's eyes, Alisa."

"Who said he's the king of the summer court?"

"He does," he said dryly.

"Which part is treason?" I asked. "Saving the trolls? Or..."

I was going to say *kissing me.*

"Both. I had tried to hide my Winter roots when I came here, and when I was uncovered…" He trailed off at the memories, then resumed his usual brightness. "Azrael's burned through all his goodwill. I'm supposed to keep my head down and stay out of trouble."

"But you can't," I filled in. He couldn't do that any more than I could have left that girl in the kitchen.

"I can't." He ran his thumb over my cheekbone, tucking a strand of hair behind my ear. "I'm not allowed to help winter prisoners out of summer to safety. And I'm definitely not allowed to fall in love with the summer princess."

Somehow those words felt like a weight, and yet at the same time, my chest was light with the same freedom I felt when we flew.

"You better get to know me before you fall in love with me," I warned him. "Apparently I don't even know myself."

"I don't think that's true, Alisa." His gaze lingered on mine, then fell to my lips.

I'd always known how to take what I wanted from men—not that I'd wanted much—but now suddenly, I felt lost.

He abruptly pulled himself away, but it seemed like an effort.

"Let's get to work," I said lightly. "Treason isn't going to commit itself."

We left the culvert outside the city, emerging into the moon-soaked woods. We journeyed toward a cave, but on our way, Tiron paused.

The two of us tilted our heads as we listened to the hush that had suddenly fallen over the forest. Were we being hunted by the king's men?

Then Tiron suddenly dragged me into the shadow of a fallen tree, his arm closing around my waist. The two of us crouched there in the darkness, hiding among the tangled roots and the scent of damp earth. The forest had gone silent, as if there were some kind of terrible predator here with us. Even the cats and the wolves had fled to their dens.

Tiron breathed a spell, the words all but silent on his tongue. I felt the rise and fall of his chest as the two of us pressed close together, huddling like children. Slowly, as the minutes dripped by in silence, the fear melted away. I began to feel ridiculous.

Then something cold rippled over my skin. Tiron bowed his head, pressing his cheek against mine, and I closed my eyes, trying to trust him even though every nerve in my body screamed that we were in terrible danger, we should run.

Something eerie seemed to pass by us. It was a ripple in the darkness, something made of nightmares, and fear prickled over my skin as if my body knew that threat, even if my mind didn't understand. Suddenly I didn't feel ridiculous for hiding anymore. A hard knot pressed into the base of my throat. I couldn't breathe, but at least I couldn't scream.

The thing in the shadows moved like a man, an enormously tall and slender man, but it was unnaturally silent. It turned suddenly, and I caught a glimpse of red eyes, a gaping mouth that could almost swallow a person whole. It stared around, nostrils flaring, as if it could scent us.

Then it began to move forward again, and disappeared quickly into the shadows.

We stayed there, holding each other close, in the shadow of that tree for a long while. My muscles tensed from the cold, then began to shake.

Then Tiron whispered, "I covered us both in cold so he wouldn't feel us here. I'm sorry."

"What was that?" I pressed my hands to my shivering arms, imagined summer magic, and the cold fled in an instant. I pressed my hands against his face, and as warmth went through him, he relaxed.

"The Shadow Man," he whispered. "I never knew he was real for sure. I thought he was a myth the Fae made us to scare children..."

"Does the Shadow Man live in the woods to eat naughty children?" I asked lightly, thinking of all those cautionary fairy tales parents use to scare their children into good behavior.

I'd never felt anything like I'd felt when the Shadow Man passed by. It felt as if evil clung to my skin, and I wanted to scrub it away.

"No," he said, his face troubled. "According to the stories, at least, when the Shadow Man hunts, he's bound to one person...one victim."

He studied me as if he thought I was that victim. My throat tightened with fear as if I could still feel the Shadow Man's eerie presence, but I pushed it down.

"We'd better get to those trolls," I said. "How many hours do you think we have left until dawn? Duncan will want to torment us..."

"We're going back to the castle," he said. "You're not wandering around the woods with that... thing...out here. The summer court needs you alive."

"And I need the one friend I have," I said. "So shut up and let's *move*."

CHAPTER FORTY-FIVE

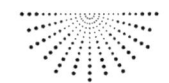

A*zrael*

S*even years* earlier

I*t was almost* the end of the year at the academy. Winter's grip had faded, and the days were becoming long. We were camping on the slopes overlooking the academy.

It was safe again these days. For some reason, the monsters that plagued this territory had all vanished.

I was chopping wood for our fire when sudden chaos erupted on the edge of camp. I'd glimpsed Alisa and Rowen together, as they so often were; summer and winter as best friends. As I headed over, it was no surprise to me that they were in trouble together, too.

But then Galic tore away Rowen's tunic. Rowen fought back, Alisa shoving Galic away. As I broke into a run, the fabric ripped, revealing the tight compressive wrap binding Rowen's chest.

"There's a girl among us," Galic shouted, pointing at Rowen.

"Which is novel. But there have always been weaklings among us," I said, which earned Galic's glare.

A crowd gathered. Alisa had already scooped to pick up Rowen's shirt, which she quickly dressed in.

But it was too late. The damage was done.

"Did you know?" Galic hissed.

"No," I said. Alisa and I had kept our secrets from each other—but only the small ones. It was better if I didn't know for sure who the other girl was at the academy.

"The punishment for impersonating a student here is death," Galic snarled.

"Hold on," I said, glancing down the hill at the academy below. I could run for Vail, but the odds weren't good that I could get back before Galic managed to carry out whatever revenge he was plotting. He'd use Rowen to hurt Alisa, and Alisa to reach me. "That's an old rule, but there's no reason to think that Vail would order an execution."

"You're always so interested in following other's rules," Galic spat at me. "How are you ever going to be a king yourself?"

I stepped close to him, pulling myself to my full height, letting some of my power radiate from my skin. Despite himself, he shrank a little, even though I saw him brace himself to face me.

"I'm happy to begin making my own rules, Galic," I told him, my voice quiet and threaded with danger.

I could have defused the situation. But Rowen chose that moment to take off.

She might've been understandably terrified about what was about to happen to her, but her movement made things worse. Fae are always two heartbeats away from their feral selves, and the second she ran, the hunt was on. The males around me transformed into predators, running to catch her. Galic grinned in delight, savoring the moment, then gave chase himself.

Alisa was running too. The two of us chased the others through the woods, blasting magic at every student who tried to attack

Rowen, knocking them down so that they collapsed in a plume of snow.

By the time we broke out of the forest and reached the edge of the cliff, most of our fellow students had been left behind, sleeping off their rage in the snow.

It was just Galic, Rowen, Alisa and me, there at the edge of the cliff, so battered by wind there were no pines growing here. The sun shone down brightly on us all, and the gray stone walls of the campus was spread below us in the distance.

Galic made a move toward Rowen, and I threw up a sheet of wind magic that blocked him. He leaned forward into the wind, trying to force his way toward us, but my wind drove him relentlessly toward the edge of the cliff. His boots slipped across the slick crust of snow, trying desperately to find purchase.

I had no mercy when someone hurt someone I loved.

Vail arrived, panting. "I saw the flare of magic—what the hell is happening here?"

I hesitated, easing up on the wind. Galic tried to speak, but he couldn't.

"Stop," Vail ordered, holding out his hand to me.

I knew he couldn't force me to stop. My magic was more powerful than his. I could send Galic tumbling over the cliff, and he would never get the chance to speak against Rowen. Alisa looked at me, her beautiful eyes wide and desperate.

But already, the first few students had managed to pick themselves up from the snow and stumble after us. They were emerging from between the trees.

Killing wouldn't get us out of this problem.

I let the wind die abruptly. Galic collapsed, landing with a bark on his knees.

There was no denying what Rowen was. But as long as I could get her off campus unharmed, I could get her safely hidden away in the autumn court. And I could shield Alisa too, from being discovered.

"Rowen is female," I said.

Alisa turned furious eyes on me.

"These fools wanted to murder her on the spot for making them look stupid," I added.

"Those are the rules," Galic muttered rebelliously.

Vail turned on him in exasperation. "You don't make the rules. You are not the one to enforce them."

I nodded.

"There's no winter court royalty here," Vail said. "You must do it, Azrael. As autumn prince, you're the closest."

He moved his fingers, and Rowen was suddenly on her knees, as if pressed down by invisible hands.

Fuck. It was going to be harder to get Rowen out of here safely than I'd expected. I hadn't thought Vail would enforce those foolish old rules.

Vail nodded at the dagger on my waist.

"No," I said. "I'm not going to do that."

"I've never known you to shirk your responsibility, Azrael," Vail said.

"I'm not," I promised. "I'm doing the right thing, no matter who is blind to what that is. Why shouldn't a girl be able to prove herself at the academy?"

I glanced around at the males who had gathered around me, keenly aware of the cliff drop off behind me, the long plummet to the icy ground below. "Are we really that timid? Are we afraid that females will shame us by doing better than we can?"

"If you want to change the law, then change the law," Vail said wearily. "Go see Herrick. Though he sent Faer here, not Alisa, so I doubt he'd see things as you do."

I felt Alisa's intention in the way she squared her shoulders, and I tried to silence her with a look. But the males were edging in toward us, as if they were going to fight for Vail's way. Rowen was still on the ground, helpless and wide-eyed.

"Is that what Herrick did?" Alisa's voice rang out, breaking the eerie silence that dominated the Cliffside.

In an instant, she tore off her tunic. "Rowen didn't do anything that I, Princess Alisa, didn't do. Are you going to cut my throat too?

For loving my land, my court, enough to fight for it, just like all of you?"

Vail's face had gone livid with rage. He controlled himself with visible effort.

"No, no one is dying today. But you won't be here by the time night falls, either."

I went with Vail when he marched the two girls down to the campus.

"Go with her, please," Alisa begged me, glancing at Rowen.

I nodded, understanding that she was the one in danger. No one was going to hurt the princess.

No matter how much it hurt to tear myself away from her, I went with Rowen, watching over while she packed her belongings.

Alisa and I never had a moment alone together to say goodbye. She looked back at me as she was getting onto her horse, and she winked at me from the distance.

My irrepressible princess.

The world felt colder when she'd left, but I knew no one would keep us apart for long.

CHAPTER FORTY-SIX

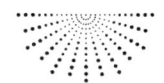

A *lisa*

NOTHING ELSE ATTACKED US, and Tiron and I reached the cave within an hour. The mouth was hidden by overgrown green branches that seemed to wilt at Tiron's touch.

As we descended inside, it grew chillier and chillier. I rubbed my hands over my arms, and Tiron noticed. He didn't seem to feel anything in the cold, but he reached out and ran the back of his hand across my arm, noticing the goosebumps. "You can fix that, you know," he said.

I nodded. It was hard at first to summon my summer magic, then I felt warmth spread over my skin and soak through my muscles. It felt like sunbathing on a beautiful summer day, and I turned my face up instinctively, seeking the sun. But we were still in the dim of the cave.

Tiron was smiling at me when I looked at him.

"What is it?" I asked.

"I thought I hated summer," he said, then shrugged. "It's growing on me, though."

"Is it?" I ran my fingertips over his arm, letting some of my magic seep into his skin.

The shimmering pastel glow of the lights reflected off the tanned skin of his bare chest and powerful arms. He looked at me with heat flaring in his eyes.

If the two of us had time, I would've tried to push him. I would run my palms over those corded forearms, letting my heat sink into his icy skin. I'd feel the ripple of his powerful shoulder muscles beneath my hands, then trace my way down the hard planes of that chest.

But instead, I pulled myself away reluctantly.

When he took my hand in his, his cold skin felt welcome against the warmth of my fingers. Who knew the cold could feel so good?

The two of us descended ever further into the caves until we reached an enormous cavern and what looked like an underground city. Magic twinkled in the sky like stars, shining soft light down on the snowy roofs of dozens of makeshift homes. Several children with pale skin and long tails chased each other between the houses, and the sound of their laughter rose up into the night.

"Welcome to the kingdom of snow in summer." He glanced at me from the corner of his eye. "Alisa, I…"

"I can't believe you trusted me with this," I said softly.

He gave me a look that I couldn't decipher. "You risk your life to protect others over and over. I think that's who you truly are."

Tears came to my eyes, surprising me. Words were just words, but the city spread in front of us showed me how he truly felt. When everyone else seemed to hold a past that I didn't remember against me, Tiron's faith meant the world to me.

"We've got to fly tonight," he said. "The truth is, I could use the help, Alisa. I've got to get them over the border. Once I get them closer to fall territory, I have friends who can take them the rest of the way."

He hesitated. "It's dangerous. If they knew I brought you with me,

Azrael would kill me, then bring me back to life so Duncan could kill me..."

"Do they know what you're doing?" I asked.

His hesitation said enough.

But then he stepped in close to me. "I've cost them enough. I don't want them to know I..."

He trailed off. His gaze was on my lips, and strange warmth suffused my skin—that had nothing to do with my own magic.

"Right," I said softly. "You aren't allowed to help winter prisoners out of summer to safety."

The rest of his words seemed to hang in the air between us: *And I'm definitely not allowed to fall in love with the summer princess.*

"Faer might have all three of us executed if I'm caught," he said. "As long as they don't know, they have an excuse... I'm just a renegade."

I wanted him to be a renegade in every way.

As if he heard my thoughts, he studied me with those green eyes. The air between us felt charged.

He leaned forward, hesitated with a breath between us. I swayed toward him. When that rounded lower lip brushed mine in the faintest, most tentative kiss, his lips were cool.

Then his hands went to my hips, gripped me hard. I twined my arms around his neck and kissed him back, those cold lips nudging mine open. He kissed me slowly, deeply, reverently.

The tip of his tongue teased against my upper lip, then slid slowly inside. My hips swayed against his as I tried to get even closer to him, and one arm slid across my waist as Tiron held me against the ropy muscle of his body.

I pulled away first, breathing hard. "Mission first."

"Right," he murmured. "The mission."

We made our way down the slick, ice-covered descent into the cave. Tiron was sure-footed, and he kept a firm grip on my hand. When we reached the bottom and he led me toward one of the houses, he didn't let go.

He pushed open a heavy curtain and stuck his head in, calling, "Abrie?"

An older woman with her hair braided back looked up wearily from where she sat with two infants on her lap. "Finally. Gior reached you?"

"He always finds a way," Tiron said dryly, and I had a feeling there were stories there.

The babies were wrapped in blankets, and it wasn't until one of them stretched that the blanket fell back. I glimpsed a white fuzzy face with big black eyes that was absolutely adorable.

"Gior started off like this?" I asked disbelievingly.

Tiron grinned and lifted one of the babies out of her arms, before he told me, "Make yourself useful."

He nestled the baby into my arms. It let out a brief cry, looking back at the woman, but when I bounced the baby against my shoulder, it calmed down.

"Ready to fly?" Tiron asked me, taking one of the babies himself.

The two of us made our way back out through the caves and into the forest. It was strange to walk back into the warmth of summer, which felt sticky and clinging after the caves.

We soared through the sky, skimming just above the forest canopy. I could hear animals howl and hoot and scream below, but it felt peaceful up here anyway. The baby curled with its head against my throat and fell asleep, arms wrapped around my neck.

"What was wrong?" I asked. "Why did you have to move them?"

"Their mother had been in a summer lord's *zoo*," he said, his voice sharp at the memory. "Her husband died helping her escape, and she was wounded too--she died in childbirth. These little ones are survivors, but they need the deep cold of the far north now. The heat will kill them at this age...Their parents sacrificed so much to make sure they survived and returned to their own clan."

"That's awful," I said. "There has to be a way to stop the summer court."

His lips tightened, and he glanced at me sideways, reminding me that *I* was the solution he imagined.

"I'll do my best," I promised him.

"And I'll be by your side," he said.

Together, the two of us soared toward the border. We saw some distant Fae flying, and Tiron whistled to me softly, then dived lower. The two of us plunged awkwardly through the canopy, whipping through the branches until we landed softly on the forest floor. Now the dangerous sounds of the forest seemed alive and threatening.

"Fae guards," he said. "Watching the border between summer and spring."

We stayed on foot for a while, both of us anxious knowing how many dangerous creatures lurked in the forest. The High Fae were not at the top of the food chain, not at night in the forest.

It was a relief to finally soar carefully back up to the top of the treetops, past eyes that shone out in the night, and then to fly beneath the starlit sky until we reached the border.

When we landed, it was cooler than before, and raining, this soft, constant mist that hung in the air.

Tiron whistled, and a pair of Fae females emerged from the forest, their light hair and pale skin bright under the moonlight.

"I'd introduce you," Tiron said, "but it's better that we all know as little about each other as possible."

The Fae couple taking them for the next leg of the journey thanked me. That was when I realized my hair was still hidden.

Would these Fae hate me if they knew who I truly was?

Some of the joy of the win faded at the realization.

But Tiron looked at me as if he knew who I truly was, and maybe that was all that mattered.

CHAPTER FORTY-SEVEN

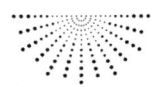

Tiron

PERIN PULLED me aside while Alisa and Dala were preparing the troll babies for the trip northward. Her voice was very soft when she asked, "Who is she?"

"She's a friend."

"You don't have any friends outside the winter court," she warned me. "Tiron, our fate is riding on you. All of us are depending on you…"

"I know," I said, because it was impossible to explain to her how complicated it all truly was. Azrael and Duncan really were my friends; hell, I'd grown so close to them the past few years they felt like brothers.

But they might become my enemies, once I began our play to save the last survivors of the winter court.

"How is the princess?" Perin asked, and for a moment, I thought she saw through Alisa's disguise. They would never trust her; hell, if they knew who she was, I'd be lucky to get her out of here alive.

I never should have brought her with me. I'd been selfish; I'd wanted to spend more time with her. I'd wanted to share the wonders of flight and winter with her.

"She's not what anyone expects," I said.

Perin snorted at that. "She's always been a master at pretending to be something she isn't."

And so was I, apparently.

Because if Alisa had any inkling who I truly was…what we were planning…she wouldn't look at me with that warmth in her eyes.

"Sometimes I think your father was right," Perin muttered. "You're too soft for what has to be done."

I fixed her with a cold look. "You'd best hope you're wrong, Perin. No one else has gotten so close to the high throne, and no one else will."

She met my gaze steadily, her expression haughty as ever. When I was a boy, Dala and Perin were my heroes. From the time I could toddle down the stone steps into the training yard, I'd go out to watch them fight with the other warriors with their shields and swords, with fists and fury. They fell, they were bloodied, but they always rose again.

By the time I was old enough to run across the yard and jump up to straddle the split-beam fence that surrounded the training yard, they'd begun to invite me in to fight with them.

I'd spent the last few years pulling my punches, pretending to be a little softer than I really was, because of *them.*

They'd saved my life more times than I could count, since war came to the winter court. But they'd done more for me than that, once I was left orphaned.

Perin searched my face, then reached out to clasp my arm, as close to an apology as she ever came. "You're right. I know you'll do us proud."

A few minutes later, Alisa and I said goodbye to them and to the troll babies, who were nestled in a basket on the front of Dala's horse.

Alisa and the baby she'd carried cooed back and forth in a goodbye, and I could've sworn Alisa's eyes were luminous with tears for a second before she joined me, smiling.

Together, she and I flew back toward summer territory.

We were sighted by another set of those damned winged guards—how many gargoyle shifters did Faer have out here to protect his secrets? We tried to dive toward the canopy, but it was too late.

"We've got to outrun them," I told Alisa, reaching out for her hand. I was afraid I'd lose her. She'd gone years without flying; her muscles had softened. But her chin set stubbornly, determined to do her best.

They chased us unflaggingly for miles, and we barely managed to stay ahead of them.

"We've got to climb higher," I told Alisa. "They can't follow us that high, but the cold doesn't bother me and you can warm yourself..."

She looked at me wide-eyed—I was asking her to do an awful lot with magic she'd just begun to unleash—but she nodded.

We soared up into ever higher, thinner, colder air. The cold invigorated me, the wind rushing through my hair, but I looked at her, worried.

"Are you all right?" I asked Alisa.

She nodded, though her lips were turning blue, vivid against her pale face.

Then one of the stone-faced shifters hurtled out of the clouds and slammed into us both.

"Fly!" I called to her, urging her out of there, but she ignored me. Of course she did.

She cartwheeled in the air, losing control of her wings as she reached for her knife. I glimpsed her blurrily, because the shifter's fingers had locked on my throat, cutting off my airway, and I felt my wings going limp.

She plunged the dagger into his side, and his grip loosened. Then another one flew into her, knocking us apart.

I shook off the one who still gripped me, that dagger buried deep between his ribs. I couldn't let him die with the knife in his body;

someone might trace it back to Alisa. Instead, I let myself fall with him, grabbing the hilt and yanked it out of his body.

"Alisa, catch!" I called.

I threw it toward her, and she caught it out of the air. She and the gargoyle shifter were spinning through the air together, jockeying for position. As she jabbed out with the knife, I kicked the gargoyle away from me and rocketed toward her, my wings beating the air furiously.

I caught the gargoyle she'd already bloodied, gripping him from behind, slicing his throat with my own knife. He plummeted away from her, falling toward earth.

I turned to her with triumph. We were a good team.

She met my gaze and smiled wearily.

Then I saw the bloody wound in her side where the gargoyle had stabbed her.

She plummeted through the air as if she were dying.

CHAPTER FORTY-EIGHT

A*lisa*

I SURFACED from the cold and darkness to find myself flying fast and low, swooping over trees, clutched in Tiron's grip.

He glanced down at me as he felt me stir. Worry was written across his face and in those brilliant green eyes. My arms hung limp and helpless, and now I reached up and threaded them around his neck, helping him that much at least.

"I can fly," I managed, although the roughness of my voice belied my words. My chest seized with a cough.

"I know you can," he said, "If you had to. But right now, I'm going to fly for you."

It wasn't easy for me to surrender control, but he was right that I couldn't fly for myself now. I let myself relax in his arms. The pain in my side was intense, my muscles felt hard and cold and I kept shivering these deep, racking shivers that were so intense they hurt.

"I had to freeze your wound," he said, sounding frustrated with himself as he noticed my pain. "I don't have much healing magic—it's not my forte—I need to get you to Az."

Azrael had told me that sometimes the more intense our magic is one way, the weaker we are in others.

Dawn streaked the sky as Tiron flew us frantically toward the castle.

"Just get me back to my room and teach me how to heal myself," I said calmly, despite the pain. "I don't want to cause trouble…"

Tiron cursed, and I would've thought he was angry at me, but instead he said, "I don't care about that, Alisa. Not now."

He dove through my window. With the next beat, his massive wings slammed into the walls of my room. He stumbled on his feet, gripping me carefully. Then his wings finally snapped into his back.

I tried to struggle out of his arms, but he didn't stop. He ran down the halls through the castle before bursting into a big room filled with commotion and laughter. I caught a glimpse around me at a room full of male and female knights in those simple black tunics they wore for training. He'd brought me into the barracks.

"Hey, is she all right?" someone started to call.

"Everything is fine," Tiron lied, right before he carried me through that common room and rushed down the hall. We burst into an oversized bedroom.

Azrael sat at a writing desk under the arched window. There was a lofted space above them, and Duncan peered down at us over the railing. A canopy bed was pushed against one corner, and heavy tapestries had been pulled back to reveal the rumpled sheets and blankets.

Azrael rose from his desk in a hurry, throwing down his pen. Worry was written across his face as he stared at the two of us, but then he crossed the floor in a few quick paces.

"Put her on the bed," he ordered. "What happened?"

Tiron lay me down on the bed, his movements careful and gentle. "She was gored by a gargoyle shifter."

"Oh, I can't wait to hear that story," Azrael muttered. His hands were quick and gentle as he touched my icy skin—which I could see but not feel. It was bizarre to know his hands were on my body but be too numb to feel them.

He called loudly, "Duncan—"

But Duncan was already at his shoulder, pulling a pendant over his head. He passed it to Azrael.

Azrael gripped the pendant in one hand as he sat on the bed beside me. "Unfreeze her, Tiron. She's going to start losing—"

"I didn't have a choice," Tiron said. "She would've bled out before I got her back here."

Azrael took in the wound. The look on his face said that it was ugly, and I raised my head.

"Don't look," Tiron warned, but avoiding how ugly reality was never healed the wound.

Ice covered the wound and clung to my skin, but nothing could hide how deep the gash was or how red it was underneath.

"If she needs a healer, I'll go get—" Tiron began.

"If she needs a healer, Faer will hang you for it," Azrael said. "Shut up and let me work."

The minute the ice faded away, I could barely hold back a scream as agony seared through my body. Maybe I'd been lucky to pass out when I had, when adrenaline had still been coursing through my body and I hadn't felt it that intensely. I gritted my teeth, grabbed Tiron's arm.

"Do you have a spell for silence?" I managed to gasp. If I couldn't hold back my screams, then it would be hard to hide what happened here. I didn't know if those knights outside would betray us.

Duncan glanced at Azrael, who was intent on my wounds. His hands were hot against my skin. He shifted onto the bed with me, one leg folded underneath his body, and Duncan and Tiron began to close the canopy of the bed around us.

Darkness enveloped the two of us, and Azrael muttered the word to summon light, tossing the ball to hang above us. The light reflected off his face, throwing it into shadow, and I focused on his cruelly beautiful mouth, his straight nose, the defined angle of his jaw.

"You can scream if you have to," he said. "No one can hear us now."

"Who sleeps in here?" I demanded, wondering why they'd have a bed enchanted so that no sound left it.

"I do," he said briefly. "Hang on, Alisa. I don't have time for a spell for the pain."

My blood was pumping steadily out under his hands. He'd thrown the pendant on over his neck, and it glowed now with the same shade of reddish-gold magic that lit his hands as he moved them over the wound.

The pain of flesh knitting back together, of my shredded body trying to come back together, made me scream. Azrael winced, but murmured, "You're fine, Alisa. You've survived worse wounds."

"When?" I demanded through gasps.

"I've always admired your strength," he told me, his voice low and soothing. I wasn't sure how much of what he said was a lie to salve the pain. Agony flooded my body, so intense that bile rose in the back of my throat and my head swam as if I might pass out.

When it was finally done, the pain faded, leaving my muscles heavy and exhausted. I ran my hand over the smooth, pink skin covering my side. As he tucked the pendant away, the glow that had lit his hands and reflected from his face faded.

The bed, the sheets, they were all soaked with blood. It was hard to believe, looking at my unblemished skin, that I'd almost died.

I knew Tiron and Duncan waited on the other side. But it felt as if it were just the two of us, alone in the world, when we were this close together, surrounded by the tapestries.

"Thank you," I said softly.

"Don't thank me," he said briskly. "If you died, so would Tiron."

I stared at him. "Have you ever considered *not* being an ass-hat?"

His brow furrowed over those dark purple eyes. "I know you're being a jerk right now. I get the gist. But I'm dying of curiosity. What exactly is an ass-hat?"

"I was this close to forgiving you after our fight, after this," I told him. "Having my life flash before my eyes put me in a forgiving frame of mind—"

"Did your life flash before your eyes?" he said eagerly. "Your memories returned?"

"No," I said. "Figure of speech."

He frowned, disappointment written across his face, then raised his hand to touch my forehead. "Maybe you're sick—maybe they had poisoned weapons. Nothing you say makes any sense."

"They're just sayings from my world," I said. "They'd make sense if you weren't such a damned…"

He quirked his eyebrow curiously.

It was amazing how quickly Azrael took me from *forgiving* right back to *maybe I'll murder him.*

I struggled onto my elbows, pulling away from him.

"I don't know why you would forgive me," he said.

I thought it was the beginning of an apology, that he realized he didn't *deserve* forgiveness, but he went on, "I'm not the one who's been insufferable."

It took me a second to even form a response to that. "You are, in fact, the most insufferable man I've ever met."

"I just healed you," he said, "and you're not remotely grateful. Who's insufferable?"

"You already told me you healed me to protect Tiron," I said, "and not because you give a damn about me."

Got you, you smug Fae bastard.

"Of course I care about you." He pulled back the curtains as he slid out of bed.

Tiron and Duncan both looked so worried. Then Duncan's face rearranged itself into his usual grim air.

I didn't have the chance to ask Azrael what the hell that meant.

Someone began to bang on the door just then.

CHAPTER FORTY-NINE

Azrael

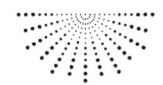

I YANKED my bloodied shirt over my head and dropped it into the basket where it would be unseen. Then I went to the door and smoothed everything over with the captain of the guard. I told him Tiron had spent the night with a prostitute and the two of them had been beaten and robbed; that story should be fun for both Tiron and for Alisa to overhear and not be able to respond to.

When I closed the door, I leaned against it for a second, trying to catch my breath. Always a new fucking disaster with this crew.

"It's a good thing everyone likes Azrael," Tiron said. He sounded cheerful as ever, and just now, that made me want to punch him.

"Well, not everyone," Alisa said haughtily.

I stared at Tiron steadily, and he dropped his gaze. He said, "I assume you'll want that story."

"Desperately," I said drily. "But right now, we need to make it seem like none of this ever happened and get about our day. Alisa has to make an appearance in the court today."

"Why does Alisa have to do that?" she asked drily.

I kept my back to her. I couldn't face her damned saucy expression and her glib words, not now when I'd just seen her almost die. I couldn't betray how I felt.

When I saw that wound—a killing wound—I'd felt as if my heart were being ripped out of my chest. I'd had to move, so that had kept the panic I felt at bay.

But I knew she'd haunt my dreams that night. I'd relive the moment with her blood all over my hands, but I wouldn't be able to save her.

I already had enough of those dreams.

Duncan took one look at my face and drawled, "Don't be lazy, Princess."

"I'll take care of this," Tiron promised, gesturing to the blood-soaked bedding. "It's the least I can do."

"Yes, it is," I said. "Not that this conversation is over."

"It's my fault," she said quickly. "I asked Tiron to teach me to fly. He tried to warn me, but I wasn't paying attention. Brought the gargoyles down on us both."

She added, "Sorry, Tiron."

"I don't care about *fault*," I said sharply. "The two of you shouldn't be sneaking out of the castle. You have enemies, Alisa."

"Everywhere I go," she said lightly.

When I turned around, I really saw her outfit for the first time, the way the gauze fell away from her narrow shoulders and exposed the long, taut lines of her stomach and the gentle flare of her hips. Her bright eyes met mine in open challenge. God, she was gorgeous. My cock was suddenly hard.

"You need to get back to your room, now," I said. "I'll meet you there."

"Fine." She didn't act as if she were annoyed by my brusque tone, but she leaned up onto her tiptoes and pressed a quick kiss to Tiron's cheek.

His cheeks colored faintly—I'd never seen the male blush before—but his arm still looped her narrow waist. The two of them shared a quick hug before she turned and sauntered toward the window, her hips swaying, and my jaw set.

I glanced at Tiron, but I had no time for the conversation I'd *love* to have with him right now. I pulled on a clean set of clothes and watched Alisa leap from the window, her wings spreading from her back.

Her gossamer wings were as beautiful as she was.

No matter how pissed I was at the moment, I was glad she could fly again.

Duncan turned to Tiron, fury sparking in his icy blue eyes, and I held up my hands. "Let's all table this conversation for now. We've got work to do."

Duncan scoffed at that, but left Tiron alone. Tiron threw me a grateful look, but wisely didn't press his luck by thanking me. Alisa couldn't be blamed for her foolishness; she didn't remember just what Faer was capable of.

But Tiron knew better. The damned wall, the bodies, rose in my mind again, and like I so often did, I imagined my friends' faces, even as I willed the thought away.

Sometimes it seemed like the more I tried to unroot the dark thoughts, the more their tendrils pushed deep into my mind.

"Later," I said again, a promise to Duncan and a threat for Tiron. I nodded goodbye to them both and headed out through the barracks. The common room was emptying out now, and I grabbed a roll to stuff with cheese and bacon to eat on my way.

I needed my strength to deal with Alisa. I stopped, sighed, grabbed a second sandwich. Doubtless she felt she needed her strength to deal with me.

"Are you joining us in the training yard today?" Calina called cheerfully from the table where she sat with a few of the other knights. "We've missed you lately."

"I wish." I smiled back at her. "Duty calls."

I could feel her gaze lingering on my back as I left the room. She'd tried to climb into my bed before, and although she was beautiful and we had fun training together, I'd politely declined.

Now that I'd shared my bed with Alisa, I doubted I could ever share it with another, no matter what fate had done to us both. I'd never be with her again.

But I couldn't bear to be with another, either.

I left behind the pleasant bustle of the barracks for the long, winding quiet halls of the palace. The servants always managed to make themselves nearly invisible.

I banged on the door to Alisa's room. She pulled the door open a second later; her lavender hair tumbled around her shoulders, sharply contrasting with her scarlet outfit now that she'd removed the cowl. Her face was pale as if she were still recovering from the wounds, but her eyes were pink-smudged against that fair skin. She hastily turned away from me.

I moved into her room and closed the door quietly behind me. "We should burn that outfit. Faer won't like it if he knows you're discovering your independent side."

She shrugged as she walked away from me toward the pool. Right; she wanted me to know she didn't care. She dropped the silky red scraps on the marble, then dove forward, her delicate muscles rippling with the movement. The water rippled around her body.

She was going to get herself killed. Faer couldn't attack her outright, but if he ever gave up on marrying her off to Raile—to make sure she could never take the summer throne—he'd try to have her murdered.

I tossed the sandwich on the table. It seemed a peace offering was pointless now.

"I'm going to sleep for a week," she said, yawning as she began to tread water. "Isn't the official story that I'm spoiled and lazy?"

She must be exhausted from being up all night, from that wound and the pain of recovering from it. But of course she would hide that under her usual light-hearted insolence.

"No, you're not. You're expected to sit with your brother as he hears appeals from the summer court." My voice came out calm and level. "If you don't appear with him, it simply feeds the narrative that you're incompetent for the throne."

"I don't want the throne." She turned over in the water, and her gaze found the bruise she'd left on my face. That girl had a powerful punch. She winced, as if she regretted those bruises, no matter how angry she still was.

"Why didn't you hit me back?" she asked, then answered her own question: "Right. You've already got your revenge. Here we are."

"You can hate me all you like, but put on your crown. You can cry about it later."

Her eyes widened. "I was not—"

"I know what you look like when you've been crying," I said.

"Did you make a habit of making me cry before?" she asked, her tone barbed.

She wasn't crying about anything to do with me. Something that happened out there with Tiron had stung her deeply, and I doubted it had anything to do with her brush with death. But she didn't want to tell me. Fine.

I shrugged. "First love. Perhaps we made each other cry."

She shook her head, as if she doubted that very much.

"You went about it stupidly, but you weren't wrong to go see the state of your kingdom," I said, my voice calm. "For all Duncan's criticisms, no one has ever accused you of shirking your responsibilities."

"Except my responsibility to marry."

My lips quirked. "Well. I'm glad you evaded that one so far. We'll see what the future holds."

"Raile talks as if he tried to marry me before. Is that why I rejected him?" Her gaze found mine. There was a glimmer of real innocence in her eyes when she asked, "Did I choose you?"

The question fractured something inside me. "Maybe you chose yourself."

"Well, that would have been wise," she muttered, climbing the marble steps. "But I've never been accused of being exceptionally *wise*."

I hesitated. "Faer is never going to give permission. If he won't let you go to the caves, then we'll have to go ourselves."

Gods, but I was a fool when it came to her.

Whatever. There would be other ways to launch our coup. We didn't have to leave her at Faer and Raile's mercy.

She faced me, her chin rising. "There would be no hiding that from Faer. You don't want to help me, Azrael. It will cost you something, and Duncan's made it very clear I'm not worth it."

"You managed to say one true thing in the midst of all that garbage," I said, because it *would* cost me something. "We can talk more later. For now, stop fussing and put on something presentable for court."

She stalked ahead of me into her room, letting the towel fall to the ground. The curves of her back, her lithely muscled shoulders and her narrow waist and the fullness of her hips, drew my gaze, just as she'd intended. She stepped out of the pants and left them behind.

"That move worked better for you this time, didn't it?" I called, ignoring how my cock twitched at the thought of her.

"I still hate you," she called back.

"I let you punch me, let you ignore me. Then I saved your life. Didn't that win me any points toward forgiveness?"

"Let me?" Her voice was sharp. She came out of the bedroom wearing a green dress, edged in gold. "I think you and I are hopeless when it comes to forgiveness, Azrael. There's just too much."

But she turned, exposing her bare back, the loose ribbons of the bodice. I began to lace up the corset, hearing the faint exhale of her breath every time I jerked it tight.

"And I don't even know what *I* need to be forgiven for," she added.

"Maybe we could start to discuss it," I said. "Tonight."

"Maybe," she agreed.

"But first, you have to get through court." I tied the last lace, then reached for her hair. Alisa had always liked for me to comb her hair, to play with it, and even now, she started at my touch for a second before she relaxed.

When I began to plait her hair, Alisa asked, "When did you learn to braid hair? Not at that military academy."

"Zora," I said. "My mother was very sick when she was little. We had maids, of course, but... Zora didn't cope well with my mother's illness. She clung to Duncan and me."

I gathered the braid in my hand and wrapped the rest of her hair around my hand, beginning to form a chignon. It was one of Zora's favorite ways to wear her hair and I'd begun automatically, but now I regretted it. I didn't need to think about Zora sentimentally; I needed to focus on the next step I had to take to keep her safe. To save the autumn court without damning the beautiful, maddening woman in front of me.

"So you learned to do your little sister's hair. That's sweet."

"Give Duncan the credit," I said. "I had to learn from the maids, so I practiced on Duncan. There's a reason he wears his hair long."

She absorbed the mental image, then laughed. "I would pay money to see Duncan with flowers braided into his hair."

"I don't think there's anything you could do to make that happen."

"Where's Zora now? Did she make it to the Sisters?"

The question made my chest tighten. "I'm taking care of Zora. Once I know she's safe, we'll leave. All right?"

"Why would you do that for me, Azrael?"

I didn't answer her. I couldn't bear to. I dropped my hands from her hair, and she turned to face me, biting her lower lip.

"I'm not as good at hating you as I should be," she admitted.

"Same, Princess. Same." I offered her my arm. "Let me tell you what to expect today."

I was ever the dutiful servant, after all.

When she walked into court, she didn't hesitate this time as everyone sank to their knees. She walked past them without a second glance before she took her place on the dais.

She greeted Faer with an icy smile—I wondered if she had thrown anything at *him*—then took her throne. Twin thrones, as much as he tried to fight their equal power behind the scenes.

I joined Tiron in the crowd of nobles that watched from near the thrones; common Fae stood corralled nearer the doors, waiting for the chance to air their pleas and grievances, and a handful of nobles in chains waited by the door since only the king—or acting king—could sentence them.

Tiron whispered to me, "Are you anxious how your student will get on?"

"I'll be happy if she makes it through the next few hours without punching Faer," I admitted.

"I'll be happier if she does," Tiron returned.

"Tuttle Longfeld is accused of enchanting a goblin den to steal his neighbors' livestock," the courtier read out loud. The courtier had a face like a mouse, covered in gray and downy fur, and he gripped the book in four-fingered hands.

The accused was dragged forward by a guard. He was dressed in fine clothing, his ears long and pointed as he bowed his morose head.

Faer listened to the first eyewitness account and half of the second, before Faer interrupted. "Sentenced to death."

Alisa frowned at Faer skeptically. I held my breath, expecting her to protest, but she kept quiet for now.

I'd suggested that this first time, she keep quiet and let Faer take the lead. I hadn't made the suggestion with an abundance of optimism.

CHAPTER FIFTY

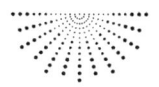

D*uncan*

I MADE my way into the back of the court. Tiron twisted to look at me, and I rested my hand on his shoulder in greeting. His lips widened in the beginning of a smile. He was so quick to forgive, and so he always expected I'd be the same way.

Sometimes Tiron's easy friendship left me thinking I should be less petty myself.

Those good intentions never lasted long beyond the next foolish thing someone said, though.

I found the nobles in the line of prisoners. There had never been so many noble Fae brought to the high court before Herrick's time. Nobility always had occasional disputes over marriage contracts or land, the rarer murder or assault. But now, there were always nobles waiting in the queue.

I didn't recognize any of them this time, and the tension in my chest eased. It was hard enough to play Faer's obedient servant.

A handful of Fae came up and requested an extension on their village's taxes, citing the many cases of illness they'd experienced recently disrupting their farming.

I saw the second that Alisa's interest caught. She leaned forward, her eyes troubled.

Faer started to say something, and she stopped him with a hand on his arm. The look he gave her was startled, then irritated, but he leaned in to hear her whispering. The two of them eventually came to terms, and Faer made a pronouncement. I imagined he was probably far more charitable than without Alisa's perspective.

Her kindness made my heart beat faster with sudden fury.

I needed her to have her memories restored, to go back to being the trickster Alisa with the cold heart I'd known. I'd thought that heart warmed for me, but that was before I learned Alisa would always prefer power over love.

Seeing Alisa as an enemy might destroy us both. But trusting her was sure to destroy me all over again.

"Enough appeals for today. Bring on the nobles for trial." Faer searched the crowd at the end of the room before he asked impatiently, "Where's the most recent?"

"All the evidence hasn't been gathered yet, sire," the courtier began, his long whiskers shaking with his speech.

"I'll make those decisions, thank you," Faer said coldly, and the courtier's whiskers wobbled even more decisively.

The courtier began to read the list of charges—treason topped the list—as the doors opened for the guards and their prisoner.

The accused Fae swaggered in, looking like a king even wrapped in chains, his chin held high. Fiery red hair topped a freckled face, his expression boyish despite the dangerous muscled power of his body.

Ander.

Azrael's jaw set. As soon as he'd tucked his hands behind his back, his chin rising high, his body turned rigid and motionless. He settled into that posture whenever he was determined not to show any weakness. I knew him well enough to know what went on behind that cold expression, though.

I hadn't been good friends with Ander, but he went to the academy with us all, and since he was a lower noble, we'd seen him at court dances and celebrations. He and Azrael had been close.

One of the guards pushed Ander to his knees. Faer asked him several harsh questions, but it was clear he barely cared about the answers. He accused Ander of treason.

There was a glint in Faer's eyes whenever his gaze flickered to Azrael, and I knew he was watching for Azrael's reaction.

"Guilty," Faer interrupted Ander's attempts to explain himself. He raised his hand to wave him away. "Traitors burn ali—"

Alisa touched his arm, whispering to him before he could finish his sentence. Faer whirled to face her, his eyes widening in fury before he caught himself. They had an audience.

She leaned forward and murmured to him, but Faer would never go back on what he'd said when it would make him look weak before the high court. Alisa was too late.

I glanced at Azrael out of the corner of my eye. He'd hate it if he knew I was worried about him.

First Alisa, dressed in blood this morning. Now Ander, sentenced to the flames.

He'd be up screaming half the night. I wouldn't be able to hear him, but that never stopped me from lying in bed awake as if I could feel the way he writhed in distress. He never wanted anyone to know his weakness. But he didn't suffer any less, just because we pretended not to know.

Sometimes I thought he must suffer even more, thrashing around in the closed-up darkness of that bed.

Faer turned his gaze to Ander. Ander's face was stony, although he'd gone pale under his freckles. He must have known this would be the outcome.

"My sister Alisa requested mercy for this boy," Faer said, his voice dry. "She thought it would trouble our autumn court friends to punish him so harshly."

I had a feeling Alisa might have been troubled that *this boy* had never even spoken in his own defense. When her lips pressed together tightly, I knew she was debating her next move.

Faer's gaze skipped right over me to Azrael. He lived to punish Azrael.

Maybe he didn't care about me, but what he did to Azrael hurt me just as much, because I had to watch my brother suffer.

"Do you care, autumn princes?" Faer asked Azrael. "Does it matter to you if this traitor burns or if I consign him to the dungeon?"

If he was sent to the dungeon, then we'd be able to release him once we wrestled the throne from Faer's hands.

Azrael began calmly, "If you were to show mercy, it would—"

Faer shook his head, and Azrael fell silent, his jaw tight. Faer wanted Azrael to admit how much it mattered to *him*.

Faer wanted him to beg, and I wanted to bury a blade in Faer's throat.

"Come here," Faer beckoned him forward. "Stand next to your lord. This is one of your subjects, is he not?"

"Yes," Azrael ground out.

Azrael started to move forward, but he stopped me from following him with a look. Faer didn't care about me; Azrael was always the one that Faer bullied mercilessly.

Faer didn't even seem to notice me. His eyes glinted with satisfaction as Azrael walked up the long aisle toward the open space in front of the dais.

I'd asked Azrael before what he'd done to piss Faer off so much. He always had a glib answer. But I had a feeling Faer hated Azrael so much for being everything he was not. Azrael was respected by the knights and even by his enemies. He was stoic, tough and calculating despite Faer's every attempt to grind him under the heel of his jeweled slipper.

Faer could chain Azrael's hands—as he did when he threatened him with Zora—but he could never truly cow Azrael. Faer hated him for that.

Azrael reached Ander, who kneeled in chains. Ander glanced up at him, his eyes wide, but Azrael never looked at him. His gaze was focused on Faer.

The less Azrael betrayed any personal connection to Ander, the more likely it was Faer would grow bored with this game.

"Why should I let him live?" Faer asked Azrael. "The evidence seems damning. He's been stealing from the summer court, despising my court's generosity welcoming nobles of other courts."

There was a soft ripple of laughter around the room from Faer's lackeys, and Faer smiled, encouraged. I gritted my teeth. We certainly *despised the court's generosity,* but we were trapped here.

"He's young," Azrael said. "A good knight. He might have made poor choices but he can redeem himself in the Rift, fighting for all the courts."

"We need more bodies at the Rift," Alisa said to Azrael, her voice cool. "Why not use the knight and show mercy to our allies?"

Faer glanced at her, a slow smile spreading across his face. "How practical you are, Alisa."

I relaxed slightly—Alisa somehow wielded more influence over Faer than I would have expected—until Faer turned his full attention to Azrael. "Is that you want, Azrael? The life of your autumn court subject?"

"Yes, your Majesty." Azrael's voice was flat.

"Then make your own appeal for his life," Faer said. "My sister has humbled herself to offer a favor to you, prince of fall, and you haven't even shown much interest in that favor."

Alisa glanced at Faer, and I willed her to stay silent. She'd pushed Faer into a position that might be dangerous for us all.

"If you want his life..." Faer smiled, revealing his mouthful of pointed teeth, "then humble yourself too."

For a long second, Azrael faced him, his back rigid and straight as his sword.

Then Azrael went down to his knees. Faer's smile widened.

"Please, spare his life, your majesty." Azrael said, his voice level. He didn't even grind the words out the way I knew I would.

Laughter rippled through the court. Across from us, some of the knights were watching, but none of them were laughing. Cora, Luca, Dere, they all stood there with cold, disapproving faces.

They should really be careful. Faer's *friends* would be watching the faces in the crowd, noticing who didn't seem loyal.

"Very well," Faer said. "Since it means so much to you, Azrael. Take him to the Rift. Let him make himself useful before he dies."

He waved his hand and began to rise.

"That's all," the courtier said. "No more pleas or grievances today."

Then someone broke loose from the crowd of common Fae. "I have a grievance, and I will be heard," he called.

A blade flashed in his hand as he ran up the steps.

I was already moving to intercept him as the guards closed ranks around the thrones.

Still the man with the blade moved toward Faer.

No, toward *Alisa*.

I ran toward him, weaving through the Fae who milled in excitement or curiosity.

But Azrael was closest. Azrael tackled him, knocking him down onto the marble just as his foot reached the bottom step of the dais.

The Fae was screaming about how Alisa had ruined the autumn court. Over the chatter of the crowd and the sight of Faer's guards rushing him away, through a hidden passage, the male shouted names. The names of those he'd lost.

Right before Azrael drove his knife into his chest, silencing him. For a second, the would-be assassin stared at Azrael, wide-eyed. He'd been killed by his own prince. Then his head fell slack against the marble floor.

Faer would have had worse ways of killing him for daring to attack his sister.

"Clear the room," Tiron yelled behind me. The guards were trying to hustle Alisa and Faer out through the side door that led away from the dais. Faer was already gone.

But Alisa stood on the dais, her face white, her eyes wide.

At first, I thought she was terrified.
And then I understood that the look on her face was horror.
For what Azrael had done.
Or for what *she'd* done so long ago that started all of this.

CHAPTER FIFTY-ONE

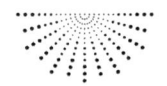

T *iron*

"Princess, we need to get you out of here." I glanced over my shoulder at Azrael. His face was horrified, mirroring hers, as if he was troubled by her emotions in a way that the simple act of killing never bothered him.

He cared about every one of his subjects. But he was from the autumn court, and autumn is a killing season, after all.

She ignored the guards who were trying to herd her out to safety, but when I scooped her off her feet and lifted her in my arms, she let me carry her. I rushed with her down the hallways and back to her room.

Duncan had beaten us there.

"The room is clear," he said, right before I rushed in with her. He glanced behind me down the hall. "Where is Azrael?"

"Probably still cleaning up."

"Who was that?" Alisa asked.

"One of the autumn court's refugees," I told her.

Duncan growled, but there was sympathy in the sound. "He'll pay for that later."

I wasn't sure who suffered more from Azrael's nightmares—Azrael himself, or Duncan, who couldn't help him.

"What happened?" Alisa said as I sat with her on one of her couches. She tried to move away, but it was a desultory move, and when I kept holding her, she rested her head on my shoulder. Her slender body shook against mine, no matter how tough she tried to be. "I know what I saw. But—what really happened? The Fae from the autumn court—"

"Had no right to try to murder you," Duncan finished the sentence for her as he moved to the bar. "Relax. We'll protect you."

"Because it's your job." Her voice carried a mocking barb, no matter how upset she was now.

"Yes." Duncan knelt next to us, offering her a cup. "Drink this. It'll take away some of your shakiness."

"I'm not shaky," she said, even though her fingers trembled as she wrapped them around the goblet. "I've killed so many monsters before, to see one person killed in front of me—"

"But that male wasn't a monster," Duncan said simply.

She bit her lower lip hard. "He would've killed me."

She was obviously struggling to reconcile *not a monster* and *person who wished her dead*.

"We wouldn't let that happen." I pushed her hand that held her goblet toward her lips, urging her to take a sip. "You're all right."

"No, I'm not." She shook her head. "Tell me what I did. Tell me everything. No more secrets, no more waiting for the caves."

"You won't want to hear it from us," Duncan said, his voice harsh. "You won't believe us."

"Then we go to the caves," she said. "We leave now. As soon as we can get ready."

"You've lost your mind," Duncan said. "Faer hasn't given his permission for us to go, and we are his knights, as much as that pisses me off—"

"How do I make you mine?" she demanded.

"Excuse me?" he asked.

She pulled a face, as if she realized how awkward the question was. "I'm just as much royalty as he is. How do I make you my knights instead of his?"

She was already coming back to life, color returning to her cheeks. She still lay against my shoulder, and I traced shapes across her back absently, first toying over the laces of her corset, then finding her bare skin above it. She relaxed into my touch.

Princess Alisa was always more comfortable when she was scheming.

A few minutes later, there was a knock at the door, and Azrael called through it, "I'm here with the prince. All's well for now, it seems."

Duncan moved to the door and swung it open cautiously.

Faer and Azrael entered, and Faer's knowing, cunning eyes found Alisa in my lap.

I expected her to move away, embarrassed, but she kicked off her slippers and drew her feet up onto the couch.

"Brother," she greeted him, "I'm glad you weren't harmed."

"I'm glad *you* weren't harmed," he said, sitting on the couch by her feet. "Were you very scared?"

She shook her head, her lips quirking.

"I heard you froze."

Her lips tightened. She didn't like that. But then she said, "Yes. I suppose I did."

She hadn't been willing to leave not because she was afraid, but because she wanted to understand what was happening. I knew that. But she went on, "I didn't realize anyone would want to kill me."

"The crown's heavy." His gaze was kind, affectionate. He was such a good liar. "You'll be safe with Raile. No one can touch him in the undersea. That's why I want so badly for you to go with him."

"Maybe." She bit her plush lower lip. "Until then, may I ask you a favor?"

"Of course," he said.

"I feel safe with the three of them," she said, glancing around the room at Azrael, at Duncan, and then at me. My lips arched in a smile, a flush of pride, despite the fact I knew she was playing Faer. "Promise me I can keep these knights until—if—I go with Raile?"

"They're yours," Faer promised lightly.

"Good," she said, exhaling slowly. "That makes me feel so much better."

Azrael was frowning, but he gave nothing away until Faer had finished 'comforting' his sister and left again.

As soon as the door had closed and Faer was gone, Azrael hissed, "What kind of game are you playing now, Alisa?"

"We're going to the caves," she said. "Tonight. Once I have my memories back, I can help you protect Zora and Ander and all the others."

She sounded sure, confident, and Azrael parted his lips to argue with her. Had she defended Ander because she was genuinely moved by his imminent execution? Or to show us what she was capable of?

Then she added, "I can't bear another day without answers. Without knowing what I've done."

I saw Azrael stumble in his feelings, no matter how solid and sure of himself he looked in front of her.

"Faer said we are hers," Duncan pointed out.

Azrael studied his brother. His face was a mask, as it so often was. The two of them looked identical.

Then Duncan pulled a face. He'd accidentally revealed he cared about her well-being. No matter what he claimed.

"I heard an interesting thing from Faer," Azrael said slowly. "About Princess Alisa's fighting prowess. Apparently she's helpless as a kitten. Can barely grip a sword in her dainty paws."

"Mm," Duncan said briefly. "And I overheard you teaching Princess Alisa about the laws regarding marriage. We both hear such interesting things."

Both of them, in their own ways, were trying to help her.
But both of them would pretend they had no interest in doing so.
Fae psychopaths.
I loved them anyway.

CHAPTER FIFTY-TWO

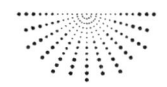

A*zrael*

Six Years Earlier

I HADN'T SEEN Alisa in a year. She'd vanished when she left the academy, and some stupid, wayward part of me had hoped at first she'd run away to the autumn court.

Even though that would have plunged our kingdoms into war.

I'd spend the last year longing for Alisa, wanting her even if it cost blood, wanting her no matter who I'd have to slaughter to take her hand.

But I'd received brief letters from her—nothing more than a few sentences telling me that our relationship was over, with no secret message or a code contained inside—and then nothing.

I'd been thrilled when I received an invitation to Herrick's latest party—in celebration of Alisa's birthday.

Even though Duncan had shaken his head at me and inssited that I was being led off to my death by my cock.

I'd told him that my cock had never done me that wrong before.

I'd been so eager to see Alisa. And now the band played cheerfully, and she was laughing by the table laden with summer wine and strawberries, with another male.

Duncan shook his head slowly. No matter how much he'd told me that I was going to get myself killed, he'd still come along with me.

I wasn't sure if he wanted to protect me or mock me. Probably both.

"Does she know I'm here?" I said, already knowing I wouldn't enjoy Duncan's response. My fingers had tightened on the crystal glass I held until it might shatter.

"I get the distinct impression she doesn't care." Duncan caught the sleeve of a passing waiter to lift a cup of wine from the tray, even though it surely belonged to someone else, as if he needed that to bear the drama that was Alisa-and-me.

"To girls who don't give a shit about you," Duncan said, raising his glass as if it were a toast, then clinking his drink against mine. "You found the one-and-only female who appears to be completely unimpressed with you."

"She didn't seem unimpressed when I was— why the hell am I talking to you, anyway?" I broke off.

Duncan was a very helpful friend to have in your corner if you needed to kill someone or hide the body after. If you wanted to talk about feelings, well, the aforementioned corpse would be more empathetic.

I handed him my glass, and he took it automatically, then gave me a scornful look.

"I'm going to talk to her."

"Good luck," he said, with a nasty smile.

I had started to walk away, but I stopped and turned back. The mean edge in his smile had told me he was *feeling* something. Duncan hated feeling things. "How much did you get to know Alisa at the academy?"

"Faer?" He made air quotes when he said the name, then shrugged. "A bit. Pompous little prick."

"Mm. And you're a big pompous prick, I can see the conflict." I tilted my head, studying him. His face was impassive, but under my gaze, he shifted, rolling his eyes. I accused, "You're jealous."

He huffed a laugh. "Of you and Alisa? Hardly."

"If you two care for each other," I said, my own heart beating faster with jealousy now even though for all I knew, he had an unrequired crush, "we can figure something out. We're all adults."

I would never want to lose these two people who meant the most to me in the world. Duncan and Alisa and I…we could make it work, if she chose us both.

"She doesn't care for anyone," Duncan assured me, "so your generosity is unnecessary. Go on. Talk to her." He waved me off.

I turned to head toward Alisa, but the space where she'd stood drinking wine was empty. A bright, happy reel was playing, and she danced by me, held in another man's arms.

I tracked her across the dance floor, trying to pull her away, but she was always in someone else's arms, always one step ahead of me. Her lavender hair flew as she spun, mirroring her silver-embroidered skirts fanning out. She was smiling, laughing, and never looked in my direction.

She was avoiding me. The realization settled like a weight in my chest.

"I've heard," Duncan drawled, his voice irritatingly near my ear; he'd managed to sneak up on me while I was focused on Alisa, and he was probably amused by that, "Herrick forbade Alisa to ever see you again."

"It's not like her to ever listen to anyone."

He put his hand on my shoulder, as if he were about to say something comforting. Then he said, "She must have decided you weren't worth it."

I shrugged his hand off and turned to face him. "Is that what happened between the two of you?"

He gave me that blank-faced look, but I had a feeling I'd struck close to the truth. "Someday you'll have to tell me what happened."

He scoffed. "Nothing to tell."

"Mm-hm." I was wildly curious, but the music was ending. Before the last notes had died away, before Alisa could slip into the arms of another man, I caught her around the waist and pulled her close to me.

There was a beat of silence between songs. She stared up at me, her lips parting in surprise. Those big, luminous eyes were steady and more somber than I'd ever seen them before. I had been growing cold and furious, but something in that gaze made me pause.

"You've been avoiding me," I chided her. I drew her into my arms, her warm, lithe body against mine.

She didn't answer me, but she pulled back, carefully separating our bodies. Her arms were stiff, holding us apart without any of the grace she'd danced with earlier; she seemed to move mechanically through the steps. Her beautiful lips pressed together tightly, her chin lifting with a spark of that old Alisa I knew so well.

"What happened to you?" I whispered. I'd almost stormed summer territory, convinced that those few terse lines meant she was in trouble. But our kingdoms were in a state of dangerous peace; all-out war would mean the deaths of thousands of Fae on both sides.

Kingdom first.

Even if it broke my heart.

But now, when she was in my arms but somehow so far away, I knew I'd chosen wrong. I should have found a way to reach her and steal her away, even if she claimed she didn't want me anymore.

She didn't answer me. Her gaze slid from mine to someplace over my shoulder. We danced as sedately as a man dancing with his granddaughter, though with considerably less joy.

She yanked her hand away from mine as if it burned, the second she could. She curtsied to me and hurried away through the crowd. Males stopped her and asked her to dance—everyone wanted a bit of her sparkling personality—but she made some smiling excuse to everyone. Then she was gone, fleeing into the enormous marble lobby outside the ballroom.

If I knew her, she was running for the gardens. She'd told me when we were lying in bed how the gardens and riding horseback had been the two places she could feel like herself, despite the pressure of being a princess. I'd told her that music and the pitch had been those two places for me. We'd been twined together, her legs and mine overlapping, and I'd stroked my thumb across the beautiful planes of that face, soaking her in as if I might never see her again. Maybe I never would truly see her again.

Maybe Herrick had done something to her.

I knew that Duncan would accuse me of embarrassing myself. Maybe I was—but maybe I should be myself everywhere, royal lineage be damned.

And I loved Alisa, even more than my throne.

I saw Herrick watching me from across the crowd. His dark eyes were flinty in that tan, ageless face; his lavender hair had long since faded to silver. He was tall and thin as a blade, the spires of his crown looking sharp enough to prick. The lavender-haired man who leaned close to him, whispering, must be Faer; he looked so much like Alisa.

When I found Duncan at the side of the ballroom, there were two females writhing around him. They were dancing; he was tolerating being pressed between the two of them, stubbornly drinking his wine with his feet planted solidly on the ground.

"You are the most joyless person I've ever met," I told him, "and I met a Soulsucker once."

He rolled his eyes. "Are you going after her?"

"Of course I am."

"Fool," he accused me. He drained his glass and handed it to one of the girls, pushing past them. They pouted behind him as he walked with me. "I'll help you get out of here unseen. Herrick's guards are tracking you."

"He wanted me to see Alisa and know for myself that she was rejecting me," I said.

"Perhaps you'll get lucky and he just wanted to torture you before the murder attempt," he said lightly. "You look as if you'd like to be put out of your misery."

"You seem so convinced he's going to murder me." Herrick might have been able to style himself High King, but his power was still precarious, no matter what he'd managed to do to the winter court.

"He wants fall territory," he said, "and you're ruining his sport."

We blocked his military from entering our land, so he had to get soldiers through the treacherous mountain pass on our east or sail ships to reach winter territory. It kept him from completely subjugating the land...and the people within it. But our army was too large to defeat easily, and Herrick valued our uneasy peace...for now.

Duncan and I played a familiar trick, changing clothes and faces—we had the same build, the same long dark hair. I stared into his face, now my own. "Don't start a war."

He flashed me a smile; it was jarring to see his smirk on my own face. "No promises."

I promised myself I wouldn't smirk anymore as I made my way through the crowd. It's not a good look. Smirking faces are punchable faces.

I waited until Duncan was talking to Herrick, until the guards' attention had wandered, and then I slipped out into the cool quiet of the hall.

I searched the gardens, passing elaborate statues—I stopped and stared at a marble princess riding a unicorn, that looked so lifelike I wondered if Herrick had transformed someone who crossed him into a statue—and lush, hanging fruit trees. In the distance the ocean thundered against the base of the castle, and I caught glimpses of moonlight shining off the furious, white-capped sea. The night was crisp and beautiful, but a storm was coming.

When I didn't find her, I thought I'd missed her. I thought about going back to the party, sure that the clock was ticking until I'd be missed. Besides, it was a terrible idea to leave Duncan unsupervised at parties. But I kept searching for her. I'd spent a year staying away doing what was best for both our kingdoms; now I couldn't tear myself away.

I found Alisa deep in the tangled woods. A wide swing hung from a wide, broad branch, and white flowers crept up the old trunk. I knew she'd loved this swing, if it were the same one. I ran my hand over the smooth polished wood, imagining her laughing in this swing, her long hair flying behind her. Was she happy now? Without me? Because if she was, then I would let her go.

I felt warmth on my skin, warmth like sun, and I looked up, searching through the thick greenery.

The princess of summer was perched up in the branches, her silver-embroidered blue gown ripped and torn. I still wore Duncan's face, and yet from the look in her eyes, I had a feeling she'd seen right through the disguise. I raised my hand, covering my features, and then I was myself. Her eyes sparkled as she looked at me, a faint smile playing over her lips, and she shook her head at my trick.

There was a flash of familiar mischief in her gaze when she peered down at me from between the branches

Right before she released the apple she'd been eating. It fell through the leaves and I shifted to one side, or it would've hit me.

I raised one finger to beckon her down. Her lips parted in a laugh and then she easily skimmed down the tree. Her skirt stuck on a branch, and she paused to jerk it free, ripping it worse in the process. Then she dropped down beside me.

"You've been ignoring me all night," I said. *"Avoiding* me."

She spread her hands as if to say, *well, you caught me.*

"Did you get my letters?" I demanded. When her replies had been so brief, I'd taken other tactics; I'd bargained to have swallows and hawks and owls carry notes to her, and they'd waited for replies. Only the first one ever came, to say not to write again. The other birds never returned, and I wondered if they'd been slaughtered by someone in her court.

She was too silent, and I said slowly, "Herrick enchanted you. You can't speak to me."

She didn't answer. But she leaned forward and brushed her lips against my cheek.

A goodbye.

That feathery soft kiss made my heart crack into two. Alisa's kisses had been so passionate and fierce, just like she was. That kiss felt like a mockery of the girl I loved.

"Gods damn it, Alisa," I exploded. "If you love me as I love you, don't just give up. We can find a way."

She shook her downturned head. She couldn't tell me what Herrick was plotting, but I was sure that she was trying to protect me or her kingdom, or both, or I doubted she could've been so cold when I said I loved her.

I stepped closer to her, catching her chin and turned her face up to mine. Her beautiful eyes swam with tears, and another one was making its way across her sharp cheekbone. Regret and fury clutched my chest, emotions more powerful than I'd felt in my life.

"I'll kill anyone who makes you cry," I said fiercely, knowing it was ridiculous, but at least it made her smile through her tears. I swiped those tears away with my thumb. "Alisa, if you want me to let you go, I will. If you want me to try to break the curse, I'll do that too."

Her chin rose at the promise and I went on, "We can play this the smartest way we can. But whether we fight or whether we play a long game… you need to hear this."

I cupped her jaw with my hand, willing her to believe me, to keep the strength to fight whatever Herrick was doing to her. "I love you. I always will. And sooner or later, you and I will find our way back together."

She stared at me with those wide, luminous eyes.

Then she pressed against me, kissing me fiercely. I smiled against her mouth because of the way she kissed me fiercely, claimingly. My Alisa, still. My Alisa, always.

Then she took all my attention and the smile fell away. Her lips stole my breath, the two of us trading wild, fierce kisses. She pushed me against the tree, her body pressing against mine. I bent my head forward, twining my arm tightly around her waist, yanking her fiercely against me. We held each other as if the sheer force of our passion could keep us together, even if the world conspired to tear us apart.

I yanked that damned gown from her body. The bodice tore under my hands, and she huffed a laugh into my mouth. It was the closest I'd come to hearing her voice, and that laugh drove me mad. My hands delved through the torn fabric, caressing the hard points of her nipples, the flat, taut planes of her stomach. My thumb stroked over her soft, downy hair, then lower, caressing her cleft. Her hips jerked against my hand. I twisted the two of us, shoving the gown down to pool at our feet, then drawing her ass against my hips. Her smooth curves pressed against my cock through my trousers, and her lavender head was under my chin so I could breathe in the honeysuckle scent of her hair.

I pinned her there, devouring her bare throat and neck with kisses and gentle bites as she tossed her head. My hand slid again between her thighs, my fingers stroking through her wet heat as she jerked helplessly under my hands. My fingers pulsed over her clit, over and over, until she moaned.

That sound... if that was the only way I still heard her voice, at least I could make her cry out in pleasure. I slid two fingers deep within her, feeling her body shudder with the movement. She bit her lower lip, her head falling on my shoulder. She was so beautiful, under the moonlight, and I paused for a second. It was so quiet in the night that I could've sworn I heard her heart beating and mine, the two of us in time.

Then I began to pulse my fingers in and out, my thumb stroking over her clit. Her thighs began to shake, and I teased her faster. She groaned, shaking her head back and forth with the power of her building orgasm. I worked my hand faster, feeling her hips try to buck under my touch but pinning her against me, until I felt her knees go weak, her channel pulsing around me. I held her up easily against my body as she cried out, her voice shattering the depth of the night.

For a few long seconds, she stayed pressed against me, her body shuddering against mine.

Then she twisted in my arms, kissing me fiercely. Her hands slid between us, trying to work my trousers. I let her shove them down, and then she was pushing my jacket from my shoulders. I helped her with the buttons as she tried to tear my shirt off, then gave up. There was a ripping sound as some of the fabric was torn, as a button sprang loose and fell into the leaves. I trampled it carelessly. She looked so gorgeous, naked in the forest as if she were the wildest of things.

I nipped at the pouty lower lip of hers, and her lips parted; my tongue swept into her mouth as my knee nudged between her thighs. I cupped her thighs, pulling her up until her legs wrapped my waist, her arms closing around my neck. The two of us kept trading kisses as I carried her toward the swing. I set her ass on the high swing, and she laughed as it swayed back and forth.

I grabbed one of the ropes to steady the swing. She leaned back, dangerously far, giving me a smile as she reached for me. She pressed my cock, tracing the places my fingers had explored earlier. My cock throbbed as she teased me in circles around her entrance, gliding easily because she was so wet.

I reached down, teasing her glistening pink clit with my thumb, and she bit her lower lip. As if she couldn't take it anymore, her thighs tightened around my waist, her bare feet pressing into my calves as she tried to reel me toward her.

And I couldn't resist. I went with her, slowly filling her. She was so tight and smelled so good as I buried myself deep into her, until my balls brushed the sweet curve of her ass. She clung to the ropes of the swing, her head falling back, exposing those small perfect breasts and sharp-looking nipples and the curve of her throat, glowing under the moonlight.

I leaned forward and captured one of those nipples in my mouth, staying buried deep within her as my tongue teased over her nipple. She let out a gasp, her thighs taut on my waist as I teased my mouth over her nipple, over and over, swirling my tongue around it. Then to be symmetrical, I moved to the other side, paying it equal attention.

She fisted my hair in her hand, pulling my head up roughly to hers, and capturing my lips with hers. The two of us kissed fiercely as I began to move, shoving deep into her over and over. She began to shudder around me again, her hair flying until she screamed and I shattered inside her, the two of us going to pieces together as the world blurred into something beautiful.

Then the two of us collapsed off the swing into the sweet-scented, thick grass beneath the tree. We lay in a naked heap, her face pillowed on my shoulder.

"I have to tell you," I murmured, "Rowen is safe with me in the autumn court. She's happy; she's going to be one of my knights. You took care of her, Alisa."

Her eyes flooded with tears, but she nodded. I held her close in my arms, savoring her body against mine, knowing we had little time left.

But I'd never give up on my summer princess, and I'd never surrender our happily-ever-after.

CHAPTER FIFTY-THREE

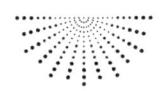

Alisa

"You need to think carefully about whether you really want to do this," Azrael warned me as he sat on my bed. He seemed to be making himself at home.

The other two had gone to prepare for our journey; Azrael had stayed behind. His primary purpose was to antagonize me while I packed, apparently.

He continued, "You'll anger Faer. If you don't return home with your memories, you'll have raised the stakes without raising your ability to cope with them."

"The Delphin said my memories would be restored at the cave," I reminded him.

"And what if the Delphin is wrong?"

"Then I'll have you to help me with Faer," I said.

He tilted his head back, studying me with those eerie eyes. The light caught the red and gold flecks in the purple, reminding me he wasn't mortal. "As far as you trust me."

"As far as I trust you," I repeated.

"I think no matter what you say, Princess, you trust me far more than is wise."

"Funny, because before I came into this world, you promised I could trust you. You said you'd be right by my side."

"And I am, in a way." The faintest lazy smile tilted one corner of his lips. "I'm your very own knight now. Loyal to you."

I jerked an armful of plain training shirts out of my dresser. "What is it that Faer has on you? Besides Zora and the autumn court? Is there something else he holds over your head?"

He shook his head. Rejecting my question, rejecting me.

"God damn it, Azrael."

He was always so controlled, so careful. It made me crazy. Even when I hit him, he hadn't hit me back; hell, he'd *let* me. I wanted to see him driven to enough passion to lash back at me.

"Tell me what happened before! Tell me what I did to you."

"When we get to the caves, you'll know," he said, his voice low and quiet. "You won't believe me anyway, Alisa."

"How do you know that?"

"Because you never do," he said, his voice heating. He suddenly rose to his feet, pacing toward me. "You want me to tell you the whole story of how things fell apart between us? Well, you can't even abide it when I suggest you were an imperfect girlfriend."

"You've made it very clear that Fae don't even have girlfriends."

"You know what I mean," he growled. "You won't believe me anyway, so why should I bare my heart to you?"

Oh. There it was. My lips parted, my own heart stuttering over his words.

Fearless prince Azrael, so dangerous with a sword and so competent in every way, was afraid I'd hurt him again.

Because I'd hurt him before.

I should say something gentle, something comforting, but when he pressed his lips tightly shut, his jaw tense, I felt my own spike of answering fury.

"Don't be a coward, Azrael," I said, my voice just as calm as his had been, even though my heart was beating fast.

"Why are you always trying to push me?" he demanded, as if he'd seen right through my cruel words. "Are you trying to push me *away*?"

"We were never supposed to be together anyway," I repeated his words from before. "I'm not pushing you away, Azrael. You and I aren't together *now*."

His jaw tensed. "It might have saved me a kingdom if you'd said that five years ago, Princess."

"I only get so mad at you when you talk about the past because *that* is all you say," I shot at him. "Just little one-liners about how I ruined your life. Tell me the whole story from beginning to end. Convince me."

His eyes glittered down at me, and after a few seconds, I said, "Be brave, Azrael."

His lips grazed my hair as he leaned down close to me, his arm going to the wall to brace himself so that his body was just barely held away from mine. Despite myself, when he was this close to me, my breath stuttered in my chest.

He breathed into my ear, "You are the worst."

I met that smoldering purple gaze. "Tell me what I've done, then."

"Sometimes I feel sorry for you," he said, each word dropping like a bomb. "But the truth is, you made this dark and horrible world, Alisa. You were a part of it, and now the monsters you created are dragging you down, and you make me feel sorry for you—"

I grabbed the front of his shirt, fisting it in my hand. "Straight line, Azrael. Start at the beginning. You're a smart man, you can do it. Tell me about the day you met me."

"The day I met you, you were a liar," he breathed. "And I shouldn't expect anything else from you."

Funny how when he insulted me, I felt as if I were the one in control. It was when Azrael was kind, when he was nostalgic, that I felt sick and dizzy about the past I didn't understand. Then I spun out of control with my desire for him.

"You can call me a liar all you want, but in *my* memory, you lied to me from the first time I met you, too."

He shook his head. "Just because you don't remember doesn't mean you aren't guilty."

"Who the hell am I now, Azrael? You can't admit that, can you?"

"You're the same person."

I shook my head. "I don't think so. And the truth is, I'm not sure you believe there's anything wrong with the person I was, or the person I *am*. When Duncan called me a Fae bitch, it pissed you off. Why?"

"Because you're the princess," he said, his voice low and dangerous. "Heir to the Fae realm, whether you deserve it or not."

"No," I accused. "Liar." My own voice was growing heated. "Because you love me, Azrael. You still love me."

"And you don't love me," he said, his voice mocking.

"Because I don't know you."

"Because you aren't capable of loving anyone else."

"No." I shook my head. "That's not true of the old Alisa, and it's not true of me."

"It is."

My hand was still fisted in his shirt, and I shook him a little with it, as much as I could move his big, intractable frame. He quirked an eyebrow, unimpressed.

"Some part of me still loves you, you insufferable, miserable *asshole* who somehow understands even less than I do, even though almost all of my life is a black hole to me—" My voice was rising.

His lips crashed down on mine. I made a small sound of surprise as his mouth conquered mine, and then I started to push him away with that hand on his chest, but I couldn't. He was unmovable.

He kissed me with heat and fire, kissed me breathless. He always looked so cold, but there was passion in those deep, smoldering eyes and certainty in his kiss.

And then I didn't want to push him away anymore.

His tongue teased against my lip, parting my lips, opening them up. I swayed against him, and his body pinned me to the wall in all the right ways this time, his knee sliding between my thighs. He kissed me, against that cold marble wall, our bodies grinding together. Everything about that kiss was rough and punishing.

His hand cupped my cheek, claiming, possessive, even as he pulled away. He studied me with glittering eyes.

"What were you bitching at me about?" he demanded.

"I think I said I loved you," I said.

"You are the worst," he said again, and then his lips were on mine again.

I twined my arms around his neck, and he lifted me easily up the wall. The bed was so close, just a few steps away, but he pinned me against the wall and I wrapped my legs around his waist.

My fingers dug deep into the powerful muscle of his shoulders. When his lips left mine, I reminded him, "I hate you too."

It was the ghost of Alisa, the ghost with the memories, who still loved him.

The woman I was now wasn't entirely certain of him.

But I did know my nipples ached against the slick material of my gown, my clit was sore and aching, that I throbbed with desire for him.

"Same, princess. Same." He murmured in my ear, right before he nipped it. His sharp teeth teasing against my lobe ignited a firestorm of want and need that rippled through my body.

I pushed off the wall, propelling him toward the bed. He yanked at the bodice of my dress, and the string of my corset pressed painfully into my skin before it exploded. The dress slipped down my shoulders.

His mouth roamed my body, his skillful mouth exploring the exposed flesh of my shoulders and my décolletage and then my breasts in ways that made my back arch with desire.

When the tip of his tongue circled my nipple, my hips jerked forward against him. He drew my nipple into his mouth, teasing it as he stroked the other nipple with his thumb. He seemed to know just how to play my body, because no male had ever done that before in my memory, but longing rippled through my body, wanting more of him.

I yanked the hem of his shirt up over his head, and he raised his arms, letting me yank it off him As I drew his shirt off, Azrael's body was a feast for the eyes; broad, powerful shoulders, defined pecs covered in tattoos, chiseled abs.

I fumbled with his trousers as he pushed my dress down around my hips. His warm palm slid across my lower back, up my spine to nest in my hair as he cupped the back of my head. My thighs tightened around his waist.

"I struggle sometimes to remember how wicked you are," he murmured, before nipping my earlobe with his teeth. He stepped out of his trousers in one smooth movement, revealing his muscular thighs and a long, straight cock that bobbed in front of his taut lower abs. His thumb slid between the waistband of my panties and my skin before he ripped those off me too.

The two of us fell back onto the bed together, Azrael still holding me lightly.

I straddled him. "Then let me remind you."

My thighs were on either side of his lean waist, pressing against his washboard abs, as I pressed his cock between my thighs.

His fingers caressed my ass, his thumbs sliding over the indentations of my hip bones, as he gripped my waist. He paused, his cock teasing against my center.

"Are you sure you want to do this?" he asked.

My body still wanted him—still seemed to adore him—even if my mind hadn't quite caught up. It was good of him to stop and check, and something fractured in me a little more.

"Yes," I said. "Shut up."

"Lovely girl," he muttered, his hand sliding across the back of my neck.

He jerked me down to kiss him. His lips met mine and he kissed me hard, his grip on my neck unyielding. I smiled against his lips. *That's right, Azrael. Keep control...we both know it's a lie.*

Azrael was as much a fool for me as I was for him, at least.

I pressed my hips down on his, taking his cock in one hand to guide him in, I brushed his tip over my throbbing opening. He looked up at me—this complicated, dark-eyed gaze in that unspeakable handsome face—and I didn't know what to make of his face.

Then his hands tightened on my hips, drawing me down his cock. As he filled me, I gasped. He paused as if he was worried he'd hurt me, but I was already rising on my knees up his cock, then driving down again.

"Gods, you feel so good," he muttered as the two of us began to move together. "I missed you so much, Alisa."

He hadn't missed me solely for the sex, and I knew that, and that was the truly terrifying thing between us.

He gripped my hips to steady me as I rose up and down his shaft, my movements languid. When my thighs met the hard muscle of his sides, I rolled my hips forward and was rewarded with the give of his breath. He bit down on that plush lip above the hard angle of his jaw, his purple eyes falling half-lidded. I enjoyed the way his face shifted as he fell under my spell—he already knew what my body loved, and maybe some part of me remembered him too.

Heat spread across my shoulders, flushed my cheeks, as the world grew warm. The constant throb I felt for Azrael turned into an all-out, wildfire.

As if he couldn't bear it anymore either, he suddenly caught me with an arm around my waist and turned us both, rolling on top of me. He buried his face in my neck, peppering kisses and then nibbles that made me bite my lip at the intensity of the desire that burned between us both, as he thrust inside me rhythmically.

My fingernails dug into his shoulders as the world went to pieces, as I flushed hot and then that heat turned into a warm glow that suffused through my body as I relaxed.

I moaned as he shattered inside me, his arm tightening around my waist, his lips parting as he was lost to pleasure.

When it was all over, when I was lying with my head on his shoulder and his fingers drifting up and down my bare skin, I said, "I don't want to fight again. But I have to tell you something."

"What's that?" he asked, his voice guarded.

"I understand you think that I betrayed you somehow, that I did something terrible to you," I said.

"Not just me," he said. "I could forgive that."

"Right. Not just to you, but to your court." I was just barely beginning to understand what a court even meant in this world. His people. The people he ruled, that he was responsible for. Perhaps they were even his kin, in a way. I sighed. This confession felt weighty, only because I knew he wouldn't believe it.

I went on, "But I don't think I could have betrayed you. Or them. That isn't who I am, Azrael. For all my faults."

"Well, the autumn court is in ruins. The winter court, destroyed completely, hunted to the ends of the earth by Herrick's monsters because they rebelled." His words were dark, and yet I felt his gaze on me was kind, as if he didn't want to say these things. "And I'm the one who gave you the key to the autumn court. I didn't give it to Faer or to your father, Alisa. Only to you. I would only have given it to you."

"A literal key?" I asked.

He nodded. "An enchanted key, so that we could be together although it was forbidden. So you could come into my castle, unseen."

Then he added, "Just as your father's men did, before they murdered mine."

"But you don't know for sure that I gave my father the key."

He sighed. "No. I don't know for sure that you gave your father the key. But there are undeniable, inconvenient facts here."

"You've hated me so much and it could have just been a mistake. A...misunderstanding. Maybe they got in some other way."

"I don't think that's the case," he said, "but I wish it was."

My lips parted, but before I could say anything else, he kissed me again. It was a deep, soulful kiss. At first, I thought he was trying to shut me up again, and then I realized that he was kissing me slowly, tenderly. There was so much affection in that kiss.

Sometimes he kissed me as if the past didn't even matter to him.

But maybe his lips could lie.

CHAPTER FIFTY-FOUR

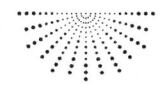

A *lisa*

Duncan stopped in the doorway, his nostrils flaring as he met Azrael's gaze. Tiron closed the door behind them both as Duncan dropped his bag of weapons with an ominous *clank* on the marble floor.

"What is it?" Azrael asked impatiently.

"The two of you had sex," Duncan said. "You love to complicate things *endlessly*, don't you, Azrael?"

"What is wrong with you?" Azrael demanded. "How can you possibly know that?"

"I know you," Duncan returned.

"Both of you, let it go," Tiron demanded.

The two of them turned to him, raising their eyebrows. Tiron raised his hands as if in appeal.

"Wait," I said, glancing between the three of them before I said to

Tiron, "If Azrael and Duncan are both princes and knights, does that make you their squire?"

"We don't talk about that," Tiron said wearily.

"How are we getting out of here?" I asked as Tiron headed past me for the balcony.

"By sea," he said. "Just for a little while. We need to clear the water before Faer realizes what we're up to, and Raile can send his storms and monsters after us."

"Raile can control the weather?" I asked skeptically.

"Only on the sea," Duncan said. "Why, are you reconsidering marrying him?"

"Not a chance," I said. "He's not my type. I'm really just attracted to big, senseless brutes of men."

I winked at him. Duncan snorted.

"So wait, are we swimming?" I asked.

"Do you remember how to do that?" Duncan asked me.

"I know how to swim," I snapped.

"We're not swimming," Tiron said, his voice exasperated. "Though swimming is an important skill set in case things go awry with our current plans."

He hummed, and a few minutes later, there was a fluttering sound as a *wing* brushed the railing.

I almost jumped back. "That looks like an enormous swan."

"Not everything here is some twisted version of what you knew in the mortal world," Duncan grumbled as he headed past me.

"He's just mad because if it weren't for him and Azrael, we could fly," Tiron confided to me.

"I don't even like flying," Duncan snapped back.

"Because he's not good at it," Tiron whispered. "If he could fly, he'd love it."

"I should have left you where I found you," Duncan grumbled.

Tiron leapt onto the back of the swan, then settled in between her wings, which forced him to fold his legs up. He held out his hand to me, and as I straddled the balcony, Azrael steadied me with a hand on my back. It was completely unnecessary, but sweet. Typically confusing for Azrael.

I slipped off onto the swan's back—it was alarming to walk across its light bones, to feel its muscles ripple under foot—and quickly sank to sit in front of Tiron.

Azrael and Duncan joined us. Then Tiron whispered to the swan, and the four of us sailed on its back across the water, leaving the bright lights of the castle behind.

I glanced up at Faer's balcony, afraid I'd find him hard-eyed, watching us go, but the lights shone from empty windows.

And even though we were heading into danger, and I was trapped in this Fae world where I was lost without these ridiculous males, as we traveled across shimmering black water, I felt freer than I had since I was carried through that portal.

I had these three unstoppable knights by my side—truly by my side now. They were mine.

And I was going to find my past.

Then I would really be free.

CONTINUE the adventure now with Alisa and her Fae knights in Lost Fae 2, Fallen Queen.

Hi! May Dawson here.

If you enjoyed Wandering Queen, please leave me a review if you can! It makes a huge difference in connecting readers with indie books, so authors like me can keep on writing!

I'd love if you joined my Facebook community, May Dawson's Wild Angels, where I share excerpts, exclusive content, news and polls!

If you'd like to join my newsletter—and receive a free copy of Their Shifter Academy—you can do that at https://BookHip.com/LPGGRR

Ready to explore the other worlds connected to the world of the Fae? Turn the page for a look at Avalon in One Kind of Wicked, a complete five book series.

Thanks for reading!

Best,

May

55

AN EXCERPT FROM ONE KIND OF WICKED

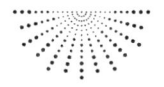

A fter my father almost destroyed my world, I was exiled from the land of mists and magic. I was just a child when soldiers of the Crown dragged me through a portal to *your* world, and I've been trying to get home ever since.

When I'm invited home to attend the academy of magic, I know there are strings attached.

Those strings may have something to do with three handsome, alluring men who befriend me.

I can't trust them, but I can't resist the pull I feel for them, either. It's been a long time since I had friends.

My chance to stay home is tied to how useful I can make myself. My father's henchmen, the True, want me to restore his wicked glory. The Crown's spies wants to use me to destroy the True. I'll have to pick a side, and fight, or I'll be exiled again. Or worse.

And in the midst of all this swirling intrigue, I'm failing both Calculus *and* Casting.

These men seem determined to tutor me, fix me and most of all, protect me.

But my deep, dark secret is that the dread magician's daughter… doesn't have her magic anymore.

When they realize how useless I am, will they still stand by my side?

Welcome to a world where redemption is possible, where friendship and adventure and magic abound, and where love means never having to choose.

One Kind of Wicked is the first in a complete five book university-age academy reverse harem series. It first appeared as Three Kinds of Wicked.

Click here to read One Kind of Wicked now, or read on for an excerpt.

CHAPTER One

Tera

THE SMELL of rain almost overwhelms the stench of garbage as I head back to the rooming house, and the thin handles of the heavy plastic bags I carry bite into my fingers. My shoulders ache, but I walk with my head held high. It's the way I was raised.

I'm going home today.

The filthy sidewalk and the buildings that close around me are all gray. I bet in Avalon, the sunrise floods the sky with pink and orange above the trees. Avalon is still half-wild in a way things aren't here. Vibrant cities stand bordered by forests, and the air carries the scent of wildflowers.

Or maybe that's all bullshit. Maybe I remember home like someone who's been exiled for five years. I don't trust my memories anymore, and I sure as hell don't trust my feelings.

Someone cries out down the street like they're being hurt. I let the bags slide down my fingers, making sure the handles aren't knotted around my hands. I need to be able to drop the bags and run.

I'm not stupid; I don't get involved. Anyway, it's probably just one criminal going after another. Someone's probably getting what they deserve.

Almost home. I'll get into my room, close the door, and finish packing my bags, and the sound of that anguished voice will fall away.

The cry echoes down the lonely street. Goddamnit, I know that voice. *Granny.* She's called good morning to me on my lonely trek back from the night shift every day in that whiskey-soaked voice. She always tells me, "You be careful out there! Be smart!"

My default setting may not be smart.

I take off running toward the cry. Staying away from the opening of the alley between the boarding house and the brick apartment building next door, I drop the grocery bags against the wall. *I'll be back for you later.* My job at the twenty-four-hour grocery stinks, but the haul of dented cans and expired bread has been good for me. And for everyone else in the boarding house.

When I turn around the corner, two teenage boys—what the hell are they doing up so early?—are at the end of the alley with Granny. One of them flicks a lighter over and over. They're threatening to light her shopping cart on fire. She's on her knees, blood smeared across her cheek, begging them to stop.

My fingers tighten into a fist. I wish I had a wand. I wish there was magic in this world so it would matter if I had a wand.

But I always find another weapon.

I run past the entrance to the alleyway. The boys are so intent on Granny that they don't even notice me. Just yesterday, Mrs. Estes complained about the piles of *basura* other tenants left behind. I nodded politely—while walking away because I didn't see anything in the trash I could resell—but I noticed there was a shovel leaning against the faded brick façade.

I grab the rough wooden handle and head back down the stairs. I feel a hell of a lot better with the weapon in my hand, even if it isn't much of one.

From behind the boys, Granny's eyes fix on me. I can't read her face. It's hard to tell if she's grateful to see me or afraid. She needs this trouble to go away. I usually make more trouble.

The boys turn, finally realizing there's someone behind them. They're young, twelve or thirteen. Too young to be so bad, but hey, my world exiled me at that same tender age for my sins.

The first one holds the lighter. The flicker of flame dies as he lifts his thumb. It'd be a small victory, except he slips it into his pocket and puffs himself up, ready for a fight.

"What are you looking at, bitch?"

My chest is tight with anxiety, but that doesn't stop me from shaking my head. "You've got a devastating wit, don't you? Leave the old woman alone."

He glances back at Granny. My chest tightens even more at the sight of her wide eyes and the blood trickling from her nose; I want to bash these kids in the head so badly. I choke my grip up on the shovel, resting the sharp metal blade against my shoulder.

"This is a woman?" he asks me skeptically, and his buddy exhales with laughter. But there's wariness in their eyes.

"If you walk away," I say, "I'll give you ten bucks. Or you can stay here and see if I'm actually capable of kicking your asses."

Frankly, I have no idea if I can kick their asses either.

"You think ten dollars means anything to me?" he asks.

Ten dollars sure as hell means something to me, so maybe. I take a step toward them, and the two of them turn and run for the back of the alley. They hit the fence and start to climb.

I'm feeling pretty smug. Then Granny points behind me, and I turn.

There's a taxi cab parked across the mouth of the alley. I don't think they're scared of the color yellow, though.

It's the driver, standing behind his door with a shotgun braced in his shoulder, who probably scared them off.

I didn't think it was possible, but my heart rate spikes a little higher.

"It's for me," I tell Granny, looking back. "Don't worry. Hey, I brought some stuff from the store—I left it on the sidewalk. Take it, okay?"

"Are you all right, Tera?" she asks me in her gravelly voice.

I shrug. I don't know yet. I'm taking a wild chance on the thing I want most, and hoping it leads me home, not to being dumped in a trash bin somewhere in this city where I've never belonged.

"Here's hoping."

"Be careful out there." Her eyes are worried as she limps toward me.

"You're hurt." I swing the shovel down from my shoulder and lean it against the wall. "I should've..."

"Be smart out there." She interrupts my vengeance fantasy.

"What are the odds, really?" I ask, more of myself than anyone.

She grabs me in a hug goodbye. She's so much taller than me that her chest presses against my cheek, enveloping me in the scent of cigarette smoke and old laundry. But it doesn't matter. I hug her back.

This world is a terrible place. But it has its rare moments of beauty too.

Click here to read One Kind of Wicked now.

ALSO BY MAY DAWSON

The True and the Crown series:
One Kind of Wicked
Two Kinds of Damned
Three Kinds of Lost
Four Kinds of Cursed
Five Kinds of Love

Their Shifter Princess:
Their Shifter Princess
Their Shifter Princess 2: Pack War
Their Shifter Princess 3: Coven's Revenge

Their Shifter Academy:
Their Shifter Academy: A Prequel Novella
Their Shifter Academy 1: Unwanted
Their Shifter Academy 2: Unclaimed
Their Shifter Academy 3: Undone
Their Shifter Academy 4: Unforgivable
Their Shifter Academy 5: Unwinnable
Their Shifter Academy 6: Unstoppable

The Wild Angels & Hunters Series:
Wild Angels

Fierce Angels
Dirty Angels
Chosen Angels

Academy of the Supernatural
Her Kind of Magic
His Dangerous Ways
Their Dark Imaginings

Ashley Landon, Bad Medium
Dead Girls Club